Journey into the Realm: The Elf Girl

Hardcover ISBN 978-1-60910-662-1
Paperback ISBN 978-1-60910-663-8

Published in the United States by BookLocker.com, Inc., Bangor, Maine.

Printed in the United States of America on acid-free paper.

BookLocker.com, Inc.
2011

First Edition

For Sofi and Aunt Kim, who taught me to believe in magic. I wouldn't have been able to write this story without their inspiration.

Journey into the Realm: The Elf Girl

Markelle Grabo

TABLE OF CONTENTS

Prologue

Everyone is different. No two babies are born alike. This fact can be explained scientifically, genetically; religiously….The possibilities are endless.

"Hi, my name's Ramsey," I said, as I sat down on the school bus seat.

The five-year-old boy beside me watched me intently for a few moments and then asked, "What's wrong with your ears?"

Sure, there are many explanations for why people are so different from one another, explanations that made sense.

Could magic be classified as one of them?

"What do you mean?" I asked, tugging self-consciously at my hair.

"They're all pointy and stuff," he pointed out, scrunching his face as if he smelled some pungent odor.

I didn't think so; not for a very long time, at least.

"So?" I challenged. "My mom says it's because I'm unique."

"Nu-uh," he bit back. "It's because you're weird."

"No, it's not!" I cried, tears forming in my eyes.

"Yes, it is!" the boy yelled, loud enough for everyone else on the bus to hear. "You're like an elf!"

I once lived in a small city in Wisconsin with my parents and sister, Dina, who was one year younger than I. My parents and sister loved and supported me, but it wasn't enough to chase away the impact others had on me when they saw me for the first time.

I lived a sheltered life before that first day of kindergarten. I didn't realize what effect my ears had on others until a little boy my age pointed it out to me.

"Elf Girl, Elf Girl!" he chanted. It wasn't long before others chimed in as well.

"Stop it!" I shouted. "Please! You're not being very nice!"

For fifteen years, everyone, including myself, knew I was different. The problem was that no one knew *why*. There were things about me that others just couldn't explain or understand, and I had so many questions that couldn't possibly be answered.

"I can't invite you to my birthday party, Ramsey," Olivia, one of my classmates in middle school, told me the day before summer vacation.

"Why not?" I asked, dreading her answer.

"Because everyone would make fun of me for having someone like you at my party," she said simply, shrugging her shoulders.

"Someone like me?"

"It's not that I think you're weird. It's just that others...well, others do, and I can't afford to lose all my friends right before high school." She patted me on the shoulder. "I'm sorry. Have a good summer."

I took a deep breath, collecting myself, before walking out of the school alone.

I never enjoyed watching T.V. or going to the mall with friends. Instead, I spent my time outdoors in the forest next to my home, the only wooded area for a good twenty miles. It was sort of a sanctuary, one that represented true beauty to me. I would run through the trees, feeling the wind splash against my face. I would sit there for hours, not speaking or moving, because I didn't need to. It was the perfect place. The place I felt most like myself. The one place in the world where I didn't feel constricted or confined, but instead felt free.

"Hey, beautiful," a boy I bumped into in the hallway said on my first day of high school.

I smiled and tucked my hair behind my ears. His expression changed from interest to disgust.

"Freak," he muttered, before stalking away.

Mom said I was like everyone else and that my looks had nothing to do with me, but I never believed her. What she said, unfortunately, never made any sense. I had already taken Biology, and I knew that the way a person looked didn't happen by chance. Genetics were involved. By the looks of it, my parents did not have the genes for pale skin, straight blonde hair, green eyes, or pointy ears. I am not even sure if that last one was a possible genotype.

No one ever said I was ugly growing up, unless of course they saw my ears. One look at the things on the side of my head, and people ran from me like Olympic sprinters. At first, it bothered me, and then I just got used to it.

"She should just cut them off or something. For her, no ears would be better than what she has," a girl snickered.

"Totally," her friend replied, checking her reflection in the mirror of the girl's bathroom. "Or she should just move to the North Pole."

The two girls erupted into a bout of giggles.

They never knew I was in the stall behind them.

Yes, I was different. Why was I? I didn't understand for a long time.

One of the names others called me stuck throughout those first fifteen years, and it wasn't simply because it was used against me so often. The name seemed important somehow, connected to me in some other way than as an insult.

No, it was something more.

That little boy on the bus was the first to utter the words.

"Elf Girl! Elf Girl!" he cried.

I put my hands over my pointy ears and realized I was far more different than I once believed.

~1~

The Water

"Ramsey, Dina, time for dinner!" Mom called one Sunday evening.

On Sunday evenings, the family *had* to eat together, no exceptions. There were no friends, no work…nothing but good old quality time. This rule was easy for me to follow, because I had only one friend, but extremely painful for Dina. I think every time my mom said no to friends, my sister died a little inside. The thought was definitely an exaggeration, but to me it was the only remark that came close to describing her feelings.

"Be right there, Mom!" I shouted back, knowing we had little time before she came up to bring us down herself. "Come on, Dina, it's time for dinner."

"Okay, I'm almost finished deciding what to wear for tomorrow. Hey, should I go with the dark denim skirt or the light?"

"Does it really matter?" I wondered, eager to get downstairs and avoid my mother's wrath.

"Of course it does, Ramsey!" With a dramatic sigh, she threw her skirts down on her bed. "I can't believe that you are so fashion impaired."

"Sorry…" I shrugged.

"Don't worry about it. Not everyone can pick out clothes like I can," she beamed, standing proud as if she would receive some kind of award for her talents.

"You got that right," I muttered.

I didn't hate clothes, but I rarely cared what I wore as long as it didn't draw unwanted attention to myself. With the way I looked, the first thing someone noticed after observing the outfit I was wearing was my ears. So I usually kept my style very plain. My outfit often consisted of a pair of dark jeans, a colored t-shirt, and a zip-up sweatshirt. The sweatshirt always had to have a hood for when I was out of school or in public places. I didn't want people staring at my freakish ears while I was out shopping. That would be beyond annoying...not to mention awkward.

"Come on, girls, dinner is waiting!"

"I'm finished. Let's go and eat!" Dina decided finally.

She ran past me and down the stairs. I followed her at a slower pace.

"So how has school been going?" Dad asked, as we all sat down to eat. He was always the first to start the dinner conversation.

"Um, it's okay," I muttered.

Actually, going to school sucked, as it did for most people my age. I mean, who actually enjoyed spending their entire day shuffling through crowded hallways and listening to boring lectures? It was a little different for me, however. School was not only boring, but also a complete waste of time. It came so easy to me that I could barely stand it. The only challenge I got was in Gym class or Spanish, but even that was stretching it.

"Honey, what happened? Are kids still making fun of your ears?" Mom asked, obviously very concerned.

"No, Mom…that was grade school. I think people have gotten used to them by now," I lied, because people actually still made fun of them. But I didn't want to get my mother started.

"Honey, remember what I told you, just because you are different…"

"It doesn't mean I'm not just like everyone else," I interrupted, touching a hand to my forehead. "I know, Mom. You don't have to explain it again." I sighed and prayed for a new subject.

Thankfully, the ringing of the front doorbell put an end to the less than lovely conversation.

"Oh, that must be your grandmother. Hold that thought, Ramsey," Mom said, and ran to get the door.

Yeah right, I told myself. That was one thought I would rather have run away.

Mom was right; at the door was Elizabeth Wilder, my grandmother. She had come every Sunday for dinner since Dina and I were both in diapers, without fail.

"Hi, Mom! Come on in, we were just starting," Mom instructed as my grandma stepped through the doorway.

"Hi, dear, sorry I'm late," she replied, giving her daughter a hug. "Ramsey, your mother was just telling me on the phone about how well you have been doing in school. It makes me very proud to call you my granddaughter."

As anyone could guess after a day in the life of me, I hated attention, even from my grandma, unfortunately. After years of receiving bad attention, the good wasn't much different.

"Thanks. Did Mom also mention that Dina made the Pom Squad?" I asked.

Because I wasn't fond of the spotlight, passing the attention to Dina helped a lot. It was always easy to get Dina going on about herself.

"Yes, she did," she remarked, graciously turning toward my sister. "I can't wait to come and see your routines!"

"Thanks! I'm so excited to start performing," Dina said enthusiastically.

As the rest of the family chatted on about Dina's school life, I slowly picked through my food, unsatisfied with the way things were. Sure, I loved my family. But it seemed as though I was always reaching for something more, yet I could never grasp what I wanted. I yearned for a life away from this place. I wanted to be away from my boring school and away from this boring life. Nothing seemed to excite me anymore. It wasn't anyone's fault, but I had a feeling there was more for me out there if I had enough strength to reach for it.

I often imagined what life would be like in the books I read, like the fantasy novels, where fairies, dragons, and mermaids reigned; where power and confidence could be found in the heart's of all, and not only in their dreams. That would be the life for me. It would be interesting, not mind-numbing like school, and I wouldn't be the only one who appeared to be so unusual. I sighed and pushed my plate away, feeling foolish and immature, reminding myself that the books were only make-believe.

They were just fantasies.

***

"Well, girls, I think it's time to say goodbye to Grandma and get ready for bed," Mother said later that evening.

"Your mother is right. Bye, dears," Grandma said, giving us each a kiss goodnight.

"Bye, Grandma!" we both replied.

Once the door shut, Dina and I climbed the stairs to our rooms. It was late, and even though this meant homework time for Dina, we always retreated into our rooms after Sunday dinner. For Dina, it created the illusion that she was actually going to sleep, not rushing through her Biology work she put off all weekend. In my case, it was the perfect opportunity to spend some much-needed time alone, especially after a long day.

I absolutely adored my room. It was painted forest green and decorated with flowers lining the ceiling. Mom had them painted on a few years earlier. They weren't girly princess flowers, but rather very elegant and beautiful.

My room had a simple layout. I had a wooden desk, a large dresser, a mirror, a queen-sized bed, and a bookshelf overflowing with books. It was rather unlike Dina's room.

Her walls were soft pinks and blues. She had a queen-sized bed like mine, but also a vanity for her makeup, a large walk-in closet, and another closet filled with all of her shoes. Her walls had posters of boy bands and movie stars. I never really liked going into her room. The word *cluttered* was a huge understatement.

It wasn't as if Dina was my parents' favorite child. I was sure that if I wanted all the stuff she had, I would get it. However, what Dina had was simply not my taste.

"Goodnight, girls," Mom called to us from the hall.

"Goodnight, Mom," I replied, the first to respond. I guessed Dina was texting on her phone…again.

"Goodnight, Mom!" Dina called, and I heard the beep of the OFF button on her cell phone.

Nights were always the worst for me. Sleep rarely came until the wee hours, when the rest of my family was sound asleep. I couldn't seem to make myself sleep for very long. I was awake until midnight and up at around four o'clock the next morning, without feeling one ounce of drowsiness.

Usually, I snuck out and went for nighttime walks, but tonight rain was quickly developing into a storm. It wasn't as if I disliked the rain; I just didn't want my clothes getting wet. It was too risky to leave wet clothes in the hamper because my parents could figure out I snuck out of the house.

I decided to read instead. An activity that was both quiet and productive. Staying up twiddling my thumbs wouldn't be the best use of my spare time. I quietly slipped out from beneath my covers and lightly tiptoed across the wooden floor to the shelf. Another reason I loved my room was that the floorboards never squeaked.

I scanned the shelf for something I hadn't read, but found nothing. I remembered the last time I went to the bookstore. Two weeks ago, I had bought three books, and as usual, I read them right away. I had planned to go today but had totally forgotten. I looked at the clock on my dresser. It read ten p.m. The bookstore closed at eleven.

Guess I'm going outside after all, I decided. I had nothing else to do, considering sleep was out of the question for at least a few more hours. I quickly threw on jeans and a large hooded sweatshirt over my pajama top, put on some tennis shoes, grabbed my phone and wallet, and headed down the stairs. I would just have to do my own laundry before anyone could notice how wet my clothes were.

Remembering I had to lock the door, I picked up the key in the basket and stuffed it into the large pocket of my sweatshirt with my phone and wallet. The door opened easily and noiselessly. I never had trouble leaving the house.

The bookstore was only three blocks from our subdivision, *Forest Grove.* The area held all two-story homes with perfectly groomed lawns the size of swimming pools. I was surprised some of the homes could even fit pools into their property. What I liked about it was the forest that surrounded us. Its tall trees and small ponds here and there made it the perfect place to spend my time.

Luckily, sidewalks led the way to the bookstore. To have a car hit me would definitely not be good. I almost ran the three blocks to the store. I loved the night, but the anticipation of being able to read was too great to walk, and I didn't want to be drenched when I walked through the entrance of the store.

I felt bad about sneaking out; I always did. However, tonight it was worse considering I had gone to church earlier. Sneaking out of the house wasn't exactly a Christian thing to do.

The silver cross that dangled from my neck bounced slightly as my hurried pace took me to the bookstore. The cross was a birthday gift from my parents, and I hardly ever took it off. It felt comfortable to wear on a daily basis. When I forgot, I felt empty.

Clutching the cross, I sent a silent prayer to God, asking for some forgiveness and understanding for leaving the house.

***

When I finally arrived at the bookstore, it was ten fifteen. I didn't worry about anyone seeing me there so late. I was a regular.

I headed straight to the teen fiction section. The object of my desire was fantasy. I had always loved the genre because it was easy to let the books take me to another world, a world where I wasn't a freak. I was just the reader watching the story unfold.

My favorite books were about fairies, and the ones that told of a Realm far away from our own world. The Realms contained beauty, wonder, magic, and mystery. Those tales intrigued me. I had loved fairies since my earliest childhood. When Dina and I were younger, my mother would tell us stories of fairies who sang in the forests. She would also say if anything was ever missing, the fairies took it. It was up to them whether they would return it or not. Mom taught Dina and me to thank the fairies every time we found something we thought we had lost.

As the years went by, my passion for fantasy grew, while Dina's dwindled. None of her friends believed, so her interests changed to boys and T.V. I kept my fascination, and I wasn't ashamed, no matter how childish it sounded. My belief in fairies had never left me, though deep down, I knew it was not likely they really existed. Even so, I liked the mystery and magic of believing in something I couldn't see.

It was easy to find something to read after scanning the shelves for a few moments; the store always came through for me. I soon had two books in my hands, just enough to get me through the week. Final exams at school were starting, so I wouldn't have much time to read between studying.

On the way to the checkout counter, a large, leather-bound book caught my eye. I was a sucker for antiques, so I stopped and touched my fingertips to the soft, worn cover, tracing the words thoughtfully. The book was brown, with green swirls making a border around the front and title. The title read, *The Mysterious Guide to Fantasy*. I had read other guides to mystical beings; usually, they were filled with random childish fluff that didn't make any sense. I always looked for books that made me think, and most importantly, transported me from the struggle of everyday life and allowed me to dream of something different.

For some reason, this book intrigued me. I knew I had to buy it the moment I saw it. Something about the book *drew* me to it. I had no idea what the reason could be, other than that it was so eye-catching, but I didn't think about it for very long. Always trying to be the smart shopper, I looked at the back for the price. I gasped. $42.50! *No way!*

This book had better be good, was all I could think. On impulse, I grabbed the book and almost ran to the checkout before I could change my mind.

When I said I was a regular, I meant it. I knew practically every inch of the store and every employee. Therefore, I was a little shocked when I saw who was behind the counter. I had never seen her at the store before, and she didn't look like the kind of girl who would even work at a bookstore.

The girl was strikingly beautiful with skin as pale as mine. Her white-blonde hair ran thinly down to her waist, and her forest green eyes flickered with surprise when she saw me. I almost dropped the books I was holding. This girl was almost my reflection. Not exactly looking into a mirror, but it was very close. She was taller than I was, and her eyes were not the same shade of green, but it still shook me. I had never seen anyone who looked so much like me before.

"Did you find everything all right?" she asked.

As I was groping for words, my mind suddenly clouded and unclear, I quickly nodded my head. I curiously looked at her nametag to see if maybe I had seen her before. *Addison.* The name wasn't familiar to me, so I decided she was probably a new employee.

She started scanning the books. When she got to the crazily expensive one, her eyes widened, and for a second they seemed to shine brighter than before. She met my gaze as if she was trying to communicate some unspoken message, but I didn't understand what it was. This night had started to get weird, even for me, the poster child for strange.

"Interesting choice," Addison remarked, holding up the book.

"Oh, I, uh, it just popped out at me," I stammered.

I couldn't believe how stupid I was acting, and it must have been obvious to her how much of an effect seeing her was having on me. *How embarrassing.*

"It's a good read."

"You've read it?" I asked.

"Yes, it's nicely written. Everything in it is true....Well, *almost* everything."

Did she just say almost everything in a *fantasy* book was true? Noticing the confused look on my face, she quickly averted my gaze and looked down at the counter. I could tell she was feeling self-conscious. *Poor girl*, I thought.

"I hope it's good," I said, trying to change the subject. "This is probably the most expensive book I've ever bought."

"The total comes to $62.35. How long have you been interested in fantasy?" she asked. Apparently, she still wanted to chat.

I handed her my debit card. "Forever, I guess. I've never thought about it. It's just always been my go-to genre. Plus, it has everything you would want in a book: adventure, mystery, romance, and sometimes even a little bit of comic relief."

"Interesting…," Addison mumbled.

"What?"

"Oh, nothing. Enjoy your reading," she said.

She waited for me to depart. I grabbed my bag and headed for the exit, but paused at the door. "Are you new here? I'm kind of a regular, and I've never seen you before."

Addison looked over and grinned. "You are very observant."

It was all she would say.

I sighed and left. The girl had acted a bit odd, and thinking of her appearance still unsettled me. However, there was no use in spending the whole night talking to strangers. I couldn't rely on the hope that my parents would never wake up and notice my absence. I checked my cell phone; the time was eleven fifteen. The store closed at eleven.

Why hadn't Addison told me to hurry up and go?

***

As I walked home from the bookstore – the now heavy rain pouring over my hood and soaking my clothes – I couldn't get my mind off the checkout girl, Addison. Something about meeting her had really gotten to me, and I couldn't think of what it was.

Lost in thought, it took me a long time to react to the long tendril of water, like a snake, that shot out from under the railing of the bridge I was crossing. It wrapped itself around my ankle. With a jolt, it pulled me to the wooden surface, my head smacking against the planks, my palms and knees scraping along the rough wood. My bag of books hit the floor and slid out of my grasp. Crying out, I struggled to get up, but the water was stronger than I could imagine.

I couldn't make sense of what was happening, and I didn't really try. The water wrapped around my ankle was icy and cold, and strong enough to pull me right off the bridge. Paralyzed with fear, I couldn't even utter a sound, let alone scream, as I fell. The rain was still pouring, the wind whipping at my face, my heart thumping violently in my chest. *Oh God, oh God, please don't let me die*, I prayed.

I hit the water. The force sent a wave of shock and electrifying pain through me, and for a moment, I could do nothing but take in the incredible agony. The freezing water caused my joints to stiffen. I could barely move.

Then my mind began to focus. I had to fight. I had to get out of here. Thrashing wildly to get to the surface, I struggled to hold my breath and stay alive. My whole body felt weighted down; I couldn't break the surface of the water. The coil of water was still around my ankle, pulling me into the depths of the small lake. Swallowing water, I coughed and spurted until my breath gave out. I was drowning, unable to understand how this could be happening.

I gasped as I swallowed more water; my throat was burning fiercely. Even if I could reach the surface, I wouldn't be able to scream. I knew no sound would come. What would I be able to do then anyway? Swim to shore? What shore? I didn't know where I was, and even if I *was* near a shore, I wasn't sure I had enough will power to swim.

My feet suddenly touched a smooth dirt surface. My first thought was that I had finally landed at the bottom of the lake. But then I realized I was being lifted. I hadn't reached the bottom. A layer of earth had suddenly appeared under my feet, lifting me up toward the surface. I didn't know how to explain what was happening, but I was grateful.

As I began to lose consciousness, I thought about how warm the earthy mud felt between my toes….

***

As I came to, my mind was crowded with thoughts of water and dirt, lots of dirt. I felt covered in it, soaking wet with mud. Every limb felt heavy and sore. My throat was dry and scratchy. My eyes stung. I wanted to open them to see where I was, but I was afraid the action would bring more pain.

It wasn't easy to do – what with the burning sensation in my throat – but I was able to breathe. I was alive. Where was I? What had happened to me?

I decided to take the risk and open my eyes. I was back on the bridge, lying on my back in the middle of the road. It was late, but there was still the chance someone could be driving home.

But I couldn't get up. There was no way. I was tired, terribly cold, and defeated. The dirt beneath me was warm, but the gusts of wind chilled the rest of me to the bone. I was shivering and my teeth were chattering. This was the only sound I heard besides my ragged breathing… nothing else.

Not knowing what to do, or even how to begin to move any farther, I closed my eyes and waited. I didn't know what I was waiting for, but there was nothing else I could do.

I simply waited.

***

The water came back. The tendril once again coiled around my ankle. It was happening again. Feeling completely overwhelmed, this time I didn't even struggle. I didn't fight. I let the water take me. I had nothing left to give. I had nothing left to do. I lay there as the water dragged me nearer and nearer, closer and closer, to the edge of the bridge – massive déjà vu.

"No!" I heard someone shout.

The voice was deep, but I didn't see anyone. I didn't care. I was about to drown anyway. It didn't matter. I had already given up.

God, I'm sorry, I prayed. *I just can't hold on any longer.*

I was slipping. I could feel it. I would fall over the bridge again, and this time no miraculous pile of dirt would lift me to the surface.

But then I realized that it was taking an incredibly long time for me to fall. I was puzzled. It was funny how my only concern at this point was why it was taking me so long to drop into the water.

I lifted my neck slightly to observe what was happening. Immediately I figured out what the problem was…for the water, I mean. Someone was stopping it from taking me. I guessed it was the same someone I had heard shouting. Catching my interest, I put my hands on the ground to stop myself from being dragged any farther by the water. I wanted to see what would happen next.

He was lithe and agile as he moved around me, trying to prevent the water from taking me into the lake once more. It was tricky to notice his exact movements. He was fast, and I was still dizzy and weak…but I did notice one thing.

This man was creating dirt with his very hands, right out of thin air, and he was using the soil to expel the water. I watched vaguely as he created pile upon pile of dirt, but holding back a little in doing so, as if he was afraid to touch the water himself. The mud seemed to be working, though, because it was slowing down the attack and prolonging my safety, but I knew it would take more than that to stop the water completely.

He tried a different tactic. He made another pile of mud and added a few rocks, which he had also created himself. Who was this person? Was I hallucinating, or was this for real? How could it be? I remembered how I had thought Addison was strange. The thought almost made me laugh because of what was going on now. *This* was strange. Addison was nothing compared to this.

Finally, the man created a huge boulder by spreading his hands wide, the rock forming quickly before my eyes. Then he dropped it on the coil of water. The boulder just missed hitting my ankle and smashing my foot to millions of pieces. I stopped moving. The water stopped tugging. Everything was quiet and peaceful.

I breathed a hoarse sigh of relief and threw my hands over my eyes, trying to calm myself down. My heart was racing from a mixture of shock and adrenaline. I still had no idea what had just happened, how it had happened, or who had worked so hard to save me…but at least I was alive.

I made no attempt to move. I wasn't sure of my legs, or how it would feel to stand, so I didn't try.

The man was before me in an instant, his dark, earthy brown eyes staring down at me. Even in the dark, I could see them clearly. He held out his hand to me. Silently, I placed my hand in his and allowed him to pull me up. I owed him my gratitude. He had saved my life, no matter how strange it all seemed.

He was tall, lean, and muscular, with messy dark brown hair, wet from the pouring rain that must have ended while I was unconscious.

When I was on my feet and standing on my own, I waited for the mystery man to say the first words. Unsure of my voice, I didn't speak. I wondered if he would explain himself. I wondered what he would say, if he would tell me the truth or not.

"Are you all right?" he asked, his eyes starting at my toes and ending at my eyes, looking me over to make sure there was no permanent damage. At least not damage that he could see. On the inside, I was freaking out. But he wasn't looking for what was going on with me beneath the surface.

"Yes…I think so," I rasped. I cleared my throat. "But I'm a little sore, a little dizzy, and *very* confused."

"You have a right to be," he replied simply.

"Yeah…."

He didn't say anything else.

"So you aren't going to tell me what just happened?" I deduced. The fact was clearly readable across his face.

He looked me over again and sighed. "Just be careful in the future," he said.

"What's that supposed to mean? How can I be careful when I have no idea why this just happened? Water grabbed me!" I cried, gesturing with my hands toward the side of the bridge where I once lay. "How is that possible?"

When he didn't respond to my questions, I probed him further, trying to get him to answer me. "What about you, with the mud and the rock and the crazy out-of-thin-air thing? What *was* that?" I demanded to know.

"It was saving your life," he said, a hint of petulance creeping into his tone. "Be careful in the future, Ramsey."

Then he took off running, and after a few seconds, he was gone from my sight.

***

Exhaustion sped through my body as I walked home. For once, I was not wide awake in the wee hours. I guess my fight against drowning and unseen forces had sapped my energy.

Who was that man back at the bridge? Why had he saved me, and how had he managed to do so? What was he? Why did he leave so quickly with no explanation? Most importantly, how did he know my name?

They were all questions I could not *begin* to answer.

I limped up the stairs to my bedroom, careful not to make any noise, and fell onto my bed, clutching the bag of books in my hand. I had picked them up before heading home from the bridge. *I'm not going to let a near-death experience take away sixty bucks*, I thought sarcastically to myself. Making jokes was the only way I could avoid thinking about the strangeness of the evening.

I was still soaking wet and muddy. I realized how bad it would be if my parents were to walk in here at this moment, or even my sister. I couldn't just stay like this.

Making as little sound as possible, I stripped from my clothes and soaked them in the sink while I towel dried and scrubbed the mud and water from my skin and hair. I changed into new pajamas and plopped the pile of wet clothes in the hamper, making sure to fit them in amongst the outfit I wore today so it would be harder for my parents to notice them later. I moved slowly as I did all of this in an effort to end the throbbing in my head and the aching of my throat and joints.

Even though I was exhausted, I wanted to read. Reading always helped to calm me down. After everything that had happened, I felt a huge need to let my eyes run through the words on a page or two. Like if I didn't, I would be missing out on something terribly important.

I had made up my mind.

I emptied the books onto my bed and threw the dirty, wet plastic bag into the trash. Curiously, none of the books was wet or

Book idea 

and responsibi

I die of period pains
and then morgan ressurects
me with quesildillas and
she stuffs me in a
bag to oklahoma and
I hide in her attic
then the taco villian
comes and turns her
into a quesildilla
and me and my
quesildilla friend frolich
into the sunset and
live happily ever after

damaged, and I was extremely thankful. I was lucky not to have lost them in the water, *very lucky*.

I carefully put away two of the books on my shelf, keeping the expensive one. I felt a strong, almost eerie, compulsion to read it.

I sat in bed and opened the volume. I immediately noticed an inscription at the top of the table of contents:

Turn to page two hundred and seventy-three. Then you will understand.
-A

I gasped. Could "A" possibly stand for Addison the checkout girl? It had to be. No other explanation seemed reasonable to me at the time. I was about to turn to the page, when there was a soft knock on the door. Startled, I dropped the heavy book, which landed with a *thud* beside my bed.

I wasn't so good with surprises. My reactions were always dramatic.

Mom opened the door and stepped into the room. I quickly reached down and pushed the book under my bed.

"Honey, are you still up? It's two in the morning!" Mom whispered.

"I couldn't sleep, but I think I'm tired now. Goodnight, Mom." I was anxious to get to that page.

Instead of leaving, she came and sat on the bed with me. *Great,* I thought.

"I'm worried about you, Ramsey," she told me.

"You shouldn't be," I replied, too hastily, though, because she sighed and shook her head.

"I don't know about that. You seem very…*distant* lately."

Putting emphasis on the "distant" hadn't made it any easier to hear. Truthfully, I guess I was somewhat distant. Feeling like an outsider didn't exactly make me want to be buddy-buddy with everyone, even the parents I loved. And especially now, I *wanted* to be distant. I'd had a close call back at that bridge. I was in no mood to chat with my mother.

"Sorry, Mom, it's finals. I'm stressed about studying," I lied, clearing my throat to make sure she wouldn't notice how raspy my voice sounded.

I wasn't going to bring up the subject of being "different" from dinner. And I had no intention of telling my mother about the frightening bridge experience. I wanted to keep that to myself, along with the water and magical Earth Man. If I blabbed the story now, my mother would probably think I was insane. Anyway, telling her would also be giving away the fact that I snuck out at night. That wouldn't go over well with either her or my father.

So, yes, I would keep this event to myself for now. It was my own bit of fantasy.

"I'm sure you'll do fine," she said, bringing me back to reality with the sound of her gentle voice. "You always do. Have you thought about what you want to do for your birthday? June seventh is only a few weeks away."

"I'll let you know soon, Mom. I promise."

"All right, now get some sleep. Mondays come too soon."

"They sure do. Good night," I said.

She stopped at the door and turned back. "I love you," she whispered.

"Love you, too," I whispered back.

Instead of getting out of bed for the book, I forgot all about it and fell asleep. Before I knew it, morning had come.

~2~

Coincidences

Mornings were, well, mornings. They were loud, crazy, tiring, and just not fun in general. Don't get me wrong, I loved waking up early. I was a morning person; Dina, not so much. Even this morning, after almost drowning, I was awake. I wasn't tired at all. I think it was because I was still so shocked. But I was surprised that an adrenaline rush could last this long. It was definitely a unique experience.

I couldn't get my mind off what had happened the night before, but I found myself wanting to get back to normalcy. Well, back to my kind of normalcy at least, Ramsey-normalcy.

Almost dying wasn't part of that normalcy. I found myself trying to go on as if nothing had happened, while still remembering the experience in the back of my mind, because I knew occurrences such as these could never truly be forgotten. Other than that, I didn't know what I would do about last night's events, or if I would do anything at all. There was no way I would ever be able to track down that man. I didn't even know his name. Maybe I would just have to forget what had happened and be careful in the future, as he had suggested to me. As for the coil of water, I would simply have to accept that there were incidences in the world I would never be able to explain. At least that was all I had to work with now....

While I quietly ate my eggs at breakfast, Dina yelled at Mom for not doing her laundry the night before. The stylish new red top she had planned to wear was in the wash and wouldn't be ready for school today. It was just an *awesome* start to the day. When the screams finally subsided, I turned to see Dina trotting happily down the stairs, sporting an even more attractive yellow tank with darker yellow spirals across the bottom. I recognized it as the present Mom had been saving for Dina's birthday in August, after buying it in New York during a weekend trip with her friends.

"Nice top," I muttered, still chewing on my eggs.

"Thanks, Mom got it for me. Totally *gorge,* right?"

I strongly disliked it when Dina shortened words. The habit just made her seem flaky and dim. I loved my sister, but she was a little low on the smart ladder.

"Yeah, it's very *gorgeous.*" I smiled and returned to my food.

Dina blew me a kiss and headed for the coffee. She added so much cream and sugar to her cup that I almost choked on my eggs and laughed. I was always amused when teen-aged girls drank coffee just to look sophisticated. They thought the taste was just awful, but if drinking the caffeinated beverage was a way to appear as part of the popular majority, it was totally worth it. In my opinion, coffee was okay, but I preferred herbal teas. I sipped mine and sighed, thinking about how strange everything was, considering my family had no idea about what had occurred last night. We were all following our normal routines, and even I was feeling oblivious to the truth.

Dad ran into the kitchen, tie slung around his neck, briefcase in hand. As a lawyer, he was always on the go. He was moving so fast he almost ran into Dina by the coffee.

"Having a late start, Dad?" I guessed.

"You got it," he said, pouring himself a cup and spilling a little on the counter. Thankfully, Dina was there to clean up the mess.

He muttered a thank you, grabbed the coffee, and left. The closing of the door muffled his goodbye.

Mom came in almost half a second later. She was dressed in a plain t-shirt and jeans. She never dressed up for work. Her baking apron would cover her clothes anyway. It was a wonder any of us could remain healthy with all the extra treats she brought home from the bakery she both owned and operated.

"Girls, are you almost ready for school?"

Dina and I both nodded. After rinsing my plate and placing it in the dishwasher, I hurried upstairs to get dressed. It didn't take me long to pick out an outfit. I chose a pair of jeans and a green and brown stripped polo t-shirt. I grabbed my bag and started to hurry out the door, but once again felt the need to look in the mirror. This happened every morning.

I inspected the strange girl looking back at me, with her white-blonde hair, which light passed through like a thin sheet of paper, and bright emerald eyes. I focused on her pale skin, pink lips, and long, dark lashes. Last of all, my eyes rested on her ears, *my* ears.

With these ears, I felt awkward, insecure, and ugly. I could put up a good front and pretend that the hurtful comments others uttered didn't matter. However, they did. They always did.

I wasn't frail. I could be brave when needed, and I could be strong, as I had been last night. Unfortunately, once my pointy ears were brought up, all the strength I knew was inside of me dwindled until it was nothing but a flickering flame. I knew that if I didn't have my cursed ears, things would go smoothly for me.

Deep inside, I wished I could feel confident about my ears. Something about them seemed right to me, as though they belonged. So far, however, no reasons for my strange feeling had manifested. I was still waiting for something positive to come out of having them.

Sighing, I combed my hair over my pointy appendages and used as many bobby pins as needed to keep it in place, hoping it would hold for a few hours. With that matter taken care of, it was time to go to school.

***

The bus was always crowded when Dina and I got on because we were one of the last stops. Dina found a seat with her friend, Julie, but I didn't sit with any friends on the bus. Dina used to sit with me, but I knew she missed her friends. Some of her friends liked me, but others didn't feel comfortable around me. I finally told her I was fine on my own. I disliked the pity Dina always felt for her socially inept sister. It only made the situation more apparent and worse.

In total, I had one very close friend and a few acquaintances. I had to admit, I was surprised when some of my classmates actually put an effort into having a decent conversation with me...without gawking at my ears.

Carmen had never cared about how I looked. Our friendship began in kindergarten, when she shared her snack with me on the first day of school. She didn't look at my ears when I thanked her. Even as a kid, she saw me as I really was on the inside, not on the outside. We had been inseparable ever since. For Carmen, it had meant earning the label "freak lover." Most of the students had become accustomed to my strange appearance by middle school, but others continued to taunt me.

At school, they stared, pointed, and whispered – not just about my ears, but all the characteristics I had that made me stand out. I sometimes found it funny how features such as white-blonde hair and green eyes were regarded as rare and interesting, but only ignored when it came to me and my ears. But today wasn't one of those days. It was a Monday, and I was not looking forward to school at all, especially after last night's rendezvous.

As I made my way down the bus aisle, I heard snickers from other students, names like "freak" and "Elf Girl," their personal favorite. Sighing and trying to ignore them, I finally found a seat in the back and put down my backpack.

"Thank the Lord," I muttered and sat down, glad to be away from the name-calling and chatter. I needed some peace and quiet this morning.

When I saw her, I literally jumped. I was not comfortable with being caught off guard. When I made it back down to earth, I had to catch my breath, my eyes wide with disbelief.

"Hello," Addison greeted from across the aisle.

Once again, I noticed our resemblance. This morning she was wearing a green t-shirt and faded blue jeans, and the green only made her eyes more prominent. I also noticed the way she fidgeted, shifting as if the clothes she wore were too tight or the fabric was uncomfortable. It was strange to me, only because her outfit appeared to be so casual.

"Sorry I got so scared," I apologized quickly. "I was just surprised to see you here. I didn't know you went to my school."

What a strange coincidence, I thought, but I didn't say the words aloud.

She smiled another bright and warm smile, the kind that made you *want* to be her friend. "I didn't until today. It's my first day at Meadow High."

"It's your first day? But school is over in two weeks," I pointed out.

"Yes…" At that moment, it seemed like she was trying to think of what to say next. "Try telling that to my parents." She laughed lightly, but her eyes betrayed her nerves.

"Did you just move here?" I wondered, still skeptical.

"Yes, we just arrived Friday."

"Wow, I can't believe you got a job so easily," I mentioned.

"It was through a family friend." I could tell she was feeling tense.

"Oh, that's cool."

"Is your throat okay?" she asked.

I coughed and nodded. "Yeah, it's fine. Just…a little dry," I lied.

I wasn't about to tell anyone about my nighttime scare, especially not someone I hardly knew. Addison would probably call me crazy or weird, like everyone else. I wasn't even sure I would tell Carmen. I mean, what happened hadn't even made sense to *me*.

The bus halted and the ride was over. Students were already pushing and shoving to get off. Addison didn't seem like she was ready to leave yet, so I went ahead without her. *What a strange girl*, I thought to myself, and then I laughed to myself. What right did I have to call someone strange?

Just like every other morning, Carmen was waiting for me by my locker. She waved and brushed her dark brown hair behind her ears. Her smooth complexion and dark eyes were alluring, and she often stood out in a different way than I.

Carmen and her family had moved here from Texas when she was five after leaving Spain when she was three. While most of her other relatives remained in Dallas, her father had gotten a job at a local university and her family had been ready for a change of scenery. I remembered that she had tried to teach me Spanish when we first met, but I completely failed at learning. I was trying to redeem myself in high school by taking a few classes, but I still didn't have much luck with the language.

"Hey, Ramsey!" she called in her accented voice, still noticeable after all these years.

"Hey C, what's up?"

Yes, I called her C. It was better than using an automobile, Car, as a nickname. I couldn't even imagine the horror. Calling her C just fit.

"Nothing really. But yesterday my family came all the way from Texas for my sister's first birthday. Can you believe it? She didn't even know what was going on! She's only a baby." Carmen rolled her eyes.

"Wait, the *whole* family?" I asked.

"Yes," she confirmed.

"I wish I could have seen it."

"No, you don't, trust me," she said seriously, which only made me giggle. "Way too many mixed accents and a whole lot of food forced down your throat. Apparently, I'm too skinny."

I laughed, and was about to comment back when the five-minute bell rang. I was going to be late.

"Crap," I muttered.

"Watch your language!" Carmen said, and then she laughed.

I sighed and grabbed the books I would need for class. "Whatever," I said sarcastically.

"See you third period. Our Spanish presentation's going to kick –"

"Language!" I interrupted.

"Ugh, whatever!" she called as I walked away.

"Bye," I replied, and hurried to my Calculus class.

I wasn't an overachiever. School just came easy for me, not that I liked it all.

It wasn't ordinary for sophomores to be taking multiple advanced placement classes, but I needed some kind of challenge in school, or I would feel useless. All of my classes were with upperclassmen, or scary-smart sophomores like me, except for

Spanish and Gym, the latter of which because I wasn't much of an athlete; more like clumsy and uncoordinated.

Calculus, my first hour, was probably one of the most boring classes I had ever taken. I could hardly pay attention enough to notice Mr. Kurt's ugly new sweater. The math was so simple it made me want to smack myself in the face. A.P. Chemistry wasn't very fun either. I was relieved when I finally made it to Spanish. At least there, I could chat with Carmen and allow her to brighten my day with some of her fun attitude. I still hadn't mentioned anything to anyone about my watery accident. It wasn't something I could bring up at school.

Carmen was already in her desk, making the final adjustments to our project, and I was relieved I wouldn't have to spend the beginning of yet another class alone, twiddling my thumbs and cursing myself for forgetting one of the books I had bought the night before.

For our project, we had to research the country Venezuela, and then make a poster on how different it was from the most popular Spanish country, Spain. It had to be both written and presented in Spanish. For Carmen it was easy, but for a foreign language-challenged person like me, it was real work. It was so unlike my other classes.

"How's it looking?" I asked, as I sat down in my assigned seat.

"*Fantastico*!" Carmen replied in her perfect Spanish accent.

She was fluent in her native language, but took Spanish to get credits and have a class with me. I loved her for that. Being alone in most of my classes had never helped my confidence level. Thankfully, I had Carmen who could always boost it back up.

"It looks amazing. We're a great team."

"Oh yeah!" Carmen replied enthusiastically.

"*Siéntese, por favor!*" Senora Peters called in her fake accent.

She wasn't Spanish at all. That bugged me a little because it didn't seem like she knew much about the language herself. She had even mentioned once that it was her backup plan for teaching, her first being math. They weren't even remotely related subjects!

Carmen saw the look on my face and laughed. She knew how I felt about school. I felt like I was wasting my time here. Nevertheless, what else could I do? Where else could I go? Unfortunately, freaks didn't fit in anywhere. That's why they were called freaks.

We were the last group to present. We did really well, and before we left, Senora Peters told us to expect an A. The day hadn't been too bad. It was the usual, mostly. I found it was easier to forget the almost-drowning incident when things were going so simply.

***

Okay, so I said that entirely too soon. The day wasn't so bad until I got to A.P. Lit. Today we were having a group discussion on *Romeo and Juliet* versus today's love stories. Mrs. Marx went through a list of questions and we had a group discussion where participation was a requirement. But that wasn't the unfortunate part. I didn't have a problem speaking out in class. It was different when the discussions concerned my education. The awful part was what came at the *end* of class.

"Now remember that tickets for this Saturday's *Last Century Ball* are on sale during lunch. Support your Music department's annual Chicago trip for next year by buying one for you and that special someone!" Mrs. Marx reminded us, pointing to the poster taped to the wall.

That was why the day went sour. The ball was this Saturday, and as an Honors Choir member, I *had* to go. The problem was simple. Freaks didn't go to balls! It wasn't as if anyone had asked me. Carmen was going with some guy she met through one of her cousins. If only I were so lucky.

But I had a dress, an amazing dress at that. Mom took Dina and me shopping a couple of weeks ago, and I found the perfect outfit. The gown was emerald green with a black ribbon around the waist that hung down the center. My black velvet choker with my name written across in green print would match perfectly, as well as some elbow length black gloves.

The Last Century Ball was kind of like prom, but for all grades. The dress had to be a gown, no exceptions, and the boys had to wear suits and ties. Yep, that was going to be fun.

However, the ball wasn't until Saturday, so I decided I would worry about it later. Instead, I focused on reviewing for finals. Most of my classes were easy, but I found I could sometimes crack under pressure, which was *why* I studied. When I got to Gym class after A.P. European History, I was ready to relieve some study stress. I almost cried out with joy when our teacher announced we were running a mile. I needed to clear my head.

While the others complained, huffed, and puffed the whole mile, I breathed evenly and let the stress wash from my mind. I actually loved running. It released all of my troubles so I could focus on just one thing, the road ahead. I was not a very talented athlete, but running was the one activity I excelled at in Gym…as long as there was nothing to trip over along the way.

I found myself remembering the man from the night before as I jogged around the track. He was young, maybe only a few years older than I was, and handsome. Something about him hadn't seemed…*human* to me. The way he moved, what he did with the dirt and rocks, how he could make things appear out of thin air. It wasn't normal, but I felt drawn to it. It was like something out of a fantasy book. I might have hallucinated; there was always the chance of that, because I *had* hit my head a few times during all the turmoil. However, I wasn't one to be skeptical about these kinds of things, and I had a gut feeling that the night before was no hallucination. Yet how else could I explain it?

I was one of the first runners to finish the mile, so I went out to the hallway to get a drink of water at the bubbler. Yes, I called it a bubbler. I was from Wisconsin…need I say more?

I actually wasn't surprised to see Addison taking a drink herself, because lately so many strange occurrences and coincidences were linked closely together. I made a coughing noise and waited to see if she would turn around.

"Hello, Ramsey," she said softly, but she didn't turn to face me.

"You know my name?" It was all I could say in return. She moved so I could take a drink. "How do you know *my* name?" I asked after I was finished.

Addison hesitated. "Uh…You paid with a debit card, and your name was on it," she said.

"Oh yeah, I forgot. Sorry."

"No problem."

"I found out your name from your tag."

"I assumed so," she said.

"Okay, then…," I trailed off.

She didn't make the initiative to leave or continue the conversation. It seemed like she was waiting for me to keep talking, but I didn't know what to say. I didn't have much experience with chitchat. We stood there, facing each other, neither of us moving or speaking.

I hated awkward silences. This was definitely an awkward silence.

"So, which class do you have right now?" I finally asked, trying not to sound too stupid.

"I have Orchestra."

"What instrument do you play?' I asked. I was glad my attempt at small talk was working.

"I play the fiddle."

"You play the fiddle? I didn't think anyone called violins by that name anymore."

"Where I come from they do," she said.

"Where *do* you come from?"

Addison looked to the side for one split second and shook her head. What was with her? She always gave the weirdest looks.

"I have to get back to class. I'll see you around, Ramsey," she said, and briskly walked away.

"Bye, Addison!" I called. I didn't think she had heard me.

My last class of the day was Honors Choir. It was my all-time favorite class. I loved to sing so much that I probably sang in my sleep. Singing was another way for me to relieve stress, and when I sang a chord with the rest of the choir, I felt like I belonged. Like I was a part of something wonderful.

We practiced a new piece today, a beautiful song about roses. By the end of class, we had gotten pretty far. When the bell rang, I had only one goal: get out before Katie saw me.

Katie. How could I describe someone like her? I didn't think I could even think of the right words to form an accurate description. She was evil smacked between two buns of cruel. *Katie.* I *really* disliked Katie.

She had despised me since the first day of freshman year. Why? I had no idea. What was there to hate? I didn't even talk to her. I never talked to anyone unless he or she approached me first. When I *did* try to talk with new people, they couldn't stop staring at my ears and asking why I was so strange. I finally got tired of it and gave up trying to make friends. I chose to stick with Carmen and the few others in school who weren't embarrassed to be seen carrying on a conversation with me.

Even worse was that Katie and her millions of minion friends liked targeting me as their punching bag – not literally, but mentally. They were the only ones in school who made fun of my strange looks every single day without fail. Others did it once in a while and I didn't notice as much. However, these girls did it all of the time.

Lost in thought, I ran right into the witch I had hoped to avoid.

"Hi, Ramsey, you did a great job in class today," she said, speaking in her sarcastic tone.

"Just leave me alone, Katie," I muttered.

"Oh, I'm sorry, I couldn't hear you. I don't have big pointy ears like you do, so you'll have to speak up," she shouted.

What a slimy little creep! I thought to myself. How could she say it repeatedly and still have it get to me?

"It doesn't seem like you have any ears at all. If you did, you would have heard how off-key you sounded today," I retorted.

Okay, so she was never off-key. Nevertheless, I had to say something back to her.

"You should bring that little attitude to the ball on Saturday. I bet the guys will be scared enough to ask you to dance…for once."

That was it. I was about ready to slap this chick.

"Katie, get out of my way," I said, brushing past her as she started to laugh.

"Okay, see you at the ball, freak," she called as I walked away.

Now I knew freak wasn't necessarily that bad of an insult, but that word always stung me. I think it was because I knew she was right. I was a freak.

Brushing away the tears that started streaming down my face, I ran to catch the bus before it left. It would really suck if I was stuck here, crying, with Katie, and my throat still sore from almost drowning.

***

I thought Addison would be on the bus home. I wanted to talk to her again. She seemed nice enough. Maybe I could finally make another friend. She hadn't said a thing about my ears, even though she had to have noticed them at some point during our conversations. Maybe she was different from the rest. Maybe talking with her could get my mind off Katie and the accident.

Unfortunately, she wasn't there.

***

That afternoon at home, I did my best to keep my mind off the accident. I tried to forget the water, the dirt, the bridge, the man…but to no avail. I couldn't focus on homework or studying. I couldn't focus on anything but last night.

Maybe I needed to see the bridge again, go back to where the accident took place. Have some closure. That was it. I needed closure, to convince myself that I hadn't dreamt it all. That it was real. What proof would I find there? I had no idea. I just had to go back, so I told Dina I would return by the time our parents got home for dinner at seven and left the house.

***

I arrived at the bridge a little before six, and the sun was just starting to set, its orange and red hues making the area seem peaceful and serene. Today, though, I didn't feel the calm. It was a scene of remembrance, panic, and danger. I felt uneasy being here, despite how badly I had wanted to come.

But now that I was here, I could just turn around and go home. However, I knew closure wasn't that easy, so I stepped onto the bridge and walked slowly and nervously toward the railing where I was pulled into the lake. I grabbed hold of the wood tightly and curled my fingers over the edge. I was shaking. I felt my eyes closing tightly, afraid and waiting for something bad to happen, but nothing did.

I knew I was acting paranoid. Whatever was here the night before was now gone. Everything was fine, but I was still panicking.

Then I saw a hand grab the edge of the bridge beneath my feet. I screamed and jumped backward, falling down in the process, my butt hitting the ground hard. I scooted backward and over to the other side of the bridge and waited, my backside throbbing and my head spinning. I wanted to scream again, but no sound came. Why was it that no one could ever scream when it was really necessary? Seeing a spider last week got a bigger shriek from me.

I waited.

Soon the hand was two hands, then a head.

It was Addison.

"What…are…you…doing here?" I cried, breathing heavily from both relief and shock.

"I…I….was…."

I stared at her, wide-eyed, waiting for an explanation. What was she doing at the exact spot where I had almost drowned? This couldn't be a coincidence, I knew, but seeing her didn't make me want to believe it.

"I was just sightseeing."

I stared at her blankly, wishing I had the guts to go over and push her into the lake. Sightseeing, what kind of lame excuse was that?

"You see, because I'm new here, I don't know much about the town. So I thought I would go for a walk and look around."

"So you go under a bridge?" I said, raising an eyebrow disbelievingly.

She nodded. "Yes. I like water. I wanted to check it out."

"That makes one of us," I murmured.

She seemed to have heard me because of her next words. "Why, did something happen to you here?"

"Why would you ask that?" I asked.

"Just wondering," she replied.

"Yeah, uh-huh," I said. "Addison, want to tell me what's really going on here?"

"Nothing, really, I was just looking around. Honest. Anyway, I have to get home. See you later, Ramsey."

Then, just as the man had done the night before, Addison ran off, away from the bridge, and away from me.

***

I looked for Addison on the way to school the next day. I wanted a better explanation as to why she was "sightseeing" near that bridge. It was strange and a little "out there" to think so, but I had this weird feeling she was in some way connected to the bridge accident. Just thinking about these coincidences and connections made me shiver.

When I looked for her on the bus the next morning, my shoulders fell when I realized she wasn't there again. I saw her during lunch and called out to her, but she slipped away before I could catch up to her. The following two days were the same. By Friday, I was getting annoyed.

I didn't know why, but there was something about the way Addison carried herself, the way she presented herself to me, that drew me to her. It was as if I was looking for an answer only she could give, but had no clue as to what it or the question was. All I knew was that I wanted and needed to talk with her again, at least about the bridge. Maybe then, I could figure out why she unsettled me so.

I had tried to keep busy studying. Carmen came over almost every day so we could help each other, but I could never get my mind off Addison. I replayed our conversations in my head, but no ideas came to mind as to why I was so determined to speak with her again. Her actions had been strange, but that wasn't all of it. For some reason, she was *important*. She became more of a mystery to me every day that I wanted to solve.

I finally got my chance to talk to her that Friday morning. She was back in the same bus seat she had been in on Monday, so I sat down across from her again.

"Hi, Addison," I said.

"Hello, Ramsey," she replied.

"You haven't been on the bus for a while."

"Oh, well, my mother had off of work, so she drove me."

Her mom took days off already after just moving here? I quickly dismissed the thought, though. Her personal life wasn't any of my business.

"That's cool," I said.

"Yes…cool," she said, a little awkwardly.

"So, do any more sightseeing lately?" I asked suspiciously.

She simply shrugged and looked away. Addison didn't seem to be her cheery self today. She definitely didn't seem like she wanted to talk about the bridge. Instead, she was giving off a vibe that was tense and serious.

"Is something bothering you?" I wondered.

"Why?" she asked, her eyes flickering from me to her lap.

"You just seem, I don't know…tense. Different."

"Oh, it's nothing. Just new school issues."

"I understand," I said, nodding slowly. "School can be tough."

"Is it tough for you?" she asked.

"What?"

I thought she had seen my ears. Hadn't she guessed it was tough?

"Is school tough for you?" she repeated.

"Well, yes, because of my looks."

"What's wrong with them?"

"You haven't noticed my ears?" I wondered.

Then it hit me. Maybe she hadn't noticed and that was why she was so nice. Now she would probably go all Katie on me and call me a freak. *Nice going, Ramsey*, I criticized myself.

"Yes, you have pointy ears. So what?" she asked, not at all getting the point I was trying to put across.

"Yeah, people usually react by calling me some kind of name."

"That's the most disgusting thing I have ever heard!" This time Addison looked like there was fire in her forest green eyes.

"Yeah, well, it's true."

"Humans can be so cruel," she muttered.

"What did you say?" I asked, completely dumbfounded.

"I said people can be so cruel," she said, too quickly to be a normal statement.

"No…you said 'humans' can be so cruel. Why would you say that? We are all humans. You sound as if you are some kind of other creature."

I had meant the comment to be taken lightly, but apparently, Addison hadn't seen it the same way. Her eyes snapped shut and her lips formed into a tight line.

For a while, she didn't say a word. It wasn't until we were almost at school that she finally spoke again.

"Ramsey, you are an elf," she said quietly.

"What?" I gasped.

I hadn't expected such a weird remark from her. She said it so seriously….

"You are an elf," she said again.

"Are you kidding me? Is this because you are mad about me making a big deal about the bridge? Is this a way to get back at me?"

What kind of a girl said things like that? Was she out of her mind?

"No. It's the truth, Ramsey," she said. "I know it sounds a little absurd, especially coming from a stranger like me, but I can't keep it from you any longer. You deserve to know the truth. The reason I'm here is –"

"Did Katie put you up to this?" I asked, ignoring the sincerity in her tone.

"Katie?" Her brow furrowed in confusion.

"Are you trying to mess with me like everyone else?"

"No!" she cried.

"I can't believe this. I didn't think you would be the same as all the other jerks in this school," I snapped. "Sure, you acted a little strange, but I didn't mind because I thought you were different."

The bus pulled to a halt. I shook my head and got up from my seat.

"Unfortunately, I'm only one thing, Addison, and it is spelled F-R-E-A-K."

I ran off the bus without waiting for her reply. I had a feeling this was going to be a long and difficult day.

***

Carmen was with her Geometry study group during lunch, so I had to sit alone. It was a great day to be upset. Nothing was going the way I wanted. Actually, most days didn't go the way I wanted, but today was exceptionally worse. At least I wouldn't ruin Carmen's day with my sour mood.

I sat alone until Addison walked into the lunchroom. I grabbed my tray to join her and hoped she would be ready to explain herself for what had happened on the bus. I wanted to confront her, give her a piece of my mind. The stunt she had pulled wasn't funny and wasn't right. She had played so nice, as if trying to be my friend. Then she had turned. It was probably my ears again, considering she had called me an elf. Elf, like I hadn't heard that one before. Yet still, it hurt, just like all the other insults.

I didn't notice Katie's leg sticking out from under her table. I tripped, and my tray went up into the air, landing with a *smack* on the floor. I tried to regain my balance, but the pasta now covering the floor was slippery and I found myself falling backward. I screamed and desperately tried to brace myself for the impact even with what little time I had to do so.

I could hit my head! I could get hurt! What had Katie been thinking? It was so first grade, yet it had worked. I was making a fool of myself, which was exactly what she wanted.

I waited for the fall to come, but it never did. Instead, I felt firm hands on my shoulders and the weight of another body holding me up. I was saved, but *by whom?* I wondered.

I looked up into the eyes of a boy I had never seen before. He had raven-black hair that went just to his chin in rustic cut-off angles and seemed to shine unnaturally in the cafeteria light. He had a strong jaw, bright green eyes, and perfect pale white skin. I wanted to touch it; it looked so smooth and beautiful. Like how marble would feel, only I detected a slight color tone in his cheeks. He was pale, but definitely a living, breathing, masterpiece. He had an intense look on his face, but I could also detect a slight grin.

This was just too weird for me. Not only was he beautiful – I mean hot, drop-dead gorgeous beautiful – but he also reminded me strangely of Addison. Like her, he looked serene, beautiful, and almost *royal*. It was as though he had a kind of power others only dreamed of, like he and Addison had something others didn't have, something that gave them an aura of incredible power and grace. He was strength, but not in a physical way – rather, in a spiritual kind of way. He was the essence of something mere mortals could not grasp.

It was weird how just by looking at him, a rush of mature and regal-sounding words came to mind.

I couldn't look away from his features, as if my eyes were permanently fixed on his face. He was just so utterly breathtaking....

But I tore my eyes away from his beauty to focus on the matter at hand. This guy had just saved me from what could have been a dangerous fall. He deserved a thank you.

"Thanks," I breathed out.

"Are you okay?" he asked in a sweet tenor voice.

"Yeah, I think so."

He helped me to stand and made sure I was on my feet before he let go. I was somewhat sad that he did. I had seen hot guys before, but none like this.

I looked over to Katie, who was still and quiet. It seemed the whole lunchroom had shut up.

"Thanks for that," I said to him, my gaze returning to his face.

"No problem," he said smoothly.

"Those were some great saving skills."

He laughed and ran a hand through his amazing black hair, as if he had done this kind of thing before. "I have been told I'm always in the right place at the right time," he remarked.

"You were this time. Thanks."

I couldn't stop saying thank you. I must have sounded like an idiot to him.

He smiled, showing perfect sparkly white teeth. *Oh my....*

"I'm Ramsey." I put my hand out for him to shake. He hesitated, then took it firmly and released.

"Stellan," he replied.

He definitely had the perfect name to match his perfect looks. This guy was sure *stellar.* I couldn't stop marveling at the grace with which he held himself. It mesmerized me completely to the point where I felt weak in the knees and an aching inside to throw my arms around him. No boy had *ever* made me feel this way. I hadn't even *thought* of anyone this way before.

I wanted to say more. I wanted to think of a way to keep him talking to me. To keep him focused on me. To make him find me as interesting as I found him, though I knew that was impossible. I couldn't compare to this. I may be attractive in some ways, without my ears of course, but not like this. Stellan didn't look weird. He looked like a dark-haired angel.

Unfortunately, the lunch bell rang almost instantly after our introduction and he turned away to leave.

"See you around, Ramsey," he said before he left.

I gasped, covering my hands over mouth, my eyes wide open in sheer astonishment. It hadn't been his line about seeing me again that had me almost gasping for air – though that sort of thing hardly ever happened and should have surprised me. No, it wasn't his words.

It was the pair of perfectly pointy ears that finally showed as he walked away that totally freaked me out. I decided that maybe he *was* a little weird. Just. Like. Me.

Things had just gotten a lot more complicated.

~3~

Elfen

Then I fell for real. By fell, I mean fainted. At least it was in a different direction so I didn't hit my spilled lunch. Sadly, this time I had no one to catch me.

I woke up in the nurse's office, woozy and in pain. They told me I had hit my head pretty hard when I fell. That was obvious. That cafeteria floor wasn't made of marshmallows.

Mom came to pick me up; the school's procedure was that I go home. Don't worry, they said; I could still go to the ball. *Woohoo!* I thought sarcastically to myself. Too bad I didn't get a concussion or something. It would have been nice to have an excuse not to go. But I wasn't so lucky.

"What happened, Ramsey?" Mom asked during the car ride home.

I decided not to mention the encounter with my pointy-eared rescuer. That would have definitely made my mother ask questions I was in no mood or position to answer. Instead, I went with an easy excuse, one that I knew would work as long as I didn't let anything about Stellan slip. I had to admit it was hard not to say his name aloud. Just the thought still gave me goose bumps. I could picture his face clearly in my mind. Focusing on his image seemed to take the pain away from my head. Then I would remember his ears, and the headache would start all over again. Things were getting very weird lately, even for me. I knew that eventually I would have to come out of this huge mess of denial, because my plan to ignore the strange occurrences that kept happening wasn't exactly working. Almost as if the more I ignored them, the more weird stuff kept happening.

"Katie tripped me during lunch, and I fell and blacked out," I said.

"Why are girls your age so mean to each other all the time? When I was in school, I remember there being mean girls, but they never did anything physical!"

"Yeah, if only we could go back to the good old days," I said sarcastically.

Why did parents always have to bring up when they were in school? As if it mattered what had happened to them. I was living in the now, and right now my head was killing me.

"Oh, stop it, Ramsey. I know your head hurts, but try not to act so foul."

"Sorry," I said.

"You know, sometimes I just don't understand you, hon."

"No one ever does...." I sighed.

"Maybe you need to open up to people more. Let new friends in."

I rolled my eyes and shook my head, which only made the pain worse. Not even my loving parents would ever understand my life. Though I probably hadn't been thinking clearly because of the pain, in the back of my mind, I had a feeling that if anyone were to ever understand me, it would be Addison, or even Stellan....The feeling both unnerved and comforted me.

Mom went back to work after I was safe in bed, so I had some time to think. What had happened today? I still could hardly believe what I had seen and what I had heard. That gorgeous guy was actually a freak like me. How could it be possible? I thought I was a genetic mess-up, an accident. Now here stood Stellan, incredibly good looking with *his* pointy ears.

I knew somehow that Addison fit into all of this. I just didn't know why all these strange things were happening all of the sudden. Why had she told me I was an elf? Surely, it couldn't be true. There was no way my life could be that interesting, that unreal. I was simply a freak. There couldn't be anything more to it than that...could there?

Something in the back of my mind was screaming to be known, but it may just have been my head begging for painkillers. The weak stuff they gave me at school wasn't doing much good. In fact, it felt like I hadn't taken anything at all. Didn't those nurses read their manuals?

Thinking of manuals finally led me to remembering the book. The book…that's what I had trouble remembering! I had meant to look at the page in the inscription, but I had forgotten all about it. I had to look through it now. I couldn't put it off. I knew somehow that this book – no matter how crazy it sounded because it was just a fantasy book – held something important for me. Being careful not to move too quickly, I slowly reached under my bed and felt around until I found leather.

Without hesitation, I turned to page two hundred and seventy-three. The sight of the picture hit me with an invisible force I couldn't describe, and I felt the woozy feeling coming back again.

It was a woman: pale-haired, pale-skinned, green-eyed, and with pointy ears. She was extraordinarily stunning, pure like an angel. Her skin was almost luminescent, glowing with an incredible light. Next to her was another woman, but this one had pitch-black hair that shined unnaturally for a picture in a storybook. The man next to them looked almost exactly like Stellan, handsome and regal.

I struggled to read the name at the top of the picture.

"*Elf*," I barely whispered.

Had Addison been telling me the truth? Was I really an elf? How? Elves didn't exist! I couldn't deny the fact that I had believed in things like fairies most of my life, but the belief had never been so close to the truth. I never expected the fantasy to become a reality, but now it appeared as though it was.

Sure, kids in school had called me Elf Girl, but I had always thought of elves as Santa's helpers. These elves were beautiful and different. They were thin and tall. They were magical. They seemed so alive, full of mystery and intrigue.

I decided to read on. I had to know every fact and every detail. I didn't know why I was buying into this so quickly, but I didn't stop to think about it.

I started with the introduction. Under "appearance," I read that elves – or elfin folk – were more beautiful than humans, either fair-haired or black-haired, had excellent singing voices, and were a lot like fairies without wings. They had pale skin and angelic physical characteristics, described as *glowing people.* They were angels without the wings, mysterious and pure.

Elves were much more gifted in magic than humans, stronger mentally but not physically, had sharper senses and perceptions, and were said to be wiser as well. They loved nature and the forest, and hardly ever lived very far from a group of trees.

It was all there. I matched everything: their appearance, singing abilities, mentality, and physical ability. It also explained why I liked the forest so much. It was all there for me in standardized print.

Yet, a small part of me didn't want to believe it, because believing it would change my life. Until today, I would have traded anything for a new life; now I wasn't so sure. I was afraid of what the future would bring if I chose to believe.

Nevertheless, how could I truly be an elf? My parents weren't like me, and neither was my sister. How could I have been born an elf randomly?

I looked under the family section to see if I could figure it out. It said elves and humans never mated because elves tended to stay in their world and humans in theirs – whatever that meant.

If they did, the elf gene would be gone, leaving the new baby completely human. An elf couldn't be born without two elfin parents. So, if it were true, I would have different parents, parents other than the ones I had shared a home with my whole life. I wondered if I even wanted to believe in the possibility….

Did I forget to mention that some countries thought elves were demons? They looked like angels, but that was to deceive humans and lure them with their magic and beauty. Yeah, that's right. I could be a demon. Once again, *great.*

Before I could shut the book and throw it across the room, another section caught my eye. It was on elf circles. I had heard of fairy rings from my fantasy books. If you stepped in the mushroom rings, you would end up in the fairy world. I had never heard of elf circles. Curious, I decided I would read just a few more lines from the fantasy guide:

"On lake shores, where the grass met the water, you could find elf circles. They were round places where the grass was flattened like a floor. Elves had danced there. It could be dangerous, and one would fall ill if one stepped over such a place or if one disturbed anything there."

I threw the book across the room and it smacked against my bookshelf before dropping to the floor. I lay back on my bed and rubbed my temples, feeling a stronger headache coming on. This was all too much for me to handle, too much information, and too much shock and confusion. I couldn't process it.

Was I really an elf? If so, what was I supposed to do about it?

Addison's name floated through my mind, and suddenly I knew with a one hundred percent certainty that she was the key to all of this. Finally, I knew the reason for my gut feeling. I knew why she had such significance.

I decided I hoped Addison would be at the ball tomorrow, because I was *not* leaving until I got some answers.

***

I tried to hide my problems from my family, but it didn't work. They knew something was wrong, just not what it was. I wanted to keep it that way. Until I had some answers of my own, I didn't want to give any to anyone else. Thankfully, Dina spent all Saturday getting ready for the ball and didn't have time to dig any deeper into my issues.

We met downstairs, both dressed in our new gowns. Dina was ready to party; I was ready to get some answers.

I had to admit, I looked good in my dress. If it weren't for my ears and the dozen questions clouding my mind, I would be just another girl excited for a fairytale night at the ball. However, that was not the case. For a brief moment, I wished I was going to the ball with someone other than my sister. Maybe someone like Stellan….The thought drifted in and out of my mind.

Dina looked gorgeous – as always – normal teen material, unlike my odd forms of beauty. Her dress was a soft peach with rhinestones decorating the top and sparkles all over the skirt. It was also strapless, making her look older and more developed in the chest region, which sparked some remarks from Mom, who didn't really approve of the dress. She would definitely get looks all around, the good kind. I would be stared at, but not because I looked good. Just because of who I was.

I was glad Dina had a date. It would keep her busy while I searched for Addison. Dina always felt it was her job to hang out with me when I was alone. I knew she meant well, but she only did it because she felt sorry for me. That just made me feel worse. My younger sister felt sorry for me. How lame.

However, tonight was different. Carmen would be there, so Dina let it go this time. I wouldn't be hanging around Carmen too much, though. She also had a date, and I had no interest in spending time with them. I wanted to find only one person: Addison.

Maybe Stellan as well, if I could....It was tricky to keep my mind off him for very long lately.

The dance was in the school gym. The theme was Medieval Times, and the huge space looked amazing. Carmen was on the decorating committee, so I figured it would be good, but I was still pleasantly surprised. Many students were already dancing when we arrived. I was glad I wasn't one of the first ones there; no need to draw attention to myself. I had to try to blend in, though I knew it wouldn't work out the way I planned. I had never blended in one day of my life. In fact, I hadn't even gotten close, but I would try my best to stay hidden tonight.

"Are you going to be okay, Ramsey?" Dina asked when we walked in.

"Of course, go and have fun," I told her, anxious to be alone.

"Okay, you try and have fun too!" Dina ran off to join her friends.

I sighed and watched her go. Finally, I could look around. I probably looked odd walking around the dancing students. As far as I could see, I was the only one on the dance floor not dancing. I tried not to pay attention to that.

Looking for Addison turned out to be incredibly difficult. The gym was pitch-dark except for the flashing colored strobe lights from the DJ booth. I really hoped Addison would be here, and part of me worried that I would never find her. Even so, I tried to stay optimistic.

I wanted to call out her name, but the roaring music didn't give me a chance. I would probably look even more out of place anyway. I decided to leave the gym and look for her in the cafeteria, where they were serving cake and punch.

On the way, I passed Dina making out with her boyfriend. *Yuck.* Oh well, you could only be young once, I guess. If my mother were there, she would probably have had a coronary. I prayed Dina would be careful. She didn't notice me walk by, and I didn't say anything. What she did wasn't any of my business. I had business of my own.

"Hello, Ramsey," Addison chimed.

Here was another one of those moments when I jumped into the air, literally.

"Holy crap, you scared me!" I cried and turned around. "I've been looking for you everywhere."

"Why?" Addison asked.

It took me a moment to speak because I was so transfixed by the girl standing before me. She looked amazing in her gown. Vibrant and full of life, her face shone with confidence, as if she had nothing to hide. I suddenly felt envious of her. She was so different from me, even though we looked so similar. She was the essence of life, while I treated every day as if it were the end of the world.

Her dress was a deep violet with slight, elegant ruffles from the waist to the bottom hem. I drew my eyes up to her face. Her pale hair hid her ears. I finally knew why, or at least I thought I knew why....

"Ramsey? Hello?" Addison looked like she was getting irritated with my lack of response.

"I need to talk to you," I blurted.

"We *are* talking," she reminded me.

"I need to talk to you alone, Addison. Please."

She seemed to understand my urgency and nodded. "Where should we go?" she asked in an almost whisper.

"In five minutes outside by the bench under the willow tree."

"All right. I'll be there," she said.

She hardly made a sound as she left me standing in the cafeteria. I wondered how she was able to be so light on her feet, being so tall.

Our meeting place was secluded enough to talk, which was good, because I needed answers. I had to know the truth so I could move on. Maybe then, I would be able to put aside the accident on the bridge.

The easiest way to the place was by going through the gym and out the front door. I was halfway through when Carmen rushed over to me, a wide smile across her face.

"What have you been up to?" I asked, still in a hurry.

"I've been with Jack. He is so amazing!"

Carmen was bouncing with excitement and her eyes were shining. She looked so *happy*. I wondered when I had last felt the same way, probably never. Carmen smoothed down her gown: layers of blue edged with black lace and decorated at the shoulders with roses.

"I'm happy for you, Carmen, really, I am. But I have to go. I'm meeting someone," I explained quickly.

"Who are you meeting?"

"No one important," I said too hastily. I had backed myself into a trap by showing just how eager I was to meet Addison. I fought the urge to curse and prayed Carmen would let it go.

She didn't.

"Who is it?" she asked instead.

"Carmen, I really have to go." I was trying my best to wiggle my way out of the mess I had created.

"Why won't you tell me? Is it a guy?"

Ignoring her questions, I shook my head. "I have to go. I'll talk to you later. Have fun with Jack." I walked away before she could protest, immersing myself in the crowd of dancing students.

I felt bad about keeping secrets from Carmen. She was my best friend, my only true and genuine friend, but I couldn't say anything about Addison. Not until I could talk with her face to face. I knew I would have to apologize to Carmen later, but now wasn't the right time.

I knew I was late when I finally reached the spot. Addison was already waiting on the bench. I didn't know how to start the conversation, so I just sat down and waited for what seemed like hours. I never was a good conversation starter. I wasn't outgoing in any way, not to mention that I was a bit awkward when talking with others. I didn't have much experience in the social department, and I blamed it on my low self-esteem and pointy ears. Sometimes I wished I could cut them off, no matter how much I needed them.

The growing silence between us was hard to handle. Finally, she spoke.

"Did you turn to page two hundred and seventy-three?" she asked seriously, her hands clasped over her lap.

I knew what she was referring to; she was the one who left the message. I had no idea how she did it, but she had. I nodded slowly.

"What did you learn?" she asked.

"I learned that I could be…"

"Could be what?"

I decided to lay it all down. "Were you really telling me the truth, Addison? Am I an elf?"

Asking it aloud sounded really dumb. I felt stupid and immature just for uttering the word. The whole situation reminded me of a cheesy television show or kid movie, or like a line from a storybook. This just *couldn't* be real.

Maybe it *was* Katie playing a nasty joke on me after all. I could see her setting up the whole thing, could imagine it in my mind. It made perfect sense. Kids had been calling me Elf Girl for years. It was just a matter of time before someone played a joke like this, especially with the huge craze over fantasy books and movies these days. Heck, there was always some way to connect what was make-believe to real life. You just had to have the brains to do it. Or, in Katie's case, the audacity and cold heart to go through with it.

Had I just walked into a trap? It was probable. *Boy, am I gullible*, I thought to myself.

Then she said the one word that turned everything around.

She said…

"Yes."

Deep down, I had expected that answer, but it still sent shivers down my spine. She said it with such a fierce seriousness, such a certainty. I knew she was telling the truth. I could *feel* it.

"How?" I asked.

"What do you mean?"

"How can I be an elf?"

"You just are one," she said, shrugging.

I bit my tongue to keep from shouting at her. If she didn't give me more of an explanation, I would hurt her. I could barely contain my confusion and frustration as it was.

"But how? My parents aren't elves, are they? They don't look like me or you."

"What makes you think I'm an elf?"

"I just guessed…"

Addison pulled back her hair to reveal her pointed ears. I sighed with relief.

"You guessed right."

"Can you answer my questions?"

"That depends on if you are prepared for the answers. This isn't a simple yes or no thing. This is your life, Ramsey." Her gaze locked on mine. "Everything will change."

I took a deep breath before saying, "I need to know what I am. I need to know *who* I am."

Addison nodded. "Your parents are not elves, and neither is your sister, as you might have guessed."

"But I read that only two elves can have an elf child."

"Actually, the correct term is elfen, which is a female elf. *You* are an elfen."

"Okay, well," I said, exasperated by the fact that she just interrupted my question only to correct my vocabulary, "I thought only two elves could have an elfen child?"

"That's right," she said, pausing and looking at me in the way a teacher would look at a kindergartener who was being informed playtime was over. "Ramsey, you are adopted."

Surprisingly, I found myself nodding. It actually wasn't a real shocker, considering my looks and all.

"Your parents found you on their doorstep fourteen years ago with *that* necklace around your neck," she revealed, pointing her finger.

I placed my hand over my name necklace, the token I always wore, feeling a connection to it as if it were a part of me.

More importantly, I knew now that it wasn't just a gift from my adoptive parents, but a parting gift from my real parents, who, apparently, were elves. Suddenly the connection I had with it felt stronger, more significant.

"When no one came forward as your parents, they adopted you. They had no idea you were an elfen."

"They took me in even though I was so weird looking?"

"Yes," she confirmed. "Your ears were only slightly pointed then. They grew more as you grew older."

"How do you know all of this?" I asked, surprised by the fact that she knew so much about me, and I so little about her.

"I knew your parents and your sister."

"You know Dina?" I inquired.

"No, Ramsey. I knew your elfin parents and sister."

"Elfin?"

"That's a term for more than one elf," she informed me.

"Oh. So I have an elfen sister too?"

"Yes, her name is Zora."

"What about my parents?"

"Their names were Carlow and Alanna. But they disappeared many years ago, when you were still very young."

"Why?"

"I don't know, but I know it has something to do with you. Something concerning you made them take you here, and then disappear."

"So, even as an elfen I am different. Even as an elfen, I'm unique." I fought back the urge to start crying. Here I thought I would finally feel normal.

"More than you know."

"Tell me more, Addison."

"All right, well I don't know *that* much about you. I was young when everything happened. After you were born, your mother kept you hidden for some unknown reason. I never understood it; no one really has. I was only one at the time, so I am saying only what I heard years later from others. Your sister was my age as well. You weren't let out of the house very often. No one knew why. I was told later that your parents were protecting you."

"Protecting me from what?"

"No one knows. All we do know is that it was something important. It was a *secret.* Some secret you had that made your parents want to keep you hidden from everyone, even their closest family and friends."

"How did I end up here?"

"Elves don't live in this world, Ramsey. You are one of a few. We have our own world. A Realm, created ages ago for elves to seek refuge from humans. They never accepted our ways in this world. We had to make our own. Your mother and father found they had to take you out of the Elf Realm. Again, no one really knows why, except for the part about your secret. No one outside your family knew what it was, only your parents and Zora.

"Your parents brought you here when you were only a year old. When they returned to the Elf Realm, they wouldn't say anything about where they left you, but everyone knew. They just didn't know *why*. Three more years passed, and your parents disappeared. They just left one day and didn't come back, and Zora was left alone. My mother took her in to live with us. Our house wasn't very crowded since my father passed, and our families had always been close. Zora told me that she knew why your parents took you to the Human Realm and why they left her behind when they disappeared, but she said she would never tell. It was a secret. She was full of them, secrets, and felt she had to guard them with her life. She knew why you needed protection, what your secret was, why your parents took you to the Human Realm, and why they left. If I asked questions about the situation, she became angry and teary-eyed. She wanted to tell me, but she couldn't. She had to keep you safe. It was something she believed in, something she fiercely wanted to keep with her, and knowledge she didn't want getting into the wrong hands."

I wanted to ask what Addison meant by "the wrong hands," but refrained. I was still processing the fact that I had a sister, an elfen sister, one who had tried to protect me all my life. I suddenly felt a little gloomy. A sister I had never known did her best to keep me safe, and I had never known.

"So why come now, Addison? Why the sudden interest in me?" I wondered.

"Because Zora is missing, and you are the only one who can find her."

"How can I help?" I asked, feeling skeptical. "I don't even know her. I didn't know she existed until just now. I didn't know who I was until just now, and actually, I still don't think I completely understand."

Nevertheless, something inside of me told me I had to try. I had to try to save Zora. Deep inside, I had a sudden, ferocious need to find her and protect her for a change, like a calling.

"When your sister was taken, we found a note."

"She was taken? Taken by whom?"

"I can't give you all the details here, but our Realm is embroiled in a war. It's our Realm against a Fairy Realm," she revealed.

"Wait, fairies? Fairies truly exist?"

"Yes, they do. Why wouldn't they? After all, you are an elfen, or have you forgotten already? Magic is real, Ramsey."

"Yeah, I just wish it had come to me sooner," I muttered, propping up my arms to rest my chin on my palms.

Addison gave me a pained look. "I'm sorry about…your situation here."

I sighed. "Let's not talk about it. I want to know more about this war, about my sister."

"All right. Well, don't ask me how the war started; it's not important right now. It would take too long for me to explain in such a short amount of time. Since its beginning, the majority of the war has been fought in remote parts of our Realm. Common village elves were untouched by the destruction and violence until just recently, when fairies started raiding our towns and cities. Three months ago, fairies that invaded our town took your sister. All she left behind was her note."

"What did the note say?"

"Find my sister and you'll find me."

"That's it?"

"That and the area you lived in, Wisconsin. I can't believe I actually found you. You could have been sent to any other place by now."

"I'm glad you found me, too. Life hasn't been easy for me."

"I can imagine. For whatever reason your parents needed to bring you here, I know for sure it was a good one. Bringing you here was a tremendous risk. They would never have done this to you if they hadn't needed to. I was afraid you wouldn't fit in."

"Well, you were right," I said bitterly.

"Don't blame your parents. They always loved you, Ramsey."

"I wish I'd known that."

"Yes, I do, too," she said sympathetically.

We sat in silence for a while. I had to take a moment to understand everything. I, Ramsey Wilder, was an elfen, a female elf. I was an elfen with a hidden secret and a clouded past. My real parents hadn't been seen in eleven years, and my sister had been captured by fairies. Why did they take her? I had no idea. Addison didn't know either. All I knew was that I had a secret that had so far doomed me to a life with judgmental humans. I thought that finally getting some answers would better my situation. Instead, I was just an even bigger – and confused – *freak.*

"So what happens now?" I finally asked. "Now that I know, now that you have tracked me down, what comes next?"

"You decide."

"What are my options?"

"Stay here with your human family and live as an outsider, or come to the Realm and help us find your sister. It's your choice, really, although I advise you to think carefully about it. I can't force you, but you have to understand that you will never fit in here. You will always be different, even more so than in the Elf Realm where your secret will set you a bit apart. If you decide not to come with me, I will leave you alone and never return. I lied about going to school here, so I can leave at any time. I only showed up when I needed to talk to you and because I needed to wait until you figured things out. I had to approach you carefully so that I wouldn't scare you off."

"Scare me off?" I laughed. "You sort of did."

Addison sighed. "I have been told that I can be a little intimidating and strange at times. But it's who I am."

I smiled. "I like that."

"What?"

"The confidence and strength you have, and how comfortable you are with yourself. I wish I had those qualities," I admitted.

"You do, Ramsey. You just haven't been able to show them yet." She paused. "Anyway, if you want to come, then we must leave very soon."

"I'll come with you," I blurted quickly.

"Are you sure? You will probably never see your human family again, or your friend, Carmen."

"How do you know about Carmen?"

"I know a lot about you, Ramsey. Remember that I came here to find you. I had to do research. I just have to say how annoying and confusing your computer system is. It drives me crazy."

"Don't worry, you aren't the first," I told her.

I thought about how much Carmen and I had been through. I would miss her, probably even more than I would miss Dina, but I had to do this. I had to go home. I had to find my real sister. I couldn't hide any longer. I couldn't escape who I was. I had to find out more. I had to learn and experience *more*. I had to do this.

"If I come with you, will I learn more about this war? Will I get more answers?"

"Queen Taryn will tell you everything, I'm sure."

"Queen Taryn?"

"Yes, our Realm still has kings and queens, lords and ladies, and more. Queen Taryn has been our queen and sole ruler for sixteen years, ever since her husband died in battle. We will eventually need to speak with her. Zora's kidnapping spread around the Realm quickly; it's not often that a common elf without a royal background of some kind ends up a hostage. And there is the obvious connection between the kidnapping and *you*. Many elves in the Realm know about your family because of what your parents did and because of your secret. You are more famous than you know in our Realm."

"How strange; I'm famous in a world I know nothing about, not the one I have lived in all my life."

Addison only shrugged, as if she didn't know how to respond. I wouldn't have either. I was only voicing my thoughts.

"Okay then, I've made up my mind. Let's go," I decided.

"And you are sure about this?"

"Yes. If, as you say, I am the only one who can find Zora, I have to go with you. And…I want to be with others like me, elves," I told her as confidently as I could.

I was nervous. I was about to put my life in the hands of a girl who told me I was an elfen. It was risky. If she were lying, what would really be in store for me?

However, Addison's smile comforted and encouraged me. She obviously believed I could find my sister. She believed in me, and I found myself believing in her as well. I would use her belief in me to gain strength and confidence. I would use her support, because I didn't have any for myself just yet.

"Okay, follow me," she instructed.

"So I can't say goodbye to anyone?"

"No, it is too much of a risk. They may not let you leave, let alone believe your story. You didn't even believe it at first. What do you think they would say if you told them that you were an elfen?"

"They would probably ask me if I was on some kind of drug."

Addison gave me a weird look. I realized the Elf Realm probably didn't have that kind of stuff.

"Um, there you go then," she said hesitantly. "Saying goodbye is out of the question. As you might have read, elves aren't very strong physically, so if they said you couldn't go, neither of us would be able to do much about it. We may be light on our feet, but we aren't vampires." She actually laughed.

"Don't tell me those are real too," I said, narrowing my eyes.

She shrugged. "I don't really know. I've never met one."

I sighed. This magic stuff wasn't going to be easy to comprehend, even if I *had* sort of believed in it already. It was different now that I knew it was real.

"Ready?"

I nodded, but didn't move. I had to think for a few more minutes. I needed just a little more time. I was afraid of the risk and the danger of what lay ahead. I was about to leave behind everything I knew to begin again. I was moving away from an isolated life toward the unknown. The consequences of my decision wouldn't be clear for some time.

This wasn't going to be easy. When I first went to Addison, I had thought everything would be solved with a few simple words. I was dead wrong. I knew now that what lay ahead of me wasn't going to be all sunshine and flowers. I wouldn't even be reunited with my elfin parents.

Regardless, a fire inside me pushed me forward to do this. No matter how difficult, I still wanted to be where I belonged. If it took saving my sister and leaving this life behind, so be it. I had to find my place, even if it wasn't in this world.

"Come on, we need to leave before midnight, or we will have to wait another day," Addison said, tugging at my hand.

I got up, but didn't let her move me any farther. "Why?" I asked.

"The Realm is open only during the first minute of midnight. We have to be at the right spot so we don't miss our chance."

"That's odd."

"It's just a fluke in magic."

"What?"

"Come on," she said, without answering my question. I nodded and followed quickly. Maybe she wasn't ready to give me all the answers I wanted yet because there were so many questions, but that would have to come soon. I was placing all my trust in her. I needed something in return. Like more information.

"Are we walking?" I asked.

"Yes. We don't have cars in our Realm. It's not that we can't. We just choose not to. Elves don't like technology."

I nodded, not too disappointed. I wasn't a huge fan of technology. I mean, I liked my laptop, but I could do without it.

"Do you have cell phones?"

"No, no technology at all. Not even those things…*televisions*." She said the word slowly, as if struggling with the pronunciation. "We've seen how your world has changed with technology. We don't want that to happen to our Realm. We are modern, in some ways more than others, but have never wanted to damage our Realm with gas guzzling cars and noisy electronics."

"How do you know so much about the Human Realm, Addison? I mean, if there are not many others out there like me, how could you know?" I asked.

"Oh, the leaders of the Elf Realm, our kings and queens, periodically send scouts to the Human Realm, just to see what's going on. We can't completely ignore this Realm, Ramsey. It's too risky. We have to make sure that no human has found out about us, because we are sort of in hiding. Humans and elves don't mix very well."

"I see. That's actually pretty smart, the no-technology thing. But you are still in a war, so there is *some* damage to the Elf Realm, isn't there?" I pointed out.

"The war has nothing to do with the way we live," she snapped.

I could tell I had upset her. Whatever this war was about, it was definitely a serious and touchy subject for my new elfen friend.

"I'm sorry, I didn't know," I apologized.

"You will soon enough."

We walked in silence for a while longer, and then I had to ask more questions. I was sick of being confused.

"Why did you come and find me?"

"I came because I owed it to your sister. She is my best friend and she helped our family a lot. She is like a sister to me. When she was taken, I was devastated. I felt like it was my duty to find you. Besides, I thought if anyone could bring you back, it should be someone who knew Zora. I thought it would make things easier if you heard the news from me."

"You are a good friend, Addison. Thank you for being there for my sister when I couldn't."

"It's not your fault, Ramsey."

"Yes, it is. If I weren't so different, I would have been there for her. My parents wouldn't have taken me here. I could have helped her, or maybe she wouldn't have been taken at all."

"You will help her, just in a different way," she assured me.

"Do you think the fairies took her because of me, because of my secret?"

Addison sighed. "Yes."

We didn't talk again after that. I didn't want to hear any more. It was too difficult. When we reached my house, I thanked God that my parents had decided to go out tonight. The house looked deserted, leaving me the perfect opportunity to pack without anyone seeing.

"How much do I bring with me?" I asked.

"Bring as little as possible, and remember, no technology."

"Okay," I said.

I opened the door with my key and rushed upstairs. In my room, I grabbed the backpack I used for trips. I stripped from my dress and decided to pack it. Maybe they dressed medieval there. I still didn't know much about the Elf Realm or its culture. I would have to see it when I got there.

I quickly changed into jeans, my favorite green t-shirt, and my black hooded sweatshirt. Then I slipped on my most comfortable tennis shoes.

In my bag, I added a family photo, a picture of Carmen and me, the black ballet flats I had worn to the ball, and *The Mysterious Guide to Fantasy.* I also kept on the necklace with my name on it and my silver cross. I had all that I needed.

I was ready to go. I couldn't believe how frightened I felt.

I had to leave *something* for my parents, Dina, and Carmen. I didn't want to tell them where I was going, because they would never believe me, but I wanted to tell them how much I loved them and that I would be all right. I just wanted to make things easier for them to understand.

I decided to quickly email Carmen and leave letters for my family. In each letter, I said only that I was going to my birth home. I thanked my parents for taking care of me and that I loved them. I told Dina to be careful as she grew up and that I loved having her as a sister. I told Carmen how much she had meant to me over the years and that I would always miss her. I left Dina's note on her pillow and my parents' on their pillows.

After sending the email to Carmen, I ran downstairs to join Addison, who was waiting just outside.

"Ready?" she asked, obviously ready to go herself.

"Yes." Still, I was fighting tears.

I couldn't believe I was really going to leave. I was leaving my whole life behind and a new one would follow. I hoped I was ready.

"It's not too much farther from here. Just follow me," she said.

I nodded and locked the door, shoving the key under the welcome mat. I hoped my parents wouldn't be out too late. I thought of Dina and felt bad that she was alone. She was probably looking for me right now. The dance ended at midnight and it was eleven fifty.

I realized we were going through the woods behind my house. Childhood memories flashed through my mind, making me want to cry even more. Then I remembered all the times people made fun of me, and of being alone, which caused me to walk faster. I didn't have time for memories tonight, not anymore. I was entering a new chapter, a new life.

"So…," I started to say, eager to keep my mind off depressing or frightening thoughts.

"What?" Addison asked.

"Your name is Addison."

"What about it?"

"It's common, for humans, I mean. I just thought…that maybe elves would have more *unique* names. Uncommon for humans, like in the books I read."

"Those are books, Ramsey. Not real life."

"Yes, I know, but why is your name so common? Do all elves have common names?"

"Have you ever heard of others with your name?" Addison asked.

"Well, no. But I *have* heard of yours," I pointed out.

"So? Names are names, Ramsey. They go back hundreds, thousands of years. However, there are periods when some names are more common than others are. Maybe my name was uncommon when elves still roamed the Human Realm."

I nodded. Her words made sense.

"But what about how you speak?"

"How I *speak*?" Addison gave me a look like I was mental or something.

"You speak English, like humans. Don't elves have their own language?" I wondered.

"We speak Common now, like most creatures from our Realm and others. Some mystical beings choose to speak in their old ways occasionally, but not the elves, at least not anymore. Not since the Dark Times…"

"The *what times*?" I asked.

Addison didn't explain. Sighing, I left it alone, but I was bothered by how easily she could stop a conversation when she didn't feel like talking any more. Still, she was helping me, and I couldn't force her to keep talking.

After a few more minutes of walking, we stopped by one of the ponds in the forest surrounding our neighborhood. It was by far the largest. Dina and I used to play in it as kids before she lost interest in the outdoors and switched to indoor malls instead.

"So where is the entrance to the Elf Realm?" I asked.

"You ask a lot of questions, Ramsey," Addison remarked.

"That's only because I still need answers. I have no idea what's going on. All I know is what you have told me."

"Isn't that enough?" she asked.

I sighed and shook my head.

"Did you read about the elf circles by the water?" she asked.

"Yeah," I said, looking around. I didn't see any sign of one. "But there aren't any here, are there?"

"No. That's because I haven't made one yet."

"Oh. Interesting," I replied.

"Watch this."

Addison took a deep breath and then began to move fluidly around in a circle.

She didn't have any music, but it seemed as though she was dancing to music from her soul. She flowed languidly in a large circle, skipping in the moonlight and drinking in the radiance of the night. I watched her in awe as she flattened the grass into a perfect elf circle.

"That was amazing," I said when she finished.

"Thanks." She smiled. She sure liked to do that. A lot more than talking or answering my questions.

"Now what do we do?" I asked.

"We wait."

"How do we know what time it is?"

"When you are an elf and live in our Realm, you know. It's just an elf thing."

"Will *I* know when we get there?"

"It takes time to learn, but for some it's easy. You'll have to wait and see."

"So what time is it now?" I challenged.

"Five minutes to midnight."

"You're good," I said.

"Thanks," she said again. She looked around and then sighed. "I hope he makes it in time."

"You hope *who* makes it?" I asked.

Addison wouldn't answer, so I didn't ask again. I counted, and three more minutes passed. Addison looked very worried.

"What's wrong?" I asked, but she didn't seem to hear me. "Addison!"

"What?"

"What's wrong?" I asked again.

"Hold on, I need to focus. Don't say a word," she told me.

I nodded and obeyed. I watched Addison become very still, her eyes closed. After a few seconds, she relaxed.

Another minute passed and Addison started fidgeting again. What was going on? I heard a rustling sound in the trees and turned to look for the source. I wondered what or who it could be, or worse, if my parents had found us. No, they couldn't have come that fast. I was nervous, jumpy because of all that had already happened tonight. This endless waiting only heightened my impatience.

"Finally," Addison sighed.

Out of the woods stepped a very handsome Stellan.

"Stellan," I whispered.

Suddenly, I remembered his ears. Why hadn't I asked about him before? He was obviously an elf as well. I couldn't believe I had forgotten. Finding out I was an elfen had obviously distracted me.

"Hi, Ramsey, glad to have you with us," he said.

"I see you have already met my brother, Stellan. He is a year older than I."

"Yeah, he kind of saved me during lunch," I admitted.

He laughed. "Yes, and I heard you fainted afterward. My good looks tend to have that affect on most elfens."

Addison slapped him on the arm and rolled her eyes.

I laughed too. "Actually, it's because of your ears. I didn't think there was anyone else like me," I said.

"Am I still good-looking?" he asked with a smile.

Before I could answer, Addison cut in. "Stop chit-chatting! We have to go. Because *you* got here so late, Stellan, we don't have time to talk until we get there. I'm starting to regret bringing you with me."

"You wouldn't have been able to last in this Realm without me, Sister, you know that. Sorry, but I had to make sure Ramsey's parents wouldn't return home before we left. They were on their way when I found them."

"What did you do?" I asked.

"Oh, just some car trouble, but it was nothing drastic," he said calmly.

"Will they get hurt?" I asked, mortified.

"No, but they will have to stop for gas." He smiled. "Interesting specimens, those cars."

I looked at him and shook my head. "*Thanks*."

"Hey, just trying to do what Addison asked," he said.

I shot a glare to Addison, but she wasn't paying attention. She seemed like the kind of person – I mean, elfen – that liked to keep things in order and take charge. I guessed she had to be during a situation like this. Especially with her hot brother saying how good-looking he was and me not having a clue about what was happening.

"We have to go now. It's midnight," Addison instructed.

"Okay, let's go," I said.

"Step into the circle, Ramsey," Addison told me.

"It's that easy?" I asked.

"Yes. I'll go first." She smiled and waved, and then she disappeared into thin air when her feet stepped inside.

"Wow," I said.

"See you on the other side, Ramsey," Stellan said. Then he waved too and vanished.

I could have left then. I could have turned away. I was scared. I was confused. However, I knew I couldn't leave. I couldn't turn away. I would follow Addison and Stellan. I would go to where I belonged no matter how scared I was and no matter what dangers I may have to face in order to save the sister I didn't remember. It was my only option, because I knew my heart didn't want anything else.

I closed my eyes, took a deep breath, and jumped into the circle.

~4~

The Elf Realm

I thought there would be some weird spiral tunnel thing that I would fall through, something like in the movies, where everything would be dizzying with millions of colors and bright lights. I was sadly mistaken. When I opened my eyes, Addison and Stellan were there with me. I hadn't even noticed the change. *So much for the movies*, I thought to myself.

Addison took my hand and smiled. "Welcome to the Elf Realm," she said, as she led me forward.

The first thing I noticed was that it was bright out, daylight. The second, the Realm was absolutely, amazingly beautiful. It was right out of a fairytale. The forest trees glistened in the sunlight. There were rolling hills filled with green grass and wildflowers, and ponds scattered about with trickling streams and shimmering stones. Not to overuse a stereotypical line, but it really was like a dream.

"Can you say something?" Addison asked, tugging on my hand.

"Thank you," I said, breathless and in awe of the glorious beauty surrounding me.

"Thank you for what?" Stellan asked.

"Thank you for bringing me here. Thank you for bringing me home." I sighed with relief. I knew this was the place for me. I could feel it. Already I wanted to soak up the Elf Realm sun and bask in it forever. I never wanted to leave this place after seeing it. It was simply too breathtaking.

"Well, you're not home yet. We have some walking to do," Addison said, starting forward.

"Why did we cross into the Elf Realm so far away?" I asked.

"Each Realm overlaps the other, which is how they were able to be created. The Human Realm is a kind of template. When we crossed from your neighborhood into the Elf Realm, this is where it overlapped. Leaving your old Realm where we did and into ours was the easiest way to avoid anyone seeing us. Not to mention our time delay...."

Addison glared at her brother, which only caused him to grin.

"Sorry," he said, although he didn't look like he meant it.

"Uh-huh, sure you are," Addison said, rolling her eyes.

I guessed as siblings, they shared this kind of banter. I wondered if I would have done the same with Zora, had I known her. I know Dina and me had, although we had been quite a bit louder during our little arguments.

"How do you know which way we are going?" I asked.

"I'm good with directions," Addison explained.

Stellan looked over at me. "It's best if you just let her be in charge. She's like that, all independent and such, a natural leader. Don't worry though. We won't get lost…I hope. It would be a shame if you got lost in this Realm after just getting here." He grinned, as if what he was saying was funny.

I liked sarcasm, and at any other time, I would have grinned back. However, his words unsettled me.

"Yeah, it probably would be a shame." I sighed. "Why is it so bright out?" I asked, pausing a moment to observe the bright sun as Addison continued walking at a brisk pace.

"There is a twelve hour difference between our Realm and the Human Realm. There it is midnight; here it is twelve hours before that," Addison replied. I noticed how she didn't turn around to face me when answering my question. She was busy focusing on our destination.

I nodded and started to follow, but Stellan lightly grabbed my arm to stop me from going any farther.

"Can I carry your pack?" he asked gently.

I felt like my legs would melt and I would collapse to the grassy floor. He was so incredible. His very voice made me weak.

"Um, sure." I smiled slightly and then he returned it with a bigger one.

I was going to take the pack off myself, but Stellan stopped me. He lifted it off my shoulders and slung it over his.

"Thanks," I said softly. My mouth was so dry I almost couldn't speak.

"No problem." Still smiling, he walked after Addison.

I followed behind seconds later, unable to say anything else.

***

We walked so long I thought my feet would fall off. Yeah, it was a dumb expression, but I was too tired to describe it in any other way. I could hardly think straight from the exhaustion, and, at one point, I almost physically collapsed.

"Are you okay, Ramsey?" Stellan asked.

"Just really tired, that's all," I said as I swayed. "I guess you were right about elves not being in shape physically. I mean, I like running, but this has been a long day and a lot of walking," I explained.

Stellan grabbed my hand to steady me and didn't let go the rest of the way. I felt warm and safe holding his hand, keeping me awake and helping me stay on my feet. He stumbled along too, because he was just as tired as I was, but we helped each other cross the mesmerizing terrain. I noticed both Stellan and Addison usually walked gracefully in fluid movements, but in this state of exhaustion they were clumsy as they walked. I wondered how I looked when I moved, and if it was in any way similar. After all, I was like them, an elfen. But it was hard to imagine myself as graceful. I had always thought of myself as awkward.

Stellan and I watched out for loose stones and logs throughout the many stretches of forests we crossed. It was as if this whole Realm were bits and pieces of different kinds of nature. Forests here, fields there, clearings as well. It was like the perfect combination of nature all in one place.

It wasn't just Stellan's hand in mine that kept my eyes open. It was the splendor of the Elf Realm, surrounding us, enveloping us. Nothing repulsive or wrong could be found throughout all that I had glimpsed thus far. Tall trees towered over us, their green leaves swaying in the wind. When the sun hit the leaves, they sparkled like diamonds. I could hear birdsong and other animals speaking to one another. Furry brown squirrels scampered up trees, their mouths full of nuts. Rabbits hopped merrily into their holes to be with their young. Deer grazed in the fields of tall grass that waved in tune with the trees, appearing as waves rippling on the ocean.

I was in awe of the wondrous beauty. I had never seen anything so peaceful and inviting. How could there be war in a place like this? It was so magical. I couldn't imagine any killing taking place here. Then again, I had seen just a small piece of the Realm so far, being there only a few hours. I had no idea if death and destruction reigned on the other side of the Realm, and I wondered whether or not I would face it as I searched for my sister.

I glanced at Stellan; my heart started to beat wildly and I felt lightheaded. Why did he make me so nervous, so different from how I normally felt around others, especially boys? Then again, Stellan was not just a simple boy. He was an elf. He was a gorgeous one at that, and the first guy to ever hold my hand.

He was also the first boy – for all intents and purposes – who didn't make fun of my ears.

Was it so wrong to feel this way about him after spending so long believing I wasn't good enough for anyone to show an interest in me? As long as I didn't go overboard, a little crush couldn't hurt. A new love interest would fit nicely with my new life, new surroundings, and completely new identity.

"Come on!" Stellan called out after walking for quite some time. He broke into a run and cried, "We're almost there!"

He pulled me along, and I couldn't help but feel excited despite my weariness. I was almost home, my real home.

A new energy surged through us as we ran swiftly through the fields, laughing and smiling all the way. It felt great to be running again, especially toward a place I knew I belonged. I could feel the excitement course through me with every quick step.

When we eventually caught up to Addison, we were standing before a lovely little town. Night had fallen, and the moon now shone brightly in the sky, but house lights and campfires scattered across the town allowed me to see a bit more clearly.

The houses appeared to be made of solid wood, attractive and simply built, like log cabins. I felt as if I were looking at a collection of summer cottages.

"Home," Addison sighed as we approached. "I sure missed it."

"Me too, Sister," Stellan agreed.

I smiled at them both, feeling invigorated and almost complete – emotions I hadn't experienced to their full extent until now. "Me too."

***

As we walked through the front gate, I gazed upon the arch above that read *Welcome to Birchwood City.* It didn't look like a city to me. In fact, the grouping of homes reminded me of a town, maybe even more like an olden-day village or colonial settlement.

"I know what you're thinking, Ramsey," Addison said, as I joined her after the gate.

"What, can you read my mind?" I inquired.

"Almost," she said, her eyes sparkling and an expression of wit upon her features. "The look on your face is enough."

"Okay, then what am I thinking?" I challenged.

"You are wondering how this place could be a city," Stellan answered for her.

"Wow, you guys are good," I admitted.

The brother and sister smiled. It was peculiar how similar they appeared even though they had mostly different appearances. Something about their expressions and mannerisms gave away their relation to one another.

"Cities here are a lot different than your old world," Addison told me. "Remember, we aren't savages, but we don't live like humans do today."

"I can see that now," I replied, fixing my eyes upon the city that would now be my home.

"But…that's what you wanted though, right? For it to be just like in your storybooks?" Addison wondered.

Sighing, I nodded in agreement. "Yes. Yes, you're right. And I love it, but what happened to elves living in forests?"

Addison's expression darkened and Stellan averted my gaze.

"What? Did I say something wrong?" I asked, wondering why they were suddenly acting so strange.

"We used to live in the forest," Addison said quietly, "but that was before…."

Stellan cleared his throat. "That was before the war began. Then all elf towns were moved out in the open to avoid fairy attacks, and we were forced to give up our ways, traditions that had lasted for centuries. You see, Ramsey, it's harder to spy a fairy in the trees, and they are always there, lurking and listening. No elves are safe in the forest anymore."

"But Zora was still taken," I pointed out.

"Yes," Addison said, sighing. "I guess we'll never get it right."

"Well, I think it's a great place, all the same," I told them, trying to lighten the mood and make them feel better.

They both smiled, and even though I knew a few words wouldn't take away the pain the war had caused them, at least it brought a little cheer.

Surrounding us were horse-drawn carriages, small stores, and dirt roads, reminding me of a field trip our school took to *The Old World.* There, a town was set up just like this to show how people lived years ago. The cool thing about this place was that people actually lived here. I would live here. It was real, but also magical. Here, the words *real* and *magical* equated to the same idea.

Addison and Stellan led me to a charming wooden cabin decorated with forest green trim and bordered with troughs of flowers. The flowers looked familiar to me, but I could detect a few subtle differences from the ones I was used to in the Human Realm. I wondered if they were the same flowers I knew from my past. Then again, maybe I was wrong; maybe they only appeared to be different. I had to admit that in the Elf Realm even the grass didn't look the same. Everything was brighter.

"Welcome to our home, Ramsey," Addison said, smiling contagiously.

"It's lovely. Who planted the flowers?" I asked curiously.

"I did. Aren't they appealing?"

I nodded. "Does the Elf Realm have different kinds of flowers than the Human Realm?"

"Just slightly. The names are usually the same, but they may look a little different. We have a few plants here and there that can't be found in the Human Realm at all. Like Elf Ear," she explained.

I looked at her questioningly.

"Green flowers that look like pointed ears."

"Why didn't I guess that?" I remarked.

Addison giggled and went over to pick a flower out of a trough. "Here, Elf Ear."

I took it and examined the flower closely. Addison was right. It was a deep emerald green and looked almost like a carbon copy of an elf's ear. Never before had I ever seen a flower so green, when usually only the leaves of plants were that shade. "Thanks," I said.

"You're welcome," she replied.

I heard Stellan huff and turned to face him.

"What?" I asked, narrowing my eyes.

"Ramsey, you need to stop staring at the flowers and come inside!" Stellan grabbed my hand again and dragged me into the house. I dropped the Elf Ear and laughed at his urgency.

Inside, the smell of freshly baked bread and fragrant herbal tea drew my eyes to a pretty elfen with long, flowing black hair and pale green eyes. She looked to be about as young as Addison was, and just as dazzling. Wearing a long brown prairie skirt and a green blouse that fit her thin body delicately, she exhibited both femininity and grace.

"Ramsey," the elfen said, setting down the bread and a tray of tea. "It's so good to have you home."

She put her arms around me and hugged me tightly, and I breathed in the floral scent of her, comforting and almost motherly.

"Um, it's good to be home," I said, patting her back and trying my best not to sound out of place.

"I am Aaliyah, Addison and Stellan's mother," she said, taking a step back. She smiled warmly and took both of my hands.

"Their mother?" It was all I could say.

This elfen could *not* be a mother! She was far too young. She didn't appear to be a day over eighteen. The family laughed as if it were some sort of joke. I watched them with a puzzled expression.

"Ramsey, did you read the entire section in your book?" Addison asked.

"No…I…I kind of became upset while reading it," I said, feeling embarrassed.

"It's quite all right. You can read more later," Addison said. "You see, after the age of sixteen, elves don't age physically. Our minds grow older and wiser, but our bodies remain the same."

"Are we immortal?"

"Sort of. We can live forever, but only if we avoid fatal sicknesses or injuries. Or…"

"What, Addison? Tell me," I urged.

"Or if we live in the Human Realm for too long," Stellan finished.

"So if I had stayed in the Human Realm, I would have become mortal?"

"You had until you were sixteen to return to the Elf Realm, because that is when we are fully grown, matured. If you hadn't, you would have lost your elfen self and lived like any other human."

"Wow, then it's a good thing you two found me. I would have never known any of…*this*."

"Yes, it is. Not only would you have become mortal, but you also wouldn't have lived very long. Elves that change to human and live in their world cannot handle the change very long. You see, we simply cannot withstand the rapid, ongoing changes of the Human Realm. We prefer a simple, easygoing lifestyle, and we need the surroundings of nature to survive, for it gives us health and happiness. Elves didn't live very long back when they lived among humans. As towns began to replace the forests, elves began dying off very quickly. You probably would have lived ten years or so after your birthday, but that is all."

My eyes widened and I felt very dizzy. I had been only a few weeks away from a death sentence. Feeling myself become unbalanced, I tried to steady myself, but I couldn't find anything to hold on to. Thankfully, my rescuer was there for me once again.

Stellan guided me to a chair where I sat down to calm myself. Aaliyah brought me a glass of water that I gladly drank.

"What happens to elves that go to the Human Realm after sixteen, like you and Stellan did?" I asked Addison, once I was able to catch my breath.

"Elves would be able to survive, although it wouldn't be easy or pleasant. Not only do elves dislike technology, but we also have trouble adapting smoothly to new surroundings. And the Human Realm is so different, so loud and strange compared to our Realm…."

"Are you all right?" Aaliyah asked me.

"Yes, I'm fine. This has just been a lot to absorb."

"We understand completely. Addison, you should take her to her home. She needs rest after all of this. All three of you do. You had quite a journey," Aaliyah instructed.

"Yes, Mother." Addison nodded and helped me to my feet.

I didn't know what they meant by "home," but my mind was on other things.

"One question before I go," I said, feeling my cheeks begin to redden. "How old are you, Aaliyah? I know it's rude, but I'm curious."

"It's quite all right to ask," she said. "I turned…what was it, fifty-two this past February?" Addison and Stellan nodded.

"I have to say, you look great for your age," I admitted whilst yawning, completely dumbfounded.

"Addison, get her home," Aaliyah said through a chuckle.

Addison nodded and motioned for me to follow her toward the door.

"Can I escort you two?" Stellan inquired.

"If you must," Addison agreed.

I smiled as he took my hand and led me out the door. It was a short walk to our next destination, which was a cabin similar to Addison's. This one, however, didn't have any flowers and appeared unused for some time, lonely and deserted.

"What's this?" I asked.

"Your home," Addison told me. "It was where your parents lived before they…disappeared." Addison said *disappeared* very quietly.

"So now…I will live there?" A sense of dread descended upon me. The idea of living alone in a home that once belonged to my absent parents was unsettling.

"Yes. We kept it in the best condition we could. Zora refused to live there, but we couldn't just abandon it. Come inside," Addison called, stepping through the doorway.

I felt weary about going into the house that my real family had once lived, a family I did not remember. I was afraid of staying in a strange place, knowing that those who had lived there had disappeared or left against their will. I think Stellan sensed my ill feelings because he nodded slowly as to reassure me. I held his hand tighter and walked forward with him into the cabin.

***

The inside was exceptionally appealing and surprisingly warm. A small fire burned in a stone fireplace, its flames licking the stone surrounding it and giving light to the main room. Finished lighting the fire, Addison got up and walked over to join us.

I could see three more doorways that led to other rooms. The main room had a small kitchen area, a large rug decorated with flowers and vines, a dining table and chairs, and a wooden couch with soft-looking green pillows. Not only did the outside remind me of a summer cottage, but the inside as well.

"Why do elves like green so much?" I asked, observing the color coordination throughout the room.

My question clearly surprised them, because neither of them was quick to answer.

"That is a very interesting question, Ramsey," Addison commented. "I'll do my best to answer it, but I don't really know for sure. I think it's because elves relate so closely to nature. Greens and browns are very close to nature, so that's why we use them. We also use floral patterns a lot. I've never really thought about it, though; it's just something we like. An elfin way." She shrugged.

"Don't forget to mention every elf has green eyes," Stellan added.

I hadn't realized it before, because I hadn't paid much attention, but Stellan was right. Every elf I had seen had some form of green eyes.

"Thanks for explaining it to me," I said, considering it all.

Addison nodded and placed a hand on the kitchen table, as though she were checking for dust. "What do you think of your home? I had Blaire come by and clean it while we were away," Addison told me, looking at her clean hands and appearing satisfied.

"Who's Blaire?"

"An elfen in the city," she informed me, but she wouldn't explain any further. "So how do you like it?"

"It's great! I love it," I gushed.

"Come, I'll show you around."

Addison took my free hand to lead me into the first room. Stellan stayed behind. I was disappointed to be leaving him, but I was eager to see the rest of my home.

The first room we entered had a large king-sized bed with a green comforter. It held another fireplace, but this one wasn't lit. Actually, the room looked very dark and sad, cold even. A large wardrobe stood off to the side, as well as a dresser with a vanity mirror.

But everything appeared lifeless, as though it had been neglected for a long time. It seemed empty even with the furniture inside. I knew right away whose room this was…or *used* to be.

"My parents' room," I guessed, hugging myself to prevent any further chills.

Addison nodded. "It hasn't been used since they left. The fireplace hasn't been lit. Their clothes are still in the wardrobe, and your mother's jewelry is in the vanity drawer. Zora wouldn't get rid of anything. She wouldn't move even one thing in this room. She never set foot in it after your parents left."

"It must have been hard for her."

"Indeed it was. That is why she moved in with us."

I nodded, feeling pity for my sister, who was left behind.

"I would like to see the other room now," I said quietly. I didn't like being in this room. I didn't feel like I belonged.

"Yes, follow me." This time Addison didn't take my hand, so I just followed her. I could tell being in this room had saddened her, too.

As we passed through the main room, I could see Stellan sitting by the fireplace adding more wood. The glow of the firelight made him appear even more handsome. I blushed, glad that he wasn't looking, and continued to follow Addison to the next room.

I was somewhat surprised to find myself standing in a bathroom. I hadn't expected flush toilets in a world that shunned technology. The bathroom was simple and pretty, with a sink decorated with floral designs and a circular mirror above. In the corner was a small shower.

"Flush toilets and showers?" I asked.

"We are somewhat modern here, although our bathroom facilities are not as advanced as you would find in the Human Realm. We are still very basic, but we aren't cave people."

"I'm glad."

Addison laughed and took my hand again. "Our Realm has become more modern in the last hundred years. Some secrets from the Human Realm just couldn't be kept secret from us. Even though elves left the Human Realm because they didn't like the humans, we never disliked *all* of their culture."

"Well, I'm glad the secret to personal hygiene was leaked into the Elf Realm, but I *am* noticing quite a lot of iron in here," I remarked.

Actually, every piece of bathroom equipment was fashioned out of iron. I was used to porcelain sinks and toilets. The scene struck me as sort of odd.

"Yes, well, iron keeps the fairies at bay. Or at least we wish it would…," Addison said, trailing off.

"What do you mean?"

"Have you ever read in your fantasy books about a fairy's greatest weakness?" she wondered.

"Yes, iron. But I thought it was just a myth," I admitted.

Addison shook her head. "Iron burns or poisons fairies, depending on the amount they come in contact with and the strength of the fairy. In the Elf Realm, we furnish as many structures as we can out of iron."

"Then I'm guessing not too many fairies stop by to use the bathroom facilities," I said, hoping she would appreciate the joke.

Addison laughed, and led me to another room.

"This was yours and Zora's room," she told me as we walked in the last room.

This room was a bit more cheery, with two twin-sized beds, each with a floral comforter. Much larger than the first bedroom, it held two wardrobes and two vanities, and had a wide, oval green rug covering the floor. A large wooden trunk with an old-fashioned padlock rested between the two beds, separating them from each other. The trunk seemed old and important, like some kind of rare antique. I peered at Addison with a questioning glance.

"We tried to open the trunk…because we wanted to know if anything important was inside, maybe a clue to where your sister is or where your parents went when they disappeared," she explained with a sympathetic glance. "Only…we couldn't."

"Have you tried using a hammer or something? Or tried to find a key?"

Addison nodded. "Unfortunately, the lock is protected by a spell. Only a Spell Master can open it, because they are the only ones who can work with locks and keys here in the Elf Realm. We believe your father, Carlow, was the one who locked it. He was a Spell Master."

"Spell Master? What's that?" I asked

"Sit down and I'll explain," she told me.

I obeyed and sat down on one of the beds. Its comforter was a green floral print. The base was a dark forest green and decorated with lighter green flowers. The bed next to it was the same but in brown.

"Every elf and elfen has a magic ability," she began.

"Yes, I read that in the book. We are gifted in magic, right?"

Addison nodded. "I see you at least read *some* of the book." She smiled and then went back to explaining. "At sixteen, elves receive their ability. Once their individual ability is identified, they go to a special school for one year to learn about controlling their power. An elf's power can be almost anything. It ranges from shape-shifting, to healing, to even using the four elements."

"What is your power?" I asked.

"I have a special way of communicating," she told me.

"What do you mean?" I asked.

"Here, let me show you," she said.

Addison got up and crossed the room to one of the vanities. She opened a drawer, took out a piece of paper, and handed it to me.

"Watch the paper closely," she instructed.

I set my eyes upon the paper and waited, sifting through the countless possibilities concerning what Addison's power could be. I heard her take a few deep, even breaths. I looked up for a split second to see her eyes closed, her face expressionless.

What happened next was truly magical, awe-inspiring.

Words began appearing before me on the paper, as if someone was writing them with an invisible pen:

This is my power. Using my mind, I can send messages to anyone I desire. The message can appear on any surface: paper, furniture, and even your very skin.

"That is incredible, Addison…but also a bit unsettling. I don't know how I would feel about words on my skin." I rubbed my arm self-consciously. Then I remembered something. "Did you use your power to send me the message in the book, about the page number?"

Addison smiled and nodded. "Yes, very good. I also used it to contact Stellan when he was late."

I remembered Stellan and my eyes widened. "What's Stellan's ability?" I asked.

Suddenly Stellan was by my side. My hand was in his again. I didn't know how he had gotten here so quickly.

"I can go anywhere I want to in an instant," he said.

"So you can teleport or something?" I guessed.

"Is that what the humans call it?" he wondered.

I shrugged. "I think so," I said.

"Then I guess I can teleport. Interesting word, though." He smiled and closed his eyes tightly.

Before I could ask what he was doing, it suddenly felt like a huge wave of air crashed over me, and when I blinked, Stellan and I were in the main room again.

"Holy crap, we just teleported into a different room!" I cried with delight, staring at Stellan in wonder.

"Nice choice of words," he said.

"What do you mean?" I asked, a little dizzy. I put a hand against my forehead.

"I don't believe any elf in this Realm has ever heard of them before," he told me.

"What? You mean the word *crap*?"

"Yes, that word."

"Oh, well it's kind of like slang," I tried to explain.

He looked at me blankly, obviously confused. "What's that?"

"Never mind, it's complicated. They are just human words, I guess," I said.

Still puzzled, he muttered, "Oh, okay."

"So what do we do now?" I asked.

Air crashed over us again.

I had to sit back on the bed to steady myself. Teleporting, or whatever the elves called it, made me very dizzy.

"That was so cool," I said breathlessly.

"Stop showing off, Stellan! Can't you see she's tired?" Addison scolded her brother.

"Wait, one more question. If you can, um, teleport, why did we walk a million miles to get here?" I asked.

Stellan laughed and so did Addison. Apparently, my confusion was very funny to them.

"For one, I wanted you to see the beauty of the Realm; and two, I can use my ability with only one creature. I couldn't have just left my sister all alone, could I?" He winked at Addison.

"I guess not. That's too bad you can't teleport with more than one elf." I sighed.

"Yes, all elfin abilities have certain limitations, like how Addison has to close her eyes when she writes to someone."

"Really, Addison, is that true?" I asked.

"Yes," Addison confirmed. "But the limitations are worse with other powers and especially worse for Spell Masters…"

"How is it so for them?" I asked.

"It's complicated to explain. Let's save that conversation for another time. Like, for instance, if you were to become a Spell Master," Addison said, smiling.

"Okay," I gave in, already wondering what my power would be. "Even though there are limitations, I still think your powers are incredibly cool."

"Cool…." Stellan looked confused again.

"That means great," I informed him.

"Oh, okay," he replied.

"Now you must go, Stellan. Ramsey needs some rest. I will come along shortly after she is situated," Addison told her older brother.

Stellan gave a loud sigh and nodded. "All right, I'll leave." He walked over to me and reached for my hand. I gave it to him and he kissed it lightly.

"See you in the morning, Ramsey." His smile almost made me melt to the floor, and then he disappeared into thin air. I couldn't breathe again for a moment.

"Show off." Addison sighed and came to sit next to me on the bed.

"He certainly is," I agreed.

"Enough about him. You need to change out of those clothes and get some sleep. I had Blaire stock your wardrobe with proper clothing. I hope everything fits. I used Zora's measurements from when she was your age."

Addison walked over to the wardrobe closest to us.

"This is your wardrobe. The bed you are sitting on was supposed to be yours after you grew out of your crib. The one next to it was Zora's. I had all of her clothes moved here from my house, as well as her jewelry and other belongings. I thought it would make you feel closer to her."

"Thank you. That's very considerate of you," I remarked.

"You're welcome," she replied. "And our house needed some space anyway." She opened the wardrobe door and pulled out a white nightgown. "Here, put this on. You'll be more comfortable. I'll leave you now to get some rest. I still have to change and go to bed myself."

I noticed then that she was still wearing her gown from the ball. I couldn't imagine having to walk in that for so long.

Seeing her dress made me think of Carmen and my family, and I had to struggle not to cry. I didn't want Addison thinking I was a baby or reconsidering coming to the Elf Realm.

"See you in the morning. Try and get some sleep." Addison gave me a quick hug and then started to leave.

That's when the events from the bridge came rushing to the surface, and I couldn't let Addison leave without speaking to her. I had forgotten all about my near-death experience because of all the excitement, but now I couldn't seem to get the images out of my head.

"Addison, wait!" I protested.

The elfen stopped mid-step and turned to face me.

"Yes?"

"We need to talk."

"Can it wait until morning?" she asked.

I shook my head. "No, we need to talk now."

She sighed and then sat down across from me on Zora's bed.

"Go ahead," she told me.

"Something happened to me the night I met you at the bookstore. I think it had something to do with my secret, or something to do with Zora. It had to be connected somehow."

I could tell my words had sparked Addison's interest. She leaned forward.

"What happened on the bridge, Ramsey?"

"Wait, how did you know something happened at the bridge?" I asked.

Addison realized her mistake and covered her mouth with her hands.

"Forget that I said that!" she pleaded.

"Too late," I replied.

She sighed. "Fine, you tell me what happened, and I will tell you how I knew it took place on the bridge, deal?"

"Deal," I agreed.

I told her everything. I told her about the weird water coiling around my ankles, how I nearly drowned in the lake, and the strange man who could make earth with his hands and his strange words of warning afterward. When I was finished, Addison looked at me, her eyes grave, and nodded.

"What you experienced was an attack from a highly trained assassin."

"What?" I asked. "I'm confused," I admitted.

"The water wasn't just water. It was a being, a creature, called a water fairy."

"A water fairy? What's that?"

"It's a type of Element fairy. These fairies have an element they use as their power. Water fairies can create water as well as control it."

"Why would a water fairy want to kill me?"

"Our Realm is at war with theirs. We are fighting the Element fairies, the ones who took your sister. They want you dead because of your secret. I already told you I didn't know much about it, and I don't. Whatever it is, it affects the Element fairies somehow, or it affects the war."

"And the Earth Man, what was he?" I asked.

"He was probably an earth fairy, one who can create earth, use earth, and master earth."

"Do Element fairies have wings?" I asked.

"Yes, they do, why?"

"The Earth Man didn't have wings," I told Addison.

Addison nodded, as though she knew the appropriate response to my statement before I even finished. "He was probably using Glamour. It's a magical skin that hides a fairy's true nature to other creatures, like humans, as a way to blend in. It covers up their true form. Every fairy can do it."

"All right," I said, satisfied with her explanation. "But if the Element fairies want me dead, why would an earth fairy save me and then tell me to be careful?" I asked.

Addison was about to speak and then looked down. "Honestly?"

"Yes," I urged.

She sighed deeply. "I have no idea." When my face fell, she added, "I'm sorry, Ramsey, but I don't know much about the war or your secret. All I know is that your sister believed you could find her, so I brought you here. The rest you will have to figure out on your own, or from someone else."

I nodded silently, not knowing what to say. I fought back tears, trying to hold myself together, but it wasn't easy. Addison, who I thought could help me through all of this, had just told me I was on my own. The realization was hard to accept, especially because I had no idea what to do now that I was here. I didn't know how to find my sister, figure out my secret, or keep myself from being killed by Element fairies. I still had no idea why the earth fairy had saved me.

I knew absolutely nothing.

Noticing my despair, Addison took my hand and her voice softened as she said, "Ramsey, I went to the bridge because I detected a heightened level of magical energy there when I left the bookstore. You see, magical creatures can detect that sort of thing. If we are in an area where magic recently occurred, we can feel it. But I didn't know what had truly happened there until now."

"Thank you for clearing that up," I said, swallowing a lump in my throat.

Addison nodded and didn't speak for a few moments. She looked deep in thought.

"You should get some rest now," she decided. "I'll see you in the morning."

"Okay," I agreed, stifling a yawn.

"I know I'm not much help, but don't let that get in your way, Ramsey. I know you can do this."

"Do what, exactly?" I asked.

"Whatever it takes to figure out the real you, I guess," she said.

Then Addison smiled, although I could tell it was forced, and started walking toward the door again. Just as she was about to leave, she turned and came back into my room.

"It could have been an elf, Ramsey," she blurted.

"What?" I asked. I was exhausted, and I'd had about enough of her vague explanations.

"The Earth Man," she explained further. "He could have been an elf. Some elves have element abilities. I go to school with an elfen whose ability is the element of air. He could have been an elf with an earth ability."

"Why would he save me? Why was he there?" I asked.

Addison shrugged. "I don't know. Maybe he is someone who knows Zora. Maybe he is one of the Queen's scouts and he just happened to be in the same area."

"How can you be sure?" I wondered.

"I'm not. But it makes a lot more sense for an elf to save you than an earth fairy, doesn't it?" She looked at me kindly, but I could tell behind her smile lay just as much confusion as I felt.

I nodded, totally unconvinced. "I guess."

"Okay, well, you should probably just forget about it for a while. It doesn't make a difference who or what saved you, so long as you are still alive. Zora is the objective now, Ramsey. That is the reason you are here." She gave me a quick hug. "Good night."

"Good night," I replied, a little dejected.

Then Addison left.

Alone, I pondered one thing I hadn't mentioned to her. I remembered The Earth Man having dark brown hair. Even in the shadows, I had still been able to make out his every feature.

Since when did elves have brown hair?

They didn't. Elves didn't have brown hair. They had pale blonde or black hair. Addison was wrong. He couldn't have been an elf. He had to have been an earth fairy. How would I prove that, though, without seeing him again? I had no idea.

And although I knew she meant well, I also knew that Addison would never have come looking for me if Zora hadn't been taken. My purpose here, in Addison's eyes, was to find my sister, not to find out my secret or anything else about me. Or, if she did care about me finding myself, it only came in second to Zora. But I wanted to achieve both. There had to be a way to accomplish all of those things. *There had to be.*

I decided just then that I would *not* forget about the bridge or the Earth Man. I didn't know why, but I felt it was important to know who he was, and why he had saved me. I wouldn't rest until I knew.

And yes, I would find my sister. I would do everything I could to figure out where she was and bring her home safely.

But that didn't mean I couldn't search for other things along the way.

However, I couldn't do any of that tonight. Not yet, not after just getting here and learning this much so quickly and suddenly. I needed some time. One night and then I would devote myself to the tasks of finding my sister, learning my secret, and everything else I felt I needed to do.

Then I finally allowed myself to tear up. I had to relieve the building stress inside me. The tears were silent, washing down my cheeks slowly as I contemplated my situation. I was only crying because I was afraid, overwhelmed. I didn't know how to proceed with anything, especially with Zora. Where would I even begin? I felt hollow and empty because of my lack of knowledge, but most of all, I felt alone. I missed Carmen, and I missed my parents. I even missed Dina, and that was saying something.

And yet, I knew that I was home. At least that was *some* comfort.

I wiped away the tears, reassured myself that I had made the right choice by coming here, and started to undress. I didn't know if

I should keep my old clothes or not and decided to put them in the wardrobe, where I found clothes of all different colors. But the common motif was obviously green and brown. Skirts, blouses, dresses, breeches, and shoes of all kinds cluttered the space. They all looked so different from the clothes in the Human Realm, but I wanted different. I craved different. This was the one chance I had to start my life over, and I wanted to do it right.

Wearing the nightgown, I slipped under the covers of my bed. Finally feeling warm and safe, I forgot about my worries for the moment. The one thing I wanted was rest. I needed to recharge before beginning the search for my sister…among other things.

I was just about to blow out the candle on the bedside table when I noticed something sticking out of one of Zora's vanity drawers. I rolled out of bed and walked over to investigate, my curiosity getting the better of me. After a slight tug, the paper came free and I unfolded it. It was a note addressed to me:

When you are ready, come and see me.
-Blaire

I remembered Addison mentioning Blaire earlier and wondered what this meant. She must have left the note while she was cleaning, but what could she mean by *ready*? Below her name were directions to her home. It wasn't too far from here. I decided to ask Addison about it in the morning. Right now, I was too tired to decide anything else. I had to sleep.

When I was once again warm and safe in my bed, I blew out the candle and closed my eyes. All traces of earlier tears gone, I reassured myself that no matter how difficult it was, no matter how long it took, I would accomplish all I set out to do. Somehow, I would get through this. I had been given this second chance for a reason, and I was determined to make the most of it.

Before sleep overtook me, I prayed silently to God, asking Him to keep Zora safe wherever she was, and to give me the strength I needed to figure out my life.

~5~

Journal

I didn't really know how I could tell, but somehow I knew it was just past eleven when I woke up. Still nighttime – I remembered reading in the guidebook that elves only slept four hours each night. Obviously, Addison and the others hadn't remembered that the rule applied to me as well. Nevertheless, I understood. It was hard enough for me to think of myself as an elfen. I acted like a human. I thought like a human. Except for my looks, I was still very human. I hoped I would become more elfen over time. Maybe then, this new situation would feel real to me, because right now everything still felt like a dream.

When I woke, I wasn't fully rested, but I was unable to get back to sleep. My mind was going crazy again, rethinking all I had learned recently like a pop song on repeat. In a matter of hours, my life had changed dramatically, and I still hadn't become accustomed to it all.

I tried to pass the night by looking around the house. Using candlelight to see, I began with my room, the one I used to share with my sister. I wanted to find out everything I could about her. If I was to find Zora, I needed to start by knowing her. I decided the best place to initiate my exploration would be her vanity drawers. I walked softly over to the vanity. I knew I was alone, but I felt the need to remain quiet. This place was still foreign to me, and I guessed still feeling cautious was wise. I wasn't used to calling this my home yet. To me, my home was still back in Wisconsin. It would take some time for me to fully adjust.

The first drawer was filled with jewelry. Gems of all kinds peeked out at me: garnets, rubies, emeralds, diamonds, sapphires, opals, and more. They were set in necklaces, rings, bracelets, and earrings. I wondered if it was normal for elves to have such expensive adornments. Sure, my family in the Human Realm was wealthy, but this was different. The only person in our home who had ever splurged on jewelry or other accessories was Dina. My mother never was much of a spender and neither was I. I only spent money on books, or hair pins so I could cover my pointy ears with my hair. Unfortunately, that had never worked very well. At least I could cross hair pins off my shopping list from now on. Having pointy ears was the style here in the Elf Realm.

The next drawer held paper and a fountain pen. I remembered Addison retrieving paper from there. I wondered briefly if Zora wrote a lot, as in letters or journals.

Thinking of journals gave me an idea. If Zora had kept a journal, I could read it to find out more about her. It could give me an insight as to who she was, what kind of girl – I mean, elfen – she was before the fairies took her. Even though it would be an invasion of privacy, I knew there was no other way. If Zora had a journal, I needed to read it.

The third drawer didn't open as easily as the others. I pulled and pulled, but it wouldn't move an inch. I put both hands on the handle, both feet against the bottom of the vanity, and pulled with every ounce of strength I could muster. The drawer opened, but not without sending me flying across the room and onto Zora's old bed. Winded for only a moment, I was soon on my feet again. I looked around for the drawer and found it lying upside down on the hardwood floor. Lifting it gently, I immediately noticed what I had hoped to find. I picked the leather book up and brought it over to my bed. In the warm candlelight, I opened the book and began to read. The title, *Zora's Journal*, confirmed that I had my sister's journal in my trembling hands. What I read below the title shocked me so much that for an instant I was breathless. Below Zora's name were two words that were more powerful than I could have ever imagined.

"For Ramsey," I read aloud to myself, my voice a quiet whisper.

Zora had written this journal for me! My heart began to race with unfamiliar emotion. A short inscription graced the next page:

Ramsey, I kept this journal for you. Read it and learn.
-your loving sister, Zora

Somehow, Zora had known or hoped that I would return to the Elf Realm. The thought sent chills down my spine. Just thinking that Zora could have predicted my return to the Elf Realm made me wonder just how involved my secret could be in her kidnapping, even in this war. What secret, I wondered, would cause my sister to believe she would be taken by the Element fairies, leading to my inevitable return?

I wasn't getting anywhere with all these questions. I needed to slow down and read the journal. Zora had written it for me, so maybe it contained the answers I sought.

I took a deep breath to ready myself. My sister's life was only a page away. A part of me didn't want to know anything. I was afraid to know my sister, because then I might feel the same way as Addison. I was afraid of the pain I would experience, the feeling of loss. Reading this journal would make her real to me, and not just the elfen Addison spoke so fondly of.

I thought of turning the page like a Band-aid. Do it quickly and it would be easier. And so I began to read.

The journal described as much as Zora could remember about her life and about elves in general. I learned stuff that I hadn't from the guidebook. I learned that elves went to bed around twelve at night and woke up at four to start their day. They never needed much sleep and rarely slept even the four hours.

Zora mostly wrote about her school life. Elf children went to school from age five to twelve, kind of like human children, except they didn't call it kindergarten through sixth grade. At five, elves were first year students and at twelve, they were seventh year students. After that, elves didn't go to school until they turned sixteen, when their powers came to them. Then they spent a year going to a special school from seven forty-five until noon. It sounded a lot simpler than being in high school for six hours a day.

From what I read, Zora loved her school days and was very popular among the other students. I noted the obvious difference between us.

As I read the description, I finally learned Zora's power:

Elves call my power beautiful, but I'm not so sure. I think it is wrong and evil. I trick people with my voice. I make them hear something beautiful and when they listen, they fall asleep.

My power is the ability to sing beautifully. I have always been a good singer, but when I turned sixteen I became amazingly good. Then I realized it was my power. When I sing, whoever hears me goes into a trance or deep sleep. Only I can break the spell. Unless an elf has protected himself with a shield ability, he can never resist. The worst part is that I love singing. Now I can't just sing when I want. If I do, all those around me will go into the trance. My power is a nightmare and a curse to me…

My heart ached for my sister. Her power was remarkable, but also extremely difficult for her to control. Elves loved to sing; I knew that much from reading the guide. I didn't know what I would do if I couldn't sing. I didn't know how I would be able to handle it if my power kept me from doing something I loved.

Then I found myself asking, "Why couldn't Zora just sing the fairies that took her to sleep?"

"She couldn't because fairies are immune to it."

I gasped and shut the journal, my eyes darting around the room in search of who made the remark. Standing before me was a burly looking elf with pale hair and the darkest green eyes I had ever seen. What really struck me was his build. He had huge muscles, muscles elves weren't supposed to have. I was beginning to feel confused again.

"I thought elves weren't strong," I commented, unsure of what else to say.

"That only applies to elves who don't have my ability: strength," he said, flexing his arms.

I ignored his arrogant gesture and moved on to the important question. What was he doing in my house, in my room, at this hour?

"Who are you?" I voiced aloud.

"I'm Cass, the strongest elf in Birchwood City." He smiled.

"Um, I'm Ramsey, the *newest* elfen in Birchwood City." I managed a smile, even though he wasn't giving me a very good vibe.

"I knew that. Why else would I be in your house?"

"You got me. I have no idea why you are here in the first place," I told him outright.

"Well," he said, "Addison told me about your arrival and I thought I should come over and introduce myself."

"Seriously? And you didn't think of knocking?"

"There aren't any locks in the Elf Realm, unless a Spell Master has one. No one knocks here. Addison told me you might be sleeping, so I just walked in to check."

"That is *really* creepy," I said, eyeing him warily. "Are you disturbed or something?"

"No…I don't think so. Why?" He gave the impression of being genuinely perplexed by my question.

"You don't just walk into someone's house while he or she sleeps. That's just weird…stalker weird."

"Oh, sorry, didn't know. Guess humans are a lot different than elves," he observed.

"You got that right," I agreed, desperately yearning for a subject change. Talking about elfin stalkers was giving me the chills. "What were you saying before…about fairies?"

"They are immune to Zora's power. Fairies can put humans in trances with their singing, even with just their looks, so it's not likely anyone could ever put fairies in a trance. Zora's power affects elves and other mystical creatures, just not fairies." He said it to me like even a monkey would know that.

"Do fairies each have a special ability like elves?"

"Some do. Different kinds of fairies have different kinds of powers."

"What kind of powers?"

"Well, the Element fairies each have an element," he began explaining.

"Yeah, Addison told me, but how many different kinds of fairies are there? She only explained about the Element fairies."

"I only know a few. Their numbers range in the hundreds, but consist of four main types and then others, called solitary fairies. The solitary ones usually live in the Human Realm. They chose to remain there when the other Realms came to be. The Element fairies are particularly harsh, though. They think they are the best because their powers are easier to access than other types of fairies. Other types of fairies must learn their magic; the Element fairies are born with both the knowledge and ability."

"Too much pride. That's one of the seven deadly sins," I observed.

Cass snorted and nodded in agreement. "Yes, I believe it is."

"I was told there were four Fairy Realms. Are there other Elf Realms?"

"No, there is just this one. Not many elves are left. Humans had killed off most of our kind by the time we made our own Realm. This Realm is vast enough to hold all of us."

"Oh. Then how can we fight fairies if there are so many of them and so little of us?"

"Well, the other fairies don't want to get involved, so that reduces the number by a great deal. Those fairies aren't interested in losing their own people."

"So they're scared, I take it?"

"You are quite right. But the different types of fairies don't always get along, so it isn't a surprise that none of the others came to the aid of the Element fairies," Cass explained.

"Elves, Realms, fairies, war, missing sisters, magical abilities, no knocking…This has been the weirdest day of my life," I blurted out suddenly.

I hadn't meant to say it, but I definitely felt it. I had to admit that it felt good to express my feelings.

Cass nodded. "I bet it has."

"It's not easy to comprehend so quickly. And Addison expects me to find Zora…It's hard."

"Addison doesn't like waiting around for things. When she wants something, she goes after it. She wants Zora back home, and she won't let you or anyone else rest until that happens."

I sighed and nodded. Addison had determination, something I had lacked until now. I realized I needed all the determination I could get if I was going to do this.

"How do you know Addison so well?" I asked when I was finished thinking.

"I'm courting her."

At this point, I was ready for anything, but not this. I doubled over laughing, my hands clenching my stomach. I laughed so hard I almost fell onto the ground. Addison was with Cass – the macho, manly, over-confident Cass. I barely knew him, but thinking of him with an organized and determined leader like Addison sounded hilarious to me.

"What's so funny?"

Through my laughter I said, "Nothing. It's just I never imagined an elfen like Addison going out with you. And for the first time today I have finally heard something remotely funny."

"I don't think it's very funny. What's wrong with me being with Addison?" he asked, sounding defensive.

"Because you're buff and strong and think you are God's gift to elves – at least that's what it seems. And Addison seems like an elfen who could hold her own and not go for your kind of attitude. She is also very kind. Do the math."

"Yes, I guess you've pinned me pretty well, but Addison isn't *that* sweet. And she likes the type of elf I am."

"I'm sure," I replied, a bit sarcastically. "I'll have to ask her exactly what it is that impresses her, the breaking and entering or the big muscles."

"It's definitely the big muscles," he said with a smile.

I still didn't feel comfortable around him because of the intrusion, but at least Cass was lighthearted and able to laugh at things, even when they were about him. I liked that in people…and recently, elves as well.

Cass yawned and ran a hand through his messy pale hair. I guessed it was getting closer to twelve. He must be tired after being up since four a.m.

"You look beat," I said. He watched me with a puzzled expression until I corrected myself with, "You look tired."

Cass finally nodded. "Yes, you're right. I had better get some sleep," he agreed. "It was nice meeting you, Ramsey."

"It was nice meeting you too, Cass. See you later."

He gave a slight nod, left the room, and then left the house. This place was weird, no doubt about it. Strangers came into your home as they pleased, there were different kinds of fairies, and Addison was dating a muscle man. Yes, this place was very strange, and it was my new home.

I knew I should probably get some sleep, but I couldn't without reading more of Zora's journal. My mind was spinning. I wouldn't be able to fall asleep now. So instead, I picked up Zora's journal and kept reading. Three hours later, I was down to the last couple of pages.

I noticed something odd while reading Zora's journal. She had written all about her school life, her interests, and her friends. However, the journal held nothing regarding our parents or me, and nothing about their disappearance.

I became alert again as I read the words, *"In closing my journal, I will explain the details of your departure and disappearance of our parents."*

I swallowed and took a deep breath. This was what I had been waiting for, and I was ready to know. Finally, I could read Zora's words, her own account of what had occurred so many years ago because of my birth:

You were one year old when they took you away. I can hardly remember it myself; I was only two at the time. I am relying on the stories of others to help me tell this to you. All I can remember is Mother saying to me, "Zora, be good while Mother and Father take your sister to safety. We will be back soon. Don't tell anyone what we are doing, okay?" I nodded, trusting that they knew what they were doing. They took me to Addison's house and had Aaliyah watch over me while they were gone. I waited for two days and then they returned…without you. They wouldn't say anything about you until three years later, when they were leaving me for good. I spent the years asking where you went and all they would say was, "Ramsey is all right now." Before they left, they told me the truth. You are special, Ramsey, so special that they needed to hide you from others of your kind. Why? I'm sorry, Ramsey, but I cannot tell you. I sense them coming here, the fairies. I know they are after me. I think they know about you, Ramsey, or at least they know you have a secret that can affect them. I can't let them hurt you, which is why your secret must stay with me until you are ready to carry it. I won't tell them anything, I promise. I can't leave any evidence of your secret behind except for one thing. You will figure out one day what that is. I know you will. For now, you must be in the dark so you can be safe. I love you, Ramsey, even though I hardly knew you when you left. I know if they take me, and keep me alive long enough, you can find me. Only you can find me.

"How can I find you?" I cried, utterly exasperated by what I had read. "How can I find you if I don't know this place? I don't even know who I am anymore!"

I felt completely, hopelessly lost in this Realm, and reading Zora's journal had brought those emotions to the forefront. I hadn't understood one word that Zora had written about me in the closing of her journal. What kind of secret made fairies care so much about an elfen? How could I be so important and not know it? How could no one else know? I didn't understand how I, an elfen who had lived in the Human Realm for so many years, could be so vital to Realms I had known nothing about until today.

My head was swarming with a mixture of pain, confusion, fear, and sadness. I was scared for Zora and for myself. I had no idea what to do. This was just too much for me to handle. I couldn't save myself from a bad life in the Human Realm, so how was I supposed to save my sister from fairies?

For the first time since coming here, I realized I was entirely alone. I didn't just feel alone, I *was* alone, even though Addison and her family were only a few steps away. But they didn't have my confusion or my heavy burden. They expected me to do this, to save Zora, and to find myself. I had no idea how I could do all of it on my own. Supposedly, I was the only one who could save my sister. I was the only one with this challenge that I didn't believe I could overcome. I wiped my eyes and buried my head in my hands, wishing I could suck it up but unable to stop feeling so helpless.

I sank to the floor, too exhausted to get back into bed, and drifted off once more.

***

When I awoke again, the room was a mixture of darkness and light. My instincts told me it was five in the morning. It freaked me out that I could tell the time already. I had slept another two hours, a colossal record for me. My neck and back were stiff from sleeping on the floor and as I stifled a yawn, I bit my tongue to keep myself from crying out in pain.

Massaging my neck, I walked into the bathroom. I looked into the mirror and frowned. I had deep bags under my eyes, the color of bruises. My eyes were still red and sore from crying. I reminded myself of a ghost, haunted. That had to change. I would have no hope of finding my sister if I continued to feel this defeated.

I splashed warm water on my face and thanked God that this Realm had plumbing, even if it was from a well I had noticed outside last night. Then I took a shower and towel dried my hair.

Feeling a bit more refreshed, I went back into the bedroom and dressed. I chose a knee-length brown cotton skirt and a short green embroidered tunic. It wasn't my usual style, but it looked fine and fit well. I wasn't worried about hiding here. I could wear nice clothes and no one would mind. I could even allow my ears to show. After brushing a silver comb I had found in my vanity drawer through my hair, I slipped on a pair of sandals and left the room.

My breakdown the night before couldn't happen again, that much I had decided. If I was to accomplish anything here, there could be no room for whining and complaining. I had to be strong, and I had to focus. I had to think of the good things, like how I was finally home. Being negative wouldn't get me anywhere. It was time to put on a smile and face the world…I mean, the Realm.

Before I left the house, I shut my parents' bedroom door. I didn't need a daily reminder that they were gone, and I would probably never meet them.

I shut the door to the house behind me as I walked onto the dirt road. The light outdoors was brighter now as the sun rose higher in the sky. The *city* – more like a small town – was already bustling with elves. As I passed them, each one turned to look at me with questioning glances. I guessed Cass wasn't the only elf who had found out about my return.

The city was charming, in a down-to-earth sort of way. Some areas were modern and other sections were not. I decided to walk around a bit before going to Addison's house. I was in the mood for sightseeing. I wanted to get to know the town, know my surroundings.

A little shop named *Songbird's Books* caught my eye as I walked, and I quickly stepped through the front door. This was my kind of shop. I had already found something to relate to in the Elf Realm. Maybe fitting in wouldn't be so hard. I had to laugh at myself for that. A bookstore wouldn't change the fact that I was so weird. But hey, at least I was finally acting a bit more optimistically.

A chiming bell announced my arrival. I browsed through the books, my eyes widening at the various titles: *My Human Best Friend* (from the comedy/fiction section), *How to Catch a Dragon* (from the informational section), and *When the Werewolf Calls* (from the non-fiction section!). This kind of bookstore would definitely take some getting used to. I doubted that I would find any fiction books on fairies or fantasy, because here, it was real.

Then I saw a section solely on spells. I remembered Addison saying the only way to open the trunk was with a spell. Could these books help me open the mysterious trunk? I started to look through the books, searching for anything that could open a lock. Sadly, most of the books were guides for Spell Masters, and I was definitely not one of those, at least not yet. I didn't know if I was going to be a Spell Master or not, because I wasn't sixteen. I didn't have a special power yet.

I wondered if any books could help someone who wasn't a Spell Master. Maybe elves had more magic than I realized. After all, I was still new here.

I continued to look, even though I wasn't very optimistic about finding anything. One, I didn't know a thing about spells. Two, I had been in this Realm less than a day, so I didn't exactly know my way around the bookstores.

I found one book that could prove to be useful. The title was more obvious than I had wished: *Unlock Spelled Locks: The Guide to Unlocking Over 100 Different Kinds of Locks.* I grinned at how funny the title sounded and picked up the book. Then I remembered I had no money. *I'll ask Addison to lend me some later*, I thought. *Or, if that doesn't work out, I'll ask her advice on how else to gather some money.* I couldn't very well spend my days here in Birchwood without any funds. How would I live on my own?

My mind set, I quickly left the bookstore and headed straight to Addison's, eager to buy the book as soon as I could.

***

I knocked three times on the door when I arrived. I wasn't going to act like Cass, whether it was normal in this Realm or not. I wasn't about to go traipsing through someone's house without being invited. It just wasn't common courtesy.

Addison opened the door right away and smiled another bright smile. *One day her face will stay like that*, I thought to myself with a chuckle. I was glad Addison paid no attention to it.

"Come in, Ramsey, good morning!" she greeted happily. I had never seen a more perky morning person in my life. Even I wasn't that easy going and cheerful so early in the day.

"Hi, Addison," I said, as I stepped through the doorway.

Aaliyah, Stellan, and to my surprise, even Cass, were all sitting at the dining table. They were happily munching on bread, fruit, and eggs, and sipping juice. I noticed Addison and Aaliyah were wearing similar brown summer dresses, while Stellan wore a white peasant shirt and brown breeches that ran just past the knee. Cass wore something similar, only his pants were black. But it didn't really matter what they wore, they were still gorgeous, Stellan especially. Looking at him made me feel faint.

"Good morning, Ramsey," Cass said, and he winked.

"Yes, good morning," Aaliyah said as well.

I rolled my eyes at Cass and took a seat next to Addison. I didn't look at Stellan. He hadn't said one word to me, and I thought it would feel awkward to say anything to him myself. I wondered if the day before had just been a fluke, or if it was how he normally acted with elves he had just met. Maybe he wasn't interested in me at all and it was just wishful thinking on my part. Still, I was a little disappointed.

However, at this particular moment my mind needed to be focused on my sister and figuring out how to find her. That meant learning all I could about elves and fairies. Regardless of Stellan's incredible good looks, I knew I had no time to be drooling over him. I sighed and shook my head to clear away the thoughts.

Looking at the food, I realized I was starving. I grabbed a roll and spread butter on it before hungrily stuffing it into my mouth. I didn't think I could ever live without breakfast. Dina had hardly ever eaten breakfast in the mornings. She thought it would keep her figure in shape. To me, that was just crazy thinking, because food was too good to pass up, especially breakfast food.

"Ramsey, eat more than a roll! Here, have some eggs and fruit and some freshly made apple juice," Aaliyah suggested.

"Thank you for being so generous," I complimented. "I will gladly have some."

Aaliyah quickly put together a plate for me and filled a cup of juice. I could hardly wait for her to put it all down before starting to eat again. After walking such a long distance the day before, I was on empty.

"I found Zora's journal," I said, between mouthfuls of Aaliyah's delicious cooking.

"She had a journal?" Addison asked. "I didn't even know…."

"She wrote it for me," I explained, noticing Addison's sorrowful expression. "That's probably why no one else knew."

She smiled slightly and returned to her food. "You must be right."

"Why did she write it?" Cass inquired.

"So I could know what her life was like," I informed them.

"Zora was always very considerate to others," Aaliyah noted.

Addison and Stellan both nodded. I wondered why he was being so silent today. Maybe he wasn't a morning person.

"Did the journal help?" Addison asked.

"Yes, very much," I said. "It taught me a lot."

I didn't mention that it had also made me frustrated and confused. I didn't want to get into that with anyone. I was afraid if I said anything, Addison wouldn't trust me to find Zora. Even though I doubted myself, I needed all the support I could get, which meant not mentioning my doubts to anyone else.

"Did you get any sleep or did you read the journal all night?" Aaliyah asked.

Cass snorted. "I doubt she got any sleep." He winked again.

"I slept until eleven and then read until around three. Then I slept for another two hours. Oh, and I had a lovely visit from your…*Cass*, Addison." I felt the urge to laugh, but thankfully was able to resist.

I was surprised to see Cass laughing. Addison hit him in the shoulder. It didn't look like it hurt him at all.

"What's so funny?" I asked curiously.

"Addison told me *not* to go over and talk to you. Shows how much influence she has in the relationship." Cass continued to laugh, and at one point almost choked on his juice.

"Don't worry, Addison, it was…*interesting* to meet him." This time I winked at Cass.

Stellan gave me a curious, *"What was that for?"* look. I ignored it. If he wanted to know something, he had to ask me the question himself. I wasn't here to interpret his confusing body language.

"Just wait until we are alone, then you'll be sorry," Addison threatened Cass, bringing my attention back to reality. She glared at him, putting her words into effect.

"Oh yes," Cass said. "I'm *so* scared." He grinned and leaned over to give Addison a quick kiss. She rolled her eyes, but her smile gave away her satisfaction.

I smiled. No matter how odd it seemed, they were a cute-looking couple.

Aaliyah took our plates and cups and started washing them in the sink. Cass left for work. I took this as my chance to talk to

Addison alone. I wanted to find out more about Blaire and to see if I could borrow some money.

"Hey, Addison, can I talk to you outside for a moment?" I asked her.

"Sure," she replied, and I followed her out of the house.

When the door closed behind us, I began. "I found a note on Zora's vanity last night. It was from Blaire. She wants me to come and see her. You mentioned her the night before as an elfen in the city. Who is she really?"

Addison sighed. "Blaire is a *different* kind of elfen."

"What do you mean by *different*?"

"She's an elfen…but isn't one."

I crossed my arms against my chest. "That doesn't make one bit of sense," I told her honestly.

"It's easier if you see her yourself. It's kind of hard to explain."

"So you think I should follow what the note says?"

"Sure. Blaire is the city's unofficial house cleaner. She cleans homes for a price if you can't do it yourself. She helps many elves take care of things if their partners are away at war. It isn't easy for a single elf to raise a family during these times. She has always kept up your house for us. Zora never liked spending time there…even thinking of your home depressed her."

I nodded, remembering how miserable I had felt reading Zora's journal. I couldn't imagine how hard it must have been for her. If I had been in her shoes, I wouldn't have gone into my house, either.

"Do you need directions to her home?" Addison asked, jarring me from my thoughts.

"No, she left them on the note. But thanks."

"Sure. Anything else you need?" Addison wondered.

"Yeah, I was wondering what I should do about money. I found a book that I wanted to buy. Could I maybe borrow some?"

Addison laughed. "I forgot you didn't know!"

"Didn't know what?" I asked.

"You are basically very wealthy," she told me simply.

"Are you serious?"

"Yes!"

"How very rich am I?" I probed.

"Your parents left everything to you and Zora. Zora wouldn't use the money and slowly saved everything she had." Addison hesitated before adding, "I think she kept it for you."

"Addison, I think she knew that I would someday come here."

She nodded. "I always thought that also. She talked a lot as if you were coming home any day. I thought it was just because she missed you. But now I do think she knew."

"I think she knew the fairies were going to come after her as well. It had something to do with me and my secret, didn't it?" I admitted.

"Don't worry about that right now," she advised, placing a tentative hand on my shoulder. "Just concentrate on finding Zora."

I nodded, both relieved and a little disappointed that Addison didn't want to spend much time talking about my secret. It was easier to focus solely on Zora for now, but it was also clear to me that Addison's main concern was for Zora only, and no one else.

"So how much money are you talking about, Addison?" I asked excitedly, trying to rid myself of any lingering doubts.

"Well, elf money is a bit different than human money. Our copper coin equals one of your dollars, bronze is worth ten dollars, silver is worth twenty, and a gold coin is worth fifty."

"So how many coins do I have?" I asked.

"About twenty thousand gold coins."

"I have one million dollars?" I asked in disbelief.

"Yes, that's good mathematics," she commented.

"So I really am rich?"

"Yes," she reassured me, smiling. "Just go to the city bank and make a withdrawal."

"Where is the city bank?" I asked.

"I'll have Stellan show you. It's probably open now considering it's almost six. Most places here are open by six a.m. each day."

"Can't *you* show me?" I asked.

I felt more comfortable around Addison than anyone else here. Even in the Human Realm, I had trusted her. She just gave off a friendly vibe that I gravitated toward. Even though she could be a little controlling at times, her leadership and strength comforted me. She was like my temporary rock until I could stand on my own two feet in this strange new world.

Moreover, I was still confused about Stellan. He was acting very strange compared to his behavior the day before, and hadn't uttered a word throughout breakfast.

"I would, but I have to help Mother around the house, do some quick errands, and then get to school by seven forty-five."

"You have to go to school?" I asked, disappointed that I would be on my own during the day…unless Stellan decided to warm up to me again.

"I'm sixteen, remember? I have to go to school to learn more about my power."

"I almost forgot!" I exclaimed. "But wait, it's Sunday, right?"

"Yes, we have school every day except Saturday. When you are an elf, you don't need many days off. We have so much time during the day that work and school aren't a problem."

"You actually *like* school here?" I asked, dumbfounded.

"Yes, I enjoy it very much. School is fun and a great way to learn about our individual abilities. At least it was fun…until Zora was…never mind." She sighed. "Anyway, let's go see if Stellan can accompany you to the bank."

I reluctantly nodded and followed her back into the house. Stellan remained as we had left him, seated at the table. When we came in, he jumped up and walked over to us. I noticed Aaliyah was still cleaning up. A fire burned in their fireplace. It was warm and comforting, and I didn't really want to leave. However, I was also excited to have money of my own in my pocket. It would definitely make me feel more content in this strange new place. Knowing I could take care of myself in the spending department would help put my mind at ease.

"Everything okay?" he asked.

Wow, he could still speak! I was amazed.

"Yes, everything's fine. Could you take Ramsey to the bank? She needs to withdraw some money."

"Sure. Let's go now," he suggested.

"Okay." I took a deep breath and followed him out the door.

"Have a great day!" both Addison and her mother called to us.

"And you also!" I called back before the door shut.

Unenthusiastically, I followed Stellan away from the house, all the while wondering why he had such an attitude and why we weren't teleporting. Maybe he just didn't want to hold my hand anymore. I found myself frowning at the thought, and I hoped he couldn't see the disappointment I knew my eyes were conveying.

We walked without speaking most of the way. As we walked, elves continued to watch me, study me. I could both see and hear them murmuring to each other. They might as well have just screamed my name aloud. I tried to ignore it, but it was difficult. Even though I had been a topic of conversation most of my life, it was different here because these were my people. They were elves, not humans.

Unfortunately, they had the same gift of gossip.

The city's cool shops and buildings kept my mind off the city folk for a while. We passed the bookshop, the market, a jeweler, a clothing store, and a restaurant. It was nice to see that this city was more modern than I expected but also had a Renaissance Era atmosphere in everything I saw.

I noted that it was the perfect combination of old and new.

***

The city bank was probably the largest building in Birchwood. It was made of stone and had a large wooden door with a brass handle. It reminded me of an abandoned mansion. However, no forms of the word "abandoned" came to mind as we went inside.

A large chandelier brightly lit the inside of the bank. Multiple wooden and cushioned couches surrounded a large three hundred and sixty degree round fireplace, making the building surprisingly warm. The back of the building had counters. I guessed this was where I could make my withdrawals. To the right side was a wall of what looked like security deposit boxes, where elves could keep important belongings and money. The left wall housed a large safe.

It was less modern than a human bank, but I still knew it was a bank just by looking around.

I hesitantly followed Stellan to one of the counters, not knowing exactly what to do. Everything in the Elf Realm had some kind of difference from the Human Realm, and I was still unused to it. Behind the counter was a dark-haired elfen with leaf-green eyes. She was wearing a brown dress with a rose pinned to the front. She smiled and greeted us with a hello.

"What can I do for you two today?" she asked.

Before I could speak, Stellan was already answering for me, which I found *extremely* aggravating.

"We need a withdrawal from Ramsey's account." He nodded to me.

The women took a second to look me over and nodded. "Yes, right away. That's right; you're Alanna's daughter, correct?"

"Who's daughter?"

"Your mother," Stellan whispered to me.

I bit my lip and nodded. "Yes," I said, angry at myself for already forgetting my mother's name.

"Such a shame that she left with your father," she remarked.

I nodded again. I didn't want to start any small talk with her, especially on the subject of my mysterious parents. Parents I knew nothing about. She probably knew more about them than I did. It was an awkward situation.

"How much would you like to withdraw?" she asked in a sweet tone.

This time I was able to answer for myself.

"Ten gold coins, please," I requested.

Stellan gave me another one of his looks, but I ignored it. I didn't want to have to come back here too often. Five hundred dollars would be fine for now, just in case.

"Of course, one moment, please." She smiled and then left to get the coins.

"Going shopping?" Stellan asked.

"I don't see how that's any of your business," I said.

He grinned, and I had to grin back. It was hard to be mad at Stellan. One smile from him and I forgot everything.

The elfen came back a couple seconds later, holding ten gold coins. She counted them for me and then put them into a red satin pouch.

"Here you are. Come again," she said, handing me the bag.

I smiled, took the bag, and tied the string handle to my wrist.

"Thanks," Stellan and I said at once.

As we walked out of the bank, a pale-haired elfen stopped us on the way. Her green eyes shone with excitement upon seeing me, making me wonder who she was and why she seemed so happy to see me.

"Hello, Ramsey. I'm Ashlyn," she introduced, taking both of my hands in hers.

"Uh, hi," I replied. I retracted my hands. Was it just me, or were elf handshakes totally bizarre?

Ashlyn smiled at me warmly. "I know it must seem strange, me just coming up and talking to you. But I have heard so much about you, and I wanted to meet you."

"What have you heard about me?" I asked, interested to learn the city gossip.

"Oh, just how…*special* you are."

"Special?" I asked, and looked over at Stellan. He stayed as still as stone. I realized he wouldn't be helping me with this at all. I was on my own.

"Yes, you know, special. I mean, your parents took you into the Human Realm. There had to be an important reason. No elf or elfen goes to the Human Realm anymore without a good reason. Not since the war began. And of course your secret is special," she said.

"Oh, I see. Well, I don't know why I am special or what my *secret* is. Apparently, only Zora knows…."

"I'm so sorry about Zora. We go to school together…I mean, we *went* to school together." Ashlyn blushed, obviously embarrassed by her mistake. "She was such a nice elfen and we were very close friends." Suddenly, her eyes lit up. "Oh, and speaking of school, I'm going to be very late if I don't get going.

Hope to see you again soon, Ramsey." She waved, turned, and sped out of the building before I could even reply.

I stood motionless as she left. Her fast-paced talking and peppy attitude had stunned me. I wasn't used to so much good cheer around me. In the Human Realm, the only cheery person I knew was Carmen.

"She's…"

"Animated?" Stellan guessed.

"Oh yeah," I said with emphasis, "but she's nice. I can tell she means well. But I didn't like how she talked about Zora in the past tense…I mean, not a very good boost of optimism for me, the one who is supposed to find her," I said.

"I get what you mean, but you have to understand that Zora has been gone for a long time, and until now there was no hope of ever bringing her home. But now you're here."

I nodded, contemplating his words. They were the most interesting and sincere phrases of the day from him. I wondered if he was finally going back to normal, whatever that was.

Lately, I was never sure what constituted as normal.

Sighing, I followed Stellan, who was already making his way toward the exit. Outside, the bustle of elves caught me by surprise. I wasn't used to being around creatures I once thought were fictional. It would be a while before I grew accustomed to the change.

"That is probably going to happen to you a lot," Stellan commented as we walked away from the bank.

"What?" I asked, admiring the scene of two elfin children playing in the street. Even though this Realm was in the midst of a war, things seemed so carefree. I could see how it would be hard for elves here to remember what was actually going on in the Realm. Zora's kidnapping must have really surprised them.

"The elves will want to introduce themselves to you. Your being special has everyone in the city interested. You see, not much happens in this town. We aren't close to the capital, so the war doesn't affect us directly. Your coming home is the biggest thing that's happened since…well, since Zora was taken."

I sighed. "Whatever. At least they won't make fun of my ears." I grinned.

I was happy that I caused him to grin, too. I wasn't going to let him do all the mesmerizing, if that's what it was.

Stellan was still being distant and I didn't know why. However, as long as he behaved civilly, I was fine with it. Besides, people hadn't acted very normal around me in the Human Realm because of my strange looks, so Stellan acting this way was already an improvement.

"So what do *you* do all day?" I asked him as we walked.

I didn't know exactly where we were going. I desperately yearned to return to the bookstore, but I decided it could wait for now. I wanted to figure out why Stellan's mood had changed so drastically from the day before, and to see if he would warm up to me again so that I could safely call him my friend. Or if I was lucky, something more….

But thinking that way was crazy. Sure, I had a special secret and a mysterious past, but that didn't make me the most eligible elfen in Birchwood City. To think that way would be delusional.

"Work," he replied.

"Where do you work?" I wondered, trying to keep the conversation going.

"*The Birchwood City Restaurant*."

"A very original name," I commented.

"I think so," he said, a hint of a smile playing across his lips.

"So when do you work?" I asked.

"My shift starts at nine and goes until five," he told me.

I giggled, and he gave me another one of his looks. That was going to get old very quickly.

"In the Human Realm, a workday is called a *nine to five*. It's just ironic, that's all," I explained.

"Right," he said, still giving me a questioning look. I needed to think about what I said before I spoke. Things were different here; expressions and sayings were not the same as in the Human Realm. I would have to be careful, or I could confuse or offend someone easily. "I have to go," he said suddenly, before I even had a chance to respond.

"But it's only seven," I pointed out to him.

"I have some errands to do," he said.

"What is with you and Addison going on so many errands?" I asked him.

"She said she had to go on errands?"

"Yes. She said she had a few errands to do before school started," I told him.

"I should have guessed she would say that. And I should have thought of something else to say…." He sighed. "Now I have a problem."

Stellan looked down at the ground and shifted his weight nervously.

"I would say so," I replied, looking at him expectantly.

"I…," he trailed off.

"So what are you two really up to?" I asked, raising an eyebrow.

"You should truthfully just ask Addison about that," he suggested.

Then he smiled, and a second later disappeared into thin air, leaving me with my mouth hanging open and feeling more confused than ever before.

~6~

Lunch Date

Since I couldn't exactly follow Stellan after he "teleported," I walked until I found the jeweler we had passed on the way to the bank. I didn't have much to do today, especially with Addison and Stellan acting so weird, so I decided to get to know the city a bit more. If Birchwood City was going to be my permanent dwelling, I should know my surroundings. This would help me blend in with the culture and feel comfortable in the Elf Realm. The jeweler would be a good first stop.

I stepped through the door to look around. The store sparkled with jewels of all shapes, colors, and sizes. The pieces were beautiful, more striking than anything I had seen in the Human Realm, another reason I already loved it here. Everything seemed to be magnified in some way, which I noticed even on my first day.

As I browsed, I wondered what I was going to say to the sales clerk when he or she appeared. I decided after coming into the store that I would talk about Zora to anyone who worked there. Her jewelry was of high quality, probably from this store. I guessed she must have bought jewelry often, considering how much she had in her drawer. Maybe the more I found out about my sister, the better chance I would have of finding her.

Okay, so I didn't exactly know how talking to a jewelry sales clerk was going to help me rescue my fairy-captured sister, but it was worth a shot. I had to start somewhere. I didn't have any other leads to go on.

I was startled out of my thoughts when I saw the sales clerk finally appear behind the counter. He looked young, about my age. However, he could be one hundred and two for all I knew. I walked over to the counter and smiled at him. The elf was pale-haired and had eyes so pale green they were almost white. He was handsome and appeared to be someone who would be a great host at a party, very welcoming.

"Hello," I greeted, trying to hide the shyness I usually expressed to others.

I wanted to seem more outgoing here. I wanted to start over now that I wasn't being made fun of all the time, now that I had a real purpose. I had a lot of work to do, but I felt confident that I could overcome my social awkwardness and be the elfen I was born to be.

Yeah, that line was cheesy, but I tried not to pay attention to that fact. Motivation and cheesy slogans just went together.

"Hello," he replied warmly.

I took a deep breath. "I have to ask you something, sir, before I say anything else," I told him.

"All right, go ahead," he encouraged.

"How old are you? I don't mean to be rude; I would just like to know, for personal reasons…." I was too curious to pass up the chance to ask. I smiled awkwardly. *What a great way to break the ice,* I thought sarcastically.

He laughed and smiled back at me. Elves and their teeth…. Their smiles were completely mesmerizing. I wondered if I smiled like that. I hoped so.

"Twenty-five just last year," he said.

I giggled and shook my head. "So, you're twenty-six then?"

"You got it. What else can I do for you?"

"I wanted to talk to someone who knew my sister, Zora. Did you ever sell any jewelry to her?"

"I'm sorry about your sister, uh...and I'm sorry again," he said sympathetically. "I'm afraid I don't know your name."

"I'm Ramsey," I told him. "And, thank you. You are the first elf I've seen who hasn't stared me down because of my past. It's been a little weird to deal with, even for an elfen who was stared at constantly in the Human Realm."

"I'm Aaron, and I am not one to pry into anyone's business, unlike many elves in this city seem to be doing these days," he explained.

"I appreciate that a lot. I understand why everyone is so interested. I mean, I'm an elfen from the Human Realm, and it seems that I have a very mysterious past. But it's still weird, especially since I have no idea what I'm doing here yet," I told him.

"I'm sure you will find your place sooner or later. This is where you belong," he said.

I smiled. "Thanks," I told him honestly. "So have you sold to Zora before?"

"Seeing as it's just me in here, I would have to say, yes."

"You work here by yourself?"

"I own this shop. It's been in my family for a long time," he explained.

"Well, you must have great business, especially since my sister had so much jewelry in her drawer," I said. "Can you tell me anything about her?"

"Sure," he agreed. "What would you like to know?"

I thought about it for a moment.

"First, how often did she come here?" I asked. Then the questions came pouring out like a waterfall. "Did you have conversations with her? What did you think of her?"

"That's a lot of questions," he remarked.

"I'm looking for a lot of answers," I admitted.

"Okay, let's see, where to begin? Zora was a regular, basically a jewelry hoarder," he joked. I smiled, realizing Zora and Dina might be a lot more alike than I once thought. Smirking, he continued with, "She used to tell me that whatever she didn't save, she spent on jewelry."

"So you *did* talk to her a lot?" I remarked, jumping into Nancy Drew mode. When I was eight, I had this month-long obsession with growing up to be a detective. Sure, the circumstances had changed, but I guessed being an elfen detective was close enough.

"Yes, we were fairly close. When someone comes in here as often as she did, you eventually start making friends with the clerk," he joked. "She would come in about once a week and tell me what was new in her life. She liked talking to people; she was very outgoing."

"Is there anything else I should know?"

"She talked to me about you a lot," he told me.

"What?" His remark stunned me.

"Every so often she would mention your name. When she bought a piece that was particularly extravagant she would comment on how much you would have loved it. She said if you had grown up with her, you both would have had the same taste in jewelry."

"Wow," I said.

I could barely feel my legs. It was difficult to hear how much Zora had thought of me when I hadn't known she existed until yesterday. I felt guilty, as if I had committed a crime or something. It sounded crazy, but I couldn't help it. Zora spent her whole life waiting for me to come home. I spent my whole life complaining *about* my life. "I need to get going," I said, hurrying to get out of the store because I suddenly felt a little sick to my stomach. "I have many things to do today. Thank you so much for your time."

Aaron nodded slowly. "I understand, and you are very welcome. Come by anytime."

"I think I'll come back sometime and maybe buy a piece of jewelry. I don't have anything like what you have here. It's amazing just how different, yet also similar, the Human Realm and the Elf Realm are."

"Although I have never been to the Human Realm myself, I understand what you mean. Many similarities exist between elves and humans. Anyway, I'll look forward to your next visit."

"Thanks for talking with me and...understanding my situation."

"No problem." He smiled.

I gave Aaron a wave and left the store. I had enjoyed meeting him. He seemed very genuine to me and I looked forward to seeing him again. Even with the countless rumors and mysteries surrounding both my past and present, he was able to look beyond that and treat me just as he would another customer in his shop.

As I headed away from the store, I started to feel even gloomier. Hearing about Zora hadn't been as easy as I thought it would be. Even though I didn't really know her, she was still my sister. It was torturous to me, knowing that she could be hurting.

But I had to put my emotions on hold for now, because finding Zora didn't leave any room for pouting. It was time to check out the bookstore again and buy the book on locks. I didn't know for sure if opening the trunk would help my search, but it was worth a try.

I must not have been used to the loose gravel on the street, because a second later I was tripping over my own feet, stumbling forward and into the arms of an elf passing by. Maybe it was fate, or just a random occurrence, but I didn't think about the possibilities very long. I looked up at him, about to apologize…but then I saw his eyes.

They were a deep emerald green, the exact same color as mine, and they glowed with an intensity I had never witnessed before. A slash of silver crossed each one, the sun's reflection making them sparkle like dancing crystals. The emerald irises appeared to be swirling in circles, creating the illusion that his eyes were never-ending. Flecks of darker emerald clustered around each pupil made my breath catch in my throat. Suddenly, my disheartened mood vanished, almost as if I had never felt sadness before. Something about these eyes held me in place, as if I had found a balance, blanketing me in a cocoon of comfort, free of worries and concerns.

I couldn't look away. I was caught up in the beauty, enchanted by it. Warmth spread through me. A rush of ecstasy overtook all other senses, engulfing me completely.

I realized how content I would be if I stayed, right here, standing in front of him, forever – and this frightened me. I had never felt this way before about anything or anyone. I had never felt so whole, especially with someone I didn't know. But those eyes – as I looked into them, nothing else mattered. They were like priceless jewels, as if they were the reason I was alive…the reason I kept on breathing.

I couldn't tear myself away to look at his face. Our eyes were locked together. I wondered what he saw as he gazed into my own. Was he seeing the same immense beauty I saw? I couldn't help but wonder as we gazed upon each other.

I found myself compelled to move forward. All I wanted was to be closer to him, to see if his heart was beating as swiftly as mine was. To see if he was breathing as heavily as I was. To see what would happen if our lips were close enough to meet.

He took a step forward as well. I felt his fingertips brush mine. I hadn't even realized my hand lifting to meet his. I took a sharp breath. Touching him set off a reaction inside of me that I couldn't put into words. I could tell that he felt it too. His eyes were smoldering, boring into mine. I had never felt so exposed, but I didn't mind. I liked this unfamiliar way he was making me feel.

Then he blinked, breaking the connection, and suddenly I was sane again, brought back to reality.

"I am *so* sorry. I wasn't looking where I was going. Sorry to bother you." I smiled apologetically and walked away quickly, still a little freaked out by how much he had affected me.

I could have sworn his stunning eyes watched me go.

***

After carelessly crashing into the beautiful-eyed stranger, I forgot all about the bookstore, and without even noticing where my feet were taking me, I arrived home. I realized saving the bookstore for another day was for the best. Finding Zora was important, but I was just too shaky and distracted at the moment to do any real good.

Once I started remembering the scene with the Stranger – my new nickname for him – I couldn't stop thinking about him. I still felt like a major idiot for what had happened. I hadn't even introduced myself. His eyes had sidetracked me from remembering the rules of common courtesy.

Had I wanted to meet him and talk to him? *Yes*. Was I feeling bad about the situation only because I had *wanted* to meet him? The answer was an even bigger *yes*. I hadn't even been able to look at his face. I was so distracted by his eyes....

Why was I so transfixed with this elf? What made him stand out from every other elf in the crowd? As I walked home, I couldn't get him out of my mind, wondering if I would ever see him again. Ever since the accident on the bridge, I had felt like everything was out of place. But for some reason, I had this strange inkling that the Stranger could change all of that. That he could make everything right again if I just gave him the opportunity to do so.

And looking at him hadn't made me feel the way I did whenever I looked at Stellan. That day in the cafeteria, I had felt like a giddy teenager with a crush when I saw his face. But I knew what I felt for the Stranger was different…more mature somehow, in a way I couldn't explain. Almost like our eyes had conveyed a deeper meaning than simple attraction for one another. But how could one look exchanged between two complete strangers determine all that?

It couldn't, of course. I *had* to be thinking foolishly. That was the only logical explanation for these bizarre feelings I suddenly had for an elf I didn't even know. It wasn't like me to behave this way. The stress and information overload that had recently begun to overtake my life must have messed with both my mind and my emotions. I needed to clear my head, or pretty soon every stranger on the street would seem important to me.

Nothing out of the ordinary had occurred between us. I had to accept that. Sure, he had beautiful eyes, but that was it. Nothing else. I had to believe that…otherwise, I didn't know what I would do. I didn't know how I would deal with that sort of situation.

But I couldn't seem to convince myself to stop thinking about him.

When I arrived home, still confused and frazzled, I opened the door to see a note on the dining room table written on a large piece of paper in elegant handwriting. Even before I read it, I recognized the writing:

I didn't want to ruin your table by using my power to write on it, so I left this note for you instead. You will be joining us for dinner at seven tonight, so don't be late!

-A

This meant she had been inside my house while I was gone. I hardly cared, though. If I were still in the Human Realm, I would be annoyed, but things were very different here. I was beginning to understand and accept that. It was barely my house anyway. I had been in it for less than a day.

I knew it was noon as soon as I thought about the word *time*. I was getting better at knowing what time it was in the Elf Realm, and the realization both startled me and made me smile. Elf stuff was weird, no doubt about that. However, I was glad that I could be a part of it, a part of *something*.

I had seven hours until dinner. It was just enough time to unwind and relax…well, maybe too much time. I would make do. I would go into my room, look through more of Zora's things and a little bit through mine, maybe take a nap, find something to eat for lunch, and then try to find a way to kill more time. Why was the day so long for elves? In addition, with no school, no work, and no one to hang out with, I was bored out of my mind. I sighed and walked into my bedroom. I kicked off my sandals, jumped onto my bed, and began massaging my temples. I needed to relax. Maybe a nap should be the first thing on my agenda.

As I began to drift off, I felt an odd itching sensation on my arm. It felt like bugs were crawling all over me, or pins and needles jabbing into my skin. I rubbed my hand over my arm but nothing was there. I continued to itch. I ran to the bathroom and turned on the water over my arm to soothe my burning skin. The cold water didn't help. Breathing heavily from the painful sensation, I tried to think of another way to get rid of the annoying, painful itch. Before I could dry my scorching hot arm and try something else, I noticed words appearing on my skin. I remembered Addison could write on anything with her mind, even someone's skin. I gasped in both pain and awe as the sentences formed:

Ramsey, I forgot to mention that Stellan wants you to meet him at his restaurant at one! Hope this didn't hurt you too much.

I washed my arm again. The words washed away as if real ink was on my arm. I dried it and took several deep breaths. *What an experience,* I thought. I held my arm close and returned to the bedroom.

I thought about ignoring the message but knew it wouldn't be right. It would be rude of me not to see Stellan. He had played a huge part in bringing me home, after all. I also didn't want to hurt Addison by hurting her brother. She was my closest friend in this place, and I didn't want to lose her. I needed all the support I could get if I wanted to find my sister. I made up my mind and decided that I was going to the restaurant at one, whether I really wanted to or not. But I was still apprehensive about spending time with Stellan. Already his erratic moods weren't easy to follow, and I hadn't even known him for very long.

I had about forty-five minutes before I would leave to find the place. I decided to use this time to inspect my room more closely. I hadn't looked through Zora's clothing yet. Maybe by knowing her clothes I could picture her better and find out where to find her. It sounded crazy and I knew it was, but I was trying anything I could because I didn't have anything else to go on. My options were limited.

I opened her wardrobe. Her clothing was startlingly bright, vibrant, and colorful. Zora obviously liked to separate herself from the pack. The *elfin* pack that is. That was another difference I noted between the two of us. However, I might have enjoyed standing out too if I hadn't been trapped in a world full of judgmental humans.

I felt each of her shirts, skirts, and dresses. Nothing out of the ordinary happened. What had I expected – some sort of telepathic link just because we were sisters? I searched through the rest of the clothes, not very optimistic. However, while I was feeling around in the dark wardrobe, my hand reached the back and crossed over a rough part of wood. I soon was able to trace the outline of a name: *Blaire*.

Confused, I let my hand drop and then backed away from the wardrobe and sat down on Zora's bed. Had my sister done this? Blaire left a strange note for me, and now it seemed as though my sister wanted me to meet with her as well. Was it an instruction or a warning? Was Blaire a friend or foe? I knew I would have to find out for myself. I decided that tomorrow I would visit the elfen who was called "the city's house cleaner."

After all, it was my first real lead.

***

For the remainder of my free time, I organized my room and used Zora's leftover stationery to write down my to-do list. I had several things to accomplish. Organization was a way to half-convince myself that I was being useful, although I felt like a fish out of water and terribly lost, not knowing what to do about my sister's kidnapping. Store clerks knew more about her than I did, which made self-doubt a whole lot harder to avoid.

Listing the tasks I hoped to accomplish (in no particular order) helped ease my stress:

1. *Visit Blaire*
2. *Speak to others about Zora*
3. *Find out what the heck was going on with Stellan*
4. *See what Addison was up to*
5. *Get the Stranger's beautiful eyes out of my head*
6. *See Aaron again and buy some jewelry*
7. *OPEN THE TRUNK!*
8. *Find my sister....*

The last one was obvious, but I felt it needed to be there. It was then I remembered the book on locks at the bookstore and quickly added it to the list. That book could possibly help me with number seven on my list: opening the trunk. Hopefully I wouldn't have anymore strange encounters with the Stranger so I could actually *go inside* the store this time. With my list written, I was fully organized and ready to go.

After a quick look in the mirror, just to make sure I looked presentable, I left the house. After only one day, the city already seemed familiar to me. I felt out of place at times, but that wasn't because of where I was. It was because of the lack of information I had about my new situation. I wasn't used to being an elfen. In time, I would grow accustomed to all of the changes this new life entailed. Other than that, the surroundings called to me. Maybe it was because I had spent so much time sightseeing already. Perhaps my elfen nature was returning. Whatever the reason, the city felt like home. I realized I would be happy to live here for the rest of my life…if I was able to.

I strolled along the streets, admiring the scenery and townsfolk. It felt good to walk from place to place. It felt right. I didn't miss the busy cars and traffic lights. Many times, I passed elves on magnificent looking horses. The elves riding them appeared confident and content. I wondered if it would take just one horse to make me feel that way. I didn't know for sure.

I loved animals, because they didn't judge me for what I couldn't control. Animals didn't look at my pointy ears or care who my birth parents were or what they had done.

Horses were especially wonderful creatures. I wasn't very keen on taking care of them, but I sure loved to ride them. When I was seven, Dina and I went to a horse ranch a few hours from where we lived. There, we rode the horses and brushed their manes until darkness fell, when our parents wanted us in bed. We returned every summer after that because we loved it so much. Even Dina stayed out of the malls long enough to spend time with the horses. Those times at the stables were when we truly connected as sisters. I fought back tears. That would never happen between us again. I had a new sister I had to connect with, if I ever had the chance to find her. Thinking of how I would never see Dina again made finding Zora even more important. I felt that I owed it to Dina. I had left her, and I wanted to make sure my leaving was worth it. It wouldn't be unless I found Zora.

I found myself wondering whether or not I would have been brought back to the Elf Realm if Zora hadn't been taken, but I swiftly realized that I didn't want to know the answer to that question. I didn't want to keep thinking about the possibility that no one truly cared about my well-being, and that they really cared only for Zora. I definitely didn't want to cry about it either, so I shoved the depressing thoughts out of my mind. Luckily, remembering the Stranger made the hurt melt away, replacing my sorrow with peace. However, I had a feeling that peace would be short lived, for I had finally reached the restaurant where Stellan worked. *How will the elf act this time?* I wondered.

The restaurant screamed one word to me as I stood before it. That one word was, *weird.* It was oval-shaped and green, and looked like a giant egg. The door to the restaurant was also egg-shaped, brown with a large oval-shaped handle.

I opened the door and stepped through the entrance. I felt a lot better inside the restaurant than outside. It looked *almost* normal. The main area had a high ceiling and oval tables with elves eating and chatting the afternoon away. I looked at the carpets and wasn't surprised at the design. Several brown and green ovals overlapped each other in various places. The only feature that wasn't oval-shaped was the bar that ran along the outline of the restaurant. That was a circle, not an oval. *Big difference*, I thought sarcastically to myself. I walked up to the host elf and asked for Stellan. He told me Stellan would come out soon, but that he was just finishing some things in the kitchen. The host instructed me to take a seat at the bar and wait.

"I'll be with you in just a moment," the bartender told me as I sat down.

He came back only seconds later. We both smiled as we recognized each other.

"So you work here too, huh?" I asked.

Cass nodded. "Yes, I met Addison here. She was meeting Stellan and he introduced me to her."

"That's so sweet. I always love chance meetings," I remarked, drawing invisible circles on the bar with my fingertips. The smudges appeared to be more like ovals than circles, proving that the atmosphere of this restaurant was already having an effect on me.

"What?" he asked, looking perplexed.

"When meetings are just by chance," I said, confused as to why I even had to explain myself.

It bothered me sometimes how simple human words often confused the elves I encountered. I found myself having to explain myself more than I would have liked. After all, I was the one who should be asking questions. I was the new elfen in town with a weird past and even weirder present. I sighed. It was difficult being the new kid, but just thinking about starting over made me giddy with excitement. This was a great opportunity; a chance to reinvent myself and decide my own future, unlike in the Human Realm, where everyone had labeled me from the very beginning. It was my turn to create the image and reputation I would now portray to the world. My frustration quickly changed to enthusiasm.

"Oh, I see what you mean. So, can I get you anything?" Cass asked.

"I don't know. What kinds of drinks are served here?"

"Well, we have juice and water. We also have wine."

"How will I choose?" I laughed.

"We don't have a huge variety. This place may look a bit modern, but it's still a Magical Realm. Elf magic does all sorts of great things, but it doesn't really affect drinks, so in that department we are still stuck in the olden days."

I laughed. "So there aren't any elves with the ability to create new beverages?"

"Not that I know of," he said with a witty expression. "So how about it, want anything?"

"Do you have cranberry juice?"

"Yes, we do," he said, so exuberantly that I had to laugh again. I was beginning to like Cass more each time I encountered him.

"Okay, then I'll try it."

"Coming right up," he said. He grabbed a glass and poured in the juice. Then he handed it to me.

"Thanks." I sipped it slowly, enjoying the taste. It was sweeter than I remembered, not as bitter. Maybe magic didn't affect the drinks here, but they were still better than ones from the Human Realm, probably more natural. I doubted that elves knew anything about juice concentrate.

"Why is this place shaped so weirdly?" I asked, speaking my thoughts aloud.

"Oh, yes, I guess it is awfully strange. The owner has a very creative mind. He wanted to build something that would stand out."

"Mission accomplished," I said.

"And he does own a bunch of pet chickens, which explains the egg shape."

"You can't be serious," I told him.

He laughed. "No, I'm kidding. Honestly, I have no idea why this place is so bizarre. I just work here."

I nodded, still smiling and feeling oddly comfortable with the elf that only hours ago had walked into my house in the middle of the night without knocking.

"So how long have you been…courting Addison?" The word for dating still seemed funny to me.

"Actually, for over a year, and it's been great."

"I'm glad," I said genuinely. "Do you think you will marry her?" I asked, propping my elbows on the bar counter and resting my head on my hands.

"What?" he asked, appearing to be a little bewildered.

"Will you ever marry her?"

"I'm only seventeen."

"I didn't say you should *now*. You could wait a few years."

"You don't understand this place very well," he inferred, putting it as more of a statement than a question.

"I guess not," I admitted. "It seems like I can't go a few hours without getting confused about something."

"Well, elves can get married anytime after they finish their ability school. But it hardly ever happens right away, or even ever."

"Why?"

"We are basically immortal. We have all the time in the world. Marriage isn't a huge thing, not for many immortal creatures. I mean, why rush it if we can live forever? What would be the point? Sure, once in a while you'll find an elfin couple that still goes by the old Human Realm traditions, but very rarely. And in the Fairy Realms, the only marriages between fairies are those of kings and queens."

"How odd," I commented.

"Well, that's immortality for you," he said.

"So marriage…isn't a big thing?"

"Nope, it's not a major concern at all," he replied simply.

"So you don't think you will marry Addison in the future?"

"It's not probable," he admitted. "I'm happy with the way things are and so is she. Marriage won't change that."

"Does anyone ever get married here?"

"Uh…Well…I don't know anyone in Birchwood who is. The Queen – Queen Taryn – she was married once, but that's because she is royal. Some of her guards, both elf and elfen, marry because it assures their place together. As long as they are married, they can both work in the same place and avoid separation. Those are the only marriages I can think of. Common elves can be married, and like I said, some do, but I don't know any."

"That's interesting."

"Why?" he asked.

"Things are just so different here, that's all. In the Human Realm, marriage is a big deal. Well, for most people, that is. Mostly it's a religious thing. Marriage is just…normal."

"Is there something wrong with the way we live?" he asked, sounding slightly defensive.

"No, not at all! I'm simply not used to it. I'm sorry if I offended you," I apologized. "I'm trying my best to get used to being here."

"Oh, it's all right. I was only confused because…well, you seem to ask a lot of questions that I haven't ever had to think about or answer before," he said.

"Sorry," I apologized. "I have been asking so many since I got here that I don't know when to stop."

He grinned. "It's okay. You'll understand everything eventually." Then he left to make drinks for other elves who had approached the bar.

Sitting alone, I realized I had a *lot* to learn about this place. I hoped Cass was right, and that eventually I would understand.

***

I was finishing my juice when I noticed Stellan walk out of the kitchen. He smiled when he saw me, and I had to smile back. I was pretty weak around this guy. His smile broke me down. I couldn't be cold with him when he did that, even though his strange behavior still bothered me.

He motioned for me to follow him without saying anything and led me to a table. I hoped he was back to being himself.

"Sit," he ordered.

"Uh, okay," I replied.

I sat down and looked up at him. I was waiting for him to say a second word, or anything. He didn't. I wasn't going to stay if he wasn't going to talk to me. I started to get up. His hand landed on my shoulder, as if he had been expecting me to try to leave.

"What am I doing here, Stellan?" I asked, slowly removing his hand.

"Would you like to have lunch with me?"

"Isn't that why I am here in the first place?"

"Yes, but I didn't really give you much of a choice, since I had Addison tell you to meet me here." He smiled, a little shyly. "So, do you want to or not?" he asked.

Should I really accept? He was acting so differently from yesterday. I was prepared to say no. My mind screamed it, but I found myself saying…

"Sure."

I wanted to punch myself in the face.

He smiled, another brilliant Stellan-the-Elf smile, and sat down. He handed me a menu and I took it. Our hands touched. I withdrew mine swiftly. I hadn't meant to be cold to him, but it was hard not to be. I didn't understand him.

"Aren't you supposed to be working?" I asked.

"I'm on a lunch break."

We didn't say any more because a server came over to take our drink order. I asked for water and Stellan asked for the same.

"So what kind of food do elves eat for lunch?" I wondered aloud to him.

"We eat the type of food from what humans call the Renaissance Period."

I looked at the menu and an uneasy feeling settled in my stomach. The food here was strange to me. Sure, there was chicken and turkey, but also pigeon, rabbit, quail, pheasant, and venison. No one hunted in my family, so we weren't big meat eaters. Also, after Dina became a vegetarian to keep a good figure, our family catered to her and our meat intake went way down. It wasn't just the meat that was different though. Even the names of other dishes seemed complicated and foreign. I took the simple route and ordered a salad. I guessed seeing the look on my face as I looked through the menu made Stellan order the same. I bet he didn't want me freaking out over what he would have ordered, like a pigeon with its head still on and its beady little eyes staring creepily as it was eaten. *Gross*.

We didn't talk while we ate. It wasn't a surprise that Stellan was being weird again, but it made me feel disappointed. I had hoped for the attitude he had the day before, when he had held my hand all the way to Birchwood City. What was the point of this lunch?

When the bill came, Stellan paid before I could stop him.

"Well, thanks for lunch," I said unenthusiastically.

"You're welcome."

I got up to leave and this time he didn't stop me. Instead, he caught up to me as I was walking down the street.

"I'm sorry," he said, appearing out of thin air beside me.

I was beginning to get used to his teleporting, but I didn't care for his strange attitude.

"Sorry for what?" I asked.

"For that horrible lunch date," he said, looking down.

"Did you just say lunch *date*?" I questioned.

I saw his cheeks turn a little red. He wanted this to be a date and I had screwed it up because of how cold I was to him.

"I'm sorry," I said.

"No, it wasn't your fault. I was acting a little…"

"Weird," I finished for him.

"Yes."

"And I was acting…"

"Rude." He raised his eyebrows.

"Yeah." I sighed. Normally I would be offended, but it was the truth. I had been a little rude. I wasn't exactly used to a guy reacting this way toward me, both distant and interested, so I used my dating inexperience as an excuse, not that I mentioned the fact aloud….

"Can I make it up to you?" he asked suddenly, stirring me from my thoughts.

"Can I make it up to you, too?"

His hand brushed against mine, and I swear, I never had so many goose bumps covering my arms. "I'll see you tonight at dinner then." He winked at me and vanished before my eyes.

My heart fluttered like a butterfly in my chest. What did this mean exactly? Did he really have feelings for me? Did I *want* him to have feelings for me? More importantly, which part of him would show up at dinner? Would it be the kind and intriguing part…or the weird and distant part?

And where did the Stranger fit into this equation? It was foolish of me, but I still couldn't help thinking about him, even with the feeling of Stellan's hand brushing against mine burned in my memory.

I asked myself these questions repeatedly until I realized I was standing on the stoop in front of my house. It still felt weird calling it mine. I was fifteen and I owned a home. I didn't think I would get used to it, at least not for a while.

I stepped through the doorway, my mind still buzzing with thoughts of Stellan and the Stranger, and suddenly my arm started burning again. I felt an agony far worse than the first time, even though I knew what was happening to me this time around. But why did Addison have to use the same arm? Couldn't she spread the pain around instead of just concentrating it in one aching spot?

I looked down when the burning stopped to read the newest message:

How was lunch? Tell me all about it at dinner!

I then decided that Addison's ability was extremely annoying.

~7~

The Elfen and the White Picket Fence

I was practically praising the Lord when seven o'clock finally came and I could go to Addison's house. I had spent the rest of the afternoon rearranging my own house…six times to be exact. I moved the couches closer to the fire and then farther away. Then I turned the table one hundred and eighty degrees and straightened out the kitchen and bathroom, trying to make the house feel more like my own. Adding a personal touch was just what I needed, even though it took me six tries to get it right….

After some more arranging, I showered for the second time that day – just to pass the time – changed into a green knee-length cotton dress, and picked out a necklace from Zora's jewelry drawer to wear for dinner. It was a simple yet stunning emerald pendant on a silver chain. The more time I spent looking through Zora's jewelry, the more excited I became about buying my own. And wearing her jewelry made me feel closer to her, even though she was so far away.

The walk to Addison's was short, and soon I was at the doorstep. Before I could knock, Cass was opening the door.

"Do you live here or something?" I joked.

"No, I just like it here, that's all." He grinned.

"I see," I commented, stepping into the house.

The delicious smell of food hit me right away, and my mouth began to water. The homemade meals here in the Elf Realm were far different from the processed ones of the Human Realm – in sight, smell, and taste.

I followed Cass to the table, where Stellan was moving a chair out for me. I smiled and took my seat, noticing the other seating arrangements. Addison sat across from me, with Cass across from Stellan. Aaliyah was seated at the head of the table.

In front of us were roasted chicken, potatoes, and bread. It looked delicious *and* normal. I felt better about eating something I knew was also prepared in the Human Realm. I could get used to the different cuisine another time. We ate and drank until we were full. I even had wine, which I learned was customary to drink at dinnertime for elves. It seemed there was no age limit for drinking alcohol. I knew many people in the Human Realm – Dina's partying friends, for instance – who would love it here because of that.

Our dinner conversation included a discussion of Aaliyah's amazing cooking skills and Addison's day at school. I gathered that everyone was trying their best not to bring up my sister, even though she was on all of our minds.

But I tried to keep my spirits up and enjoy the time I had with my new friends.

Part way through dinner, I learned about the orchard Aaliyah owned a half mile away, where they picked apples, pears, and oranges. I recalled the tasty fruit from this morning, noting that it must have been their own. When I showed interest, Aaliyah told me she would take me there tomorrow and we could even have lunch. I was glad I would have something fun to do, because I knew the rest of my time would be spent on both my sister and my secret.

Cass left after dinner. He had to get home or his mother was going to "make him sleep in the stables." We all laughed at that one. Apparently, although there was no age limit on drinking, there were still curfews.

When he left, Addison made tea and we took a seat in front of the fireplace.

"How are you, Ramsey?" Aaliyah asked.

I shrugged. "I'm okay."

"Are you sure you are comfortable being alone in that house? You could sleep here if you want," she offered.

"Thank you for the offer, Aaliyah, but I feel closer to Zora there. If I am to find her, I have to know her."

"We understand," Addison said, as she took my hand and smiled.

Does she really, or is she just saying that? I wondered. I felt I could trust Addison, but I was also wary of her because a part of me believed she had brought me here only to find Zora; that she was only concerned for my sister's wellbeing. I could trust her to help me find Zora, but could I really trust her with my life? I wasn't so sure I could, not yet anyway.

We sat in silence for a few moments, no one knowing what else to say. This situation seemed to occur every time the subject of my sister came up during a conversation.

"I just remembered a question I had for you, Addison!" I blurted out, finally breaking the silence. "Stellan told me to ask you about it."

"He did *what*?" Addison shot a worried look at her brother.

"I wanted to know why you guys liked doing errands so much," I told her.

I was smiling, but the whole room went completely silent once more. I bit my lip and looked down. "What?" I asked.

"You should start sharing things with her, Addison. If you want her to help find Zora, she has to know what you're up to," Aaliyah suggested, resting a hand on her daughter's shoulder.

"Yes, Mother, I know. I just wanted her to settle in first. She's had a tough couple of days," Addison explained.

"That's no excuse, Addison," Aaliyah scolded. "She can't be kept in the dark. It isn't fair. She needs to know."

"Yes, but we didn't want to worry her," Stellan commented.

"Worry her? Confusing her is worse," Aaliyah said, shaking her head.

My frustration, mixed with a pinch of confusion, built until it got the better of me. "I'm right here, you know! What are you all talking about?" I asked, looking over at Stellan.

"Once again, I'll let Addison explain this one," he said, leaning back against the couch.

I sighed. "Addison?" I asked.

Addison sighed. "*Fine*," she said, and took a deep breath. "The reason we have been sort of…*avoiding* you today is because we are making arrangements for a little trip."

"What kind of trip?" I wondered.

"In three days we are leaving for Tarlore," she said bluntly.

"To see Queen Taryn?" I assumed, remembering that Tarlore was the capital of the Elf Realm.

"Precisely. If we want to find Zora, we'll need the Queen's help," Stellan informed me.

"But what will she do? I thought I was the only one who could find Zora," I said, and suddenly I felt a rush of disappointment. *Are we going because Stellan and Addison don't think I can find my sister on my own?* I wondered. I knew the odds were against me, but I had been counting on them for support so I could do my very best to find her.

"We are quite certain that Zora is in the Element Fairy Realm because that is the Realm we are fighting against. We will need protection if we are to search for her there. It's very dangerous for elf soldiers to be there, and even more dangerous for untrained elf civilians," Stellan explained, unknowingly reassuring me that this had nothing to do with their faith in me.

"It's also against the law to cross over into a Fairy Realm. Ever since the war began, going into any Fairy Realm was decreed too dangerous," Addison explained. "We'll need the Queen's permission to go to the Element Fairy Realm."

"What about the Human Realm? Is that okay?" I questioned.

Both siblings avoided my gaze. I could tell that I had hit a sore subject for them. Stellan looked up at me, worry creeping into his green eyes. "No. Leaving our Realm and going to any creature's Realm is against the law, unless you are a soldier, a royal, or a scout. Especially the Human Realm," he said gravely.

"Yet you went into the Human Realm," I reminded them.

"That is another reason we must go to Tarlore. Queen Taryn must decide if what we did was right…and worth it," Addison said quietly.

"If what was worth it?"

"We need to prove to Queen Taryn that bringing you back was important enough to break the law. Zora is not a royal, but you are a different story. Your unusual past is what gives us time to search for her, but it is a limited amount of time. If you can't find Zora soon, we will all be put on trial," she explained.

"And if we go to trial, we will probably go to prison," Stellan added.

"How did she know that you went into the Human Realm?" I asked.

"Queen Taryn's ability is to be able to see in her mind's eye what any elf is doing or has already done. She has trained herself to notice when anyone crosses over into another Realm. When we went to find you, she knew right away. She has others like herself in her service, so even if she misses something, she will know sooner or later from one of them," Addison told me. "The only reason we haven't been apprehended by royal guards as of yet is because…well, *so far*, she trusts you."

I blinked hard and tried to keep my breathing even. "Okay, then this is a lot of pressure on me," I said.

"Yes, it is. But if Zora believed you could find her, you will," Aaliyah said encouragingly.

"I hope so," I whispered to myself.

I realized that even though I had been brought here only because of my sister – and also that if she hadn't been taken, Addison probably wouldn't have come for me at all – I couldn't let Addison or Stellan down. They had risked their futures to help find her, and I decided *that* alone was good enough for me.

***

While Aaliyah and Addison cleaned up, Stellan led me outside. The evening was crisp and cool, and the breeze felt good against my skin. It was almost midnight and the stars shone brightly in the sky.

"I'll walk you home," Stellan offered.

I nodded. "Okay."

He took my hand and walked slowly with me down the dirt road. I guess he didn't feel like teleporting tonight. I took the time to think about my situation. I had just returned to my real home and in three days, we were already leaving.

I knew I needed to find Zora, and quickly. Addison and Stellan didn't risk everything for me to fail. If I didn't find Zora soon, I would ruin their lives. They had pretty much saved me from a terrible life in the Human Realm, and now it was my duty to save them.

Seeing Blaire had to be first tomorrow before going to the orchard. If she knew something about Zora, I needed to know the information before I left. I also needed to buy that book on how to open locks. I had a feeling that what was in that trunk could help me figure out my secret. It might also be able to help me find Zora.

I was glad Stellan didn't want to talk. My mind was swarming with so many thoughts and ideas that I was afraid my words wouldn't make much sense if I spoke.

I looked up to see a shooting star flying through the night sky. I felt an incredible excitement spread through me, as if it were falling just for me. I wondered if shooting stars were a common sight in this magical place.

I had always believed shooting stars weren't just a child's tale. I believed if you wished on them, your wish would somehow come true. I couldn't know for sure how the process worked, but it didn't matter so long as my wish was granted. I took the opportunity and wished for a way to find my sister.

"I believe you can find your sister, Ramsey," Stellan said in front of my door. It was as if he had read my mind.

Elves have a way with reading people, I noted to myself.

"Thank you. I think I can find her too…if I have an idea where to look," I muttered.

Stellan smiled and released his hand from mine. It felt colder without him. I looked down and sighed. How did he feel about me? How did I feel about him? What was this? Was it just a friendship or something *more*?

When I looked up, he was closer to me than before. I could feel his warm breath on my face. My heart pounded and my knees felt ready to buckle. I shivered, but not because I was cold. I had never been this close to anyone before. The scene was so…intimate. I could barely think, let alone make sense of what was happening.

Stellan took both of my hands in his. Warmth spread from them to my heart. I looked into his eyes as he leaned even closer. My breath quickened as his lips pressed against mine, and at first, I was apprehensive. But as he kissed me gently and slowly, a feeling of sheer bliss passed between us, and I forgot about everything else, all of my worries. I simply let myself be swept away by the closeness we both felt.

When the kiss ended, Stellan squeezed my hands one last time and vanished into the night. I stood breathless against the door, my heart pounding and the rest of me feeling faint and woozy. I didn't move for what seemed like a long time, even though my internal clock told me just minutes had passed. My mind was finding it hard to comprehend what had just happened. I couldn't stop *thinking* about what had just happened.

I had just had my first kiss…with an elf. I had to giggle at how absurd the sentence sounded in my head. But it was true.

Stellan had kissed me. Stellan really did like me. Did I like Stellan? I definitely liked his kiss. What would happen now? Would he court me like Cass and Addison? Did I like Stellan that way?

Yes, I decided.

A boy had never reacted this way toward me before. No boy had ever *liked* me this way *before*. The feeling was new and wonderful. Even though I knew this was probably moving too fast, I couldn't stop myself from falling for him. It was completely, utterly inevitable. I didn't want this rush of feelings to end, and I already wanted to be with him again. I yearned to be near him, to feel his warm hands entwined with mine. Being away from him, even so soon after our kiss, was beginning to make my heart ache.

Stellan and Ramsey, elf and elfen, confident and confused, outgoing and shy, *beautiful and beautiful,* all words to describe what we were, and I liked the sound of that.

I *really* liked the sound of that.

***

The next morning I woke at exactly four on the dot. Feeling happy and rested, I took a shower and dressed in a pale yellow sundress. I had a smile on my face from the minute I woke up, remembering the kiss I had shared with Stellan last night.

Before heading over to Addison's I looked in Zora's wardrobe and found a brown shoulder bag to carry my money and the directions to Blaire's. *Today is going to be a very long day,* I realized. However, it would be worth it if I found out anything more about my missing sister.

When I closed the front door and turned to walk away, something colorful caught my eye. I looked back to see the most gorgeous flowers surrounding my house. They looked dazzling, and just as lovely as Addison's flowers. I smiled and knelt down beside the troughs. The flowers smelled heavenly. Each one was different, which made the house look unique. It brightened up the "unused" look the house had yesterday. It actually looked like someone lived there, like a real home.

With an added bounce in my step, I walked briskly to Addison's. I found her kneeling by her own flowers. She held a tin watering can over the troughs, her green skirt smudged with spots of dirt. Her short-sleeved blouse was already brown, so the mess didn't show as much. I knelt down beside her and gave her a hug.

"Thank you," I told her.

"You're welcome. I take it you liked the flowers?"

"I love them!"

"I'm sorry they are all different. I didn't know what kind you liked, and I wanted to surprise you. I thought it would cheer you up a little, take away the stress."

"They're perfect," I assured her.

Addison stood up and brushed the dirt off her skirt. I got up as well and followed her inside. Aaliyah met us as we walked in.

"Aren't the flowers beautiful?" she asked.

"Yes! I swear, Addison has a gift and I'm not talking about a kind of ability."

"Okay, enough with the praise, please!" Addison laughed and went to wash her hands in the kitchen sink. "They're only flowers," I heard her mutter as she took a seat at the table.

"Sit down for breakfast, Ramsey. It's almost ready," Aaliyah encouraged.

"Thanks, but I feel bad for eating all of your food. I should start buying and making my own meals."

"Don't feel bad at all! I'm not a very busy elfen, and I like cooking. The only job I have is selling fruit at the market down the street every few days."

"Even so, I *do* want to go to the market and stock my fridge with *some* food; at least just enough to get me through the few days I have before we leave for Tarlore. I'd like to try my hand at cooking elf cuisine myself. Maybe if I'm good enough, I can have you over for dinner too."

"That would be lovely." She smiled. "Here, eat some breakfast before you go."

Aaliyah set down a bowl of her orchard-grown fruit and some buttered bread. While we ate, I discussed with Aaliyah when we would go to the orchard. I still had to visit Blaire, stop at the market, visit the bookstore, and go to the jeweler. We decided on meeting back at her home at eleven. She would be waiting with a packed lunch for both of us. Addison would spend her day at school. I didn't ask her about our upcoming trip, but I knew that after school her mind would be focused on what we would need to travel. I wanted to help somehow, or at least know what she was doing, but I didn't say anything. I had enough on my plate already, and I didn't know how I could help her anyway.

I thanked them both for preparing breakfast again and left for Blaire's. I was in a hurry because I wanted to make sure I accounted for everything on my list.

However, before I could take more than five steps away from the house, Stellan appeared before me, stopping me from getting a head start on my busy day.

"Where were you this morning?" I asked.

"I was…thinking," he replied.

"Thinking about what?"

Instead of answering, he took my hands and kissed me on the cheek. I looked up at him and frowned.

"What?" he asked.

"You missed, Stellan. I didn't think you were *that* uncoordinated."

"I apologize. I guess I'm still a little tired, or maybe I was unfocused by your beauty."

I rolled my eyes and blushed simultaneously. He smiled and kissed me on the lips this time, and I was glad to see his wary attitude gone once more. Maybe the more time we spent together, the more comfortable he would feel, and the happier he would stay.

I felt warm and cheerful as his arms moved to hold me close to him. I wrapped my arms around him and sighed.

"What?" he asked, as he removed his arms from around my waist.

I smiled. "I'm happy," I said, a little surprised that it was the truth. I had thought with my sister missing and my mind jumbled with unanswered questions, I would be depressed and moody. That was not the case. Although I was a little overwhelmed at times by the huge responsibility of finding my sister, I was also grateful for all I had already gained. That included Stellan.

"I'm glad you're happy," he replied.

"So…what *is* this?"

"This?" he asked.

"I mean, what are we? What does this make us?" I asked.

"Like…relationship wise?"

"Exactly, are you…courting me now? That sounds so weird…." I looked down, feeling embarrassed. His fingers lifted my chin as he planted another kiss on my lips.

"I'd like to," he said sincerely.

"What does that mean? Is it like dating?" *Man, is this conversation awkward*, I thought.

"Dating?" He looked confused.

I tried to find the right words to explain. "It's a human thing. We go on dates. We go places together, we kiss, and we have a relationship. What is courting? Isn't that like preparing for marriage?"

"Not really. It's close to what you are saying. It's only for marriage when the parents arrange something, and anyway, elves don't get married often. It's just an old age term we took from the English back in the Human Realm."

"I see. Then I would like it if you did court me."

I still giggled at the thought, and couldn't stop myself from blushing. It just sounded weird. It reminded me of old movies, like the ones that represented the fifteen-hundreds or something.

"Good," he said.

I checked my internal clock and realized the longer I stayed with Stellan, the more behind I became on my duties. I sighed, wishing I didn't have any responsibilities and could spend the day with Stellan's arms around me. However, my better judgment won the internal conflict inside of me and I realized, with a pang, that I *had* to go. Finding my sister was more important than exploring my new relationship with Stellan.

"It's after five and I really have to get going. I'm sorry," I told him, frowning.

He shook his head. "No, it's okay. I'll see you later at dinner."

"Okay," I said.

He squeezed my hand and then I was off to meet Blaire. All the while, my heart was pounding and my mind was on Stellan.

***

Let's just say Blaire's house was not what I expected. Instead of the normal brown and wooden style décor I had become accustomed to seeing in the Elf Realm since I had arrived, it was all white, with a white picket fence and flower pots lining a walkway leading up to the door. It looked too modern for this Realm, and just like the kind of house a woman dreamed about after she got married.

Confused, I walked up to the door and knocked. The door was forest green and the windows next to it trimmed with green as well. These were the only elf-like details about the house, which seemed quite odd to me.

If I thought that was strange, what came next was far beyond that. The door opened to reveal a tall pointy-eared elfen with lovely green eyes. That was the normal part.

She also had a warm tan glow to her skin and brown hair that reminded me of my sister Dina's, chestnut and shining. It flowed over her shoulders in long waves. I covered my hand over my mouth in a gasp and blinked to make sure I was seeing correctly.

Elves did *not* have brown hair or tan skin.

"Are you Blaire?" I asked, shocked.

"Come on in, Ramsey, and we'll talk."

I nodded, still in shock, and followed her in. It was a lovely house, but once again felt too modern for an elfen. Then again, Blaire wasn't just any elfen. That was obvious already. Addison had been right when she said Blaire was different from other elves.

"Sit down, please. I'll go and get the tea," she told me.

I sat down, still unable to speak. She came back moments later with a tray, teacups, and a kettle. She poured us each tea that smelled like a mixture of peaches and an herb I couldn't place. The soothing aroma calmed me and relieved the shock of seeing Blaire for the first time.

"Before we really talk, I'll set some things straight," she said, in a businesslike manner. "I'm an elfen."

"That relieves *some* of the confusion. I think." I half-smiled. She didn't smile back, so I cleared my throat and looked down, embarrassed. Apparently, there wasn't any room for jokes here. Instead, Blaire continued speaking.

"My parents were both elves. I am some kind of genetic mistake. At least that is how others explain it." She pointed to her hair and brushed a hand over her arm to show off her tan skin. "I just call it different. Humans are different. They have different hair and skin color. I never understood why elves couldn't. My parents ignored it at first, saying that it was just a 'baby' thing and I would grow out of it. I turned five and I still hadn't changed. No one knew what had caused it. I was the freak among elves. Funny, right, considering they are supposed to be mythical creatures?"

She didn't pause long enough for me to respond to her sarcastic statement.

"When I was six, the town made a decision. I would have to go to the Human Realm. I didn't fit in here, so I would have to be sent somewhere that I could. Someplace where being different was just fine, at least that is what the elves thought."

"What? How? I thought it was…."

"Illegal?" she inferred.

"Yeah," I said.

"When it happened to me, Queen Taryn hadn't begun ruling yet. The law hadn't been made. Everyone knew you were there already. They thought it would be as simple as dropping me off and never looking back. When you left, you were only one year old, but when I left, I was six and I had a mind of my own. My parents took me to the Human Realm and found a family to take me in. After they got over the whole elfen thing, they were ready to be my new parents. However, I was not ready to be their new child. I waited a year, gathering all of the information I could about elves. I waited, I was patient, and I put off returning in hopes that the elves of Birchwood might forget me, because when I returned, I wasn't planning on leaving again."

"What did you do then?"

"When I felt the time was right, I waited for midnight, made an elf circle, and came home. It took me a while to find Birchwood City again, but soon I was back on my doorstep. However, there was one little problem. It wasn't my doorstep anymore. My parents had left after sending me away. They were so overtaken with guilt that they couldn't live in Birchwood anymore without remembering what they had done to me, how they had just gotten rid of me. I could have followed the footsteps of my parents and relocated to their new city, but I quickly dismissed the whole idea. I didn't want a family who rid themselves of their own daughter and then ran away because they felt guilty… No offense."

"It's okay," I told her, swallowing a lump in my throat.

"Your situation is completely different, Ramsey. Your parents loved you," she reminded me.

"I know," I agreed, though I couldn't help but feel a bit of resentment toward my birth parents even so.

Maybe Blaire was wrong; maybe everyone was wrong. Maybe my parents hadn't loved me. Maybe that was why they sent me to the Human Realm, and for no other reason than that. Maybe I wasn't so special.

Then, I dismissed the terrible thoughts. I had to be special, somehow. How else would I be able to find my sister? I had to have some kind of an edge. Maybe my secret would be what would lead me to Zora. I had to hold on to that.

I felt ashamed when I realized Blaire was waiting for me to pay attention so she could finish. I had somehow drifted off, my head in the clouds. After I muttered a quick apology, Blaire resumed her story.

"Anyway, I was left alone and without a home. The city, feeling ashamed, decided to raise me together. I stayed with various families at different times. They accepted me as different and tried their best to ignore it. Unfortunately, when my sixteenth birthday came around and my ability was non-apparent, everyone questioned what kind of elfen I would be as I grew older, or if I was an elfen at all. Then an idea came to them. With the war raging and most elf men – and some elfens – racing off to battle, the city was in shambles. Elfen wives and mothers were finding it hard to keep up with the cleaning while taking care of their children and the men who lived in the city had to work. Their solution: Have Blaire be the city's personal "maid." In exchange, I could acquire my own house, food, clothes, and personal items free of charge. So here I am, twenty-two years old and a house cleaner."

"The war has been going on for over twenty years?"

It was all I could ask, because I didn't know how to respond to her story. It was awful, and I didn't know what to say to comfort her. I could detect tears in her eyes, and when Blaire caught me looking, she quickly brushed them away with the back of her hand.

"Twenty-nine years, actually," she replied.

Trying to keep the subject away from straying back to her parents, I asked, “So why do you have such a different house? Did the elves here actually build you a house like this?”

“No, I decided what it would look like. Then I paid elves to build it for me. I liked the houses in the Human Realm. My belief is that if I’m different, I should embrace it; different elfen, different house.”

“I’m sorry for what happened to you, Blaire. Believe me; I know what it’s like to be different. It’s not that my life is any harder, but being different as an elfen, or as anyone for that matter, is hard. I know that.”

“*That* is why I am going to help you,” she said, clearing her throat, all traces of earlier sadness gone. She was serious now.

“How can you help me?” I inquired.

“Zora and I were close friends, believe it or not. She wasn’t like the others.”

“I believe that,” I realized, a little stunned at how well I was beginning to know my sister without even meeting with her face to face.

“Before she was taken, she knew they were coming for her,” Blaire confirmed.

“She hinted on that in the journal she wrote for me,” I said with surprise.

Blaire responded with a nod. “One week or so before she was taken by the Element fairies, she came to my house to ask me for a favor. She wanted me to give you something just in case something bad happened to *her*. I asked her what she meant and she said it didn’t matter. I just needed to promise. I was the only one she trusted with this task.”

“Did you accept?”

“Would you be in my house now if I had not?” she asked me.

“I guess not,” I agreed. “So what was the promise?”

“I promised I would give you *this*.”

She pulled a velvet box from her skirt pocket and opened it. Inside, shining like a falling star, was a slender, diamond-shaped crystal. Blaire took it from the box, revealing a thin black cord attached to it.

"What is it?" I asked, admiring its beauty. "It's gorgeous."

"It's called a Mood Diamond," she said.

"Is it like a Mood Ring? We have those in the Human Realm. They change color depending on your mood."

"It's not quite the same thing," she said, her face showing the same confused expression as Stellan's did when I talked about human things. "For two people who are bonded or related by blood like you and your sister, this necklace serves as a connector. Zora wore one as well, at least during the week they took her. It's a tool elfin Spell Masters created years and years ago, as a way for loved ones to keep in contact over long distances," she explained.

"What do I do with it? Will it help me find her?"

"It might, if it's strong enough."

"What happens when I wear it?" I asked.

"You can connect to her. When it glows, it means you will have a vision."

"What do you mean by a vision?"

"If the diamond is strong enough, Zora will sense you. She can use the connection to show you where she is. You will experience an out-of-body feeling. You can be there with her, but only spiritually, not physically. Then, if the bond is strong enough, you can connect and become one being. For example, if you connect with Zora but she can't speak to tell you where she is, you can become one with her and she can tell you with her mind."

"How can that happen?" I asked with wonder.

"Elf magic is wondrous…and utterly complex. You would have to ask those who created the diamond to fully understand it, but I must also warn you to be ready for whatever comes. The connection may not be pleasant."

"I will do anything I can to find her, Blaire, no matter the cost. She is the only real family I have left...that I know of," I added. "And many other elves are counting on me."

"I trust you will do whatever you can. Wear the diamond, Ramsey. With luck, Zora will be able to connect with you and tell you where she is. Then you can find her and bring her home."

"Thank you for this, Blaire. I won't forget it," I told her. I reached over and placed my hand over hers. "And I won't let you down. I'll make sure the promise you made to Zora was worth it."

"You are just like your sister, Ramsey. You are compassionate and you truly care about others." For the first time since meeting her, she showed a genuine smile. "You are a *good* kind of different."

"It makes me glad that others think that, because being different has been so hard for me to accept."

"It's true," she replied.

I smiled and nodded, feeling a new surge of hope and self-confidence from her words.

***

We finished our tea, and it was time for me to go. With the Mood Diamond fastened around my neck, I got up to leave.

"Ramsey, I must say one more thing before you leave,"

"Yes?"

"I do not know your secret – Zora does – but I do know one thing. If the Element fairies find out about you, our Realm could fall into the Dark Times once again, and you can't let that happen. Everything depends on whether you find Zora or not, for she is the key to unlocking your secret before the Element fairies do."

"The Dark Times," I repeated, pondering. "What was that?"

"They began shortly after all the Realms were created. They were a time when goblins, trolls, and dark spirits arose. All were evil things, filled with darkness and hate."

"What happened?" I wondered.

Blaire's message was both fascinating and ominous to me. I was interested because I wanted to learn more about the Elf Realm, but fearful because of how terrible the Dark Times sounded. I hadn't even heard all of it yet, and I didn't know how I fit in.

"Some say the Dark Times were created by the same magic that made the Realms. All magic has mistakes, or loopholes. That great amount of magic had the power to make countless mistakes. Those mistakes were the Dark Times."

"What exactly occurred during the Dark Times, Blaire?"

"The dark creatures bound together. The goblins were grotesque and hateful, the trolls giant and merciless, and the dark spirits cruel and mysterious. Other lesser beings followed them, creatures filled with light that succumbed to their evil ways. The dark creatures vowed to rule our Realms and destroy us. They wanted to dominate every Realm, even the Human Realm."

"How would that ever be possible?" I asked.

"Have you ever heard of the mysterious plagues that have hit the Human Realm over many hundreds of years?"

"Yes. I learned about them in school," I remembered.

"Those were the dark spirits. They did not know how to travel to the Human Realm, so they used their sorcery to kill. They sent evil magic to the Human Realm. Every creature in the Realms fought these evil beings. It took over one hundred years to achieve peace. Those were the Dark Times."

"Are the dark beings dead now?"

"They are either dead or imprisoned throughout the Realms," Blaire explained. She sighed. "At least that is what I've heard. You never know what can happen when it comes to magic, but since then, our Realms have become more modern."

"Why?"

"If any dark magic arises again, we will be prepared. We need some of the skills and tools humans have so we can be one step ahead."

"But the Magical Realms are not as modern as the Human Realm, are they?"

Blaire shook her head. "No, and they will never be. No matter how much we want to be safe, some things will never change. Most of the creatures throughout the Realms would never allow technology to destroy our beauty and peace. Elves don't want to lose their culture. The fae – the general grouping for all types of fairies – despise modern things even more than elves. You don't find many things modern in those Realms. The fae also can't bear the touch of iron, because it burns their skin, so that leaves metals out."

I nodded, remembering my conversation with Addison my first day here, when she explained why the bathrooms were fashioned out of iron.

"Too much technology and modernism would hurt us more than one million dark beings, because it would change us completely. No one here wants that. We live and breathe our own cultures," Blaire explained.

"I understand completely. But how can my secret make something worse than the Dark Times happen?" I asked.

"If this war goes on much longer, every Realm will be involved. They cannot hide from it forever. One day, each Realm will have to choose a side, elfin or fae. Once every Realm is involved, no one will survive. That much magic released into the Realms…." She sighed. "No side will come out of the destruction alive. Even the humans may find a way inside it."

"How can I stop a war, Blaire?"

"I don't know, Ramsey. Only Zora knows. That is why you must find her. All I know is that you have a secret within you that the Element fairies would kill to posses. You can't let that happen to Zora or to you."

I nodded silently and looked down at the Mood Diamond hanging from my neck. "I don't know about ending a war just yet, but I *will* find my sister."

"I believe you will," she said.

Blaire and I hugged and she wished me luck. I told her I would see her again when this was over, if it ever was over. She said she would like that. I knew I would. Blaire was just another me. She was different in one place and different in the next. She had learned to accept it. I suppose I would have to accept it, too.

Nevertheless, how would I stop a war? How could my secret hold the key to so many lives? How could I, an elfen so new to this Realm, ever hold that much power? I pushed the thought away. I wouldn't understand any of it until Zora was safe. She was the key to all of my questions, just as Blaire said. I would have to find her to open the doorway. I would decide the rest afterward.

I promised myself to stop thinking about the war and focus solely on my sister instead. I felt a little guilty for abandoning all that Blaire had shared with me, but I couldn't do everything at once. Zora was the "first clue." It had to start with her.

Slowly walking away from Blaire's modern home, I realized it was time for me to stop by the jeweler and see Aaron again. It was next on my list.

The walk there took longer than I expected. I was anxious about the Mood Diamond. I didn't know when a vision might come, or if any would come at all. I wanted to be prepared, but what happened if I suddenly had a vision in the middle of a street? I was afraid something would go wrong, and that didn't do good things for my already piling handful of worries. I tried to focus on the present, but it was difficult.

Seeing Aaron smiling from behind the counter lightened my spirit as I entered the store. I walked over and smiled as well. Then I noticed his eyes fixated on the Mood Diamond hanging around my neck.

"Is that…?" he started to ask.

"It's a Mood Diamond, if that's what you're asking," I told him.

"And Zora has one as well, I take it?"

"You are a very good guesser," I complimented him.

He ignored my comment. "What you are doing could be dangerous; you know that, right?"

"What do you mean?" I wondered.

"If Zora is feeling any pain when she connects with you, you could receive it," he informed me.

"I could really feel what she feels?" I asked.

"Yes," he said gravely.

"Blaire forgot to mention that one…but I don't care," I admitted. "I have to find her, and I have to bring her home."

"I just hope you know what you're doing."

"I do," I told him. "And even if I don't, the most interesting parts of life are the ones that surprise you." I smiled, trying to shrug off his negative attitude.

But Aaron would have none of my optimism. He shook his head and sighed. "You need to be careful, Ramsey. This is an entirely different world to you. You can't just jump right into it and expect to know all the tricks."

I shut my eyes tightly. "I have to trust that I can do this, Aaron."

"I know you're strong enough to find your sister," he explained. "I just want you to be aware of your limitations along the way."

I breathed in deeply. "I grew up believing magic has no limitations."

Aaron half-smiled. "I may have been wrong before. Maybe you know more about this Realm than I realized."

***

The day was glorious as I stepped out of Aaron's shop, bag full of jewelry in hand, this time avoiding any run-ins with beautiful-eyed strangers. The sun shone beautifully through the fluffy white clouds, and the birdsong filled me with delight. The day was getting a lot better, and I felt optimistic about things…for once. But who knew how long that would last?

Like I mentioned to Aaron, life was full of surprises.

~8~

The Orchard

The market Aaliyah had referred to was bustling with elves and venders when I arrived. Walking through it was like going through a giant maze. Fruit, vegetable, bread, and pastry venders had stalls everywhere, gathered in clusters like peas in a giant pod. Every food in the Elf Realm seemed to be on display and ready for sale. It was crazy trying to maneuver around all of the elves, and I browsed as slowly as possible without being trampled. I wanted to see everything before buying. I made a mental note to come back to the venders I was drawn to, and made sure to stray away from the meat venders. I wasn't confident in my ability to avoid meats that would disturb me, because everything looked the same to me.

While searching, I noticed how many elves watched me, staring curiously as I browsed. I remembered Stellan had said that many elves would approach me often just to talk to me, but so far, they were only staring. I would have preferred the talking. Being stared at put an uncomfortable feeling in my gut.

With a basket full of groceries, I headed for home. It was only one hour until my picnic with Aaliyah. I was excited to spend time with her. She seemed wise, and I wanted to know a lot more about my sister – and the Elf Realm in general.

As I started putting away the food, I noticed a large piece of paper and a small velvet bag on my kitchen table. There was also a huge flowering plant in a lovely painted green pot. I walked over, curious to know what the letter said and who had left the gifts. I guessed it would be from Addison or Stellan. Yet, why would Addison leave me a letter when she could just write on my arm again? *It must have been Stellan*, I decided.

When I reached the table, I picked up the letter and was surprised to see that it wasn't from Stellan at all. It was from Ashlyn, the spunky girl I met at the bank with Stellan the day before:

Dear Ramsey,

Here are some things that Zora left at my house. They are her favorite writing pen and necklace.

Zora always told me that the necklace stood for "sister;" I just wanted you to know that. No matter where she is right now, I know she cares about you.

Anyway, I'm sorry for stopping by your house unannounced. I had to get to school on time, and when I saw that you weren't home, I decided just to leave everything here. I hope you are not too upset with me!

I also hope that we can get together soon. Zora was my friend, which makes you my friend as well. If you are ever having trouble with the plant I gave you just let me know. My ability is to bring life to nature. However, that does not give you the right to neglect it! Remember that! Water it every day, keep it in the sunlight, and sing to it. Plants love when you sing to them.

Have a wonderful day!

Your friend, Ashlyn

I smiled. Ashlyn sure was flamboyant, but also very sweet. Knowing I had another friend warmed my heart. In the last two or three days, I had made more friends than I had in a lifetime.

Sighing happily, I put the beautiful plant on my windowsill. It would get plenty of sunlight there. Then I opened up the velvet pouch and dumped its contents onto the table. I noticed the lovely black writing pen and a silver chain necklace with an "S" pendant at the end. Looking at it made me feel a little empty, and low.

Time, and time again, I was told about how much Zora cared for me. I had never thought of her once. Even though I knew her when I was too young to remember, it still made me feel terrible. I couldn't help it. She walked around with a necklace in memory of me, and I walked around complaining that I was a freak. What a sister I was....

I promised myself I would make it up to her. I would find her, rescue her, and then spend the rest of my life being the kind of sister I would have been if I had never grown up in the Human Realm.

I put Zora's writing pen in the drawer with her stationery and put the "S" necklace in my shoulder bag. I wanted it with me so when I did find Zora, I could give it to her and thank her.

What I really wanted was to have all of my problems out of the way so I could enjoy being myself. I wanted to find Zora. I wanted to find out the supposed secret I had.

After that, I wanted to start my life, my real life, in the Elf Realm. Yet I knew that would not happen until Zora was safe.

I finished putting away my groceries and was relieved when the time came to meet Aaliyah for our picnic. Any more time alone with my rambling thoughts and I would go crazy. My mind was clouded, and I needed someone to help clear it. I knew she could; my impression of her was that she could be a friend and mother to anyone.

As I headed out the door to meet Aaliyah, I couldn't stop worrying. What happened if I wasn't able to find my sister? If I failed, Addison and Stellan would go to prison. What would happen if they sent *me* to prison? I had to make things move faster, but I wasn't sure how. Blaire said to give it time, but I didn't have much left. *God, what am I going to do?*

What was there I *could* do? Besides waiting around for the Mood Diamond to work, I could do nothing to help the situation.

I was certain that Aaliyah could ease my mind, even if her advice didn't bring me any closer to finding Zora. I wasn't looking for someone to solve my problems. I just needed someone to *listen* so I didn't feel like I was all on my own.

Aaliyah was waiting outside when I arrived. She held a large basket that carried the delicious aroma of food. When she remarked about the Mood Diamond, I had to promise her, as I had to Aaron, that I would be careful.

Arm in arm, we walked to the orchard. It was a long way to go, but I didn't mind. The scenery was beautiful.

On the way I saw herds of deer, ponds filled with baby ducklings following their mothers, and robins searching for worms. These were the same wild animals from my old home, but here they looked happier, more peaceful. The modern craziness of the Human

Realm didn't touch them. Instead, they were living in balance with nature, as it should be.

Lost in thought, it took me a moment to realize that we had finally reached the orchard.

It reminded me of farms in the Human Realm. Row after row of fruit-bearing trees stretched out before me. I could spot the oranges, pears, and apples. My mouth watered at the sight. Even from far away, I could see that the fruit was luscious and ripe. One thing I wondered was how oranges could grow in the same region as pears and apples. In the Human Realm, this wasn't usually done. I asked Aaliyah that same question.

"Do you know the story of the Garden of Eden?" she asked.

"Yes, Adam and Eve," I recalled.

"Well, when Adam and Eve broke God's law, the real beauty and magic of the Human Realm was taken away. However, humans had broken the law, not elves or fairies. So when our Realms were created, we had the beauty and magic that God first gave to the Human Realm. That same magic in this Realm allows anything to be possible. We have no need for regions or specific climates, and we are provided with all that we need to plant orange trees with apple trees. "

"But God didn't create these Realms," I commented.

She smiled. "Yes, that is true, but these Realms would not have been possible if God had not gifted the creators with the ability to do so. But how did you know that?" The gentleness and amusement of her voice gave away the fact that she was not mocking or insulting me, but generally curious.

I bit my lip. "Well, I sort of assumed so. Whenever an elf mentions the creation of the Realms, they never mention God. I didn't even know elves believed in God," I remarked.

"Why wouldn't we?" she asked.

"Because you aren't human," I explained. "In the Human Realm, mythical creatures are thought to have their own gods."

"It's called fantasy, Ramsey," she explained. "The real fantasy is what others have made up about our kind. We believe in God just as any human would. Sure, other magical beings believe in different things, but we believe in Him."

"What do the others believe in?"

"The majority of elves, gnomes, dwarves, etc., believe in God. Some don't. Just like with humans. We believe in Jesus, but we do not worship Him as the humans do. For you see, He was not our savior. He was the savior of the humans."

"That makes sense," I told her.

Aaliyah nodded and continued, "The fae creatures believe in Fae. They were named after her. She is their goddess, their supposed creator. They believe God exists as well, just that He didn't create them. Fae did."

"So God created humans, elves, gnomes, etc., and Fae created the fae?" I asked, just making sure I understood what she was explaining to me.

"Yes. That is what we believe."

"Any other religious beliefs I should know about for future references?" I asked.

"Well," Aaliyah replied, pausing a moment to think, "I know the mermaids believe God had a wife. When God created the earth, He created her as a companion. Her name was Mer. Legend says that when God created the oceans and seas, Mer fell and was lost in the depths of the water. To save her, God made her legs into the tail of a fish so she could swim up into the heavens to be with Him. However, Mer decided she loved the sea and wanted to stay there. When God changed her legs to a tail, Mer felt she was completely changed. She belonged in the sea. However, she didn't want to be lonely and asked God to help her make more of her kind. Legend says He did, and together they created a whole sea full of new, wondrous creatures. That is supposedly where *Mer*maids and *Mer*men come from."

"Do mermaids have their own Realm, separate from elves and fairies?" I inquired.

Aaliyah nodded, moving the basket of food from one arm to the other. "Their Realm is Atlantis, also referred to by humans, as 'The Lost City of Atlantis.' The reason their Realm was created was to keep the sirens under control; otherwise, they may have stayed in the Human Realm. At first, Atlantis was an island in the Human Realm. The mermaids who lived there had the power to be either a mermaid or human. It was their choice. When the mermaids moved Atlantis to their own Realm, they returned to their true forms. Humans now believe Atlantis sank to the bottom of the ocean after some failed attempt to take over the Greek city of Athens. We mystical beings, of course, know this is not true. However, humans sometimes have ways of covering up what they can't explain with a story, lie, or legend. It's difficult for a being without magic to accept that magic truly happens."

"I see," I said. "Don't sirens lure sailors to their deaths with their looks?"

"Precisely," she confirmed. "Sirens also have the most beautiful voices of all mystical beings, even more beautiful than elves and fairies, and that says quite a lot. They are all women, and undeniably stunning. A siren can be born from two mermaid parents, or from a merman and a siren. Before the Mermaid Realm, sirens swam through the seas looking for anyone weak enough to prey on. When things started getting out of hand, the Mermaid Realm was created to protect the mermaids and to avoid problems with humans."

"Wow, so many stories…so many beliefs. And I thought the Human Realm was complicated…."

"Ramsey, all that matters is what you believe," Aaliyah told me.

"I believe in God."

"Then that should be enough," she said, patting my arm affectionately. "You can sift through the rest of the information another time. Right now, focus on what you believe, and use those beliefs to give you the strength to find Zora and discover your secret."

I nodded, taking her advice to heart, and followed her into the orchard.

***

"You made it home to the Elf Realm just in time, Ramsey. Everything here is in season," Aaliyah commented.

"It looks wonderful," I said.

"Come, I'll show you where we will have lunch," Aaliyah said, taking my hand and leading me through the fruit trees.

I looked up in awe at the vibrant colors of the fruit. I noticed different kinds of apple and pear trees, and even Clementine trees nestled among the normal-sized orange trees. It was the most fruit I had ever seen in my life. It was all beautiful, like precious jewels, only edible. I giggled to myself. I would never have compared food and jewels to each other before this day. In the Elf Realm, everything was different. I was thinking of new thoughts and enjoying new experiences.

Soon we came to a small clearing where Aaliyah draped a large blanket over the grass. She placed a large bouquet of flowers in the middle of the blanket.

"Addison's," she commented, gesturing to the flowers. "She always says you can't enjoy food without flowers as the centerpiece. They make the experience all the more enjoyable."

"Interesting thought," I remarked.

"That's Addison for you," Aaliyah replied with a smile.

I breathed in deeply and admired our surroundings.

"It's like a fairyland here," I said, and then gasped. "Sorry, I didn't mean that kind of fairy…."

"Don't worry about it, Ramsey. What you said is true. The Elf Realm is beautiful, but if you went to the Golden Fairy Realm, I don't think you would want to leave. I hear it's too beautiful for words."

"What is the Golden Fairy Realm?" I asked.

"Four kinds of fairies make up the foundation of the fae. Dryads, nymphs, and pixies are fae as well, along with other fairies that fit in here and there, but these four fairies are the most powerful and plentiful," she said as we sat down. "All four have their own Realm. The other fairies fit in wherever they choose, or remain in the Human Realm. The Golden fairies are the royal ones. Queen Titania lives in the Golden Fairy Realm. She is known as the High

Queen because she is queen of the Golden Fairy Realm as well as the ruler of the entire fae population. Some even believe she rules over all the Magical Realms."

"Do elves believe this, too?" I asked.

Aaliyah winced. "No, we believe that because we were the first to create a Realm, we do not need to bow to Queen Titania," she explained. "We were the ones to come up with the idea of separate Realms in the first place. However, she *is* the most powerful being of the Realms. An elf would be foolish to cross her....I don't believe any elf would, no matter how he or she felt about Titania. She is dangerous, stunning, and wondrous...many words can describe her and not all of them very good. So even though our Realm does not acknowledge her as supreme ruler, we *do* respect her."

I nodded. "Why are the Golden fairies considered royal?"

Aaliyah flattened a part of the blanket that was ruffled and flicked away a few pieces of grass. "They are the most beautiful of the fae, the most magical, and the most powerful. Golden fairies have honey golden hair; soft, tan skin; and lovely golden wings and can have many abilities instead of just one like the elves. They also have the ability to perform spells, create charms, and mix potions. Golden fairies have their powers all of their lives, far reaching abilities stronger than most can imagine. The possibilities are endless. However, these powers vary for each Golden fairy. They are a wondrous sight to behold and equally just as threatening. Their powers, unlike the elves and other fae, are limitless. I do not know one creature who has ever challenged a Golden fairy. Any who would do so would most likely pay for it with their lives."

"Sounds like they can do almost anything," I remarked, feeling a little intimidated just hearing of the Golden fairies.

Surprisingly, Aaliyah nodded. "Almost," she said rather quietly.

"What about the others?" I wondered.

"Well, the next step below Golden fairies is the Element fairies."

"Yeah, Cass told me a little about them my first night here."

"Oh, did he really?" she asked, raising a pale eyebrow.

"Yeah, how they each have their own element," I remarked.

"Yes. They have water, earth, air, or fire, and they are truly exotic beings. Their looks correspond with their element. For example, a fire fairy usually has red or dark hair. Element fairies use their specific element as their power, and they have it all their lives like the Golden fairies do. Actually, fairies always have their powers. It's only elves who must wait until sixteen," she explained.

Aaliyah paused to open the picnic basket and examine its contents, as if contemplating what to remove first. I fidgeted as she did so, eager to learn more, to know more about the wonders of magic, of this place.

"I want to know more," I blurted. I knew I probably looked like a kid in a candy store, eyes sparkling with excitement and urgency in my tone. Every piece of information Aaliyah gave me was like another door opened. The more I learned about magic, the greater attraction I felt toward it, realizing it truly was a part of me.

Aaliyah smiled and shut the picnic basket. "Then the food can wait," she decided. "Let's see…after the Element fairies come the Woodland fairies. They are the common folk of fairies. They look a lot like we do, except they have translucent silver wings on their backs. They don't have abilities like we do, but they have different magic that is born within them. This magic includes abilities like Golden fairies: to use spells, potions, charms, and other oddities that deal with magic. However, they are not nearly as powerful as Golden fairies are. Woodland fairies love the forests and do not meddle in any affairs unless they involve dancing, drinking, and merrymaking."

"It sounds like they love to party."

Aaliyah stifled a giggle. "Yes, they do," she agreed.

"Go on," I urged.

"Just below the Woodland fairies are the Flower fairies, or as they are also called, Butterfly fairies. They are pretty and dainty little creatures that wear clothes made of flowers and are often confused with pixies. Flower fairies, however, are much smaller than pixies. Their wings are like a butterfly's, colorful and delicate. Flower fairies embody a type of flower. Depending on the flower, the fairy will receive a certain type of magic, a power. They like the presence of animals and keep to themselves. I have never had a chance to learn much more about them for that reason."

"I think I like the Flower fairies best. They seem less likely to start a war because they keep to themselves," I remarked.

"Yes, they are a nice folk. The Woodland fairies are as well, for the most part. The only disturbing thing about them is that they are unaffected by sadness or despair," Aaliyah said, as she opened the basket.

"What do you mean?" I asked.

"Most of the fae don't feel sadness. They do not look upon death the same way we do. They celebrate life and do not understand feelings of pity or remorse. They have no guilt, and only know happiness and fun. This is how every Woodland fairy that has lived in their Realm feels."

"Wait, would they feel that way if they lived in our Realm?"

"No, once they have left their Magical Realm, they change. You see, their Realm is like a cloak. It covers up feelings of sorrow. However, once they have crossed into the Elf Realm, the cloak is gone and those covered feelings are revealed. In our Realm, they can feel sadness. That is why elves always went to the Fairy Realms before the war and not the other way around. Who would want to feel sad while visiting a Realm? The fairies surely would not. The reason our Realm is uncovered is because elves believe all feelings are a part of life."

"That all makes sense, but the fae sound so cruel. So different from what I used to believe…."

"They are not really cruel, Ramsey. They just do not see things the same way we do. Their magic separates them from other beings, like elves and humans."

"I guess it could be a good thing, not feeling sadness, but I couldn't imagine not caring if you, Stellan, or Addison were to die. That's just terrible," I said.

"Yes, it is, but the fairies cannot experience this in their Realms, especially the Woodland fairies."

"How do the other fae feel?"

"They do not feel much sadness, but they can feel some. For instance, when King Oberon, Queen Titania's husband, died, every Golden fairy cried for days on end."

"What about the Flower fairies and Element fairies?"

"The Flower fairies are too filled with innocence to feel such a way. They are like children. As for the Element fairies, I believe they once felt sad feelings, but have hardened since the war began," she explained.

"How can the Element fairies get away with war? Why doesn't Queen Titania stop them? Is she really that concerned for her own fairies?"

"Actually, she is. The Element fairies are very powerful. They are only one step down in power from Golden fairies. Titania doesn't want to fight with them, so she stays out of it. She believes it's better to let the Element fairies deal with their problems than get every Realm involved. The fae have always tried to get along with each other. Titania doesn't want a conflict. If she were to get involved, there would be differences in opinion among the fae, leading to great turmoil. She truly just keeps the best interests of her folk in mind. Her subjects mean everything to her."

"I think I can understand that," I decided aloud. I sighed. "I'm sorry to be bothering you with all of these questions, Aaliyah."

"It's quite all right, Ramsey. I'm happy to tell you about the other Realms. It's high time you knew about them anyway. This is just as much a part of your culture and history as mine."

While Aaliyah went back to digging through the picnic basket, I took a moment to absorb everything she told me. It was amazing how much I still needed to learn. Playing with the loose threads on the blanket, I realized it would probably take more than Aaliyah's wisdom for me to become accustomed to the reality of magic. *That will come with time*, I decided. *Right now, the most important thing for me to do is to find my sister.*

"Thank you so much for explaining these things to me," I said to her gratefully.

"Well, that was just a brief history. As you grow older, you will learn more. I have just told you the basics, which is good enough for now."

"Should we eat then?" I suggested.

"Oh, yes!" Aaliyah agreed, while removing the various foods she had packed from the basket.

I looked at the food warily. Aaliyah brought several kinds of meats, some of which I didn't recognize. My stomach churned.

"Stellan told me how uneasy you were about the meat here. I wanted to bring you some different kinds to try. I promise you don't have to eat anything you find unappetizing, but I thought it might help you become accustomed to our eating habits."

"What kinds are there?" I asked, as my voice slightly rose higher in pitch.

"I brought chicken, pheasant, venison, and lamb."

"No rabbit?"

"No," she assured me, shaking her head.

I breathed a sigh of relief. "I'm sorry. I know you eat it here, but I could never imagine eating a bunny."

"It's okay, you don't have to apologize. We don't eat rabbit very often. Elves that hunt usually eat a wider variety of game. But I do not, and neither does Stellan or Addison."

"Then I will try all four. They sound normal enough. I have already had two of the four anyway."

The meat tasted great – it didn't make me queasy or anything. I used the bread and meat together as a sandwich and everything tasted fine. For dessert, Aaliyah had baked a cake filled with the taste of honey, and we each had a piece. I learned later that it was a fairy recipe, one that Aaliyah was given by Woodland fairies before the war began.

"What was Zora like?" I asked, as we finished our meal. "I mean, elves have told me she was caring and friendly, but what else?"

"Would you like to see?" she asked me.

"What do you mean?" I was confused. How could I see Zora if the Element fairies had her?

"I see Addison hasn't told you about my ability. I can show others my past memories. I could show you one of Zora."

"Really, you would do that?"

"Of course I would," she said. "Here, give me your hands."

I nodded and slowly put both of my hands into hers.

"Now close your eyes and repeat Zora's name over and over in your mind."

"All right," I said.

I focused my thoughts on Zora and waited.

Suddenly a million colors flashed in front of my closed eyes. They swirled and danced before me. Then they started forming into images.

I saw a pale-haired elfen kneeling beside a trough of flowers with her back to me. I recognized the house as Aaliyah's and, at first, I thought the elfen was Addison. Then she turned around.

She was definitely not Addison.

She had the same hair, but her eyes were a glowing emerald, like mine...but they weren't my eyes. They were Zora's.

"Zora," I whispered in awe. I couldn't believe I was actually seeing my sister for the first time.

"Yes," Aaliyah confirmed for me.

She was glowing, with a dazzling white smile. She looked like an angel, someone warm and inviting.

"Aaliyah, Addison plants such lovely flowers. I wish I had her skill," Zora said. Her silky voice was like a bird singing. "It seems whenever I plant my own something always goes askew."

"She does keep up a great flower garden," Aaliyah replied, laying a hand atop my sister's shoulder.

She sighed happily. "We are so lucky to have such a great gardener." Zora laughed and then got up, brushing the dirt off her clothing.

"Yes, and soon you will have to start paying me for the great job I do!" Addison said as she joined the two.

"I'd rather not," Zora disagreed, and gave Addison a playful shove.

"Come on, you two, it's time for school. If you don't leave now you will surely be late."

"You're right," Zora realized, nodding swiftly. "Come on, Addison, let's get a move on!"

Zora took Addison's hand and ran with her away from the house and away from my mind....

Everything was dark again as the memories left me. I felt tears in my eyes. I didn't want the pictures to leave. It would be wonderful to linger in those memories, even to live in them; to have Zora truly there, just sitting by the flowers, not held prisoner somewhere. Life would be a lot simpler that way.

"Thank you," I said, letting out a breath I hadn't realized I was holding.

"You're welcome, Ramsey."

We didn't speak much after that. I *couldn't* speak much after that. I was too wrapped up in Aaliyah's memory of my sister. The sole memory I now had of her.

***

After our meal, we went off into the orchard to pick fruit. Aaliyah used her basket, and I used my shoulder bag. She told me to help myself and take as much as I could carry home. As we passed one of her many pear trees, I saw Aaliyah frown. Wondering what could be wrong, I watched as she bent down to inspect a pile of what I assumed were rotten pears collected at the base of the tree. Picking up one by the stem, she shook her head disappointedly. "Nasty little hobgoblins," she muttered. "Sometimes I wonder if the war has changed anything at all. We still have certain types of fae running amuck, causing trouble in our Realm."

"Why do they come here?" I asked, remembering that hobgoblins were nothing like fairies, but were still considered fae folk.

Aaliyah sighed. "Well, like I said before, fae that do not belong to the four major groupings fit where they like. Most see the Fairy Realms as their boundaries, and a large percentage never even left the Human Realm when the Magical Realms were created, but others…"

"Not so much?" I presumed.

She nodded, dropping the rotten pear and wiping her hands on her skirt. "Exactly."

"Now, you said the fae fit in wherever they please among the four *Fairy* Realms. What about in our Realm? Are there other magical creatures here besides the elves? And I'm not counting the troublesome fae." I thought about it for a moment. "Like dragons, for instance?"

"Yes, there are dragons. However, they are usually found only at the capital, Tarlore, where Queen Taryn can protect them. Dragons, like us, are very scarce these days. In the Human Realm, they were hunted and killed. Only a few hundred managed to escape with our help. For that reason, dragons live here in our Realm. You can find dragons in the Fairy Realms occasionally, but most choose to stay with us."

I didn't ask any more questions. I decided I'd had my fill for the day, and even though Aaliyah said she didn't mind, I didn't want to bother her *too* much. After a while, we separated. She needed to find the elves she hired to manage the orchard and pay them for the month, which left me to explore on my own.

I had meant what I said earlier. The orchard *was* like a fairyland. The sun shone through the trees and made small patches of sparkling light on the grass. The leaves were healthy and green and swayed lightly in the afternoon breeze. I picked fruit after fruit until my shoulder bag was too heavy. I felt like my arms would fall off from the weight. Occasionally, as I explored, I sat beneath a tree and admired the beauty of the orchard, resting my shoulders.

I soon realized it wasn't as bright out as before, and my internal clock told me it was getting late into the afternoon. I decided to go and find Aaliyah. I didn't want to be here alone after dark.

Finding my way back proved to be difficult. Everything in the orchard looked the same. After taking a wrong turn countless times, I sat down to rest. I needed a breather before trying again. Just as I found a comfortable spot beneath a Macintosh apple tree, I felt something hard hit my head. The object made a *clunk* that sent waves of pain through my body. My hand flew up to feel a small bump forming on the back of my skull.

"What in the...?" I trailed off. I got up to look around.

Could an apple have fallen from the tree? Was it just a coincidence that the apple fell on my head just when I sat down? I didn't think so.

I got my answer when I spotted a small man, only about two feet tall, sitting in the tree, his tiny legs swinging in the air.

"Did you just throw an apple at me?" I asked.

"Of course not! Why would I do that?" the little man cried.

"I'm pretty sure you're not telling me the truth."

"Alrighty then, ya caught me," he said, jumping down from the apple tree. "I just wanted to get your attention."

"A simple hello would have sufficed," I told him.

"It wouldn't have been as much fun, though!" he replied, smirking at me.

I looked down at him and shook my head. I had never seen such a small person before. Then the realization struck me. He must be a gnome.

It was plain to see, with his short body, long white beard, and funny, cone-shaped hat. Almost like a dwarf, but not as hefty. He wore a red shirt and jean overalls. Small brown leather boots covered his feet, and he held a wooden staff in one hand. He was just like out of a storybook.

"You're just like the stories," I whispered aloud, not really meaning to.

"What? What did you just say to me? *I'm from a story?*"

"I'm sorry, I didn't mean to be rude. I'm just surprised that the Human Realm could describe you so well in their books," I explained.

"Yeah, well, I was once part of that Realm myself," he told me, pulling at his overall straps.

"You were?"

"Aye. About two hundred years ago, I lived there among the human folk. We gnomes used to be plentiful there until we found the other Realms. We don't go back to the Human Realm much nowadays. The people there aren't always that friendly to our kind."

"I can understand that," I told him.

"You can? How so?" he wondered.

"I grew up in the Human Realm. I just came back home a few days ago. It was hard to live there. Different isn't always accepted."

"You must be Ramsey!" he realized.

"Yeah, how did you know?" I asked.

"Word travels fast underground among the gnomes and the dwarves. We are always 'in the know.' You may not see us, but we know about you."

"That's a little unsettling," I told him.

He shrugged and then shook his head. "I'm sorry, I haven't even introduced myself. How rude of me. The name's Mac."

"Well, it's nice to meet you, Mac. Do you live in the orchard?" I asked.

"Live? Ramsey, I don't live anywhere," Mac explained, pulling at the straps on his overalls. "Like them other gnomes and dwarves, I'm a nomad, so everywhere is my home. I've just come here from the Element Fairy Realm. 'Tis a strange place, that Realm. Lots of fightin' and crazy things. I was sick of runnin' around, so I came here for some peace."

"The war's pretty big, isn't it?"

"Big? Elfen, you ain't never seen a bigger war than this one. I don't understand why your kind and the Element fairies just can't get along," he said with a sigh.

"Don't ask me; I don't even know how it started," I admitted to him.

"You don't? Well then, I had better tell you about it, you being an elfen and all. You should know what kinds of things your folk are involved in."

I remembered Addison saying that Queen Taryn should explain the war, but if I didn't take my chance now, I may not know for some time. I was very curious, and my impatience got the better of me.

"Go ahead, please," I urged. I hoped I wouldn't regret my decision later.

"Alrighty then." He leaned back against the apple tree, readying himself to tell the tale.

"It all started about thirty years ago," he began. "All the creatures could go to and from each Magical Realm as they pleased, no trouble at all. One day everything went and changed. An elfen, a fairy, and a fairy child caused the whole war. That's all! You see, there was this Woodland fairy babe, just born 'bout a year or so before the war started up. The mother of the babe had died durin' the childbirth and the babe was left alone with its daddy. Unfortunately, the daddy didn't know how to raise a child and didn't know what to do. The father knew an elfen girl who was a friend of the mother and asked for some help around the house. She gladly accepted and left the Elf Realm to start caring for the fairy child as if it was her own. She even named the child, for the father was still grieving for his deceased love. She named her Elvina, which translates into 'friend of elves.' Funny, eh?" he asked, but didn't wait for me to respond before continuing.

"She cared for Elvina for a whole year, and they formed an unbreakable bond until one sad day. The daddy didn't want the elfen to stay anymore. He had found a new mate to take care of Elvina. He told her to say her goodbyes and return to her own Realm."

"That's terrible," I muttered, and then urged him to continue. I had to stop interrupting people. Unfortunately, it had always been a bad habit of mine.

Mac gave me a look and then nodded. "So after a tearful goodbye, the elfen left. However, she couldn't go far without feeling the pain of her loss. She felt robbed of someone she loved dearly. She had become like a mother to the child when the father wouldn't be a father. She decided to do something…well, something quite drastic."

"What?" I asked.

"She stole Elvina that very night and took her back to her Realm. Her ability was to make protective shields around herself and others. She shielded them both and ran to the safety of the King."

"Did the King help her?" I asked, astonished.

"He was her father!"

My jaw dropped.

"Yes, and that means the Princess of the Elf Realm stole a fairy child, and the King stood by her. What else could he do but stand by his daughter's side? He kept the child hidden for a while, but it was no use. The Element fairies soon found out about it and declared war over their stolen child," he told me in a serious tone.

"But I thought Elvina was a Woodland fairy?"

"Yes, her mother was and she had passed on the gene to Elvina, but the father was a fire fairy and lived in the Element Fairy Realm. His gene wasn't passed on to her, but she was still considered part of their Realm after the mother died. Anyway, the King accepted the declaration and the war started and hasn't ended since. All because of one little babe."

"Sounds like a dumb reason to go off killing each other," I said, disturbed by what I had just learned. "Why doesn't Queen Taryn end it?" I asked.

"She won't because those two are sisters. When their father died, Queen Taryn promised to take care of her sister and continue with the war. She would never go and break that promise. And she loves Lady Cora – which is the name of her sister – too much to even consider betraying her."

"What about Elvina?" I asked.

"She lives there with them."

"Why doesn't she leave and go back to her father?"

"She loves Lady Cora far too much to leave her. The Elf Realm is her home now."

"Do the Woodland fairies have a problem with Elvina being taken?" I wondered.

"Nope, no problem at all. They think war is wrong. They would never take it that far. They forgot the whole thing almost as soon as it happened. However, the Element fairies have always been very prideful. They won't give up on something so easily. That is what war is, Ramsey. It's all about the pride," Mac explained.

I thought about what he said and decided Mac was right. War was just pride covered with a huge mass of fighting and death. Even in a beautiful place such as this, I realized there was just as much terror, fear, and hate as the Human Realm.

Why had I thought it would be any different?

~9~

Diamonds

"So what is your part in all of this?" I asked Mac after he finished telling his tale.

He raised a bushy eyebrow. "What is my *part*?"

"Whose side are you on?" I wondered.

"I'm not on anyone's side! We gnomes and dwarves are neutral in this sort of thing. We have our own lives underground. Think of us like that country in the Human Realm…um, oh yeah, Switzerland! Yes, we are like Switzerland."

"That sounds like the best side," I said, suppressing a sigh, "and the easiest."

"You better not go around sayin' that to your kind, Ramsey. You could get in some mighty big trouble," Mac advised.

"I guess I could. I keep forgetting I'm actually an elfen."

"Hey, before I finally left the Human Realm I thought I was a human kid with a beard," he said with a hearty chuckle. "You will get to know who you really are. Trust me, I did."

"Thanks, Mac. You've sure cleared a lot of things up for me," I told him.

"Don't mention it. We small folk like to help others who need it. I'm just doin' what I do best."

"So where are you headed now?" I asked.

"I thought I'd spend some time here and then go over to the Flower Fairy Realm. It's all peace and quiet there, no war. And it's easier being around other small folk."

I nodded. "Well, I have to get back to my friend, but I hope I see you again some time," I said, sad to be leaving my new friend.

"You will, young elfen. I travel around a lot, and maybe I'll take a peek around your city sometime soon," he assured me.

"If you ever do come to Birchwood, look me up," I told him. I had always wanted to use the "look me up" line from the movies. It was a geeky thing to say, but I trusted he didn't know much about human movies, so I was probably safe.

"Will do," he replied.

"Hey, do you by any chance know the way to the center of the orchard? That's where I'm meeting my friend. I'm completely lost," I admitted.

"Sure I do. Just go straight ahead. You'll find her easily that way. Just don't change direction!" he instructed.

"Thanks, Mac."

"Bye for now, Ramsey!" he said, and then the little gnome turned around and climbed back into the tree.

"Bye!" I called.

I heard Mac start to hum a little tune as I walked away. I was very glad that I had met him. Now I finally understood more about the war. I hoped Addison wouldn't be too upset.

Thinking about the war made another question pop in my mind. What did the war have to do with me? In her journal, Zora said that the Element fairies knew about my secret but didn't know exactly what it was. What kind of secret could I have that would make the Element fairies kidnap my sister, especially when the war was nothing but extreme overreaction and misplaced pride?

I succumbed to worrying once more. My meeting with Mac had preoccupied me for only a short time. What else could ease this? *Nothing*, I decided. Until I found Zora and figured out this "secret," my mind would not rest. I would have to put up with it.

I was lost in my thoughts as I walked back to where Aaliyah was waiting for me. I knew I wasn't paying attention to my surroundings, which was never a good idea. But I couldn't keep a clear head. As I headed to the center of the orchard, my mind a jumbled mess, I heard a weird fluttering noise every couple of seconds. I shrugged it off at first as nothing more than a harmless bird, returning to my thoughts, and then the noise became clearer and closer to me. I clenched my fists and quickened my pace from a walk to a slow jog. I didn't understand why I was so frightened, but something about the sound made me shiver with fear.

Something red passed near me. I whipped my head around to…nothing. I wearily surveyed the area. When I found nothing out of the ordinary, I continued walking back to Aaliyah. Was I just being paranoid?

I noticed another flash of movement. I turned and looked around again. This time, I didn't like what I saw.

It was barely recognizable behind a pear tree, but I knew what I was looking at. I could see the tips of the shining red wings. I was looking at a fairy. I wasn't too keen on fairies myself, but I guessed this fairy was an Element fairy by the color of its wings. The element was most likely fire.

I didn't stay long enough to observe the fairy any more. I fought the urge to scream, turned back around, and ran. I didn't know where I was running; I had lost my sense of direction after spotting the fairy. All I knew was that I had to get away from there, and fast.

***

It was a little after five when I got back to the clearing. Aaliyah was patiently waiting for me with her basket full of fruit. I smiled and waved as I approached, still unsettled but feeling safer now that I wasn't alone. However, I knew that it wasn't safe for us to remain in the orchard.

"Aaliyah, I think I saw a fairy on the way back to the clearing," I blurted when I reached her, knowing I couldn't keep the sighting a secret.

"What?" she cried.

"I saw the tips of red wings, heard fluttering, and then I ran to you."

Aaliyah's eyes shone with fright. "This is dangerous, Ramsey. We should leave now. Come on." She took my hand and pulled me through the orchard.

"What if it sees us leaving?"

"We will go around the outside instead of straight through the orchard," she explained to me in a hushed voice. "We have to leave somehow. Just standing around is not a good idea."

I nodded silently and followed her quickly out of the orchard. All the while, I was afraid the fire fairy would jump out to attack us. I couldn't believe a being similar to one that took my sister was so close to my home. It unnerved me deeply.

When Aaliyah thought we were far enough away, she relaxed and slowed down to a walk. I sighed in relief and followed suit.

But even though the sun was shining and the birds chirping, I couldn't pay attention to the beauty. I was still wary of the Element fairy.

Aaliyah, on the other hand, appeared to be worn out, probably from walking around the whole orchard. Her eyes looked tired and it seemed as if her arms were struggling to hold up the basket. Not feeling as tired, I took it from her to carry. She mouthed a *thank you* and smiled.

"So I met a gnome, Mac, who told me about the war," I said, trying to get our minds off the Element fairy in the orchard.

"Everything about the war?" she asked.

"Yes. *Everything*," I replied.

"Addison won't be happy about that," she warned me.

"Why is it so bad that I know?" I asked.

"She wanted an elf, particularly Queen Taryn, to explain things. You are new to this, Ramsey. We don't want you thinking that all elves are awful because of Queen Taryn's sister."

"Look, it's okay. Everyone does things they aren't proud of, and everyone makes mistakes. I'm not going to be scared away that easily."

Aaliyah took my hand and smiled. "Good."

I nodded, but I wasn't feeling so good. Sure, we had escaped, but seeing the Element fairy had suddenly made my dangerous situation very real to me. Now that I had seen one, I knew it was inevitable that I would meet more in the future, especially if I was to rescue my sister. I didn't know how I would handle my fear, or if I would be strong enough to face such dangerous foes as the fae.

"I can tell you're stressed, Ramsey. I can't imagine what this must be like for you," Aaliyah mentioned as we walked together into Birchwood City.

"I have no idea what to do, Aaliyah," I admitted.

"You will. Believe in yourself and believe in Zora. If she said you could help her, then you can. I've said that before, and I'll say it again. I see Zora in you, Ramsey. I see her gentle nature, her free spirit, and her courage. I will always be there to help you, and don't forget that Addison and Stellan will be as well. Zora was like a daughter to me, and I feel as if you are one, too."

Her kind, sincere words brought tears to my eyes. "Thank you, Aaliyah, for saying that. You have helped me so much today, with everything. I am so grateful."

"I mean it," she said, smiling warmly. "Thankfully, we avoided the fairy. I will have to speak with Stellan and Addison about it, though. It isn't safe with Element fairies anywhere in the Realm, in Birchwood especially, because you are here. You need protection so you can find your sister and avoid being taken instead. Don't worry, I will take care of everything. I advise that you just go home and rest for a while. It will help you to clear your mind and rejuvenate."

"I will. Thank you so much, Aaliyah."

"You're welcome."

I was relieved and thankful. It didn't matter now if Addison had only brought me back for Zora, because Aaliyah was here for me. I knew she cared for me, and not just because of Zora. As I walked home, I knew talking with Aaliyah had been the right thing to do. I felt surer now of which direction to take. She had reassured me of my place here. My mind was at peace. Sure, there were many problems with my life now, but I knew I could overcome them. I just needed to figure out how. I laughed. *If only it was that easy to accomplish,* I thought to myself.

When I finally walked through the door, it was near six, and I still had time before I had to be at Addison's house. I walked into my room and sat down on my bed. Aaliyah told me to rest, but I felt as if I should be doing something.

After a few minutes of running ideas through my head, I went to the wardrobe and took out the bag I had brought from the Human Realm. For the first time since coming to the Elf Realm, I reached inside and grabbed my copy of *The Mysterious Guide to Fantasy.* I wanted to see if the guide held anything on Element fairies.

Unfortunately, the only section on fairies was very general. The descriptions reminded me of what Aaliyah told me of Flower fairies. Butterfly wings and flower petals weren't going to enlighten me on the habits of my new enemies.

I shut the book, dismayed at the lack of information on Element fairies, and tucked it under my bed. Then I realized how tired I was, and finally decided to take Aaliyah's advice and nap to pass the remaining time. What else was there to do?

I lay down on my bed and closed my eyes. I didn't bother changing into a nightgown. I would be sleeping only for a little while. I hoped I would wake up in time for dinner, because there weren't any alarm clocks here. I had closed my eyes for only a few seconds before I was dreaming.

Even though everything was dark, I knew I was dreaming because I could no longer feel the comfort of my bed, and I certainly didn't smell my flowery and herbal scented room anymore. Instead, the smell was musty, and reminded me strangely of hay. There was even a faint scent of blood in the air. I was standing, instead of lying down. Was I having some kind of nightmare?

I braced myself for some man-eating monster or a blood-crazy vampire, but everything was silent. Then, like a lit match to my skin, the Mood Diamond resting on my chest started to burn. I could see it glowing at my neck. The fire was almost too much to bear. I could barely keep from screaming. Soon, my whole body felt insanely hot; images of flames flashed behind my closed eyes, shut tight to fight off the pain. My fists clenched to stop the spasms pulsing through me. What was happening? How could a dream be so painful? How could a dream be so real*?*

Finally, the pain began to ebb away, and I was able to open my eyes. I gasped, finding myself standing before my sister.

She was lying against a wooden wall, her eyes closed and her mouth slightly open. Her hands clutched the Mood Diamond tightly against her chest. The horror finally reached me as I took time to look at her closely. She was nothing like the beautiful memory

Aaliyah had shared with me earlier that day. This view was the complete opposite. It was more terrible than anything I could have imagined.

Until I saw Zora, I hadn't believed anyone could be any paler than I – or any other elf for that matter – could ever be. She appeared stark white, dead white. I sighed in relief when I noticed the slight rise and fall of her chest that told me she was still alive – although just barely. Dressed in brown cloth rags that hung limply on her thin frame, I had never seen anyone look so...well, anorexic was the best way to describe it. But this seemed even worse.

Zora had patches of dirt and grime from the tips of her shoulders to the ends of her toes. The patches looked like soot from a fireplace or some kind of burn. Several cuts that reminded me of lashes from a whip were still bleeding on her hands and wrists. Her pale hair was ragged and dirty. I realized with horror that she had severe burn marks on her neck, face, and upper arms. She was also sweating with fever.

I reached out to touch my sister. I hoped that if I touched her, I would wake up, like splashing a hand onto a reflection in a pool, and the terrible image of Zora would disappear. Maybe this would all go away, just a nightmare. Unfortunately, touching her didn't wake me up. My hand rested on hers, and she opened her eyes slowly and stared into mine. The emerald irises were empty of their glow, replaced by fear, grief, and pain.

"Zora," I choked. "Zora...what happened to you?" I was barely able to ask. The sight was just so horrible....

Tears fell silently from my eyes and ran down my cheeks. I wiped them away with my free hand, trying to appear stronger and more in control than I felt.

"I'm so sorry, Ramsey. I'm sorry," she kept repeating, over and over again, her own tears leaving lines of pale skin where they washed away the grime.

Tears clouded my vision again. I blinked them back and shook my head. "You have nothing to be sorry for," I assured her.

"Yes, I do. I should have found you sooner. I should have told someone...," Zora trailed off.

"All of that is in the past now. It doesn't matter. What matters is getting you away from here. Come on." I grabbed her hand as gently as I could and started to pull, but she wasn't trying to get up.

"I can't leave, Ramsey. This is only a spiritual connection, a vision...a glimpse. You aren't here with me, and I'm not there with you. You are still in your room. I connected with you using the diamond. It took a while...but it finally worked."

"Then what can we do?" I asked her.

"Find me, Ramsey. Look around and remember this place. Then come for me. You must hurry. I don't have much time left before they finish me. The Element fairies want to learn your secret, but I won't tell them. I promise, Ramsey," she said, her eyes fierce and determined, appearing more alive than before. "I will die before I tell them anything about you. But as soon as they realize that, they will kill me."

"That won't happen. I will *come for you," I promised her. Then I had an idea. "What is the secret, Zora? Please tell me now. Maybe it can help save you."*

Before she could respond, I heard the clanging of a door opening. I tried to find a place to hide, but tripped in the darkness. Trying to steady myself, I allowed one of my hands to fall on top of Zora's Mood Diamond. Suddenly, the scene changed. I was still in the room, but now I was sitting against the wooden wall. Pain came at me in great waves. I looked down and gasped in shock at my hands, covered in slashes and my knuckles raw, blood oozing slowly. The smell made me queasy. I could tell right away that they were not really my hands. They were Zora's hands. The Mood Diamond had connected us further. I was seeing through Zora and feeling what Zora felt. I struggled to stay conscious. The pain was making me dizzy and weak.

A dark figure fluttered through the door. His red wings glistened like the blood from Zora's hands. His thick dark hair flowed from the wind his wings created as he flew over to us. I knew right away he was an Element Fairy, and his element was fire. Was he the fairy I had seen in the orchard? I wasn't sure.

The fairy was dressed in a red peasant shirt and ragged, cut-off red shorts. His feet were bare, his arms toned, and I could see his muscles tense as he saw the horrible state of my sister. He was terribly beautiful, both attractive and menacing. He reached a hand down and caressed my – I mean, Zora's – cheek. I could feel Zora's body stiffen. Just the nearness of him made me feel cold. Although his looks were striking, I could detect the cloud of darkness that surrounded him, a warning not to be deceived by his beauty.

"You poor thing, I didn't know my friends and I had harmed you so badly. I am sorry about this, really sorry," he said darkly.

"I find it hard to believe you are sorry," we seemed to say together.

It was weird because even though I wasn't thinking of the response, I still knew what to say. Everything Zora thought and said, I did as well because of how close we were connected. Unfortunately, every word brought on more pain and burning.

"Zora, you know what we want. All of this can end if you just tell me about your sister. We know she is valuable."

"How could you possibly know anything about my sister?" Zora challenged.

"Ah, Zora, you are so naïve," the fire fairy said with a hearty chuckle. "You have no idea what happened to them, do you? You have no clue as to what happened to your parents."

Chills ran through us. Fear settled into the pit of Zora's stomach. I could feel her unease and worry. She and I both were expecting the worst.

"You see, Zora dear, when your parents abandoned you it wasn't long before they were caught...by my soldiers." He strode forward and knelt down in front of us. Cupping Zora's chin in his hand, he grinned maliciously. "You want to know how I know about your sister? Why she is so valuable to us?" He paused, obviously for effect. I waited with grim anticipation. "Well, your father told me so...before he died."

"No," she whimpered, shaking her head. But she knew, just as I did, that the fire fairy wasn't lying. Hearing the news saddened me, but I couldn't feel heartbroken. I hadn't truly lost my father, only

the hope that we would someday meet again. Zora's despair went deeper. She had really known him. I hadn't. I didn't remember our father the way she did, and I was too busy concentrating on the immense pain I was feeling to feel much else.

Zora started shaking, but her sobs were barely audible because of the pain her movement was sending to the both of us. The agony clouded my entire mind, engulfing me. When it was finally too much to bear, Zora fell silent, unmoving. Anymore stress on our bodies, on our hearts, and we would surely break. She had to stop grieving, because if she didn't, we would die.

"Finn...you monster...," we said, hardly able to speak through the burning.

I now knew the fairy's name. Even though it was hard to do because of the strong connection with Zora's mind, I said it repeatedly so I would remember it in my own mind for the future. Finn shook his head silently. "I'm no monster, Zora. I only did what was necessary."

"I...will...never...tell...," we told him, determination in our joined voices.

"I don't believe you, Zora. Your father told me even though he said he wouldn't. Of course, it wasn't enough information, because if it was, I wouldn't have needed you. He only told me that Ramsey had a secret, a very powerful one at that, concerning both fairies and elves. You need to tell me what that secret is. I know he told you. I could see it in his eyes that he knew, and I can see it in yours that you know as well."

"NEVER!" we screamed.

We had made a huge mistake. I didn't think the pain could get any worse, but now it was an icy kind of fire, freezing our limbs as it washed through our very veins. It would have been easy to succumb to the darkness, let go of what tied me to life. I couldn't give up, though, because so many depended on me, especially Zora. But it was tremendously difficult to stay conscious. I had never felt such torture. I was running out of words to describe how miserable these feelings were. I imagined they were even worse for Zora, because she was actually experiencing the pain, not just feeling it like I was.

Finn chuckled. "I can see that your life is dwindling. You will tell me soon, Zora. When you do, your life will end quickly and there will be no more suffering. I know you don't want to bear this for the few days you have left. Let me know when you have had enough. Wynter is just outside as always. Just speak her name and she will call for me," Finn said.

He turned and flew out of the room. Without the fiery light from his wings, the room returned to partial darkness.

After that, everything was thrown into chaos. Suddenly released from part of the connection with Zora, I fell over onto the wooden floor. I wrapped my arms around my body, trying to pull myself together. I was afraid of falling apart if I let go. My breath came out in sharp gasps. I could barely breathe. I looked over at Zora. Her eyes were closed tightly, and she was slowly rocking back and forth, as if she was trying to fight the pain. I knew just by looking at her that it wouldn't work. Her condition had worsened. She was broken. Only I could put her back together again, by finding and saving her.

If I didn't accomplish this soon, she would die this way.

"Find me, Ramsey," she said, almost too quiet for me to understand.

"I will, Zora. I promise that I will save you…no matter what it takes," I told her.

The room began to spin, and the Mood Diamond glowed brighter than before. I shook my head to keep away the dizziness, but nothing changed. The room just spun faster and faster.

"Zora, what's happening?" I cried.

"Don't look for me in the...Realm!" she screamed with every ounce of energy she had left as the room continued to spin around before my eyes.

"Which Realm?" I asked her.

"The…"

Before she could say any more, everything was total darkness once again….

Screams echoed from my lungs as I sat up in bed. My hands flew over my heart and pressed against it tightly. I felt like it was going to burst out of my chest. The burning subsided, but in its place was a terrible aching, the aching of loss. I had finally experienced what everyone else had when the fairies took Zora. I now knew what it was like to lose her. I hated the feeling. It hurt even worse than the burning fire and Zora's pain put together, because this pain wasn't physical. It was emotional. And it wouldn't end. Nothing could make it go away, nothing, except to have Zora at my side.

The connection was the worst thing I had ever experienced. I was afraid. I couldn't believe it had been so *real*. I was terrified; I never wanted to feel that way again. The pain, the burning, the way Finn's eyes glinted in the darkness of the room…all were images I couldn't erase from my mind no matter how hard I tried. I couldn't stop feeling this way. I felt as though fear was now a part of me, and that scared me more than anything else did. *Fear of fear….*

The burning was still there, only it had now concentrated around my neck area where the Mood Diamond still lay glowing. I wanted to rip it off, but I couldn't remove my hands from my heart. I was too afraid of the risk, afraid of the pain that could ensue.

I hadn't realized I was still screaming until Stellan – Addison and Aaliyah following closely behind – ran into my room. The screaming turned into sobs as Stellan sat on the bed and cradled me. He wrapped his arms around me, trying to stop me from shaking. I wanted to stop. I was begging God to let me stop. I couldn't. The shaking continued and the sobbing continued as Stellan rocked me back and forth. Seconds, then minutes passed, and nothing changed.

"Oh my God, Stellan, look what that Mood Diamond did to her! What had Zora been thinking by giving her that necklace? It could have killed her!" Addison cried.

I could see through my tears that she was pacing back and forth in the room. Her clenched fists made her knuckles paler than the rest of her skin. It reminded me of Zora and my sobs grew louder.

"She won't stop, Mother. What can we do?" I heard Stellan ask.

I could hear the pain in his voice. *Seeing me like this must be killing him*, I thought, surprised that I could still think coherently. But I could do nothing to end this agonizing trance.

"I…I don't know," Aaliyah said.

"Give her a memory. Give her something that can make her feel better," Stellan suggested.

"I think that would make things worse," Aaliyah admitted.

"Just do something…anything! I can't take seeing her this way!" Addison screamed.

I could feel Aaliyah's hands slip into mine. I tried pulling away, because I didn't want my hands to leave my heart, but she only held me tighter.

"Think of the orchard, Ramsey. Think. Believe."

I couldn't do what she asked. My mind couldn't wrap itself around the word. Images of Finn and Zora assaulted my mind, creating a barrier to Aaliyah's ability. I cried out, louder, in frustration. *Please let me see the memory!*, I begged. Aaliyah started repeating the word "orchard." Soon she was almost as loud as my screaming. But the terrible images of blood and fire lingered, resonating within me. The sultry voice of the fire fairy, Finn, echoed in my mind. I shut my eyes tighter, but the pictures wouldn't go away. I prayed to see the orchard, but I just couldn't break through the barrier of horror that was blocking me from seeing beauty.

Then, finally, my prayers were answered.

A beautiful image...the orchard fairyland. Sunlight streamed through the trees, making the grass sparkle. Everything was peaceful and serene. The beauty soothed my pain. I saw the plump, ripe fruit, and patches of flowers here and there, and I felt that I could breathe again. Little animals ran around and burrowed deep into their holes. In the distance, I could hear Mac humming his cheerful tune...

I was myself again. I could control my thoughts. I could stop shaking. My sobs continued, but they became quieter and less frequent. I whimpered softly in Stellan's arms.

"There," Aaliyah said, releasing my hands from her tight grip.

I instinctively placed them around Stellan's neck and buried my face in his chest. I wanted to run away from the pain that was slowly departing from me. I wanted to hide from it so it couldn't come back.

A dull ache still flickered in my heart. I understood it wouldn't go away until I found Zora. It was crazy, but I decided I wanted this pain to stay for a while; having it would motivate me and make me stronger. I could bear this pain, because it would push me farther than before.

"Thank you, Mother. I don't know how much more I could have taken. Hearing her like that…it was awful," Addison said, shivering.

I watched, although my vision was blurred by tears, as Addison covered her face with her hands and fell back onto Zora's bed.

"Yes, it was, Addison. However, do not blame Zora. She did only what she had to do," Aaliyah explained quietly.

Stellan remained silent as he focused on soothing me, still rocking me like a small child. I was afraid to meet his eyes. I didn't like being so vulnerable, but his hand lifted from me as he stroked my sweat-streaked hair, and I let go of my pride, allowing his comfort to soothe and heal me. My eyes closed.

The last thing I heard before falling asleep was, "Everything is okay now."

No matter how much I wanted to believe Stellan, I knew he was terribly wrong.

~10~

It isn't Nice to Stare

Sunlight streamed through my window and brutally struck my eyes like a punch to my face. I winced at the brightness and covered my face with my blanket. Could it really be morning already? I focused on the time and realized it was almost five.

Yawning, I sat up in bed and stretched. I had to blink a few times to adjust to the bright light of morning. I was stiff and aching all over. At first, I couldn't remember why I ached so much. It took a moment for me to remember everything from last night. The realization hit me harder than the sunlight.

I shut my eyes tight. *No...the pain won't come back again,* I told myself. I wasn't so sure of that, though. I placed my right hand on my chest. Nothing there. The Mood Diamond was gone. I guessed Stellan or Addison took it when I fell asleep the night before. I would have to get it back. I still didn't know where Zora was, so I would have to try again, even though I dreaded what might happen. Nothing mattered except finding Zora. I had to go back and experience the vision again, no matter how painful.

At that moment, however, I was glad I wasn't wearing the necklace. The terrible vision could not return until it hung around my neck once more. I needed time before I tried again; time to recuperate, gather my thoughts, and collect myself.

I rubbed my eyes, sore from crying the night before, and got out of bed. I had to steady myself to keep from falling over as my feet hit the ground. I shook my head to clear away the dizziness. Last night's connection with Zora had taken a huge toll on both my body and my mind. I walked quickly to the bathroom and jumped in the shower. The steam I breathed in cleared my head, and the water massaged the tension in my back. If only I could stay in there forever....

It took a good twenty minutes to feel clean again. Even though it had only been a vision, the time with Zora in the dirty room had left me feeling disgusting and unclean. After wrapping myself in a towel and combing my hair, I left the bathroom to get dressed. As I walked into the bedroom, I came face to face with Addison.

Her sudden appearance made me jump. "Holy crap, you scared me!" I gasped, taking two steps back.

"Sorry, Ramsey, I didn't mean to frighten you," she said.

Her eyes looked full of worry and concern. She reminded me of my human mother for a brief moment. I had never experienced this side of Addison. I wondered if last night's occurrences had led to this, or if I just hadn't noticed the tenderness she had within her until now when I was really paying attention.

"Sorry, I'm easily spooked," I said. "What are you doing here?"

"I've been here all night," she said.

My brow furrowed in confusion. "What?"

"You must be really out of it. I stayed in Zora's bed last night. I couldn't let you sleep alone. Not after what happened…."

"You don't need to remind me," I told her, looking down at the wooden floor beneath my feet.

"I know," she replied, averting my gaze so we were both looking at the floor like it was the most interesting thing in the room.

I sighed and my shoulders slumped. "I'm sorry."

"About what?" she asked, looking up at me.

"Being like this. Being vulnerable and out of it."

"It's not your fault, Ramsey! What happened to you was *not your fault*."

"Stop saying that like it's true, Addison. Stop acting like none of this is my fault. I should have handled it better. I wasn't prepared. I had no idea…."

"No one can know what a connection is like until they have experienced it. *No one*," she emphasized.

"How could you possibly know that?" I asked her.

"I know…because it happened to me," she said quietly.

Startled, I took a step away from her. "With who?" I wondered aloud.

"My father. He and my mother each had a Mood Diamond once. When he left for war, they used it to keep in touch. Not all connections are bad, Ramsey, as long as you handle them carefully. These connections are used often for long distance relationships. However, they can turn horribly wrong in an instant. One day I took my mother's diamond and wore it. I missed my father, and wanted to see him again. I hated him being at war and not able to take care of me as he used to. I concentrated on him and a few minutes later, I was in a war zone. There was fighting all around me. Element fairies and elves in a swarm, swords clanking, blood everywhere. The stench of death hung in the air. I saw my father fighting with a water fairy. It was the first and last time I saw him kill someone."

Addison drew a shaky breath and leaned against the wall for support. I went to put a hand on her shoulder, but thought again and decided not to bother her. Telling this story was difficult for her, and interrupting her in the middle of her thoughts wouldn't help her finish sooner.

"When he saw me, he ran and scooped me up into his arms. I hugged him tight and told him I wanted to go home. I touched his Mood Diamond by accident. It was then that we truly connected. I found myself seeing through his eyes. I screamed and cried. I wanted so badly to be back at home. I was confused and scared. I was so upset I didn't see the earth fairy come and shove a rock-sharp spear into my father's chest."

Addison was weeping. Large teardrops fell from her eyes and hit the floor. For a moment, it made me feel uncomfortable to see her like that; she usually appeared to be so rock solid and invincible. Then my compassion kicked in when I realized no one could be stone all the time. Vulnerability was just a part of life.

"Addison, I had no idea," I said. I put my arms around her and then released, knowing now was the time to comfort her. "I'm so sorry."

She ignored me and continued. I knew she needed to finish before she could succumb to any kind of consoling. "Never before had I experienced that kind of pain. I don't think I'll ever experience it again. It wasn't just the pain of the sword, but also the pain of loss. We fell to the ground, bleeding to death. Except I wasn't really bleeding. When we parted, I crawled over to him, barely able to stay conscious, and I pressed my hands to his heart to stop the flow of blood. As his eyes closed, I found myself back in my room. To this day, I can still smell his blood on my hands. A ghostly reminder that will never cease to haunt me."

"You do understand," I realized.

Addison nodded slowly. "I really do."

"It's not your fault, Addison. You were young. You didn't know."

"It's not your fault either, Ramsey. You didn't know either. You've been here only two days. There was no way you could have known."

I nodded. She was right after all. Nothing but the experience could ever tell you what a connection might end up like.

"I'm going to get dressed. I'll meet you at your place for breakfast," I told her.

"Okay," she said.

Addison walked past me and left the house without another word.

Left standing speechless, I felt guilty and selfish. Here I was complaining about my vision, when Addison had witnessed her father's death as a young child. I felt terrible. All I wanted to do was curl up in bed, close my eyes, and hide away forever.

Instead, I dressed in tan shorts and a green blouse, put on a pair of brown sandals, grabbed my shoulder bag, and left the house.

Crying wouldn't save my sister.

***

The house was awkward and silent when I walked in. Addison sat at the table next to Cass, his hand on the small of her back as if to comfort her. His face was stone cold and very serious, more so than I had ever seen. His usual sarcastic smile was gone, replaced with a tight frown and eyes glinted with caution, as if he was preparing himself for anything bad that might happen. He was

Addison's protector, and for a moment, I wondered if he was protecting her from me. Dismissing the thought, I surveyed the rest of the room. Aaliyah sat at the head of the table. She looked like she hadn't gotten any sleep. Her head hung just above her cup of tea. They all appeared to be lifeless.

Stellan looked like he had been up all night as well. His eyes were slightly bloodshot and his hands shook. He almost didn't notice me when I walked into the house. It took a few seconds for him to respond. Did I do this to them? Was this my fault? It had to be. I wanted to die. Seeing them like this was torture.

Stellan jumped up from his chair and hurriedly walked over to me. He crushed me against him, his arms wrapped tightly around me as he planted a kiss on my head. Safely in his embrace, I breathed a sigh of relief, and he did the same. I was glad he wasn't angry with me, but I still felt guilty for making him worry so.

But I wasn't in his arms long before I began to tremble awkwardly. Even his very touch hurt. Stellan pulled away from me and looked into my eyes. His own were sad and dull. I could feel unwanted tears forming in my eyes. I wiped them away and looked down. He lifted my chin and kissed me gently. It wasn't a passionate kiss, like the first one we shared outside my house. Rather, it was filled with comfort and the reassurance that he was here to keep me safe.

Out of the corner of my eye, I saw Addison, Cass, and Aaliyah all watching our encounter. I cleared my throat and stepped away from Stellan. I clasped my hands together and went to take a seat.

Aaliyah got up as soon as I sat and filled a plate of food for me. She must have guessed that I wouldn't be hungry, because she only put a few pieces of fruit and some bread on the plate. I mouthed a *thank you* to her and started picking at my meal, but not really eating much of what was on my plate. I couldn't think of – let alone eat – food at a time like this. Stellan moved to sit beside me.

When I gave up on eating, we sat in silence for many moments. No one knew what to say. Cass finally broke it.

"What exactly happened to you last night, Ramsey? We all want to know. We need to know. I understand it's hard, but it's important."

"I know, Cass," I replied.

"Don't make her talk, Cass. She has to decide when to talk," Addison said, giving me a sympathetic glance. I returned it.

Although Addison and I had very different personas, we were similar in our experiences. We were the only ones in this house who knew how horrible a connection could turn.

"Well, if she doesn't, Addison, we won't be able to find Zora," Cass said sternly.

"Don't," I snapped. "Don't push me, Cass."

"What? Ramsey, stop being selfish. We need to know what you saw!"

"Cass! How dare you?" Addison cried.

"Don't call me selfish, Cass!" I shouted. "You weren't the one to see Zora like that! You didn't feel all of the pain. I did! You weren't there. I was! Therefore, if I were you, I would shut up right now. You have no idea what it's like!"

The anger bubbling inside of me made the pain worse. Soon I was breathing heavily.

"Addison, take Cass home," Aaliyah instructed.

"I need to be here for Ramsey," Addison protested.

"Fine, I will. Let's go, Cass," Aaliyah demanded.

She grabbed his hand and pulled him toward the door.

"I'm sorry," he said quietly, realizing the mistake he had made.

I didn't turn to look at him as he left. I didn't want to see his face, no matter how sorry he was. Stellan was rubbing my back and Addison handed me a glass of water. I drank it and felt better.

"Sorry about the episode there," I apologized, once I was able to speak again. "I just…."

"It's okay. Cass understands. It was wrong of him to push you like that," Addison said soothingly.

"But he's right. I need to tell you about the vision so we can find Zora. I'm supposed to be helping, not hurting. But that's all I have been doing…hurting people."

"Then tell us, but only if you are ready," Stellan advised.

"I want to," I said. "I really do." But I knew my tone of voice was still conveying uncertainty.

"Do you want to wait a while?" Addison asked.

I shook my head. "No, it's best that I just get it over with now," I told her, making up my mind.

I swallowed the lump in my throat and told them everything. I told them about the room, about Zora's condition, and about Finn. I left out the part about the "Realm." It hadn't made sense anyway.

Another awkward silence followed. I was getting sick of silence. Stellan held my hand, but it wasn't enough to make me feel better.

"We have to leave early," I decided aloud.

"Do you mean to Tarlore?" Stellan asked.

"Yes. Zora doesn't have much time left. She will be dead soon if we don't find her."

"How can you know for sure?" Stellan asked.

"I'm sure because she told me. And I believe my sister," I told him harshly.

Stellan nodded without saying anything.

"Ramsey is right, Stellan. We have to leave. We must also remember that Ramsey saw a fairy yesterday. It is too dangerous for her here," Addison agreed.

"What if that was not what she really saw? What if she made a mistake?" Stellan asked.

I sighed. I knew I hadn't made a mistake. It was obvious to me that Stellan didn't want to go to Tarlore – although I didn't know why – and his desperation didn't make me feel any better.

"We can't take that risk," Addison said.

Stellan sighed and nodded slowly, realizing he wasn't going to win this argument – not with two against one. "When do we leave?" he asked.

"We will leave tomorrow morning at five. We need a night's rest," Addison replied, looking at me closely.

"Good idea. I'll get everything ready and let my employer know I'm leaving. After school, you can help," Stellan said to his sister.

"What should I do?" I asked.

"Try and take it easy," he advised.

I had no idea what he meant, but I didn't ask again. I had just remembered what I had to do, and it had nothing to do with taking it easy. However, I wasn't going to let Stellan or Addison know that.

"Well, I'm going to get out of your way," I said, getting up.

"I'll take you home." Stellan placed his hands in mine and we were in front of my door. Waves of dizziness hit me, adding to my aching joints.

"That is probably not the best thing to do so early in the morning," I admitted.

He chuckled and bent down to kiss me. I smiled and put my arms around his neck. Kissing him made the ache dull a bit. I tucked a curl of black hair behind his ear.

"See you soon," I said softly.

"See you," he said. "Be careful."

He kissed me quickly on the cheek and vanished before my eyes.

I waited for a moment before heading down the dirt road, just to make sure he wasn't going to come back. I didn't want Stellan or Addison knowing I was going to spend my day running around the city. I had a lot to accomplish in a day. We were leaving for Tarlore tomorrow, which moved up all the plans I had been saving for the next few days.

First, I had to stop at the bank. I had no idea if I would need money on this journey, but I had to prepare myself for anything. Then I had to talk to Cass. I wanted to be on speaking terms with him before leaving. I hated keeping grudges. Finally, I needed to go to the bookstore and buy the book on locks. It was time the lock on my secret was broken…literally.

***

The trip to the bank took less than an hour, and soon I was standing inside the restaurant. I asked the host for Cass and he led me to the bar. Cass was pouring a few drinks for an elfin couple, appearing tired and upset. I felt bad, even though he was the one who had stepped out of line.

"Hey, Cass," I said, unsure of how to start apologizing.

"Hello…oh, Ramsey, it's you," he muttered.

"Yeah, it's me."

A few silent moments passed.

"I'm sorry," he said quickly.

"Me too," I replied.

"I didn't mean what I said. You're not selfish. I was just upset. Addison came in this morning crying, and I hated seeing her like that."

"I understand," I told him.

"So did you tell them about it?"

"Yes," I said carefully.

"You don't have to tell me," he said.

"I won't," I said, shaking my head. "I can't talk about it again today. It was bad enough the first time." I paused, wincing from the pain of returning memories. "But you can ask Addison if you really want to know. I just wanted to clear things up between us before I left. We are leaving for Tarlore at five tomorrow morning."

"That soon, huh?"

"Zora needs me," I told him.

"Enough said. I'll come by for dinner tonight to say my goodbyes then."

"So you're not going?"

"No. I have to work…and I'm not really a part of this. I wasn't as close to your sister as the others were."

"Won't you miss Addison?" I asked.

"Of course I will miss her. But I know she can take care of herself," he said. He was probably right. Although Addison had shown her vulnerability this morning, I also knew how strong she was. "You don't need me causing trouble on the way," he added after I didn't respond.

I nodded, and had to smile at his last comment. "I guess you're right. Well, I have errands to run before tonight. See you at dinner."

"Goodbye, Ramsey, and remember what I said. You aren't selfish."

"Thanks." I faked a smile and left.

Talking with Cass was awkward now. Our fight had changed things. I didn't believe his apology any farther than I could throw him, but I was glad he had at least tried. He wasn't a bad elf, and up until now I had liked his witty humor and the protectiveness he had for a strong elfen like Addison. But I knew what he thought of me was said at the breakfast table. He loved Addison, and my making her upset had put a rift between us.

Even so, I felt lighter now and less stressed. Sure, I still had to meet the elfen Queen in Tarlore and find Zora, but things seemed a little bit easier.

However, my fight with Cass earlier had unnerved me. I had never once lost my temper like that. I didn't like what I was becoming. All of the tension and stress related to the war and to Zora was turning me into a different person, I mean, elfen. Change scared me sometimes. I never knew how it would affect me, good or bad.

Yet change was inevitable, right? This was my real home. Must I change to fit in?

I wasn't up to analyzing this confusing topic just yet. I would wait until things calmed down before I thought about it again. My whole life needed to revolve around Zora until she was safe at home. I had to deal with that one goal. Thinking about life that way would make bringing her home seem much easier.

Once I bought the book, I could open the trunk. I was hoping the contents of the trunk could shed some light on where to find my sister and reveal my secret. It might even have something to do with my parents.

Thinking of my parents made me remember what Finn the fire fairy said: "*Your father told me so…before he died.*"

I shuddered and hurried on to the bookstore, trying to convince myself that my father's death didn't affect me as much as Zora because I had never known him.

But no matter how hard I tried to pretend otherwise, it did.

***

By the time I reached the store, I was in desperate need of something to distract my mind from thinking terrible thoughts. I needed something good to happen today. Maybe the book would help me accomplish that. If just one thing could go right, maybe I wouldn't feel so bad. Even so, I doubted it.

Except for the sales clerk, the bookstore was empty. I headed straight for the area where I had seen the book. I searched the bookshelf for where I had hidden it behind a few of the other books on locks. *Please let it be there*, I prayed silently. Sure enough, it was just where I had left it.

Almost squealing aloud with joy, I picked the book up and hugged it. Yes! Something good had come out of today! I was just about to go to the sales counter when the front door opened. A chime sounded, and I looked up out of curiosity. Was it really curiosity? Was it fate, or was it just a creepy coincidence that I was in the store at the exact moment *he* came in?

The Stranger walked through the door casually, obviously not looking for anything in particular. The only problem was that he was heading *my* way. I didn't think he saw me, but he definitely would soon if I stayed where I was.

Once again, drawn to his eyes, they held me for a moment and I was unable to move. I had no idea why, but something about this elf held me in place. When I saw him, he was all I could think about. The feeling was both a good and a bad one. Good because he made me stop thinking about bad things. Bad because I didn't know how to stop thinking about him when I saw him. I had no control.

He looked up as he walked closer, and for a moment, we just observed each other. I felt my cheeks go red hot. "*It isn't nice to stare*," I heard my human mother saying in my head. I turned my head away and slowly backed up into another section. I knew it was obvious that I was avoiding him, but what else could I do? I was totally gawking at an elf I had literally run into two days ago. I was embarrassed.

No, this wasn't just embarrassed. This feeling went way beyond embarrassment.

The fear of what would happen to me if I allowed myself to come too close to him hit me. Without any control, what actions would I regret later?

Then, as I thought about it more carefully, I realized I wouldn't care what I did with him, so long as I could still look into his eyes….

I went as far back into the store as I could before bumping into the back wall. Three books fell to the floor, making three loud *thuds*. I hurried to pick them up and stuff them back on the shelf. During the process, my own book fell to the floor as well. *Great*, I thought. *Could this get any worse?*

It did get worse. It got a lot worse. As I reached for my book, someone else beat me to it. *He* beat me to it. I looked up to see him holding the book out to me. If I had a mirror, I knew what my face would look like – horrified: 1) I was completely embarrassed; 2) I couldn't stop looking into his eyes; 3) He was right in front of me and I didn't know what to do.

"Drop something?" he asked, trying to suppress a smile but failing miserably at the act.

I nodded and smiled back at him sheepishly, unable to find my voice to respond in any other way.

"Interested in locks, I see," he commented.

I nodded again.

"Well, here you go," he said, and he handed the book to me.

I nodded. *Oh crap, why did I just nod? Take the book!* I screamed inside my head. *Take it!* I took it slowly. He kept looking at me, smiling.

"Thanks," I muttered.

"Hold on, wait," he said, as I turned around quickly, almost running to the counter. I reluctantly ignored his calls of protest. The temptation of going back to talk to him was great, but I was able to resist.

"Find everything all right?" the elf asked.

"Yes," I said hurriedly.

I paid the clerk, grabbed my bag, and rushed out of the store. As I walked back home, I told myself repeatedly that I was wrong about today turning good. Today was definitely bad.

I couldn't get the Stranger's eyes out of my mind as I returned home.

And I couldn't help but wonder what would have happened if I had listened to him…if I had gone back to face him.

***

"Ramsey, are you okay?" Addison asked while we were having lunch later that day.

But I wasn't paying attention. I was thinking about the sequence of events that led me here. After my episode with the Stranger, I ran home, threw the book in a drawer, and high-tailed it over to Addison's house. The trunk would have to wait because I couldn't stand being alone anymore. It left me with too much thinking time. I needed distractions.

Since Addison hadn't arrived home until noon, I talked to Aaliyah about the orchard, drank tea and nervously munched on freshly baked cookies. I did anything I could to distract myself. I was already as freaked out as I could stand.

"Ramsey. *Hello*?" Addison yelled.

"Sorry, what did you say?" I snapped out of it and finally turned my attention to the elfen girl sitting across from me at the table.

"Are you okay? You seem very out of it. Even more so than you were this morning," Addison noted.

"I'm just stressed."

Okay, that was kind of the truth. I just hoped she didn't ask why. I did *not* want to tell anyone about the Stranger.

"Why? Tell me about it," she suggested.

Crap.

"I, uh, it's hard to explain," I blurted.

"Try me."

Double crap. I didn't want to answer.

"No, it's okay," I finally said.

"Ramsey, just spit it out!" Addison cried.

Triple crap.

"It's Zora," I lied.

Well, I wasn't really lying. Zora was a huge part of my stress, just not the center of it…at this moment. I felt stupid for thinking like that. Of course, Zora was at the center of it! She was *always* the center of it. She had been ever since I stepped through that elf circle and into the Elf Realm.

"Oh," Addison said. She stopped talking after that.

I was thankful my semi-lie had saved me. Then I realized how often I had been lying to avoid subjects I wasn't interested in discussing. It wasn't a good thing for me; another change. We ate in silence until Aaliyah asked if anyone wanted more tea.

"I'm fine, thank you," Addison said politely.

"I'll have more, please."

"Ramsey, this is your seventh cup!" Aaliyah commented.

"Yeah." I didn't know what else to say.

Aaliyah poured the tea and sat down. She reached across the table, and I jerked my hands away. I didn't want any memories to calm me down like a bottle of pills. Nothing could help right now. Only finding Zora could help.

For a brief moment, I actually wished the Stranger were here, because I knew he would be able to calm me down. I didn't know what it meant for me to believe something like that; all I knew was that it was the truth.

"Ramsey, please," Aaliyah begged.

I reluctantly put my hands in hers. If it would make her happy and leave me alone, I would give in and let her try.

A picture flashed before my eyes.

It was of a baby rocking in a cradle. Her delicate face was smiling and her hands were waving in the air. Her emerald green eyes were full of happiness and wonder. She was dressed in a green cotton dress that reflected her cheerful eyes. A tuft of pale hair was on her head, held together by a brown bow. Everything about the memory was nice and simple. It was just a happy memory. No strings attached.

When the memory left and I opened my eyes, I was a little disappointed. I had enjoyed that memory. I hadn't wanted it to leave. I never wanted Aaliyah's memories to end.

"Do you know who that baby was, Ramsey?" Aaliyah asked.

"No, should I?" I asked.

"It was you," she informed me.

"That was me?" I was stunned.

"Yes. You were almost a year old at the time."

"Thank you, Aaliyah. I think that of all the abilities I have witnessed so far, yours is my favorite. You sure know how to cheer someone up."

Addison snorted and smacked me in the shoulder. "Hey!" she cried.

"Sorry, Addison, but it's true," I said. I winked at her and smiled. "Aaliyah's ability doesn't hurt people or destroy furniture."

Addison pouted and muttered, "It's not my fault if you're sensitive and your table is cheap."

"Don't feel bad. I'm sure Ramsey likes your ability second best," Aaliyah said, patting her daughter on the back and laughing when Addison gave her a look of disdain.

"No way, she likes mine more!" Stellan said, as he appeared by my side.

"Aren't you supposed to be working?" Addison asked.

He smiled slyly. "We're leaving tomorrow, so I took the rest of the day off to get ready."

"Good idea," Addison commented.

I got up and hugged Stellan tightly. I had missed him a lot today, and it felt good to be back in his arms. It felt safe and normal, unlike my interactions with the Stranger. We sat down together, our hands intertwined.

"So what kind of planning do we have to do before tomorrow?" I asked, getting down to business, all traces of my crazy mood finally gone.

"Not too much, actually, but let's go over how this is going to work," Addison suggested.

I nodded. "Okay."

"The three of us will leave tomorrow morning at five. Getting to Tarlore takes about two or three days, so we will pack enough food for the journey. When we arrive, guards will probably take us to Queen Taryn. After a night's rest, she will want to discuss all of our options. Then whatever we decide, we will do."

"I've got one question."

"Yes?" Addison and Stellan said in unison.

"Do I wear the Mood Diamond again?"

"No!" they both replied.

"She should," Aaliyah said quietly.

Stellan and Addison glared at their mother.

"I agree," I said.

"No, no, no, no, no, no," Addison screamed as she got up and started pacing, "absolutely not!" I noticed she liked doing that whenever she was upset.

"I won't let what happened last time happen to her again, Mother," Stellan said sternly.

"It's the right thing to do," Aaliyah replied.

"The right thing? Are you kidding me?" Addison asked, disbelief wracking her features. "Since when is putting Ramsey in danger the *right thing*? What happens if she gets hurt, or dies? Who will save Zora then? Who will save Ramsey?"

Stellan turned to me and shook his head. His eyes were full of worry.

"I have to wear it, Stellan. It's the only way to figure out Zora's location. I'll be okay. I know what to expect now," I assured him.

"But what if you don't? What if you get hurt or killed? Don't do it, please, Ramsey," he pleaded.

I squeezed both of his hands. "I have to, and you know it."

Addison was still yelling "no," while Aaliyah tried calming her down. I looked into Stellan's eyes and nodded. He leaned over, took my hands in his, and kissed me softly on the lips. Then he sighed and nodded as well.

"Okay, but you can't wear it until we reach Tarlore. That way you can be looked after better, and if you do get hurt, help will be nearby," he told me.

"Deal," I agreed.

We shook hands.

"What?" Addison shouted after hearing us. "What does 'deal' mean?"

"I will wear the Mood Diamond when we are safely in Tarlore," I told her.

Addison didn't reply. I knew I had won.

"Fine," she snapped.

"That sounds like a fair deal," Aaliyah agreed.

"Then it's decided. So where did my Mood Diamond go, exactly?" I wondered aloud.

She smiled mischievously.

"Addison, give me the diamond!" I pleaded.

"Not a chance. You can't set eyes on it until we reach Tarlore!" she said happily, dancing around in a gleeful circle.

My response was a frustrated groan. "Why do you have to be so difficult?" I cried.

Her only reply was a bow, and then she disappeared into her room.

I shook my head and looked at Stellan.

"You won't win that one," he told me.

I had already known that.

"I know," I sighed. "But can you blame me for trying?"

~11~

Fate

Dinner that night was part happy, part awkward, and part depressing all at the same time. We were happy to be together, yet anxious and wary about leaving. Cass was there, and I hardly spoke to him all evening. I wasn't upset with him; I just didn't know what to say to him. He seemed at a loss for words as well, and kept his attention focused on Addison. No, dinner was not a picnic at the orchard. Trying to eat was complicated enough, especially when I knew that my sister was getting closer and closer to death with each passing minute – and my internal clock only made me more aware of those passing minutes. How could I enjoy anything with this on my mind?

Stellan remained by my side the entire evening, and I was grateful to have him with me. I didn't want to be alone so soon after my connection with Zora. Even though I didn't have the Mood Diamond on anymore, I was still anxious. To make matters worse, the Stranger subject was still floating through my mind.

Stellan was the only distraction I had left.

"See you at five tomorrow morning," Addison said, as we hugged each other goodnight after finishing our meal.

"I'll be here," I promised.

"Make sure to pack only the things you need," Aaliyah advised. "You don't want to be carrying too much on this kind of journey."

"Are we walking?" I asked.

"Unfortunately, yes. We didn't have enough time to arrange for horses," Addison told me.

"Why can't Stellan just teleport us?" I asked.

"I can't teleport *that* far. My ability is limited to how many miles I can travel," he said. "I guess I'm not strong enough yet. Abilities grow stronger with age, and I've had mine for less than two years."

I sighed. "Bummer, but I guess we can manage,"

"Don't worry; we will get there in time," Addison reassured me.

"I hope so," I said.

I hugged Aaliyah and turned to Stellan. He smiled and took my hand in his.

"Let's go," he said.

"Okay. Are we teleporting?" I asked. "Please tell me so I can prepare."

"No, let's walk instead," he decided.

He led me out the door and onto the dirt street. As we walked, I took in the cool night air. In the Elf Realm, everything was clearer. This place made me feel alive. I wished I could enjoy it without the stress. My head was the only thing not so clear here.

"Ramsey, is everything okay?" Stellan asked, his expression full of concern.

I blinked at him and thought about my answer.

"Just thinking," I replied.

"About?"

I exhaled. "Everything."

"I see."

A moment of silence passed between us.

"Are you scared, Stellan?" I wondered.

"Scared of what?"

"Going to prison, for one," I reminded him.

"I'm not going to prison."

"That's a little overconfident, don't you think?" I asked, bumping him in the side with my hip.

"Not at all. I know you will find Zora in time," he told me.

I sighed, taking in his response. "Thanks for the faith, but I don't deserve it," I told him.

"Yes, you do," he said, looking intently at me with those big green eyes. I tried not to, but I couldn't help but notice how much his eyes paled in comparison to the Stranger's. But that was wrong. I shouldn't be comparing Stellan to someone I didn't know, especially since we were, well, together. What was wrong with me lately? You would think that after years of being shunned by guys, I wouldn't take Stellan for granted. He made me feel…well, he just made me *feel*. What it was, I couldn't exactly put into words, but it was better than anything I had ever felt before. I had to stop thinking as though my interests could be divided. I was with Stellan, and that's how it would remain, how I *wanted* it to remain. Stellan brushed a gentle hand against my cheek, bringing me back to reality. "You may not see it yourself, but I do."

Realizing I would never win this argument, I nodded slowly. "Well, thanks."

"Of course," he replied.

We were at my door after that, so we didn't continue our conversation. The house was cold and empty as I stepped inside. It didn't soothe me one bit. Stellan lit a fire as I changed in my room. I could feel its warmth already spreading through the house. I could see the firelight dancing on the walls as I walked out into the parlor.

"I guess I'll go home now. We all need rest," Stellan remarked.

My stomach clenched. I was nervous, but I had to ask. I didn't want to be alone tonight, no matter what. I was too afraid. It was stupid, but I couldn't shake the feeling that I wasn't safe alone anymore. After what had happened the last time I was alone, I wasn't ready. I just felt too uneasy.

"Stay," I told him.

"What?" he asked. He looked stunned, and a little confused.

"Don't go home. Stay here with me. I don't want to be alone," I pleaded.

"What exactly do you want me to do?" he asked, still looking confused.

"Just sleep here," I said, nervously looking down at my feet.

"You mean *with* you?"

When I realized what he was getting at, I gasped. "Not that way! My God, Stellan! I'm not *that* kind of girl…I mean, elfen. I meant like on the couch or something. Jeez, just in the house so I feel safer and not so lonely."

His face reddened. "Oh…yes, that makes sense."

I nodded, laughing despite my worries. It was amusing to see Stellan, who was always so cool and collected, become so embarrassed.

"So can you?" I asked. "I hate being in this empty house. It gives me the creeps."

He let out a deep breath and nodded. "Sure."

I beamed. "Thank you!" I wrapped my arms around him and gave his waist a light squeeze.

"Yes, yes, I'll be on the couch," he said, hugging me back and sighing. "I hope it's comfy."

"I'm sure you'll live," I said, and winked.

He sighed again and went over to his new "bed." I waited until he settled in before retreating to my own room.

"I knew you would say yes," I said, as I walked into my room and got into my own bed.

"You did?" he asked, his voice muffled and distant because we were no longer in the same room.

"Yeah, I did," I called.

I heard him chuckle. "You seem to be a lot more confident than you let on."

"That's the point," I retorted, my smile wider than it had been since the vision with Zora.

I heard him laugh again. "Goodnight, Ramsey."

"Night, Stellan!"

I yawned and drifted off quickly, no longer afraid.

***

I was back in the city bookstore. This time, everything looked different. Books were floating in the air like birds, as well as sitting on shelves. I realized then that I was dreaming.

I grabbed a book out of the air and began to read. It was a story about an elfen who didn't know she was an elfen. She had lived in the Human Realm until she was found and taken back to rescue her sister. She was just about to go on a journey to the capital....

It took me a while to realize that the book was about me. I closed it, tossed it on the ground, and then picked up another.

That one was about an elfen girl who met an elf and they connected right away. He was a little odd sometimes, but he was handsome and kind. He always knew how to make her smile. I threw that one to the ground as well when I realized it was about Stellan and me. I didn't need to read stories I already knew.

The last book I picked up had a picture of the Stranger on the front cover. Although his eyes were not nearly as beautiful in my dream state, they still took my breath away. I opened it up curiously and there was one word written in a large, bolded font: FATE.

"Ramsey, it's time to go," Stellan said softly, as he woke me from my slumber.

I struggled to open my eyes against the sunlight that was streaming slightly through my windows. I rubbed them and yawned.

"Sleep well?" I asked.

"Horrible."

"What?" I said. My eyes widened.

Instead of continuing to be serious, he chuckled.

"So not funny," I told him.

I punched him in the arm and got up from bed. He was still dressed in his clothes from last night. I wondered if he would bother to change. I grabbed a beige peasant shirt and a pair of brown knee-length pants from my wardrobe. It wasn't very attractive, but I guessed it was good for traveling purposes. I grabbed my bundle and headed for the bathroom. Once inside, I washed my face, dressed, and went into the parlor to see Stellan sitting at my table. In front of him was a bowl of fruit and bread and butter waiting on two plates.

"He made breakfast?" I wondered aloud, putting a hand over my mouth to stimulate a look of amazement. "I'm impressed."

He chuckled and gestured to the open chair beside him. "Come sit and eat. We have to leave in a few minutes."

I sat down beside him and ate as quickly as I could manage. He did the same, and soon we were both full enough to survive. I ran back into my room and pulled on a pair of brown boots I had found in the back of the wardrobe. Then I stuffed my money, Zora's journal, some paper, a pen, and a navy blue summer dress into my shoulder bag. I didn't know exactly what I would need, so I just grabbed the basics. I put on my silver cross and decided to add some fruit from the kitchen into the bag as well. I had everything I would need.

"Ready?" Stellan asked when I arrived at the door.

"Ready," I confirmed.

He took my hand as we stepped outside. Before he teleported us to Addison's, I took one last look at my home. I was a little sad to be leaving it so soon. I prayed I would return to enjoy it.

In a matter of seconds, we were inside his house. Aaliyah was drinking tea in the kitchen. She pointed to Addison's room and rolled her eyes. I could tell she meant Addison was still getting ready. The similarities between the elfens here and my human sister Dina were actually beginning to pile up.

"Elfens…," Stellan muttered.

I glared at him and he apologized by giving me a kiss on the cheek. *What a guy*, I thought.

While we waited for Addison to join us, my mind trailed back to my strange dream. It was normal until the Stranger part had come into play. I wondered why I had thought of the word *FATE*. Why was the Stranger becoming such a significant part of my life? What was his role in all of this? Why did I feel so strongly about him in ways I couldn't explain? The dream had completely unnerved me, and I wondered if it meant anything. Maybe it was just random, with no significance to my life whatsoever…or maybe it was more. But I had no idea. I realized I wouldn't have time to figure it out when Addison walked over, repeating, "I'm ready, let's go!" numerous times.

Stellan and I nodded and we turned our attention to Aaliyah. Addison and Stellan each hugged her and she wished them well. When she got to me, she took both of my hands in hers. For a short moment, I saw the happy, glowing Zora. I couldn't help but smile. It was nice to have a new image of her in my head. After my connection, all I could see was the fatally thin and miserable Zora. Now I had the lovely, carefree Zora.

"Bring her back, Ramsey. I know you can," Aaliyah said.

"I will, Aaliyah. I will do everything possible to bring her home," I promised her.

We hugged and then the three of us walked out of the house, leaving Aaliyah behind. It was then I remembered the book on locks still lying in my room. I wanted to go back for it, but I knew we didn't have time for books or mysterious wooden trunks. The real journey was beginning. I just hoped that the trunk didn't contain anything vital to our search for Zora.

I didn't know which way we were supposed to go, so I followed closely behind Addison, who led the way. Stellan held my hand most of the time.

When we were out of the city, I paid more attention to my surroundings. We walked through beautiful fields; vibrant wildflowers and bright green blades of grass dotted the countryside. The wind made the long grass tickle my legs as it swayed back and forth. The sun, high and shining brilliantly in the blue sky, made me warm; everything around me seemed brighter. The blue sky was cloudless and serene. However, because of the sun, we were soon very hot. The closest trees were only a thin line on the horizon.

After admiring the fields, I passed the time by thinking. It probably wasn't a good idea, because thinking always led to worrying these days. I didn't feel like talking, however, so it was the only option left. I thought about what my secret could be. Was I going to have a special ability no one else had? Would I have a power that could end the war? Maybe I was royalty or something. I thought of several possibilities, but nothing seemed to fit right. What was I? Why was I special? I wanted so badly to know.

All of this led to Zora. She knew my secret; she had confirmed that to me many times. When I found her, she would have to tell me. She had to, because I *needed* to know.

I stopped thinking once we reached the forest. I recognized all the trees as tall birches. Various green and leafy plants grew beneath the trees. Not many flowers bloomed, so the only color I really noticed was green.

"This is Birchwood Forest. It surrounds most of the city except to the west," Addison told me. "No other types of trees grow in this forest."

"That's right! I noticed that the forest we went through to get to Birchwood that first day was full of birch trees. I hadn't put it together then, because I didn't know the city's name," I remembered.

"It's beautiful, isn't it?" she asked.

"Magical."

Addison smiled and nodded, then continued to lead. Stellan had remained quiet most of the way. He looked deep in thought, and I wondered what was going on in his head. I didn't ask, though, because I didn't want to badger him. I could feel his hand tighten on mine. What was making him so tense?

I found it hard not to trip over the various white logs and stones in the forest. I loved hiking and spending time outdoors, but I had never been in a forest as wild as this one. It was a good experience, but a tough one. As I tramped along, I noticed how many animals appeared and scurried around the trees. The wildlife here was plentiful and happy. I couldn't believe how the Human Realm could ever have let this slip away. I knew that I would *never* go back, nor want to go back. Even though I was more stressed here than I had been in my whole life, I knew that would all go away once my sister was safe. Then I would have the chance to fully experience this incredible place.

We traveled for several uneventful hours. I found myself losing focus and becoming unaware of my surroundings. I noticed the time passing as we walked. Ten, eleven, twelve, one, two….We stopped every few hours to catch our breath and rest our feet, and we lunched together around two. We ate dried strips of beef, which I noticed were just like beef jerky from the Human Realm, and munched on bread. I decided we could have the fruit I brought another time. What we had was enough to keep us going. We traveled until it became too dark to see and looked for a place to spend the night.

We finally settled down in a small clearing. Stellan built a fire while Addison and I laid out a few blankets for each of us. Together we found a way to cook some of the meat using a slab of rock and creatively propping it up over the orange flames. A stream nearby gave us plenty of water, and after we ate, Stellan roasted some nuts he had brought along to eat the next day. Then Addison brought out an instrument that was long and circular, with the neck of a violin.

"What's that?" I asked her.

"It's a medieval fiddle. It's different from your string instruments. Humans used these a long time ago as well."

"Will you play?" I asked.

"Of course I will! Why else did you think I brought it?" She giggled, placed the fiddle at her neck with bow in hand, and then began to play.

The melody was beautiful and flowed elegantly from the fiddle, warming my heart. Strangely, I felt the urge to sing along, but didn't know the words. Instead, Addison sang, her lovely voice ringing in the darkness of the night:

The lonely elf in the forest wood,
Will never sit in the dark.
He likes to sing a little tune,
That keeps the firelight on.

He plays his tune on his fiddle and,
He never stops until morning comes.
He will not sleep by the firelight,
Because that would mean ending his song tonight….

Stellan and I watched in awe as Addison sang her beautiful tune. In my heart, something stirred, an emotion I couldn't explain. Remembrance, recognition, I felt as if something about this song – or this tune – was important somehow, but I didn't know what it was or why:

The elfen who was all alone,
Walked through the wood and saw him sing.
He gave her a grin and continued then,
He wouldn't stop so she sang along.

Sing; sing out you elves nearby,
Join in the tune of our fiddle's cry.
Shout to the night and heavens above,
Then find a new friend and again you will sing.

Don't end the tune right away, hold up your fiddle and play...

The song ended and we all clapped. I felt oddly overjoyed and happy. The song had helped ease my worries, taking away my stress and replacing it with warmth. I could see that both Addison and Stellan felt more at ease as well by the smiles on their faces.

"That was lovely, Addison. You play an excellent fiddle," I said. "And your voice is beautiful as well."

Addison blushed. "Thank you."

"I sort of recognize that tune," I said. "And now that I think of it, the melody reminds me of a song we used to sing in church at Christmas time."

"What was it called?" Stellan asked.

"'What Child is This?' It was one of my favorites," I said.

"That's so odd," Addison commented.

"Why?" Stellan and I asked in unison.

"Well, your mother used to sing a song just like this one, but it had different words. Maybe the tune has always stayed in your mind, and that is why you liked the human song so," she said.

"Can you sing the other song? The one my mother sang to me?"

"No," Stellan said sternly.

"What harm would it do, Stellan?" Addison asked him.

"Others could hear you," he said.

"What others?" Addison challenged.

"It's not safe," Stellan warned, his eyes clouded with anger.

"What is so bad about the song?" I asked.

"It's about an elf and a fairy, but it's harmless. I can assure you of that. It's just a song," Addison told me.

"Sing it softly," I suggested.

"The trees," Stellan pointed out through clenched teeth.

"What are you talking about?" I asked.

"Dryads," Stellan explained.

"What's so bad about them?" I wondered.

"They, like other fae, should be in the Fairy Realms, but you never know when one could slip into another Realm. If they are on the side of the Element fairies and ever heard us singing of elves and fairies in harmony…I don't even want to think about the consequences. Element fairies could be alerted and on us in a matter of seconds."

I realized he was right; the trees could listen. Dryads could be anywhere, within any tree. And with no way of figuring out which trees they were in, we would be taking quite a risk by allowing Addison to sing.

I nodded slowly. "I understand."

Stellan relaxed, but to my surprise, Addison started playing the tune anyway. I had always pegged her as stubborn. Now she was completely proving my thought.

She started singing, her voice velvety and her fiddle soothing, and then suddenly, I realized I knew the song as well. I could sing along. I was amazed, and soon I was singing along with Addison, our voices blending in one beautiful harmony:

The lonely elf in the forest wood,
Will never sit in the dark.
He likes to sing a little tune,
That keeps the firelight on.

He plays his tune on his fiddle,
And he never stops until morning comes.
He will not sleep by the firelight,
Because that would mean ending his song tonight.

A fairy with her wings of bright,
Flew through the forest to the elf.
She asked him what song he sang,
He told her and she beat her wings.

Before the song could draw to a close, a rustling rang out through the trees. Fear gripped my gut. Had the dryads heard our song? Were we in danger?

Then, something miraculous occurred. Leaves began to float from the trees, gathering around us like a dome of dark green shapes. They twirled to and fro, creating a kind of light show as the glow of the moon shone between the moving cracks. The sight was astonishing. I felt chills as I witnessed magic I had never believed could be possible until now. The wonder of what was occurring left me breathless, but after getting over the initial shock, I realized that we had to continue singing. The dryads *wanted* us to sing.

I gestured to Addison, and she quickly took the hint. As we resumed the song, the leaves appeared to be swaying in rhythm with our voices:

Sing; sing to my love nearby,
He plays his fiddle and then I cry.
Play; play forevermore,
My love, my elfin sweetheart.

We watched in wonder as the leaves departed, returning to their trees. Moments of silence passed. We were all too stunned to speak. Even Stellan appeared mystified.

"How did you know the song?" Addison finally asked.

"I don't know. I guess I just remember it from when I was a baby. Some weird sudden realization, I guess."

Addison smiled, and Stellan was impressed, although he was trying hard not to show it because he was still upset.

"What does the song mean?" I asked Addison.

"It tells of a loving friendship between a fairy and an elf. It was what the Realms were like before the war."

"It's beautiful," I commented.

Stellan grunted and shook his head, obviously frustrated with her for playing the song against his orders.

However, Addison ignored him. "It is," she replied, "which is probably why the dryads approved." She shot a glare toward

Stellan, as if to rub it in his face that he had been in the wrong. It was a sisterly thing to do. Sighing, Addison began to pack her fiddle away.

"No, don't stop. Play more," I urged.

Addison nodded and for a long while, she played her fiddle. Sometimes she would sing, and other times the fiddle would be enough. Stellan refused to join in on any of the songs. I didn't let this bother me; I was enjoying myself too much. The dryads never reappeared, but I could tell by the rustling of the branches that they enjoyed the entertainment.

As midnight approached, Addison and I agreed it was time to stop and get some rest. Stellan muttered something I didn't catch and went to his blanket to sleep. I shook my head and lay down on mine. *What a fun guy*, I thought sarcastically. Couldn't he ever just stay happy and smile his perfect smile all day long? I wished. His mood swings were getting annoying.

I closed my eyes and tried to clear my head. I didn't need any bad dreams tonight.

***

Fortunately, I was too tired to dream, and slept without any disturbances. I woke up around four to Addison humming as she cooked breakfast on the fire. I noticed Stellan was still sleeping. I stretched and went over to sit with Addison and put my hands in front of the fire to warm them. The morning was nice, but a little chilly.

"Good morning, Ramsey," she whispered.

"Morning," I replied.

"Hungry?"

"Oh yeah," I said. "Is that bacon you're cooking?" It sure looked like it.

"Bacon? What's that?" she wondered.

"Never mind," I said, shaking my head. "What do you call this?" I asked instead.

"Strips of pork," she told me.

"That's called bacon in the Human Realm."

"Interesting," she said, moving the "bacon" around with a stick.

"So when is Stellan going to put on his happy face again?" I asked.

Addison rolled her eyes. "Who knows? I wish he would, though. It isn't fair to you. You have enough to worry about."

"Thanks," I said.

"It's only true," she replied.

I saw Stellan move, and we both ended the conversation. He got up and walked to the stream for a drink. I held my breath as he walked away.

"Do you think he heard us?"

"I hope he did," Addison said, "because maybe he will get the hint and cheer up."

I nodded in agreement as I watched him walk back. He still looked tense but better than last night. I could detect the hint of a smile, a sign that he was in a better mood. That was enough for me.

He sat down near me and put his hands in front of the flames the same way I had. Addison told us to watch the fire while she went for a drink. I moved the bacon while Stellan and I sat in silence. Then he gently turned my head and cupped his hands around my face.

"I'm sorry," he said softly.

"Sorry for what?" I asked.

"I'm sorry for the way I acted before. This whole situation is difficult for me, for all of us. I'm so afraid for you all the time. I'm worried that one little mistake could cost you your life. I hate going through this when we just found…," his voice trailed off.

"Found what?"

"Each other," he finished, half-smiling.

I kissed him, reveling in the sweetness of his lips pressed against mine. "I forgive you," I told him.

Our lips met again, and this time our kisses grew longer and deeper. His hands moved to my waist as he pulled me closer to him, and I ran my fingers through his hair, caught up in the heat of the moment. Pressed tightly against one other, I put everything I had into those kisses, revealing to him just how much he meant to me, even after only a few days of being together. He seemed to be doing the same, pouring out everything he had inside as our lips moved together.

Finally, we parted, both of us breathing heavily from our embrace.

He smiled, so I smiled – my cheeks probably flaming red – and everything was okay again. Sure, our little tiffs were bothersome, but at least it was easy for us to make up. Addison returned to see Stellan's arm around me – and me smiling like a little kid opening a present on Christmas morning.

"Welcome back, brother," Addison greeted, eyeing us curiously.

Stellan rolled his eyes and I laughed.

"I think the bacon – I mean, strips of pork – are ready to eat now," I guessed.

"You're right. Stellan, could you please take the meat off the rock for us?"

"Afraid you'll get burned?" he asked.

Addison gave him a long look, but didn't reply.

"All right," he said, gingerly taking each piece off and laying it on another rock to cool.

We ate quickly, eager to continue our journey. Addison predicted we would arrive in Tarlore by tomorrow morning if we stopped twice. Once for lunch, and once to sleep. I was pleased we had only another day's walk ahead of us.

"Did anyone ever tell you about Tarlore, Ramsey?" Addison asked me, after a few hours of walking. She was the first to break the silence in quite a while.

"No," I answered.

"Stellan, could you do the honors?"

"I would love to." He cleared his throat and began. "Tarlore wasn't always called Tarlore. It used to be named Breena."

"Why was it changed?"

"You see, every city in every Realm, except for the Human Realm of course, was named by fairies."

"Every Realm was? Why?"

"Why do you think? Because there were more of them, and even today, no one challenges a supreme order from Queen Titania, not even elves. She was one of the reasons the Realms came to be in the first place, because of her powerful magic. The fairies took the naming into their hands even though creating new Realms was the elves' idea. Fortunately, they soon realized it was wrong to control everything and everyone. So they left the elves alone and paid attention to naming their own Realms. However, after taking so long for every city to receive a name, our Realm just kept the fairy names. *Breena* is Celtic for 'fairyland.' When Taryn became queen, she changed the name right away. She didn't want her Realm to support fairies if she was at war with them."

"But we are only at war with Element fairies!"

"That was a good enough excuse for Queen Taryn," Stellan explained. "She renamed the capital Tarlore, after herself and her husband, who died in the war. His name was King Lore."

"That's a powerful first move as queen," I remarked.

"Yes, it was, but she's Taryn, powerful and very determined," Stellan said.

"Sounds scary," I admitted.

"She's a little intimidating," Addison agreed.

"Have you met her?" I asked.

"Yes. She came to our city when the fairies took Zora," Addison replied.

"Oh." I looked down, sorry our light conversation had taken a drastic turn.

"Stellan, continue. Tell her what Tarlore is like," Addison suggested, obviously trying to lighten the mood.

"Tarlore is a wonderful city. The capital lies in a huge valley, surrounded by rolling hills of the brightest green grass you will ever see," he explained, excitement creeping into his tone. "At the edge lies the Queen's palace. It's amazing. I cannot even describe it properly. You'll have to see it for yourself. But believe me, the capital is probably the utmost best place you will ever visit in the Elf Realm."

"I can't wait. But I wish it was just a visit," I admitted.

"Me too," Stellan said, and squeezed my hand.

"Me too," Addison agreed.

Stellan continued to talk about Tarlore for a while after that. Addison piped in every now and then, too. I learned the main reason every elf loved Tarlore: it wasn't modern one bit. How ironic. In the Human Realm, anything not modern was either mocked or cast aside. Seeing Tarlore would definitely be interesting. Stellan described it as "Renaissance." I used to go to a Renaissance Fair in the Human Realm. I had always wanted to live in a place like that. I thought Birchwood City was similar, but it sounded like Tarlore would be even more like the fair. While Stellan didn't describe the palace in detail, he did say that it was almost the same as a castle with some elfin touches. I looked forward to seeing that as well.

We stopped for lunch around noon and then resumed our travels. As we walked, Stellan whistled and Addison hummed a tune. I was too anxious to do anything musically. I was like a little kid. I kept asking Addison how close we were. I knew Zora didn't have much time left, which meant Addison and Stellan didn't have much time left either. The closer Zora got to death, the closer they got to prison. I was impatient to reach the capital because I felt useless just walking. I wanted to do something more to find my sister. Tarlore wasn't coming soon enough.

I was concentrating so hard on my thoughts that I didn't realize what was going on around us until it was happening for many moments.

I felt the wind pick up, circling rapidly. I knew right away that it wasn't a normal occurrence. At first I thought it was the dryads again, but quickly dismissed the idea when I realized none of the trees were moving, it was just the air around us. I tightened my grip on Stellan's hand. I had a bad feeling about this. I saw a shadow moving out of the corner of my eye, and then I felt as if wind was wrapping around me. I gasped and whirled my head around to see what was going on. Nothing was there, but I saw more shadows.

"Oh no," Stellan whispered.

"What? Stellan, what's happening?" I cried. "What's with all the wind?"

"Run," Addison decided for us.

"Why, what's going on?" I asked.

"Just do it!" Stellan pulled me forward.

We went into a sprint and ran as fast as we could. I stumbled and tripped, but still Stellan dragged me along. We were all breathing heavily. Elves were not physically fit. Where was Cass when we needed him?

I could feel the shadow, or whatever it was, following us as we ran. I felt the air whisking around behind us. I could even hear the air because it was so strong. As it got closer, I could hear Addison's cries as we tried picking up the pace. However, it was no use. We couldn't run any faster. It wasn't enough.

"Stellan, can you teleport us out of here, or is it too far to Tarlore?" I asked, as I ran blindly through the trees.

"Yes, but I can't teleport all of us at the same time!" he reminded me harshly.

"Then go with Addison and come back for me," I suggested.

"No!"

"You have to!" I cried, my breath coming out in short gasps.

"I won't leave you with that thing!"

"What is it, Stellan?" I finally asked.

"It's an air fairy," Addison informed me, her breathing labored.

I gasped and then made up my mind. "Take her, Stellan, please. They want me. Maybe I can stall long enough for you to take her to safety so you can come back for me," I suggested.

Stellan looked from me to Addison and then nodded.

"I will be right back." We stopped running. "Sit by this tree."

"I will," I promised.

"I…." Stellan looked at me with a deep worry in his eyes.

"Just go," I told him.

There was no time for tears, remorse, or second thoughts. If we were to survive this, we had to do it fast.

He nodded and took Addison's hand. Within a second, they were gone. I finally realized what I had done. I had sacrificed myself, but I couldn't have let Addison stay behind with the risk of being hurt or killed.

I felt the air again before I saw the fairy. It was cold and chilled me to my bones. I wrapped my arms around my chest as I waited anxiously for Stellan. *He should be back by now*, I thought to myself. Had something terrible happened to him? Had something happened to Addison as well?

Then I saw *her*. She flew toward me, blonde hair flowing in the wind she created around herself. She wore a flowing white dress that went to her knees. It sparkled like thousands of white diamonds. Her feet were bare. She looked like an angel. If only she *was* an angel, and not a dangerous enemy.

In another instant, she was right in front of me.

~12~

After Effects

"Ramsey," she greeted, in a delicate, light voice. I could see how satisfied she was, finally able to reach her catch.

"Yes?" I asked, as I looked up to meet her icy white eyes, trying hard to hide my fear.

"My name is Lura," she said.

"Okay…hello," I said, as calmly as I could.

Where was Stellan?

"Do you know why I came for you?" she asked sweetly, although it didn't sound very convincing to me.

"Sorry, a little new to this Realm. You will have to fill me in," I told her.

She laughed a bubbly little giggle that made me feel sick. She was my enemy, and she was laughing? What was wrong with her? Was she crazy? Maybe all Element fairies were….

"You're special, Ramsey. You must know that. We just want to know *why*," she explained.

"You mean the Element fairies want to know why, or just Finn?"

"How do you know about Finn?" she asked crossly.

"So you know him?" I probed her.

"Yes, I do. How do *you* know about him?" she asked.

"A wild guess," I said sarcastically.

"Look, Ramsey, I don't want to make things difficult," she said, glaring at me. Her sweet attitude had vanished in an instant, replaced with annoyance.

"Then leave. That's a great solution for you right there," I suggested to her.

"I can't do that."

"What *are* you going to do?" I asked.

"I just want to have a talk with you. That is my only job," she informed me, clasping her hands together. I wondered if that was the only way she could keep from lashing out at me.

"Then start talking," I suggested.

"Do you know what your secret is?" she asked.

"How is that any of your business?" I wondered.

She smiled sardonically, her eyes narrowing into slits. "Everything about you is my business, Ramsey."

"Sure it is," I said, rolling my eyes and crossing my arms against my chest. Goosebumps pricked my skin. I didn't know whether it was from fear of her or the bitter cold she radiated, causing the temperate around us to drop several degrees. Most likely it was a combination of both.

"Do you know your secret?" she repeated.

"No,"I told her out flat.

"I can tell you are not lying."

"Really, you're that good?" I asked, believing her to be stranger by the minute.

"Yes," she said. "Thank you."

"You're welcome," I replied, not knowing what else to say in response.

"Do you know where Zora is?" she asked this time.

I thought for a moment and shook my head. It was best not to say anything about my sister, just in case. "No," I said.

I sort of lied that time.

"Are you sure?" she asked.

"Yes," I said.

"How did you know about Finn?" she asked.

Unfortunately, my eyes widened enough for her to notice. How would I explain knowing Finn without telling her about the connection?

"Someone told me about him," I lied.

"You're lying," she guessed right away.

"No, I'm not," I replied in defiance. But my tone was too defensive for someone telling the truth.

"Yes. You *are* lying." Lura's eyes burned with aggravation.

"It doesn't matter how I know about him," I snapped.

She smiled. "Oh, but it does," she expressed. "You found out about him in a very peculiar way, didn't you?" The tenor of her voice was both teasing and insulting.

"Did I really?" I retorted, throwing some of her nasty attitude back at her.

She ignored my question and asked another of her own. "Where are you headed?"

"A place you're not welcome," I told her.

"I'm not welcome anywhere in your Realm," she pointed out.

I shrugged. "I guess you're right."

"Where are you going?" she asked again.

"Where do you *think* I'm going?" I wondered.

"I'm getting really annoyed with your answers," she said fiercely.

"That's not my fault," I said in my defense. "You wanted answers, and I gave you some. It's your problem whether they are the ones you are looking for or not."

"Are you going to the capital?" she asked.

"Maybe, but why would I tell you? You're my enemy."

"Stop messing with me!" she shrieked.

It was the worst sound I had ever heard; shrill and terrifying, but also terribly beautiful. I shrunk back against the tree. Her eyes were blazing with rage, and they reminded me of Finn.

"Sorry about that," she said, fixing her hair and flattening down her dress. "Fairies have very good lungs for singing *and* for screaming when necessary."

"I can tell," I said, still shaken.

"Now, what are you going to do in Tarlore?" she asked.

"I'm going to party. I've never been to a capital before, and I've never met a queen."

I smiled at her. She scowled, but then her eyes brightened.

"Ah, so you admit you are going there."

I refused to be fazed.

"I love partying and sightseeing. Why wouldn't I go there?" I asked her.

"What are you truly doing at the capital?" she demanded.

"I'm meeting the Queen. She wants to meet me," I said instead.

"All right, that is all then. Thank you for your time." She straightened herself and turned to leave. Her white wings started to beat.

"Wait!" I cried.

She stopped and turned back to face me.

"What?" Lura asked.

"That's it?" I asked.

The white beauty watched me for a moment before replying, "Yes."

"You really just wanted to talk?"

"For now," she said. She smiled deviously and flew off, the beating of her white wings the only sound other than my swiftly beating heart.

I was stunned. What had just happened? She'd had a chance to take me, or even kill me. She hadn't. Why? Fairies were becoming more intimidating and confusing by the minute. How could I have ever thought they were dainty little creatures who liked to live in my garden? I was so naïve.

In addition, where in the Realm was Stellan? He promised he would be back! How long would I have to wait? I knew it would be wrong of me to start searching, because I could get lost, and then he might never find me.

I buried my head in my lap, frustrated, but something shiny made me lift it seconds later. Sitting on the ground in front of me was a Mood Diamond. It looked just like mine, but I knew it was not the same one. Addison still had mine.

I understood everything now. The Element fairies knew I had made a connection with Zora, and Lura left me the Mood Diamond for a purpose. They wanted me to connect with my sister again. They wanted me to go to them. It didn't matter that Lura had found me. It was Finn who really wanted to meet me.

Should I do it? Could I? There were huge risks, and I knew it. I could die. I knew it. They could kill Zora right there, and I could die with her because of the connection. I knew it. Yet I had to go through with it. I knew that as well.

After all, I had to connect with her again if I wanted to figure out where she was. I might as well do it now. I couldn't sit idly by as she lay suffering in a room somewhere. I had to act. I feared where this connection would lead me, but I had to go through with it.

Against all better judgment – and before I could change my mind – I picked up the necklace and put it around my neck. Then I focused on Zora. I repeated her name aloud. I concentrated on no one and nothing but Zora. Then the burning came as it had before. It wasn't as bad as the last time. This time I was prepared for it. It wasn't as fiery; calmer, but still painful.

I waited for the darkness.

***

As both the darkness and the burning subsided, I found myself standing in front of Zora once more.

"Ramsey...why did you come?" she asked. Her voice was shaky and hoarse.

"Because I had to," I said.

But had coming here been the right choice? Did I even have any good reasons to support my decision? Had I not thought about it enough?

Yes, coming here was necessary. I had to trust that instinctive feeling. Besides, this opportunity might help me identify Zora's prison.

"They...they...wanted you here," Zora said.

"I know that," I told her.

"Go while you still can."

"I would like to, but I can't leave you yet. I still don't know where you are, Zora."

"I'm...," Zora trailed off, coughing and placing a hand over her chest in pain.

I cursed under my breath. If I didn't figure out where Zora was now, I would never find her.

I heard the door open; in came Finn and another fairy with a beautiful oval face, short blue hair, a sparkling blue mini dress, and blue high-heeled boots that went to her knees. She was radiant, even though she sort of reminded me of a Hollywood pop star. Her eyes, however, shone with strength and fierce determination. This fairy meant business. With all the blue, I knew right away that she was a water fairy.

The two exchanged a few words in a language I didn't recognize. I remembered Addison's remark to me about old languages, how some fae still spoke in their own tongue as well as in Common. When they were finished with their little chat, they turned to face us.

"Hello, Zora," Finn greeted.

Zora didn't answer. I kept quiet as well. They couldn't see me – only Zora could – but I knew they could probably hear me if I said anything.

"Hello, Zora," the water fairy greeted as well.

"And hello, Ramsey," Finn added.

"Yes, welcome, Ramsey," the water fairy said. "I am Wynter, if you hadn't noticed already." Her voice was both beautiful and haunting.

Ah, so this was Wynter, the famous guard fairy. She didn't look tough, but the power in her voice and the coldness in her eyes told me otherwise.

"Ramsey's...not...here...," Zora whispered, her voice breathy and scarcely audible.

"Don't try fooling us, Zora. We know she is here. We put a spell on the Mood Diamond. Well, actually, one of our Woodland fairy friends did. When she connected with you, we knew right away," Finn explained.

"Good thinking," I admitted.

I probably should have thought of that earlier. But I wasn't too keen on fairy spells to begin with, so I probably would never have guessed. Another reason why I shouldn't have come, *I found myself thinking.*

Both fairies looked around, their heads moving violently as they unsuccessfully attempted to find me.

"Don't try looking for me," I said, moving a ways to throw them off my trail. "You know I'm here, but you won't see me," I reminded them.

"We know," Wynter snapped.

"Calm down, Wynter," Finn instructed, laying a hand on her shoulder.

Wynter stiffened. "Sorry," she muttered.

"Why did you want me here?" I asked.

"You must know," Finn said.

"Like I said to your friend, Lura, I'm new here, so you're going to have to explain things to me in a little more detail," I told them.

"You are here so we can learn your secret. Zora is going to tell us. I thought you would want to know it as well...before you died, at least," Finn explained.

I shivered, very glad that neither of the fairies could see my fear. I collected myself and said mockingly, "How considerate of you."

"We thought so," Wynter responded coolly.

"Aren't you feisty," I muttered.

Before either of the fairies could question my words, Zora had regained her voice.

"No...I won't tell. I promise, Ramsey...," Zora said.

"Yes, you will, Zora. If you want Ramsey to live, you will tell us," Finn told her. Wait, now wasn't that just a little contradictory? Hadn't he just said I would die after I learned my secret? I hoped Zora wouldn't buy into his games.

"What are you going to do?" I challenged.

"I am going to burn her, Ramsey." Finn said this without emotion, as though he tortured others on a daily basis and I should accept that fact graciously. It made me sick, and gave me the urge to slap him right across the face. Unfortunately, I didn't have much experience in the slapping department, and I doubted I could even

inflict any damage upon him. I was, after all, just a ghost here. "I will burn her, and it will burn you because of the connection. I will kill her and you as well, unless she tells me your secret," Finn explained slowly.

"Why does my secret matter so much to you?" I asked.

"It may be the key to winning the war," Finn informed me.

"How could you possibly know that?" I asked.

"We have spoken to many witnesses," Wynter said.

"You mean our father, you heartless monster!" Zora cried.

"Yes," Finn said, shaking his head. "The poor lad, it took quite long for him to die, to burn. You will die the same way, unless you tell me your sister's secret," Finn said.

I was horrified.

"No! You will not kill her!" I screamed.

"It's up to her," Wynter said.

"Wynter is right. Zora will tell us if she wants to live...and if she wants you to live," Finn stated.

"Zora, I'm sorry. I knew this was wrong," I apologized

I was panicking. I needed to find a way out of this, but I didn't know how.

"I won't tell...," Zora repeated.

"You have to, Zora. Please. It's our only chance." Although I sincerely doubted that either of us would make it out of here alive. Still, I had a small glimmer of hope, and it was all I could count on at the moment.

"They...will kill...us...anyway. Get out of here while you still...can," she gasped.

I could tell that it was hard for her to speak through all of her pain.

"I won't leave you," I told her.

My sister ignored me. "I...will...tell you...the secret...if you let her go," Zora told the fairies suddenly.

"I don't believe you," Finn said.

"I don't either," Wynter agreed.

"She'll do it. Please, believe her," I begged them.

"I'm probably...your...only...chance at ever finding out," Zora said weakly. "I'm the only one left that knows and would even think of telling."

Finn and Wynter exchanged glances. They believed Zora. I did too. But I wondered what she had meant by her last phrase: "I'm the only one left that knows and would even think of telling." Who else knew – our mother? Or was she dead like our father?

I didn't have enough time to think about it. I had to focus on getting out of here.

"We know that, but we can't risk you going back on your word," Finn said.

"I'll make an oath. I swear to you...in five nights' time, after you tend my wounds...I'll tell you about Ramsey," Zora said.

I knew the "tending wounds" part was really just Zora's way of stalling so I would have enough time to find her, if I even managed to do so. I nodded slowly in agreement.

Suddenly, a light radiated around Zora's body. Fear gripped me as I thought she might be dying, going to the white light. But then the light formed into a large ball of glowing fire and flew from Zora and into Finn's chest. He shook for a moment and then went still. Finn nodded to Wynter.

"She has sworn. Elves cannot go back on their word. It is one of the strange curses they carry. In five nights, she will tell us," he confirmed to his guard fairy. Then Finn turned to face me. He was looking directly at me, though I knew he couldn't actually see me. Somehow, he could feel my presence. "Go home, Ramsey," he said, "and don't bother coming back. We will find you next time."

"I'm sure you will," I said sternly. I turned to Zora and whispered in her ear as quietly as I could so only she could hear, "I will save you."

She nodded and then tried to smile. It didn't look like much of a smile. She was too hurt to even fake happiness or hope. I still had hope, though, and that hope would lead me to her. I believed in that, even if it seemed impossible.

"Goodbye for now, fairy friends," I said, and then I concentrated on going back.

It took me until now to realize how much pain I was in as well, being too worried about Zora to notice prior to my leaving. Now her wounds cut deep into me. I couldn't breathe. I focused as hard as I could on going back, afraid I wouldn't make it and be stuck here, dying from all the pain.

But darkness finally washed over me one last time.

***

I opened my eyes slowly – and painfully – to the sounds of voices all around me. I could tell I was being carried on some kind of stretcher, but I didn't know to where or by whom.

"How long has she been out?" a voice asked.

"A little over an hour," I heard Addison reply.

I recognized her voice at once. I prayed Stellan was with her, that he was all right.

"Why can't we remove the diamond?" I heard a worried Stellan ask.

I sighed with relief. He was okay. But was I?

"It could kill her," the voice from before said. "If she were still connected, she would be stuck there in spirit form. She wouldn't be able to survive very long after that."

"We have to get her out of this. They could be killing her," Stellan pleaded.

"We have to wait," another voice told him.

"Her eyes are open!" Addison gasped.

I saw all four faces peering down at me. The burning was subsiding, but I was still in a great deal of pain. I didn't want to move or respond, even though I wanted badly to tell them what had happened. I was afraid the throbbing would become worse if I tried to speak.

"She has come out of it. Take off the diamond," an elfen voice instructed.

I felt Stellan taking the diamond off. My skin was on fire from his touch, and not in a good way.

"Give it to Gavin," the elfen told Stellan. "Gavin, fly back to the palace and give this to Queen Taryn. She needs to have it inspected for spells and magic. Then she will have it destroyed."

I saw the elf beside her nod and take the necklace from Stellan. He was an elf; how could he fly to the palace? His next move explained everything. He shook a little, and then in a flash a small hawk sat in his place. It was holding the Mood Diamond in its beak. The bird screeched and flew away. The sight was puzzling and odd to me. However, I couldn't watch much longer before an elfen's face came into view.

"Ramsey, my name is Danica. I'm a close friend of the Queen's and part of her special guard. We are taking you to the palace so our chief healer can help you. You have several injuries, if you hadn't realized," she told me.

"What?" I gasped. "You're serious?"

I had real injuries? *How?* I was only supposed to feel the pain, not actually have wounds, after a connection. I didn't come back with wounds after the first meeting with Zora.

"The fairies put a spell on the Mood Diamond," she explained.

"I knew that already. It was so they could know when I arrived," I said.

"They put on more than one spell," Danica revealed. "One was to alert them of your arrival, and the other was to have you share all of Zora's physical and emotional injuries. They don't want you to find Zora, so this slows you down. You have severe burns on your neck, face, and arms, and cuts on your hands. You are also extremely dehydrated. Luckily, the spell wasn't strong enough to give you the full extent of Zora's pain. You have a mild case, and our healer is excellent with his ability."

"Yeah, it isn't as bad as in the connection," I added.

"But it *is* still dangerous. We need to have you healed very soon. I said our healer was exceptional, but only if we can get you to him quickly," she explained.

"Okay," I said, trying hard not to panic or cry. Nervously, I prayed that we would make it to the healer in time.

"Try not to talk," Danica suggested. "Save your strength so the healing can be successful."

I nodded just enough for Danica to understand. It hurt too much to do anything else. The three of them carried me in silence. Danica asked Addison and Stellan not to say anything to me in case I would try to respond. Yet I could see clearly what they wanted to say to me by the expressions on their faces. They were scared for me, angry with me, and in pain because of me. I was hurting them again, and it was more painful than any of my wounds put together. I was feeling guilty for what I had done, and what I had caused.

I felt tears fall from my eyes and run down my cheeks. I wanted to wipe them away, but the injuries on my arms felt like hot, burning flames.

Stellan used a free hand to wipe the tears off my cheeks for me. His hand lingered on my face. I smiled. He didn't smile back. I knew he wouldn't. He was too upset. Instead, he kept looking ahead. I could tell he wanted to talk to me, but Danica had made it clear that he couldn't.

The injuries hurt badly. However, this pain was different from before. Last time I hadn't felt Zora's injuries in the same way. They were more like ghost pains. This time it was for real.

I winced each time the stretcher moved too much. I swear I received one million apologies from Addison and Stellan. It was all they would say to me. I kept my mouth shut and stayed as still I as I possibly could. I knew listening to Danica was crucial, and I trusted her judgment.

I drifted off quite often. The pain made me delirious and too dizzy to keep my eyes open. Soon after I would drift, though, someone would wake me up. I knew it wasn't a good idea to sleep after sustaining serious injuries, but how could I help it? The pain was both tiring and nauseating. Sleep was my only comfort.

"You need to talk to her," Danica decided later. "She needs to stay awake. It's too risky for her to be sleeping at a time like this."

She sounded a little upset, but I could tell that it was just out of worry for me. I was very grateful for the care she was giving me.

"I'll talk to her, Addison; just focus on communicating with Queen Taryn," Stellan told his sister.

"Okay," Addison replied. She nodded and briefly closed her eyes.

"You're trying to reach the Queen?" I managed to ask.

"Addison is sending the Queen messages on how you are doing and how far away we are. Before you ask, we are a few hours away. Remember how I told you Tarlore lies in a valley? Well, before the valley is a long stretch of grassland, and before the grassland is the forest we were in when the air fairy attacked. Right now we are walking across the grassland. That is the only way to get to the valley. And yes, we are tired. But you are worth it."

I smiled and this time he returned it. I instantly felt a little better.

"But why aren't we teleporting?" I asked.

"It's too risky to move you so quickly. You become dizzy when you teleport *normally*. In the state you are in now, there's no telling what aftereffects you may experience."

"I see. Your power has a lot of limitations," I commented.

"All abilities do. You just have to work with what you are given," Stellan told me.

I nodded, taking his answer into perspective.

"I bet you are wondering what happened to Addison and I after we left you," he guessed.

I had totally forgotten about his strange disappearance. Now I wanted to know. I nodded for him to continue, eager to have his story take my mind off the pain.

"After we left, we were ambushed. I don't know how they found us so quickly, or how they knew we would be there, but they did. We were at the edge of the forest, right before the grassland. Element fairies were already there, waiting for us. It struck us as strange because we had no idea how so many of them could have crossed into the Elf Realm. Our Realm is usually quite protected, and most of the war has been fought in the Element Fairy Realm. Anyway, we would have died if Danica and Gavin hadn't come along, because we were completely outnumbered and defenseless.

Danica receives her power from the stars. At night, she absorbs energy from them and during the day she uses the energy. She can basically use the energy as a kind of 'light beam.' It burns worse than fire. And I know that you know what fire burns like."

I winced. Fire hurt a lot. I couldn't imagine what Danica's would be like.

"Anyway, she killed the Element fairies, all seven of them. We are eternally grateful to her," Stellan finished.

"I just hope no more come. I used up all of my energy, and now I am recharging. I wouldn't be able to take another seven so quickly. Killing fairies is not easy. They are tough little creatures," Danica informed me.

"Thank you for saving them, and then coming for me," I said quietly.

"You're welcome, but you should really be thanking Addison. She was the one who sent me the message. She was lucky Gavin and I were in the area on a patrol. As I said before, we are a part of the Queen's guard. She handpicked twenty elves she thought were good enough to protect her and be her closest confidants. We go on patrols, attend to her, run errands, or anything else that requires our help. We are like special servants, with powerful abilities and high ranks."

"You must feel special, being picked by the Queen," I commented.

"I do," Danica said, sighing. "Now, no more talking, Ramsey, just listen."

I nodded.

"Danica and Gavin helped us, and then I came back to you," Stellan said, continuing with his story. "Gavin flew, and I took trips taking Addison and Danica. We found you lying against the tree with your eyes closed and the Mood Diamond glowing around your neck. We knew right away that you had connected with Zora, though we didn't know how. Addison still has your first diamond. We watched as the burns and cuts appeared on your body. It was horrible." Stellan shook his head, as if trying to chase away the memories. "You were gone for a little over an hour."

"The air fairy gave me the Mood Diamond," I told him, disliking the look on his face as he described how hard it was to see me getting hurt. "And it wasn't an hour to me," I added.

"Traveling to and from the connection took more time than you realized," Stellan told me. "Queen Taryn is waiting to speak with you about it. This recent activity changes things. She is going to put more faith in us because of you. Even though what you did was reckless, we are thankful. The Queen trusts that you can find Zora because of your strong connection. Also, you have seen where she is being held more than once. She is confident you will come through."

"Five nights," I choked out.

"What?"

I cleared my throat. "We have five nights until they kill her. She did some weird thing where she swore that she would tell my secret in five nights."

"She swore an oath. If an elf swears on something, they can't break the promise. We are an honest kind. Right now, that is a bad thing."

"Yeah, thanks for telling me," I groaned.

Stellan sighed. "When you are healed, we will decide what to do," he assured me. "Try not to worry so much now. Focus on staying awake…and…"

"Alive?" I guessed.

Stellan shook his head. "I was going to tell you not to worry about anything else…but do that too," he said.

I nodded, and a slight smile stretched across my face.

"Will you go on trial?" I asked then, my smile disappearing.

"So far, it is only a maybe. The Queen has decided that what we did was right, but she must be completely sure before she can clear our names. If you can save Zora, we will be free. If not, she will have a lot of thinking and deciding to do. I'm hoping she won't have to."

"Me too," I told him.

He squeezed my hand gently.

"No more talking now. Obviously she cannot listen to orders," Danica demanded. "She will have to stay awake on her own."

Stellan and I both nodded. It was easier to stay awake now. The pain was still bad, but talking to Stellan had cleared my mind of some of my confusion. That helped. There was also hope that Stellan and Addison would not go to prison. That helped as well.

They carried me for another hour. I could tell all three were exhausted. I tried to keep my mind preoccupied with something other than Zora and my guilt, but it was very difficult. No thoughts were strong enough to keep me focused. Then I realized only one thought could.

The Stranger, I thought to myself. Would I ever see him again? Would I ever know his name? Would I ever act like a normal elfen in front of him or just a clumsy human-adjusted elfen? More importantly, what was the Stranger's significance to me?

I thought about it and decided I didn't know. It wasn't something I could explain. The Stranger was just there. But why did he have the power to hold all of my attention? *How* did he have that power?

Again, I didn't know, but the only thing I was sure of was that he *was* important for some reason unknown to me: simply significant.

I was jarred from my thoughts by a prodding in my shoulder. I opened my eyes to see Stellan staring at me.

"What?" I asked. I was somewhat annoyed. I had finally found something to think about and he ruined it.

"You were sleeping," he said.

"No," I told him, "I was just thinking. I was thinking a thought that you just interrupted."

"Sorry," he said, frowning and brushing the hair out of my face.

I sighed and closed my eyes again. I couldn't seem to return my thoughts to the Stranger, so I chose to keep my eyes shut tightly and wait.

***

"She's getting worse," I heard Danica say.

I had been slowly drifting off ever since Stellan disrupted my thoughts about the Stranger. Now I became fully awake once more.

"What do you mean?" Stellan asked.

I didn't say anything. I knew I wasn't allowed to talk.

"She's drifting," Danica pointed out. "And who knows what kind of pain she could be in right now…."

"Why don't we ask her ourselves?" Stellan proposed.

Danica rolled her eyes and looked down at me.

"Ramsey, you are still not allowed to talk, but do me a favor and blink once if you are feeling a lot of pain, twice if you are feeling better than before."

I found that I had to blink once. While I was drifting, I hadn't noticed the pain, but now it was back, and in full force.

"See?" Danica said to Stellan.

"Is there anything else?" Stellan asked me, ignoring Danica's comment.

"Wet. I feel wet," I told them quite out of the blue.

I hadn't noticed the feeling until now. I hadn't noticed a lot of things until now. Danica put her hand on my stomach, and then on each of my sides.

"Oh no," she said.

"What?" Stellan and I asked at the same time.

"She's bleeding…a lot," Danica said, peering intently at my abdomen. She cursed. "I can't believe no one noticed…."

The news was big enough to stop Addison in the middle of communicating with the Queen. Her eyes flew open and she peered down at me, concern clouding her green eyes.

"Will she be okay until we reach Tarlore?" Addison asked. She had barely spoken since I had awakened from the connection.

"I don't know," Danica replied, shaking her head. "It's hard to tell. There is a lot of blood, and a deep cut wound on her stomach that I hadn't noticed earlier. She's becoming paler by the minute."

I wondered just exactly how pale I was. From what I remembered, I was pale enough already. How could I get any worse?

"What can we do?" Stellan asked. His voice was cracking with every word.

I felt tears sting my eyes. We were all scared for my life.

"I…," Danica trailed off. "Wait, I've got it."

"What?" Addison demanded.

"The tree nymphs," Danica whispered.

"What about them? They aren't on our side," Stellan reminded her.

"Not all of them. But some are," Danica explained.

"How do you know?" Addison asked.

"A few live in the forest you traveled through, right before Tarlore. Just a few, but they are allied with the elves," Danica said.

"Why?" Addison repeated.

"They want to protect Elvina, the fairy child who started the war. They don't want the Element fairies to take her to their Realm. They believe either she belongs in the Woodland Fairy Realm, or she belongs here; and since she's not going to the Woodland Fairy Realm any time soon, they choose to watch over her in this Realm. They provide us with any news they hear that might be useful to Queen Taryn, and they watch over Elvina whenever she is out of range of the palace," Danica revealed.

"Can you call them?" Stellan asked.

She nodded. "Yes, but we are far away from the forest. It may take a while."

"We don't have much time," Addison reminded her.

"I know," Danica replied. She looked down at me gravely, her words sending a chill through my battered body. "But we have to try."

~13~

Tarlore

"How do you call them?" I asked, knowing I wasn't supposed to be talking but doing so anyway.

"All guards to the Queen have small flutes they carry with them in case they need to call a nymph or two," Danica told me. "If I play the three notes right, the nymphs will hear it no matter how far away they are. But it may take a few moments for them to arrive…or more. I don't know for sure. I have never needed to call them from this far away."

I nodded. "Okay. Proceed with the calling," I suggested.

"Right," Danica said.

From her belt, she produced a brown pouch. Out of that pouch, she withdrew a small flute, just as she had described. It was shiny and smaller than any flute I had ever seen before, even smaller than a piccolo. It looked more like a whistle with holes on top. She put the flute to her lips and blew into the mouthpiece three times, each time covering a different little hole. The sound was beautiful, pure, and surprisingly quiet, but I trusted that Danica knew what she was doing.

"Now what do we do?" Stellan asked.

"We wait," Danica replied.

He nodded. I noticed they were no longer moving, just standing in place as they held me. I guessed it was so the nymphs could find us sooner.

I felt myself slipping faster. I tried to get a grip on consciousness, but it was extremely difficult. I just wanted to sleep.

"I hate waiting," I said.

No one replied, but they *did* shush me, so I didn't say anything else.

Finally, I heard a rustling nearby. Praying it was the nymphs, I turned my head slightly to the left to see what was coming. Sure enough, two figures were walking – no, floating – toward me in a delicate fashion. When they came closer, I could see they were both female, and lovely. Both wore brown dresses, with tree vines and flowers draped over their shoulders and around their necks. Their feet were bare and their hair long and flowing, laced with flower petals and leaves.

Though I could see them clearly, they also looked almost transparent, like vibrant shadows. After all, nymphs were the essence of spirit. From what I knew, they were like dryads, but they did not embody one tree. Instead, they were spiritual protectors of the forest. They protected nature, making it grow, and dedicating themselves to living among the wildlife.

The nymphs finally reached us, and I felt a surge of anxiety rush through me. I could tell Danica was eager for their help as well. Her eyes darted from the nymphs to where I lay bleeding on the stretcher, as if assessing each and every possible move before taking action. Gently, she and Stellan lowered the stretcher to the ground. Then she walked forward to meet the newcomers.

"Welcome. And thank you for coming," she greeted them.

One nymph, with dark hair and even darker eyes, nodded slowly. "We came as soon as we heard your call," she said. "What is it you need?"

"Protection," Danica replied.

"What kind of protection?" the other nymph, one with pale hair and light brown eyes, asked.

"Protection from death," Danica told them quietly.

Though I had known what she would say, Danica's words still sent shivers down my spine.

"I see," said the dark-haired nymph. "Who is it that desires protection?"

Danica pointed down at me. "Her name is Ramsey, and she is badly injured. We have a healer waiting for her at the palace, but we are afraid we won't make it in time."

"It's *her*," the fair-haired nymph said, almost in a whisper, the corners of her lips pulling up into a sweet smile.

"What are you talking about?" Addison asked.

"The one, the Chosen Daughter," the other explained. "She is the one who holds the future in her palms."

"What do you mean?" I asked, wondering if it had something to do with telling the future, because of her mention of "palms." I also couldn't help giggling a little at her words. Was it just me, or were mystical creatures really into cheesy movie lines? Had a few movie writers visited a Magical Realm or two in the last fifty or so years?

"Hush," the fair one said, caressing my cheek with her soft hand. "Save your strength."

Her companion nodded and looked back up at Danica. "We will help you," she said.

Danica, apparently just as confused as I was, nodded in return. "Thank you," she said.

"What exactly are you going to do to save her?" Stellan asked.

"We will give her one of our charms. It is an eternal life charm, one that all nymphs have to preserve their spirits. It keeps us bound to nature, so we do not move on to…well, Heaven. Nymphs are the spirits of fairies and dryads, you see," the blonde explained.

"Wow, I never knew that," I admitted. "But I always wondered how nymphs were able to stay connected to the forest even though they didn't embody trees like dryads."

"Our charms are what keep us here," she said, her words directed mostly toward Danica. "For now, it will keep her alive. But the charm should not be used long-term. Not unless you want her to turn into a nymph," the dark-haired beauty warned, giggling faintly.

"Thanks for the warning," I told them.

The two nymphs smiled at me warmly. Then the dark-haired nymph removed one necklace of flowers that looked to be a combination of Aloe Vera and some type of lily. As she placed it over my head, she told me, "The Aloe Vera is to keep you alive physically, and the Blue Water Lily will keep your emotions intact, keeping you alive spiritually. The combination of the two will preserve your life until you reach your healer."

I nodded, taking in the soothing scent. I didn't feel completely healthy, but more like time had stopped. My injuries were frozen in place, put on hold. And that was enough for now.

"Will you be okay without your charm?" I asked.

"I will need it back soon, but I will be all right as long as I stay near my sister nymph. Have another guard bring it back when you are finished with it," she advised.

Danica nodded, and then we all thanked the nymphs for their help. Before they could leave, I had to ask them one last thing.

"What did you mean when you called me the Chosen Daughter?" I asked.

The nymphs looked at each other and smiled. Then they turned their heads to face me again.

"We are not the ones to answer that, Ramsey," the dark-haired nymph explained.

"Then who is?" I asked desperately.

Instead of answering, they each blew me a kiss, smiled, and faded away into the wind, their spirits one with the breeze.

I was left dumbfounded, and more exhausted than before. Why hadn't they answered my question? And how would I ever know the answer?

Baffled and worn out, I decided that closing my eyes wouldn't be so bad…now that I was preserved for the time being.

***

Okay, so closing my eyes and waiting may not have been the best idea, because when I woke up I was dizzy and confused. It took awhile for me to remember what was happening. I *had* slept a long time, much longer than I realized.

"Ramsey, you can wake up now. We are entering Tarlore," Danica told me.

My eyes flew open. I tried to sit up, but Stellan stopped me and gently pushed me back onto the cot.

"You can see the city sights another time," he said through gritted teeth.

"Fine," I grumbled.

Luckily for me, I could still see even when lying down. It was evening, so everything was dark. But the city was filled with lanterns, illuminating the areas we traveled through. Tarlore appeared to me like a city of fireflies.

I could see elves running in all directions, eyes peering intently at our group, obviously trying to catch a glimpse of me. I understood why. Being carried in on a cot with one of the Queen's guards must have looked strange to anyone watching.

"We will be at the palace in less than twenty minutes," Danica informed me.

I nodded and kept my eyes on the city. Even in the dark, I could see how medieval it was. The houses were much more rustic than those in Birchwood City, and the people dressed in simple clothing. I could hardly distinguish elf from elfen. They each wore the same kind of clothing: trousers and peasant shirts. It was strange, yet fascinating at the same time. I looked closely at Danica and realized that she was dressed almost exactly like Robin Hood. I would have laughed, if I were not in such a dizzying haze.

She wore a long green tunic and tight brown pants tucked into green knee-high boots. A brown rope belt holding a small dagger circled her waist. The only thing missing was the green hat and red feather! The outfit suited her well, however, and she appeared more like a fierce beauty than a Robin Hood.

I looked down at my own clothes. Twigs clung to my shirt and pants, but my boots were in good shape. The clothing was dirty and ragged, probably from lying on the ground against the tree. My sleeves were pulled up to reveal several burns and cuts. I clenched my teeth at the sight. I looked, and felt, horrible. What had made me do something so irresponsible? I didn't really think about my answer, because I already knew what it was.

Zora had.

A great deal of cacophony caught my attention to the left of our little procession. My eyes settled on a large tavern not too far away, where it appeared as though two elves were arguing. One, an exquisite elfen beauty with dark hair, was laughing and hiccupping. The other, a sour-looking elf dressed in the same way as Danica, was lecturing her loudly. The elfen didn't seem to mind his anger, however, because she did a little curtsy and continued laughing.

Then the elf pointed at us, whispering a few words that I couldn't make out. Finally, the elfen listened to him, following the direction of his outstretched arm until her eyes rested on me. Her unblinking gaze unnerved me, although it didn't appear harsh or angry. She curtsied in my direction, looked back to the elf, and gestured ahead of her. Taking the hint that she was finally ready to listen to his instructions, he led her away from the tavern. I couldn't tell where they were going; the darkness swallowed their forms shortly after they began walking.

I didn't think anyone else noticed the strange display, except for maybe Danica, because her voice was stern and disapproving as she said, "The palace is just ahead."

But she hadn't needed to tell me. I saw it for myself. The palace was magnificent. It was lit even brighter than the city, and shaped like a square with a slanted roof to form a smaller square at the top. The top was flat and I could see lights there as well – torches with bright orange flames that flickered in the night breeze. I wondered if elves went up there at any time. On each of the four corners was a large cylindrical tower. Three of its roofs were cone-shaped, but the front left tower was flattened at the top. It reminded me of a look-out tower. The palace was just like a castle, as Stellan had described.

Color-wise, the castle was a pale gray. I always thought gray was a boring color, but it suited the castle magnificently. The roofs were gray but looked almost black. I strained my eyes to observe more. Flowers and greenery surrounded the structure, making it appear more lively and colorful. I didn't need to ask her first – I had already noted Addison's favorite part of the palace.

I heard rushing water and realized I was being carried over a bridge. It wasn't the usual draw bridge. Instead, it was built into the ground and curved up and over the water. No moat surrounded the structure. A series of streams and small ponds ran in zigzags around the palace. I saw the lights reflected off the water, and they danced in tune to the ripples. It truly was a magical place.

I looked to the front to see two elves walking toward us. We slowed down a little so they could catch up to us before we got too close to the palace, and stopped at the middle of the bridge.

"Welcome back, Danica," a handsome elf greeted. He was wearing the same guard clothes as she, but they were more masculine like the elf at the tavern.

"Thank you, Thane. Let me introduce you to some *friends*. This is Stellan, Addison, and…," she looked down at me, "this is Ramsey."

"I'm pleased to meet you all. I would formally greet you, but I see you have your hands full," Thane said.

Thane was dark-haired, with a sly look to him. He reminded me of a fox, but a very good-looking fox. His pale skin shone in the moonlight, his green eyes were so dark they were almost black, taking in the sights before him. Elves were always so breathtaking.

"It's quite all right," Stellan replied.

Addison hadn't uttered a word for some time. I could tell she was still communicating with the Queen.

"Friends, this is Gabriel. We are both members of the Queen's guard," Thane explained, gesturing to the elf standing next to him.

Gabriel was a different story. He had a gentler look to him, but he also seemed focused, concentrated, as if he were carefully processing things at every moment, being sure not to leave anything out.

Stellan and Addison nodded to him. I weakly lifted my hand.

"Nice to meet the both of you," I said.

Strangely, Gabriel took both of my hands and gave them a slight squeeze. When he released, I retracted them slowly. Then Thane did the same. I remembered Aaliyah and Ashlyn making the same gestures. I still didn't understand why, and I always forgot to ask. I started to speak, but then I remembered my condition, and refrained. I didn't want Danica yelling at me for uttering unnecessary questions.

"Follow us. We will take you to Galen, our most gifted healer," Thane told us.

I was carried across the streams and ponds, and soon we were in front of a large stone door. Thane and Gabriel opened it and motioned for us to go first. Inside the palace, I gasped in awe. It was glorious; a sight right out of an enchanting fairytale.

The interior was decorated in a Victorian style, with the signature green, brown, and tan elf colors. The floor was stone and covered mostly by a green rug that reminded me of the Hollywood red carpet. Glorious, shining chandeliers hung from the ceiling in many places, and portraits of elves hung on the walls. I almost forgot my situation as I admired the beauty of the palace. I was lost in the wonder of it all. Even Stellan and Addison seemed mesmerized.

"Galen's quarters are just down this hall," Thane told us.

"Good, because she won't be conscious much longer," Danica explained. "The Nymph's charm has been around her neck for too long." Gently, she removed the charm. "This will make her vulnerable."

This was news to me. I thought I was better off than before because of the charm. Then I remembered that the charm only preserved me; it didn't make me stronger. Now that the charm was gone, I realized I could feel myself slipping, losing the protection.

"Danica is right," I mumbled.

Stellan stiffened.

"I'll be okay," I assured him.

He relaxed, but his face still shone with concern. We finally reached the healer's quarters a few moments later. I could immediately feel the calming aura that filled the room. Candles provided light, and the scent of herbs wafted around my nose. I felt oddly safe here, even though I didn't know this place. I realized how different this environment was from human doctors' offices. I had never felt this comfortable with my pediatrician. The bright white rooms and smell of disinfectant never comforted me like this particular atmosphere.

An elf, who I assumed was Galen, came out from behind a silky brown curtain. He was barefoot and wore knee-length tan pants and a forest green shirt. He was pale-haired and had large, friendly green eyes. He appeared to be very welcoming and seemed...*warm*. He also gave off the impression that he was ready to work, focused and alert. I liked that. The perfect balance, like a healer *should* be.

Danica pulled back her black hair and looked at me with her almond-shaped, olive green eyes.

"You are in good hands now. I hope to see you again soon so we can have a chance to talk about things other than you staying awake." She smiled.

I was surprised by her sudden warmth. She hadn't struck me as the friendly type, but I guess I was wrong. Though she had a tough exterior, she had feelings inside as well. She reminded me of Addison.

"I'd like that, Danica. Thank you," I told her.

She nodded and left the room. Gabriel quickly followed.

"I'll be right outside," Thane informed us.

I inferred that he was probably our guard, here to make sure we didn't do anything troublesome or out of line in the Queen's palace.

Trying not to be offended by his presence, I turned my attention to Galen, who was now standing before me.

"Hello, Ramsey," he greeted. "My name is Galen, and I am the Queen's chief healer."

Galen held out his hands. It was another one of those weird handshakes. I put my hands in his, and he squeezed them lightly. Though I was getting used to the action, it was still foreign and unfamiliar to me.

"Thank you for seeing to me," I said, instead of questioning him.

"I would heal any elf in need, especially you," he revealed.

"Why is that?" I asked.

"The Element fairies are not the only ones interested in your secret," he said, smiling. "I have a bed prepared for you. You there, Elf, help me get her onto the bed, please," he asked Stellan.

"My name is Stellan," he told Galen. He held out his hands and they shared the same handshake.

"Help me to move her please, Stellan," he asked.

Stellan nodded, and they both lifted me as gently as they could, although any kind of movement still hurt, no matter how gentle. When I was comfortably on the bed, Galen went over to a table and started mixing something in a small bowl. Stellan sat on a chair next to me. Addison, who had still not said anything, was rubbing her temples by the door.

"Addison, you can leave if you wish. I know all of the communicating has made you tired. See the Queen and then get some rest," Stellan advised.

Addison nodded and walked over toward the bed. She took my hand.

"Get better, all right? And stop worrying me so much."

She smiled, and I half-smiled. I couldn't fully smile because it hurt too much. I could feel the pain increasing the longer I remained unhealed."I'll do my best. I promise," I told her.

Without another word, she left the room. I hoped she would get the rest she needed. Everyone needed to relax after our journey.

"I'm going to start you off with some herbs that will soothe you. They will prepare you for my healing. It can be somewhat uncomfortable at times," he told me. "Especially with *your* injuries."

He handed me a warm cup. It smelled like tea, but tasted very bitter. Even so, I drank all of it, listening to the healer's instructions. The bitter herbs left me feeling warm, but with a bad aftertaste in my mouth.

"Now I will do the actual healing. Stellan, could you leave the room for a moment? She needs to change into clothes that will expose her stomach and arms."

Stellan nodded and walked out. I didn't want him to leave, too afraid he wouldn't return. Telling myself I was behaving foolishly, I focused on the task at hand. I was feeling this way because of the connection; both episodes had left me shaking and needy.

Galen helped me remove my top and change into a short, strapless tan shirt that reminded me kind of like a swimsuit top. He left me for a moment, and I was glad to see him return with Stellan.

He took a seat on the chair once again, and Galen returned to my side.

"Why does my stomach have to be exposed?" I asked.

"You have a gash there, caused by a burn that has opened."

I nodded, remembering. "That was the reason I needed the charm," I told him.

"Yes, that's right. I almost forgot about that," he said. "It was wise of Danica to remove it, because the charm would have interfered with the healing process. Now remember, this healing may feel a bit uncomfortable."

"Okay," I replied.

He placed his warm hands onto my abdomen and closed his eyes. I heard him inhale deeply and then exhale. I could feel myself becoming hotter by the second. Then I felt a part-burning and part-tickling feeling. It wasn't terrible, but Galen had rightly predicted my discomfort. He remained in this position for about two minutes. Then he lifted his hands a few inches, and I saw that they were glowing with a soft green light. Soon, the burning and tickling faded. I looked to see a thin line in place of the gash.

"The scar will be completely gone in a day or two. Now I'll heal the other burns and scratches. They will take only a few seconds," he said.

He was right on the mark. The pain was completely gone in under fifteen seconds, and the only lingering scar was the one on my side that would fade soon. I sighed with relief. And the healing hadn't even been that bad.

"Thank you," I said.

"You're welcome."

"Does healing tire you out?" I asked curiously.

"It did when I first started practicing, but now it's simple. I become weak only when I have to heal elves who are close to death."

"That would be Zora," I told him.

Galen and Stellan both nodded without saying anything in reply.

Then Galen broke the silence. "It's time you got some sleep. Stellan and Thane can help you to a room. Come back if you feel any other pain."

"I will. Thanks again," I told him.

Galen nodded and then walked back behind the curtain.

Thane came back into the room. He and Stellan wanted to put me back on the cot, but I refused. I could walk now that I was healed. I was still weak but could stand on my own two feet. They finally agreed, but refused to let me walk by myself. With an elf on each side holding an arm, I slowly walked down the hall and up a flight of stairs.

"The palace has four floors," Thane explained on the way. "The first floor houses the guards, cooks, healers, and other personnel. The second floor is the ballroom, dining hall, library, kitchen, and parlor. The third floor holds all of the guest rooms. The Queen enjoys having company for extended periods of time. She will also allow the guards to have family and friends visit once or twice a year."

"That's very kind of her," I commented.

"She is a wonderful leader. You will like her, I'm sure. The fourth and last floor houses the quarters of the Queen, her daughter, her sister, and her sister's...well, *child*." He said "child" very delicately, and I could tell the subject of the Woodland fairy was a sore one for him.

"You mean Elvina?" I guessed.

"Yes," he said softly.

I wanted to change the subject and stray away from anything to do with the war.

"I didn't know Queen Taryn had a daughter," I mentioned.

"Yes, she was born shortly after King Lore died. Princess Brielle just turned sixteen a few weeks ago. She will be attending the ability school next fall," Thane said, sounding very proud of his princess.

"She's close to my age," I remarked.

"Is she really? Well, I'm sure you will meet her sometime soon. She is quite a handful."

"What do you mean?" I asked, as I was helped up another flight of stairs.

"She finds it difficult to warm up to elves. She is very isolated and doesn't always relate well to others," he explained, "*at least in the palace, that is....*"

"Interesting," I commented, wondering what he had meant by his last statement.

We stopped in front of a pretty wooden door down the hall. Flowers were carved into the wood, which looked recently polished.

"Here is your room, Ramsey. Your friend Addison's is to your left, and Stellan will be to your right."

They walked me inside. I sat down on a lavish purple bed. It was the first color I had seen other than shades of green or brown. The walls were lavender and the rug was a deep violet. The room had a wooden dresser, and I could see a bathroom through an open door. It was quaint and beautiful and reminded me of a five star hotel room, not that I had ever been in one....

"Each room has a different color scheme. Queen Taryn likes her guests to experience more than the traditional elf colors during their stay," Thane told me.

"I'm beginning to like the Queen more and more," I whispered, to no one in particular.

"Speaking of which, I have to see to the Queen now. Try to get some rest. Danica will be here to take you to Queen Taryn at five tomorrow morning," Thane said.

"All right. Thank you, Thane."

"Yes, thank you," Stellan agreed.

"You're welcome and goodnight," he said. Then he left the room and closed the door softly behind him.

"Nice place, huh?" Stellan asked.

"Nice place? That is a *huge* understatement, Stellan."

"Yes, you're right." He took my hands in his and kissed me tenderly. "Get some sleep, all right?"

"I will! How many times do I have to promise that?" I asked with a laugh.

"That's the last time, I promise."

Stellan smiled and then turned to leave.

"Goodnight!" I called as he shut the door behind him.

For the first time since waking from the connection, I was alone. It didn't feel right. The room felt suddenly empty. Fortunately though, I knew I was safe here. It was strange being alone after the hectic events of the night. However, a positive attitude would keep my spirits up. I was healed, and tomorrow we would meet with the Queen and finally start searching for my sister.

Feeling weak and very tired, I pulled back the purple covers and slipped into bed. I fell asleep thinking of the palace, and my dreams were filled with beauty.

It wasn't until Finn's menacing face appeared that I bolted upright, gasping for breath.

~14~

The Elfen Queen

After the nightmare of Finn's haunting face, my sleep was much better. I woke up at four the next morning feeling slightly weak, but rested. Getting out of bed, I made my way across the room, moving slowly because I was still sore from my injuries. As I opened the soft lavender window curtains, I could see the sun rising, taking its rightful place in the cloudless blue sky. I looked down at the capital before me and smiled. It was even more glorious in the morning light. I couldn't wait for the chance to explore, if I ever had the chance. I didn't know how busy I would be in the coming days.

I turned and noticed my shoulder bag hanging from the bathroom door. It was a little dirty but still in good shape. I was pleased to see it, and until now I had wondered if I lost it when I was taken to Tarlore. Someone must have dropped it off in my room.

After making sure everything was still inside the bag, I went into the bathroom. I was grateful that the palace had plumbing. It was probably the only modern thing I would find here. After taking a long, hot, and much-needed shower, I dressed in my navy blue summer dress and towel-dried my hair.

Once I was dressed and ready to go, I spent the remainder of the hour inspecting the room and looking out the window at the beautiful city. I found myself lost in the wonder of Tarlore, even though I was watching from a distance. It was strange to admit how great it felt to be here, like I was on vacation. That feeling quickly left me when I remembered what I was here to accomplish.

Find Zora.

A knock at the door brought me out of my thoughts. Sighing, I got up to open it.

"Good morning, Ramsey," Danica greeted.

"Good morning," I replied.

"I am to take you to the dining hall, where you will have breakfast with your friends. Then I will lead you to the parlor to meet Queen Taryn."

"That sounds great," I said. "Lead the way."

I followed Danica down the hall and down one flight of stairs. She led me into a huge room with a long wooden table, with a dozen chairs on each side and one chair at the end. The single chair was more ornate than the others, and I guessed it was for Queen Taryn when she dined here. Stellan and Addison were already seated and waving me over. I bid farewell to Danica, who had already eaten, and took my place next to Stellan. Addison was seated across from me.

"How are you feeling?" he asked.

"Much better," I replied. "A little sore, but healed."

"Good. I'm glad you're okay," he said, lacing his fingers through mine.

"Me too," I replied after taking a sip of juice. "How are you feeling, Addison?"

"I'm rested, but last night wasn't easy," she said. "It's been a long time since I've had to use my ability for such an extended period of time."

"Last night wasn't easy for any of us," Stellan pointed out.

"You're right," I agreed.

We sat in silence for a few moments.

"So how do you like your room?" Addison asked.

"It's so cool! All the purple reminds me of royalty." I smiled, remembering the lovely room. "What color is yours, Addison?"

"Pink. It reminds me of the flowers from home," she replied. She smiled and popped a raspberry into her mouth.

I turned to Stellan. "What about yours?"

"Red. It's nice and manly," he said, flexing his arms.

The three of us laughed, the mood finally lightening up a bit, and then turned our attention to eating. We had until six before we met with Queen Taryn. It was long enough for us to finish eating and continue discussing the wonders of the palace. Danica returned right on schedule to fetch us.

It was time for me to finally meet the Queen.

***

The parlor was only a few steps away from the dining hall, so it wasn't a very long walk. I tried to prepare myself for the meeting by breathing in and out slowly, clearing my head. I didn't think it helped. I was still nervous. I hoped Queen Taryn would like me. She needed to like me for Stellan and Addison's sake. Most importantly, she needed to like me for Zora's sake.

Danica knocked briskly at the door. It was opened by an elfen with chin-length black hair and pale moss-green eyes. She wore an outfit similar to Danica's, but she didn't look as feminine. Instead, she looked nimble and almost birdlike. Elves had such unique forms of beauty.

"Aditi," Danica addressed.

"Danica," the elfen replied. "Come in, please."

We followed Danica into the room, which was cozy and inviting, but also very elegant. A fire in a stone wall fireplace warmed the parlor. The floors were a deep, solid mahogany. Artwork covered the walls, portraying the magic and beauty of the Realm.

Settled upon one of the many seats and couches was an elfen wearing a long green gown that shimmered from the lighted chandelier above her. She had beautiful black hair pinned up in a fancy bun, and wore a solid gold crown with green swirls. Her pale face was long and serious; confidence and power radiated from her being. She sat on the couch with her hands clasped on her lap. Already, I was feeling intimidated by the Queen's presence.

Next to her sat another elfen with long black hair reaching almost to her waist. What struck me most about her were the two strands of pale blonde hair that hung loosely down both sides of her face. Until now, I hadn't met any elves with two different hair colors.

Her gown was similar to the Queen's, only in a different shade of green. The fabric was darker, but shimmered in the same way.

She wore a golden tiara with a large emerald at the center. A gold chain necklace with a pendant of deeply colored jewels adorned her neck. I had never seen such an elaborate collection of jewels in one necklace.

The young elfen appeared much more relaxed than Queen Taryn, but the resemblance between them was striking. I knew I was standing not only before the Queen of the Elf Realm, but also the Princess.

Aditi addressed the Queen and her daughter with admiration in her voice: "May I present to you, Queen Taryn of Tarlore and her daughter, Princess Brielle."

Danica stepped forward toward the Queen. "Queen Taryn: Ramsey of Birchwood City and formerly of the Human Realm. With her are the siblings Stellan and Addison of Birchwood City." Danica nodded once and then retreated to stand with Aditi and another elfen at the door.

The elfen with Aditi looked about the same as she did. She had cropped black hair that accentuated her small face. She looked just as birdlike, but slightly smaller.

"Aditi, Wren, leave us. Danica, you may remain. I will need a word with you shortly," Queen Taryn said, her voice filled with authority and grace.

The two elfen guards left quickly. No one said anything until the door had shut. Queen Taryn rose from her seated position and walked over to us. Her daughter followed in step behind her.

Princess Brielle seemed antsy, as though she were trapped in a cage, wanting to break free. Her eyes darted to and fro, especially at the door. I guessed living in a palace must be difficult for her, because she probably wasn't able to roam the city as she pleased, at least not without guards at her side.

"It's lovely to finally meet you," Queen Taryn said, reaching out her long arms to greet me.

"Thank you for the privilege of meeting you, Queen Taryn," I said.

I put my hands in hers and we repeated the same gesture I had observed frequently here.

She released my hands and then Addison and Stellan exchanged the same greeting. Princess Brielle stepped forward. She held out her hands and I gave her mine.

"It's a pleasure," she said coolly.

Our eyes met, and I had to resist the urge to gasp. Standing before me was the elfen I witnessed drunkenly misbehaving last night outside the tavern. I recognized the intense look in her eyes. I was so shocked that I barely regained my bearings in time to respond.

"It's a pleasure to meet you as well, Princess Brielle," I said, stammering slightly.

She must have realized that I remembered her inappropriate display, because she winked at me, quick enough for no one else in the room to notice. Then she turned her back to me and sat down without even a glance at Stellan or Addison. Suddenly, meeting the Princess wasn't so much of a pleasure. After recognizing her from last night and hearing her cool tone, I wasn't feeling any pity for her now.

"Please sit down, all of you," Queen Taryn told us with a smile.

I went to the couch across from Queen Taryn and Princess Brielle. Stellan sat on my right and Addison at my left. Stellan's hand reached for mine as the Queen began to speak.

"We have many important things to discuss, so let's begin. First, Ramsey must tell us of the two connections she shared with Zora."

Princess Brielle's bright green eyes sparked with interest, and instead of keeping her eyes trained on the door, she now watched me with an unreadable gaze.

"Okay," I agreed nervously.

I took a deep breath and then I began. Even though it was painful, I recalled everything I could remember from both of the connections. I told them of Finn, Wynter, and Lura, and everything that had occurred during my time with Zora. I described how wounded Zora appeared to be, which was the worst part of it all.

Afterward, I learned from Queen Taryn that Finn was a very important fairy to the Element Fairy Realm: a general. He and his followers did the dirty work for King Vortigern, the King of the Element fairies. Female fairies were highly respected in the Realms, so it was far more usual to have fairy queens. King Vortigern was an exception; the only fairy king in the last hundred years at least. I found this to be both humorous and interesting. Fairies were *very* different from humans, who held men high on their pedestals.

While she spoke of the Element fairies with great pity – because up until Vortigern's reign, they were genuinely good-natured fae – she described Vortigern as soulless and cruel, horrible from the beginning of his rule. He was immortally alluring and hauntingly dangerous. Just the thought of being near him caused me to shiver with cold fear.

Even so, I was grateful to Queen Taryn for sharing so much information with me. I was finally beginning to see the big picture, the whole picture. Since my new home was a Magical Realm at war with another, immensely powerful Fairy Realm, I felt it necessary to have knowledge of my own Realm and my supposed enemy's, as well as a familiarity of my surroundings. The clouds of confusion that surrounded me began to lift.

"We must decide what to do about Zora," Queen Taryn said when we were finished chatting.

"Ramsey can find her, Queen Taryn. I know she can," Addison said.

Queen Taryn nodded. "Yes, I believe so as well. Ramsey, you share a very strong connection with your sister. Do you know where she is?" she asked.

"I'm afraid not, your highness. All I know is that she is in an old room with wooden walls," I admitted, which didn't really help our cause.

"We can assume she is in the Element Fairy Realm. Finn would want to keep her there to make it difficult for her to be rescued," Queen Taryn suggested.

"Are you sure? Wouldn't he expect us to know that?" Princess Brielle asked, making a valid point.

"Well, she isn't here, that's for sure," Stellan reminded. "Otherwise we would have found her already."

"Maybe she is in a different Realm, like the Woodland Fairy Realm?" Addison suggested.

"She could be. I tried to use my own power to detect where Zora was taken, but there are strong spells surrounding her. I have no way to get through them. I am guessing that Finn hired a string of Woodland fairies to do his spell work for him," Queen Taryn added.

I kept quiet for this portion of the conversation. I didn't know as much about fairies *or* their Realms. I left it to the others to decide.

"I will summon a small group of soldiers for a secret visit to the Element Fairy Realm, and then to the Woodland Fairy Realm, if necessary. They will be ready in two days time," Queen Taryn decided.

I wanted to scream out that it wasn't good enough. Zora would die in four nights! That meant two days of searching. It wouldn't be enough time. Nevertheless, I held my tongue. It wasn't my place to fight with the Queen. I could only pray that I was wrong.

"In the meantime, I will need Addison with me so I can send messages to summon the soldiers. Stellan, you are not to use your ability anywhere or at any time while you are here. You will be under the care of Thane, the guard whom you met last night." She saw the look of confusion on Stellan's face. "I know it seems harsh and an annoyance, but you and your sister are still suspects of disloyalty. I can't let any of you roam without supervision. Ramsey, I have a guard who will tend to you. You are to remain in the palace. Explore, look around, do whatever you see fit for yourself. But *do not* walk out of my palace doors."

I nodded. It could have been worse. She could have locked us up in a room until they called upon me to search for Zora. As far as I was concerned, she was being gracious to all three of us, especially to Addison, trusting her to assist with the summoning of the soldiers. "I will not leave, Queen Taryn."

"Good. Stellan, you are dismissed. Danica will take you to Thane," Queen Taryn said. "And then return to me, Danica," she added, "so I can have a word with you."

"Yes, Queen Taryn," Danica said.

Stellan and Danica left the room. I watched Stellan leave with a heavy sadness in my heart. I didn't want to be apart from him. However, I knew the Queen's word was law. I had to obey her wishes. If that meant keeping me from him, so be it. I didn't want to get into any kind of trouble here. I had to find my sister. That was the most important thing.

"Addison, please tell Ramsey's guard she may join us," Queen Taryn instructed.

Addison nodded and closed her eyes. After a few moments, she said, "The message has been sent. She'll be here shortly."

Three minutes later, there was a quick knock at the door.

"Come in," Queen Taryn invited.

The door opened and in came a dark-haired elfen with large green eyes. She stood very straight and her head was held high. Her hair was pulled back into a knot. She wore the palace guard attire. Her lips were in a tight, serious line. I could tell just by looking at her that she was strong, for an elfen at least. She sure was bodyguard material.

"Ramsey, this is Jacqueline. She is one of my most skilled guards. Her ability is to create walls at any time. She will protect and watch over you. You are both dismissed," Queen Taryn said, introducing us briefly.

I nodded, said thank you to the Queen and her daughter, waved goodbye to Addison, and followed Jacqueline out of the room. Outside, we exchanged the strange greeting.

"What would you like to do, Ramsey?" she asked.

"Why do elves do that two-handed shake?" I wondered aloud to her.

"I beg your pardon?"

"In the Human Realm, we shake only with one hand. Why is it different here?" I asked.

"Oh, I see," she said, pausing for a moment afterward to asses my question. "Elves touch both hands in greeting so they can discover each other's power," she explained.

"Why?" I asked.

"So there are no surprises. If you are formally meeting someone, you want to trust him or her. When elves join hands, they can identify each other's ability."

"How? I couldn't," I said, baffled.

"You learn the skill at ability school. Elves must have their power to know what another's is through the greeting. The same goes for elves who shake hands with others who do not have a power yet. I couldn't tell what your power is because you haven't received one."

"Then why do the gesture?" I wondered.

"It has become a common greeting for all elves, not just those with abilities," she said.

"Oh, well, thanks for explaining it to me. I was so confused, and every time I wanted to ask, it didn't seem like the appropriate moment. But I felt like an idiot not knowing exactly what it meant," I admitted.

"That's quite all right. Now you know. Do you have any other questions for me?" she wondered.

"So what *am* I allowed to do here?" I asked.

"Tour the palace," she replied.

"Lead the way then," I suggested, knowing it was my only option, considering I was basically under palace arrest.

Jacqueline nodded and started walking down the hall. I followed her quickly. It was hard to keep up with her. She walked very fast.

Our first stop was the library. It was the most impressive collection I had ever laid eyes on. The walls were completely covered with books, with four large round tables and a few couches crowding the room for reading and studying. Candles and a fireplace gave the room a bright glow, and the scent of books filled the room. The atmosphere was comforting, and reminded me of the many times I lost myself in the wonder of books.

After spending as long as I could in the library, Jacqueline told me we had to keep moving. The ballroom was next. It was a glorious room with a rich hardwood floor. Chairs to sit on between dances lined the walls and instruments sat on a stage at the back, consisting of a grand piano, a harp, and a few fiddles. Imagining the room filled with dancers and music made me wish I had come to the palace for a ball, instead of the real reason I was here.

Jacqueline also took me through the kitchen for a quick look. It wasn't fancy at all, a huge change from the rooms I had seen so far. Jacqueline explained that kitchens needn't be fancy, because only a few elves besides the cooks worked within its walls. I met the head cook, an elf whose power was the ability to move things with his mind. He said that it made retrieving ingredients and cooking multiple dishes incredibly simple. I agreed.

Afterward, we went to the first floor, where I was introduced to the guards who occupied the palace today. I saw Aditi and Wren, and finally understood why they looked so unusual compared to the other guards. Their ability was to shape-shift into birds. Aditi could be a hawk, and Wren could be a small falcon. Now I knew how Gavin had changed into a bird when I was being taken to the capital.

I learned that shape-shifters were a valuable part of the war. They could travel fast and attack from the sky as well as the ground. They explained that all shape-shifters were important in the war. However, Aditi, Wren, and Gavin had been chosen out of hundreds of shape-shifters to be part of the Queen's guard.

Thane was a shape-shifter as well, but he took the form of a fox, which explained his sly look. The only other shape-shifter was an elf with army-green eyes named Arnold, who we met as well. He took the shape of an eagle. I saw Gabriel again, and asked about his power. I had only seen him for a short amount of time the night before and hadn't had the chance to ask. Jacqueline told me he could see up to five miles away. He was chosen by the Queen to be her extra set of eyes.

I hadn't expected a tour of the palace to be so interesting, but after meeting with the guards and learning more about elfin abilities, I wasn't as disappointed with being unable to leave the castle. I lunched with Jacqueline in the dining hall around noon. Stellan joined me, and as we ate, I told him about the guards I had met. When I asked him what he had done all morning, he only shook his head. He was simply following Thane around as he did various jobs. I felt bad for his lack of adventure, but he told me not to worry. I didn't like the fact that all three of us were separated during our stay. With Stellan courting me and Addison practically a sister, they were the closest elves I had to family here.

After lunch, I reluctantly hugged him goodbye and went with Jacqueline once again, hoping Stellan would be able to do at least one interesting thing today. Together the elfen guard and I toured the entire palace except for the fourth floor. I was even shown the other guest rooms. My favorite, besides my own, was the blue room. It reminded me of the ocean. Jacqueline informed me that the blue and purple rooms were the favorites of the guests.

"What now?" I asked her once we were done.

Before she could respond, Gabriel approached us and tapped Jacqueline on the shoulder. He handed her a note and then departed without saying a word. Jacqueline opened the folded piece of parchment and her already large eyes widened.

"You are to go to the fourth floor to Lady Cora, Queen Taryn's sister. She wants to meet with you," Jacqueline whispered. She looked surprised, as if this was an odd request.

"Is that a good thing?"

"She never asks for visitors," she informed me grimly.

"Why? Doesn't she like visitors?"

"I'm afraid the visitors are the elves who don't enjoy her company very much. Not the other way around."

"Because of what she did with Elvina and how she started the war," I guessed.

"Yes. She rarely leaves the palace. Most of the elves in Tarlore are forgiving, but some are not so kind," she explained.

"It's terrible that she has to hide away like that."

"The *war* is terrible. Lady Cora has a great life compared to those who have lost theirs fighting for the mistakes she made," Jacqueline said angrily.

I could tell what Jacqueline's view on the war was now. I wasn't sure what my thoughts on the subject were as of yet, but I would probably have a better opinion after meeting with the Queen's sister myself.

I followed Jacqueline up the two flights of stairs and into a nicely furnished Victorian style room. It was all green, with hints of brown here and there. I could see two doors, one that led to a bathroom and another that might be a second bedroom. The main room was not only a bedroom but also a parlor, complete with couches, a table, and chairs. It reminded me of an apartment, a very *well off* apartment.

I followed Jacqueline over to a sitting area where Lady Cora herself greeted me. Her black hair was pinned up like Queen Taryn's, but not as fancy. She wore a simple brown dress with gold lace trim. Her attractive green eyes watched me intently. She stood up and I put my hands out to her. Now that I knew what to do, I didn't waste any time greeting her. She took my hands and then we parted.

"Thank you for coming, Ramsey," she said in a sweet voice. "As you probably have already assumed, I am Lady Cora."

"Thank you for asking me to meet with you. I hear you don't often have visitors," I said.

"Jacqueline, you are dismissed," Lady Cora said, as I sat down in a chair across from her. Once Jacqueline was gone, Lady Cora responded to my earlier statement. "No, I don't have visitors often. I don't invite visitors, either. For an elfen in my situation, visitors can be unpleasant."

"Then why did you summon me?" I asked her.

Lady Cora sighed. "Because I know you are different."

"How so?" I asked, wondering how she could possibly know anything about me without meeting me until now.

"You do not see things the way other elves do," she told me.

"That's because I have been here only for a short time," I reminded her.

"No, Ramsey, it isn't just that. You are who you are for other reasons," she said.

"Like my secret?" I guessed.

"Sure. That's one."

"What are the others?" I wondered.

"Living in the Human Realm has given you the chance to look at things differently. You view fairies as more than just evil; I know that."

"How?" I asked.

"It was merely a guess, because of your previous living situation. Am I correct?"

I looked down and then back at her. I couldn't find it in me to avoid the truth. "Yes, you are."

"You shouldn't be ashamed. You have the right to your own beliefs and opinions. Don't allow a needless war to destroy your images of the Realms." She paused. "Even so, you must think of me as a terrible elfen."

"Actually, I…I don't," I admitted.

Lady Cora smiled. "I'd hoped you would say that."

"How do you know so much about me?"

"The knowledge I have gained is written across your face," she explained.

"It is?" I asked, a little skeptical of her explanation.

She nodded. "Yes."

"I thought your power was making bubble shields," I remarked.

"I *learned* to read faces. It isn't a gift or a power," she explained. "It is not a difficult skill to master, once you learn to understand how emotions are displayed."

"I see," I said, wishing I had a cup of tea or a cookie to fill the awkward silence growing between us.

Before I could find a way to fill the silence, Lady Cora leaned closer to me, her green-eyed gaze locking onto mine. "I wanted you to come here so you could learn the other side of the story. I wanted you to know firsthand why I did what I did. That way, you can decide for yourself what to think. You are a special elfen, and you deserve to know as much as you can about your Realm and the Realms around you, especially because of your past *and* your secret. I want you to have all the facts. And I know if anyone could understand what I did, it would be you."

"Tell me then," I suggested, both intrigued and wary of what I might learn.

So she began her story.

~15~

Lady Cora's Story

"I had been very good friends with Elvina's parents for almost ten years when she was born. When elves and fairies socialized, I traveled often to the Woodland and Element Fairy Realms. I was treated like family. When Elvina was born, everyone was devastated over her mother's terrible death. Her father couldn't manage taking care of Elvina alone, and he was too heartbroken to be around the baby for a long time. When he asked me to live with them and help, I immediately said yes. Elvina's mother had been my best friend. It was the least I could do after she died. I also cared deeply for Elvina. She was a beautiful Woodland fairy baby, without one trace of her Element fairy father's nature. Not that I had anything against Element fairies at that time," Lady Cora assured me. "Caring for her was my life. I never thought of anything else. I even chose her name….My world revolved around her. I felt as if she were my own child and my own flesh and blood. I never loved someone so much."

I thought of my own parents, the ones I never knew. Had they loved me in the same way, even though they had abandoned me?

"We were never apart," Lady Cora continued. "Her father wasn't around that much because he was still grieving. When he did come around, we behaved like a family. Everything was perfect. Life was simple and wonderful. Then one day, everything in my life changed." Lady Cora stopped for a moment, collecting herself. Then she went on. "Elvina's father came to me and advised that I return to my own Realm. He had met someone new who would be his partner, and who would take care of Elvina. He thanked me for all I did and then told me to leave. I was not only heartbroken, but also confused. I had no idea what I would do with my life without Elvina. Like I said before, she *was* my life.

"I left, but I had to come back. Ramsey," she said, her features expressing nothing but honesty, "believe me, I never wanted to hurt anyone. However, I couldn't just leave her there. I couldn't live with myself knowing she was going to be part of a family that would never care for her as well as I had. I used my power to take her back to the Elf Realm. Things seemed fine until a week later. Then King Vortigern contacted my father and told him that the Element Fairy Realm wanted Elvina back. They wouldn't just allow a fairy child to be stolen. I begged my father to refuse. He knew how much I cared for her, so he agreed. The declaration of war came swiftly. The elfin people begged my father to reconsider, but he wouldn't. He was a very determined elf, never backing down from a challenge. Then he died....Queen Taryn wanted to end the war. But she was full of pride, and she cared for me and Elvina too greatly." Lady Cora wiped tears from her eyes.

I understood Lady Cora now. I could see the love she felt for Elvina in her eyes. She had done what she thought was best, not only for herself, but also for Elvina. She put her love for Elvina before anything else. She had true courage because she followed her convictions and made the only choice she thought possible. And she couldn't have predicted that a war would start as a result of her decision.

Hearing this, I knew I could not judge her for her actions.

"I'm deeply sorry I started this war. I wish I had thought of another way to stay with Elvina," Lady Cora explained. "It seemed like it was my only option at the time."

I nodded. "Where is Elvina's father now?"

"The last I heard, he was living a comfortable life with his new partner and their children."

"He doesn't want Elvina back, does he?" I guessed.

"No, he doesn't now that he has his own family. It's all about pride now, just pride. No love is involved," she said, with an edge of scorn to her voice.

I nodded slowly, then reached my hand out and placed it over Lady Cora's.

"I understand why you took Elvina," I told her. "And although it is very unfortunate and disturbing that this ridiculous war even started, I'm not angry with you. I...I admire you."

"Your support means a lot to me," she responded quietly.

We sat together quietly for a while, neither of us knowing what else to say. But Lady Cora's face brightened as the sound of an opening door broke the silence.

"Elvina is back from the city. I'm glad you will be able to meet her," Lady Cora remarked.

I turned my head, and my eyes widened as I watched the Woodland fairy enter the room. Her feet hovered just above the ground as she flew over to join us. I could see her iridescent wings fluttering as she neared us. Her long, shiny auburn hair was wavy and cascaded over her shoulders. She had pale skin and pointy ears, reminding me of the similarities between Woodland fairies and elves. Her warm brown eyes sparkled when she saw us.

"A visitor, I see," she commented, as she sat down beside Lady Cora.

"Elvina, this is Ramsey, the elfen I was telling you about."

"Oh, yes! I'm very sorry about your sister. I have prayed to Fae for her safe return every day since I heard she was taken."

"I heard about Fae back in Birchwood City. Do you pray to her like elves pray to God?" I asked.

"Oh, yes. If anyone can help you find your sister, it will be Fae."

"Why?" I asked.

"She can help because she loves all creatures, even elves. If you let her, she can guide you."

"But I'm not a fairy," I said.

Elvina smiled. "As long as you trust her, she will lead you."

I nodded, taking in her words. "Well, thanks. That's very thoughtful of you," I said.

"No need to thank me. It's the least I can do. This whole war is my fault anyway…," Elvina sighed, trailing off.

"Don't say such things, Elvina!" Lady Cora said, her voice raising an octave.

"If I hadn't been born, none of this would have happened, and you know it," Elvina pointed out.

"But Lady Cora is right, Elvina. This war isn't your fault. The way I see it, the war was a huge mistake from the beginning. The confusion on all sides cannot be solved with fighting, so the war continues only because everyone is too stubborn, proud, or afraid to make the necessary decisions to resolve the conflict. You can't blame yourself for that."

"I have never heard it expressed that way, Ramsey. How does one with limited knowledge of our history have so much insight?" Elvina asked.

"I don't know. It's just how I see it," I admitted.

"Thank you," Elvina said, immense gratitude filling those two little words.

The brilliance of her clear, sparkling wings took my breath away, sometimes hurting my eyes to look at them. I tried to avert my gaze, but I was drawn to their immense beauty. For a moment, I wished I could have them as well. I wondered how it felt to fly.

Straying away from touchy subjects like the war, Elvina told me about her life as a Woodland fairy in the Elf Realm. She said that elves accepted her very well; it was Lady Cora they shunned. They believed the war wasn't Elvina's fault because she was just a child when it began twenty-nine years ago. Every day she went into the city and worked as a street vender. She sold floral arrangements as well as fairy cakes that she made herself. She called her vender cart *A Taste of the Fae,* which I thought was a clever name. She was also popular among the elves, despite her differences. I envied Elvina. In the Human Realm, I had not been the least bit popular, and I had been different as well.

A wave of nostalgia suddenly washed over me. I remembered my loving human parents and my foolish, hormone-driven sister. I remembered Carmen and my favorite bookstore. No matter how much I loved the Elf Realm, a part of me would always miss parts of my old life. I would just have to try to get over the sadness creeping up inside me. I had more important things to do than feel homesick.

Before Jacqueline returned to the room to escort me to dinner, I learned more about Elvina. Most important was that she desperately wanted to visit the Woodland Fairy Realm. Since coming to the Elf Realm, she had not set foot out of Tarlore. She wanted to be around her own kind for a change, and to be free to go wherever she desired. I felt sorry for her. I couldn't imagine what life must be like for her, not ever being able to go home. Kind of like my situation in the Human Realm, only I hadn't known the Elf Realm was my real home then.

As if she had read my mind, she told me before I left, "No matter what has happened in my life, I am happy. Would I be happier with my own kind? Who knows? Maybe I would. But I can live with not knowing for now."

I admired her ability to accept her situation. Someone else had decided what sort of life she would live, and in turn, she managed it the best she could, without complaints. She reminded me of Blaire. I knew I should probably follow their examples, but it was hard. I had gone from a simpler life to one that was difficult and complicated. Yet I knew that if Elvina could manage her life, I could too. I would just have to try harder. I had met others with difficulties, and they had managed to adjust.

I would have to do the same.

***

"You have fifteen minutes to freshen up before dinner," Jacqueline told me when we arrived at my room.

"Okay, thanks, Jacqueline," I replied.

She nodded and stood guard by the door. I shrugged and went inside. Jacqueline still hadn't warmed up to me yet, and I wondered if she even trusted me.

I almost cried out with fright when I saw a big hawk sitting perched on one of the end tables. I was too surprised to scream, so instead, my mouth hung open soundlessly, and I shook with fright.

Before I could call Jacqueline, I saw the bird begin to quiver. It grew larger and then its shape started to distort. I backed against the wall, ready to scream at any moment. Then I noticed the hawk was turning into a shape that looked oddly elf-like. The hawk must be a shape-shifter.

I almost smacked myself for being so dumb. I had just spent half the day learning about shape-shifting, and I couldn't even recognize it. I couldn't believe I had acted like such a coward.

I recognized the elfen as Aditi. She shook out her cropped hair and walked toward me.

"Sorry for frightening you, Ramsey," she said in a hoarse voice.

"Your voice!" I exclaimed.

"I'm sorry, once again. The change back to elfen takes some time. My voice hasn't returned just yet," she apologized.

Fortunately, I could hear it getting better.

"What are you doing here?" I asked.

"I was making a delivery," she explained.

"What kind of delivery?"

"Look on your bed," she told me.

I walked over to my bed. There, lying neatly on top of the covers, was my emerald ball gown from the Human Realm.

"How did you get this?" I asked bewilderedly.

"When Queen Taryn realized you had nothing to wear for dinner, which is usually a very formal affair in the palace, she sent me on an errand to Birchwood City. Addison told us that she remembered you had a dress from the Human Realm."

"That was a fast delivery," I remarked.

She shrugged, like a trip from the capital to a small town was no big deal, even though it had taken us over two days to get here. "I was gone for most of the day."

"Well, thank you," I said.

"You're very welcome," she replied.

I stared at Aditi for a moment, still marveling over what she had accomplished. She went all the way to Birchwood City just because I needed something to wear for dinner. She went because the Queen asked her to. Now *that* was loyalty.

"I'll see you at dinner," Aditi said, jarring me from my thoughts.

"Do the guards eat at the same time?"

"Only a few of them do. You know the Queen has twenty guards, right?"

"Yes."

"Well, there are ten high guards and ten low guards. The high guards receive the most important and trusted tasks and dine with Queen Taryn. The other ten perform tasks that are usually just as important, but smaller. They do not dine with the Queen. They eat on the first floor with the healers, cooks, and others."

"Ah, I see. Then I'll see you at dinner," I agreed.

Aditi nodded and walked out of the room. I heard her exchange a concise greeting with Jacqueline, and I was surprised the guard didn't question Aditi's presence in my room. I guessed everyone in the palace was probably used to her and the other bird shape-shifters popping up at odd times.

Realizing I had about ten minutes to get ready, I stripped from my dress and hurriedly began putting on the gown. As I picked it up off the bed, I noticed that my black ballet flats were there as well. I was thankful I wouldn't have to wear my boots, which were my only shoes, to tonight's dinner.

I put my dirty clothes from the day before in the sink and turned on the hot water. I scrubbed them with soap and then left them to soak. I hoped they would be clean for the next day, for I had nothing else to wear. After running through my hair with a comb, I was ready to go. I met Jacqueline outside of my door, and we walked down the hall and down one flight of stairs to arrive at the dining hall.

I was embarrassed when I walked in and found everyone already seated. I was the last one to dinner. I was *late*. I took the open seat beside Stellan, and Jacqueline sat beside me. I had no idea what to say, so I kept quiet. I was afraid I would be speaking out of turn.

To my surprise, no one seemed to care that I was late. Instead, everyone turned his or her head to Queen Taryn, who was starting to speak.

"Let us pray before we eat," Queen Taryn said, and bowed her head.

I followed suit and so did everyone else.

"Lord, thank you for this meal tonight. We pray that you continue to watch over this palace and this Realm." She raised her head and continued, "High peace to all."

"High peace to all," I heard the elves repeat.

I found out later that "high peace to all" was like a human saying "amen" after a prayer. It just meant that everyone should have peace. I wished I had known that. Instead of repeating what the elves said, I had remained silent and confused.

It was another elfin custom I would have to absorb.

As the cooks brought in the first course, I looked around at the table to see who was dining with us. I saw Princess Brielle seated near her mother. Across from her sat Lady Cora and Elvina. I saw the guards Danica, Aditi, Wren, Gavin, Arnold, Thane, Gabriel, and two others I hadn't met. The Queen, knowing I hadn't exchanged words with them yet, introduced them as Kayden and Eder.

Kayden was pale-haired with dark green, almost black eyes. He looked deep in thought as the Queen introduced him. His power was using his mind to make things happen. He explained that it wasn't like telekinesis when the Queen finally got his attention. He didn't *move* things; he just imagined them happening, and they happened. As a demonstration, he imagined Stellan picking up his plate. I gasped in surprise when Stellan did the motion without even knowing what was happening. I liked Kayden's power very much. The only drawback was he could only make others do things when they were not ready. Otherwise, they could prepare for the attack mentally if they knew it was coming.

It seemed strange to me, but Kayden said that I would have to experience it to understand completely. He also mentioned that he wasn't able to end the war. Many others had asked if he could because of his ability, but he didn't have enough power to accomplish something of this magnitude.

Then Queen Taryn introduced the dark-haired Eder, who had the element of earth as his ability. He seemed intense, and his dark green eyes made me feel uneasy as he watched me. It seemed as if his eyes were trained on me, and they rarely looked away throughout the dinner. It was very uncomfortable.

For dinner, we feasted on meats of all kinds, fruits, vegetables, soups, and salads. It was a wonderful meal. I had never eaten so royally in all my life. Everything tasted fresh and delicious.

It was also comforting to be with Stellan, our free hands joined during the meal. I had missed him during the day, and I could tell he felt the same. Addison, who was sitting near the Queen, frequently smiled in my direction. I took it as an "everything is okay" gesture. I hoped she was right.

For dessert, we had cake that I learned was a fairy recipe from Elvina. No one seemed bothered by the dessert. I assumed it was because it came from Elvina. She was not only popular among the city folk, but also among the guard.

I had never had such a dessert before. It tasted like sweet honey and smelled like flowers. No matter what fairies did to us now, they would always be the best cake-makers. No one could deny that.

Toward the end of dinner, I noticed Eder watching me once more. I frowned, wondering why he was so interested in me. Every time I caught his gaze, he seemed more familiar to me than any of the other guards. Something about him struck a chord in my memory, and it wasn't until I heard him speak that I figured it out, responding to a question from the Queen about the perimeter of the palace.

"All clear," he said, in a familiar deep voice.

It all came crashing down on me – the intense eyes, the familiar voice, the earth ability….

I was sitting across from the very man who had saved me from drowning in the Human Realm, the night I met Addison. Only he wasn't just a man, he was an elf. He had different hair; tonight it was black, not brown, but I may have been wrong. After all, I was close to unconsciousness at that time. I was *sure* I was mistaken now. This was definitely the Earth Man, my rescuer.

Here in Tarlore, he was a high guard to the Queen. I could hardly believe my eyes. This elf had saved me, and he hadn't mentioned anything about it. I was sure he recognized me, knew me. He had known my name before.

Why didn't he say anything? Why did he simply stare at me?

I didn't know, but I wanted to know. Feeling a little shaky, I got up from my chair.

"Queen Taryn, may I please be excused for just a moment?" I asked.

"Of course, Ramsey, you may be excused," she consented.

"Are you all right?" Stellan whispered.

I nodded. Then I stared across the table until my eyes found Eder's.

"I just need some air," I said.

I turned and walked away quickly from the dining hall, praying Eder would follow.

~16~

An Earthly Encounter

I found a spot to wait right outside the palace doors. I could see a few guards patrolling the perimeter, probably the reason I was allowed to venture outdoors. Queen Taryn trusted me because there were guards to watch me.

It took Eder only a few minutes to join me outside the palace doors. I noticed how he looked in the moonlight; handsome, like all elves were, but something about him was different, something foreign that I couldn't explain.

"I was afraid you wouldn't take the hint," I admitted.

He didn't say anything in reply, but his eyes watched me intently, like he was trying to figure me out. I bit my lip and wished he would say something…*anything*.

"You saved me that night on the bridge," I said, hoping this would get him going.

He looked as if he were in deep thought. He still refused to speak.

"Why didn't you say anything about it at dinner?" I asked.

"Because…," he trailed off. It seemed as if he were trying to choose his words carefully.

Why? I wondered. *What did he have to hide?*

"Because no one else here at the palace besides me knows about that night," he revealed.

"Why not?" I wondered.

"I wasn't supposed to be there," he explained.

"You mean in the Human Realm?" I asked.

He nodded. "Yes. I didn't have permission to leave Tarlore, let alone enter a forbidden Realm."

"But surely the Queen must have known you were there, because of her power, right?" I asked.

"Not exactly. There's, well, a reason I could hide from her power."

"Care to shed any light on what that reason may be?" I asked, raising my eyebrows.

"I can't tell you, at least not now," he said. "I'm sorry."

I sighed, wondering if I was wasting my time by bringing him out here. "Okay, then. How about you tell me the reason you were in the Human Realm to begin with," I suggested.

"No, unfortunately I can't tell you that either."

"What *can* you tell me, Eder?" I asked, becoming annoyed.

"Not much, I'm afraid."

"Well, tell me what you can," I told him. "Please. I deserve to know."

He nodded, contemplative once more. I guessed he was deciding on what to tell me…and what *not* to tell me.

"All right," he said, "I *can* tell you that I didn't mean to leave so suddenly after I saved you. I had to return to the Elf Realm before I was discovered."

"Um, well, thanks. But that's not what I really want to know. I don't care that you had to go; I understand that. I want to know how you knew my name," I said.

"Everyone knows your name, Ramsey," he said. "You're famous in these parts because of your parents, your sister, and your secret."

"How did you recognize me?" I asked.

"Who else in the Human Realm has pointy ears?"

He was right, of course. I sighed with growing frustration. "What were you doing at the bridge?" I asked.

"I sensed magical energy coming from it, like most magical beings can," he explained.

"You seem to have an excuse for everything, but they are all pretty vague," I remarked.

"I can't help it if you don't get the answer you want," he said.

"Right," I muttered. I suddenly felt a twinge of déjà vu. After all, I had used that same line with Lura the wind fairy not too long ago.

"So are we done here?" he asked.

I was shocked. "Excuse me?" I couldn't believe how easily he was dismissing me.

"I'm sorry. I just don't want anyone getting suspicious. If the Queen found out about my visit to the Human Realm, I would be in a lot of trouble."

"Well," I said, "maybe I should just rat you out."

He looked at me blankly.

"Oh, sorry," I said, rubbing my eyes because I was suddenly exhausted from our tense conversation. "It's a human expression. It means maybe I should tell the Queen what you did," I explained.

He nodded. "But why would you do that?" he asked.

"Because you aren't giving me the answers I want."

"I saved you. You should be grateful for that," he snapped.

"Sure, but why? Why did you save me? Why were you there?" I asked.

Eder looked down at the ground and shook his head. For the first time, I noticed how strong, yet also how frightened, he appeared. It was a strange combination. As if he were ready for anything, but was afraid of it coming. His gleaming eyes held determination, but when they met mine, I also saw worry in their depths.

"Ramsey, you can't know about some things yet; my intentions, and the reason I was with you that night on the bridge," he said simply. "And it's for your own safety, your own good."

"What is that supposed to mean?" I asked.

"What it means is that there are bigger things than Zora happening out there right now. She is only one piece of the puzzle. But right now, you need to focus on finding her," he explained.

"When will I learn about those 'bigger things'?" I asked.

"When Zora is safe. When the time is right," Eder told me.

"And I take it that you are involved in those bigger things somehow?"

He nodded. "But in what way? I can't tell you that either," he said.

"Why am I not surprised?" I said sarcastically, crossing my arms against my chest and sighing deeply.

"Look, Ramsey, you need to forget about this meeting for a while. It's not as important as finding Zora. Right now, you need to focus on finding your sister. It's imperative that you do."

"Why does it matter to you?" I asked.

"What happens to you matters to everyone. And without your sister, you won't figure out your secret. Without your secret being revealed, the war will continue, and elves and fairies will continue to die. And without Zora, without your secret, you will never know why I was there that night on the bridge."

I nodded, finally understanding his reasoning, although it was still mystifying and unclear.

"Okay, so when I find Zora, everything else will play out?"

Eder sighed, looking down at his feet. "I hope so."

"And you won't tell me anything more?"

He shook his head. "I can't. I'm sorry."

"I know. Thanks," I said, still upset.

He turned away and began to walk back into the palace.

"Eder, wait," I called.

He turned back around. "Yes?" His eyes were hopeful.

"I won't say anything, to the Queen, to anyone. I promise," I said.

"Why not?" he asked.

"For some reason I trust you. I don't know why, but I do. And you're right. I need to find my sister. That's the most important thing right now," I agreed.

For the first time, I saw Eder smile. I liked him more when he smiled. He seemed more…genuine to me. And in the moonlight, he looked almost serene – like an angel, my guardian angel. Although he was vague, he *had* saved me. He had protected me. I had a feeling that later on he would protect me again, or at least be a significant presence in my future.

"Thank you," he said finally, and I knew he meant it.

"Yeah," I replied, wondering why in the Realm I was letting him just walk away. I didn't have the answers I wanted. I hardly knew anything but vague fragments of an explanation, yet there I was, letting him go.

He disappeared into the palace, leaving me pondering what had just occurred between us.

Then I remembered something. Back when he saved me, Eder's eyes were brown. Just a minute ago, when we were talking, they were green.

I shook my head and walked back inside the palace, not knowing what to believe anymore.

***

I was surprised to find everyone still in the dining hall when I returned…except Eder. He was nowhere to be seen.

Dessert dishes were being cleared away, and elves began rising from their chairs. Before leaving, Queen Taryn approached me. I quickly forgot about Eder and turned my attention to her.

"I heard that you don't have anything to occupy yourself with after today," she said.

"Who would say such a thing?" I asked, trying to be polite.

Queen Taryn was right, though. Tomorrow I would be bored out of my mind. I had toured the castle, met a bunch of elves, and even a fairy. What else was there to do?

"I have my sources, Ramsey. And I have decided you will be allowed to go into the city tomorrow, so long as you return at least an hour before dinner, which will be at eight."

"Queen Taryn, thank you. I promise I will behave," I told her.

"I'm quite sure you will." She smiled at me. "Just know that Jacqueline will be with you wherever you go."

"That is perfectly understandable," I agreed.

"Then I hope you have a good time. Goodnight, Ramsey."

"Goodnight, Queen Taryn," I said.

I waited for her to leave before leaving myself.

I was going to the city! My wish would come true. I had hoped that I wouldn't leave for Birchwood City without seeing the sights. Now I could spend the whole day there. I wasn't too keen on having Jacqueline with me everywhere, though. I wasn't a baby. However, I did understand why she had to accompany me. If Stellan and

Addison were still suspects, I was one as well. They couldn't risk me bolting before we even tried to find Zora. I hurried past several guards until I reached Stellan. Placing my hand in his, I whispered in his ear, "I can go to the city tomorrow."

"Good; at least one of us will be having a good time," he remarked.

"You don't have to be with Thane again, do you?"

The look on his face said it all.

"I'm sorry," I told him softly.

He squeezed my hand. "Don't be sorry, Ramsey. I don't mean to sound so upset. It's just…." He shook his head. "Can I walk you to your room?"

"Of course," I replied.

He led me up the stairs, Jacqueline close behind. I was just glad Thane wasn't there. That would have been creepy; a weird guy that I hardly knew following us up the stairs would have been awkward. We didn't speak as we walked down the hall. Stellan didn't look like he was open to conversation. Sometimes he acted like a two-year-old, and his behavior was growing old. I didn't want to date – or court – a two-year-old. I was about to say goodnight when we reached my door, but instead he turned to Jacqueline.

"Can we have a moment, please?"

Jacqueline looked uncertain. I nodded to her.

"Very well, I will leave you," she said. "I will see you tomorrow morning, Ramsey."

I nodded in response. "Thank you," I said.

As Jacqueline walked away, Stellan took both of my hands in his. "Ramsey, I need you to promise me something," he said.

"What? What is it?" I asked, bewildered by his sudden seriousness.

"I need you to promise me that whatever happens with Zora and Queen Taryn, you won't forget that I care about you."

"Why would I forget?"

"Ramsey, just please promise me. No matter what, I don't want to lose you."

I put my arms around his neck and looked into his eyes. I could see the fear inside them. Why was he so worried? Why did I have to make a promise that I knew I would keep?

"I promise," I said.

I decided it was better just to make the promise. I didn't want to make him worry any more than he already was. It didn't matter if it was useless worry or not.

He pulled me closer as I kissed him, his arms wrapping around my waist, holding me tightly. For some reason, I was a little hesitant. One part of me felt carefree and content in his arms. Another part was worrying over what he meant when he said, "no matter what happens." My head was buzzing with confusion. I could barely focus on the kiss. I pulled away from him and opened my door.

"Goodnight, Stellan," I said. I was anxious to be alone, a first for me.

"Goodnight," he replied.

He smiled, then turned and walked away from where I was standing.

I hoped I hadn't revealed any of my uncertainty. I wanted to keep those feelings to myself until I had time to sort through them. I shut the door and walked into my room. I grabbed the nightgown I noticed hanging on the coat rack, reminding myself to thank Aditi the first chance I got. Her only task had been the gown, but she had obviously thought beyond that. If it hadn't been for Aditi, I wouldn't have been able to sleep very well.

I was about to change when I remembered my clothes soaking in the bathroom sink. I wanted them to be dry and ready for tomorrow, so I knew it would be best to take them out now. I walked into the bathroom and gasped, covering my mouth with my right hand and dropping my nightgown.

My clothes were no longer in the sink. They were hanging over the bathroom tub. I felt them, and sure enough, they were already dry. They were ready for tomorrow, but I hadn't put them there.

Who had done this for me? Was it Aditi? No, I washed the clothes after she left, right before dinner. Who else could have gotten into my room in that short amount of time? For a moment, I thought of Eder, and then discarded the thought. It was silly. The elf was strange, but why would he hang up my wet clothes?

A noise came from the bedroom. I whirled around and slowly crept out of the bathroom.

Princess Brielle was sitting on my bed, her legs crossed and her hands clasped over her lap, her long hair pooling over her shoulders. She smiled at me.

"Hello, Ramsey," she greeted.

"How did you…?"

"After living in a palace for sixteen years and only being allowed to go into the city on weekends, you learn to pick locks. How else would I get out of here?"

"Um…thanks for telling me how you escape from the palace, Princess."

"Don't act so surprised. I know you saw me last night at the tavern." I bit my lip and felt my cheeks redden with embarrassment. I had hoped the Princess would forget that I saw her last night. "Yes, not my finest moment, I'm afraid, but it sure was fun to mess with Arnold. He was the guard who escorted me home. And cut the Princess stuff. It's Brielle, all right?" she said.

I nodded. "Okay…why are you in my room…Brielle?"

"Well, for one thing, I had to hang your clothes. If I hadn't taken them out, they would still be sopping wet in the morning. Do you even know how to wash your clothing?"

I ignored her snide remark and returned to asking my own questions. "How could you have dried them so fast? I saw you at dinner. You left only a few minutes before me."

"Let's leave that for me to know. The point is that they are dry," she told me.

"What's the other reason you are here?" I asked, feeling both uneasy and suspicious of her sudden appearance in my bedroom.

"I heard you were going to the city tomorrow."

"And for some reason that interests you?" I asked.

"Want some company? Surely, you can't be happy about Jacqueline following you all day. She is quite a bore. I mean, all serious and such. No real fun involved. Since tomorrow is Saturday, I can escort you. I won't have to sneak out of the palace at all."

"You must have a guard with you when you go to the city," I said.

"We can sneak away. I'll find Jacqueline and tell her she is off tomorrow. You can come with Danica and me."

"Danica is your guard?" I asked.

"Yes, she is. Queen Taryn chose her because she is an elfen and not a shape-shifter."

"Why can't she be a shape-shifter?" I asked.

"Shape-shifters are needed on a whim for missions and tasks. The Queen said I needed someone who could watch over me."

"Obviously Danica wasn't the right choice, since you can slip away from her," I pointed out.

"Don't be too hard on her," Brielle replied, playing with the folds of her gown. "Danica has more important things to do, like be with Thane, for example."

"What?"

"Oh, you didn't know? I guess Thane guarding that elf you are with takes up most of his time. You probably haven't had a chance to observe them together. Usually they are all over each other. That's how I can get away. Danica gets distracted by her fiancé quite easily." Brielle smirked and tucked a piece of hair behind her ear.

"Thane is her fiancé?"

"Yes, their wedding is in July," she told me. "They want to make sure they can never be separated, not that the Queen would ever even think of dismissing them, but it's good to be cautious during times like these."

"Wow, I had no idea," I remarked.

"You haven't been around the two enough to know."

"You have a pretty good thing going then, don't you?" I guessed.

"Sure I do! I can do as I please most of the time. It's only when Queen Taryn is around that I have to act my best," she explained.

"I see."

"So how about it?" she asked.

"I don't know....Couldn't we get into some kind of trouble?" I asked her.

"Trust me, Ramsey. I know what I'm doing."

"Okay," I said. "Will you talk to Jacqueline and the Queen?"

"Yes, of course. I'll see you in the morning. Come to my quarters at six," she instructed.

"All right, I guess I'll see you then."

"Goodnight!" Brielle said and walked toward the door.

"Goodnight," I replied. As she opened it I added, "And please don't break into my room again without warning me."

She laughed and shut the door behind her. I sighed and went back into the bathroom to dress in my nightgown. Looking at my dry clothes, I shook my head and walked back into the main room. I blew out all of the candles except for the one by the bed. As I got under the sheets, I thought about the Princess. Brielle was an odd elfen. That much was true. How had she dried my clothes? Why was she so secretive? Was it just what Thane said, that she was isolated?

More importantly, why did she suddenly want to spend so much time with me, when earlier she was so cold and uninterested? I didn't even know why I had accepted her offer to accompany me into the city; I hadn't been able to say no.

I decided there had to be more to her than mere social issues and I would have to figure her out sooner or later. For now, all I wanted was sleep. The day had been filled with too many surprises. My room was broken into twice, I met a fairy who was actually nice, I had a strange conversation with Eder, and Stellan said some things that totally confused me. What would tomorrow bring? I shuddered and blew out the last candle.

I would wait until tomorrow to think about that.

~17~

Party Like a Princess

That night I had disturbing dreams filled with confusion, blood, and horror. They included Zora. *Her pain-stricken face swirled behind my closed eyes. I reached out to her but I couldn't grab hold. She was slipping away. There wasn't any time left....*

When I woke suddenly, my eyes and face were wet with tears. Wiping them away, I got out of bed and ran into the bathroom. After being sick for a few moments, I washed my face and sank onto the bathroom floor. I shook from the horrors of the nightmare. Seeing Zora again like that and not being able to help had made me sick to my stomach. Burying my face into my knees, I tried to stop the sobs from coming. They rose up and out of my throat. I could do nothing to stop them. I stayed that way for a while. I didn't realize how much time had passed. As my sobbing quieted and I picked myself off the floor, I finally noticed the time. It was five in the morning. I had only one hour until I met with Brielle.

I dressed into my newly cleaned clothes and rushed out of my room to the dining hall, trying to forget my horrid nightmares. On the way, I almost collided into Jacqueline. After my quick apology, she escorted me to breakfast. Addison wasn't there when I arrived and neither was Stellan. I was relieved, and guilty for being content with their absence. I didn't want Stellan to ask me for any more promises. I also didn't want to reveal my nightmare to either of them. Nor did I want to be around anyone until I met with Brielle. I ate quickly and quietly. I didn't want to be late to Brielle's room. Whether she was strange or not, she was still the Princess of the Elf Realm. Being late would certainly not do.

Jacqueline informed me that the Princess had spoken with her and that I was to accompany Brielle and Danica to the city. I could see the suspicion in her eyes as I nodded and rose from my seat. After a polite goodbye, I was on my way to Brielle's quarters. I was thankful Jacqueline trusted me enough to go on my own.

I found myself in Brielle's "apartment" minutes later. She told me to make myself comfortable and she would be ready in ten minutes. I sat down on one of her plush brown couches and looked around. The room was beautiful. It was full of colors, and I admired how different it was from Lady Cora and Elvina's. I guessed Brielle wanted the colorful guest rooms even more than Queen Taryn.

The bedspread was a shade of blue with swirls of red and green, with a blue canopy. The curtains were brown and blue, and she had two couches. One was brown and the other green. I looked down at the carpet and I swore I saw every color imaginable. Brielle was more unusual than I thought. Sure, the colors were beautiful, but they were also highly unnatural for any elf, straying away from the traditional colors of simple brown and green.

When she was ready, I asked her about her interesting room. She said she wanted color in her life. The thought of being trapped in a room during the week with no excitement made her want to gag. I laughed when she said it, but then I realized she was serious. Although she sometimes managed to sneak out of the palace, most of the time she was unable to leave.

"Danica is right outside," she told me. "We should be going."

"How do you know that?" I asked.

"Just a feeling," she replied.

"Okay," I muttered.

Brielle was getting stranger by the minute.

I followed her out the door. Just as she predicted, Danica was waiting for us outside. She led the way down the three flights of stairs and out the castle doors. As we walked over the bridge, I was once again taken aback by the beauty of the palace and what surrounded it. I could see the glistening streams and ponds more clearly in the daylight. When I looked back at the structure, I couldn't believe I was a guest there. It was the most beautiful place I had ever seen, more spectacular than I had imagined it to be.

When Brielle saw I was lagging behind, she grabbed me by the hand and pulled me forward. Now walking very fast, I didn't have much time to admire the scenery. However, I did come to one conclusion: Tarlore was amazing! New sights to see beckoned to me from every direction. We passed street venders, markets, and bakeries. Busy elves surrounded us.

The city wasn't modern, but it was definitely a city. When I pictured Birchwood City, I thought of the nineteenth century. Looking at Tarlore was like going backward to the seventeenth century. Buildings were constructed out of stone or crude wood. Even though the shops and homes were rustic, they were also soothing, pure and natural.

Still dragging me along, Brielle walked around with an air of confidence, looking at things here and there. I wondered when we would try to break away from Danica, who was following close behind us. Brielle said we would leave her at some point. I pushed the thought away and focused on the city. Brielle could decide what to do about Danica on her own.

Twenty minutes later, I saw Thane walking toward us.

"Danica, we have a slight problem," he said after they embraced.

"What is it?"

"You know how you wanted me to find the wedding invitations and send them off with a few of the shape-shifters? I'm sorry to tell you the invitations have disappeared."

"How?" Danica cried.

"I have no idea. All I know is I have looked everywhere and they are nowhere to be found!"

I noticed Brielle was smirking. Did she have something to do with this?

"You probably didn't look hard enough. They need to be sent out today if everyone is to get them in time. I'll have to come and help you look."

"What about Princess Brielle and Ramsey?" Thane asked.

"We can take care of ourselves," Brielle interrupted. "I've been to the city numerous times. I can look after Ramsey."

"I don't think that's a good idea," Thane said.

"We'll be fine, I promise," Brielle reassured them both.

"We really need those invitations sent out," Danica admitted.

"Are you sure we can trust them alone?" Thane asked.

"As long as Queen Taryn doesn't find out, I believe everything will be fine," Danica said.

"What if she *does* find out?" Thane asked.

"We won't say a thing to her, Danica," Brielle promised.

"All right, but remember to be back an hour before dinner, okay?" Danica asked.

"You can trust us!" Brielle called as the two ran off to the palace.

I looked at Brielle, completely stunned. How had she gotten to those wedding invitations? How had she known Thane would come looking for Danica? Moreover, how could they have fallen for her scheme?

"Don't look at me like that! I told you we would get away, didn't I? Well, we did."

"But how did you…the invitations…*how?*" I asked.

"Lock picker, remember? I just went into Thane's room, took the invitations, and hid them. Don't worry, they will find them in time. I just placed them in a place I knew Thane wouldn't check."

"Where did you put them?" I asked.

"I put them in Danica's closet. You wouldn't believe how disgraceful it is! She is quite a slob! I knew Thane wouldn't have the heart to go through it, so I shoved them to the back," Brielle said, smiling and obviously very impressed with her skills.

"You really are something, Brielle," I told her.

"I'll take that as a compliment," she replied. She smiled and then took my hand.

"What do we do now?" I asked.

"I'm going to show you the best parts of the city!" Brielle cried, pulling me along.

I kept up as best I could, though it was hard to run around so much in the early morning. My nightmare had deprived me of sleep, so I was still tired.

Brielle took me to various venders and shops. I helped her pick out some jewelry and learned she was a jewelry hoarder like Zora. It made me sad for a moment to think of my sister, but then I was whisked away again to another shop. Brielle knew how to keep me distracted. She also knew how to have a great time.

She even took the liberty of buying me a new shoulder bag, among various other accessories. The bag was dark brown with bright green floral designs and a large emerald jewel at the center. Her reasoning: my bag was too old and worn out to be seen in Tarlore.

After refusing her offer for more than fifteen minutes, I gratefully accepted it. I transferred all of my own money, jewelry, and Zora's journal into my new bag and thanked her countless times. Later at lunch, she asked me about the journal.

"Do you think it will help you find her?" she wondered.

"I don't know. But I thought I should keep it with me just in case," I told her.

"Don't you have any idea where she is?"

"Not really. God knows I wish I did. She has only three nights left," I said quietly.

"Can't you connect with her again?"

"The last time it happened I almost died. I was told not to come back. If I did, the Element fairies would probably kill both of us."

"What about trying to remember details of the previous connections? Is there something you saw that could let you know where she was, anything at all?" Brielle asked.

"Even if there was something, I probably wouldn't know what it was. I have no idea how to distinguish one Fairy Realm from another."

"I still think you should try. Maybe think about it later tonight, all right?" she asked.

"Okay," I agreed uncertainly.

I liked Brielle's encouragement, but I highly doubted I would figure out Zora's location just by thinking. Pushing the thoughts aside, I tried to enjoy my lunch with the Princess.

It was four when we finished shopping, and we had to be back at the palace by seven. Brielle said we had one more thing to do before we left. Following her down the dirt roads, she took me to a large wooden building that I recognized as the tavern from the other night. The sign across the front read, *The Hall of Drink and Dance*. I looked at Brielle, confused, and she smiled in return.

"What's this?" I asked.

"*This* is fun," she told me.

Inside, the place was filled with elves dancing, laughing, and drinking the late afternoon away. I noticed a large dance floor and a bar at the back. Musicians played on a stage in the middle. Brielle squealed with delight and beckoned me to follow her to the bar. After taking our seats, Brielle asked the bartenders for two glasses of their finest wine.

"Are you allowed to be here?" I asked her.

Brielle looked at me and grinned. "If Queen Taryn knew her daughter spent her evenings drinking and dancing with complete strangers, she would have my head!" She winked. "But even that wouldn't stop me from having a good time."

We got our drinks moments later. I looked around and sighed. Who could have known the Princess of the Elf Realm was such a rebel? I certainly hadn't until today.

"Come on, Ramsey, let's dance!" She tugged me away from the bar and pushed me onto the dance floor.

At first, I was nervous and didn't want to participate, but Brielle wouldn't have it. She taught me a few elfin dances, which I picked up surprisingly fast. It wasn't long before I was laughing and dancing along with her. My stress melted away for that short time and I felt completely free.

The music was loud and wonderful, and I danced and danced until I couldn't dance anymore. Brielle even found us a few elf partners. It was nice to be around elves who were so carefree. After numerous songs, dances, and sips of wine, I reminded Brielle of our time arrangement. After one more song, we said goodbye to everyone and headed out the door.

With both of us feeling a little tipsy from the drinks and tired from the dancing, it took us a long while to get back to the palace. The sun was beginning to set as we walked through the city.

"Brielle, I just wanted…to say…thank you," I said, breathing heavily.

"For what?" she asked, giggling.

"For everything! Today was amazing! I had so much fun." I coughed and then continued. "I haven't truly enjoyed myself since I arrived here. I always have my guard up because of Zora. But today…you showed me how great this Realm can be." I smiled as I staggered just a tad.

"When Zora is safe, you will see just how great *everything* is here. Right now, your eyes are covered, but soon the veil will lift and you will enjoy yourself again. I promise."

"How do you do it?" I asked.

"Do what?" she wondered.

"You are a princess, your mother is the Queen, and your Realm is at war. That must be so stressful! How do you keep smiling through it all?" I asked.

"What else can I do?" she asked, almost tripping over a few loose stones. "Crying over things that can't be changed won't help. Just because I want the war to stop doesn't mean it will. The most important thing is to keep living no matter how hard life is. That's what I do."

"I underestimated you, Brielle," I admitted.

"Most elves do," she said, smiling.

Then we both erupted into giggles.

***

It was exactly seven when we crossed the bridge to the palace. Brielle said she would stop by my room before dinner and give me some tea that would help the throbbing ache in my head from drinking so much wine. I thanked her and we parted when we reached the third floor. While she went up the stairs, I went down the hall to my room. I walked inside and was relieved no one was there waiting for me. I wasn't ready for any surprise intrusions. My head pounded and my legs were wobbly. I was a little unsteady. The room was fuzzy. I was about to change into the red velvet gown that Brielle had picked out for me for dinner, when I suddenly couldn't stand anymore. I flopped down on the bed and closed my eyes. I wasn't used to drinking, and it had affected me greatly. I decided I would rest until Brielle brought me the tea.

While I lay on the bed, I remembered what Brielle mentioned to me at lunch. She told me to remember my connections with Zora. Maybe I would figure out where she was if I really thought about them.

I wasn't optimistic, but it was something to do until Brielle arrived. It could also make me forget about my aching body for a while. I took a few deep breaths and thought about my first connection. The room was musty and dark. The only distinct smell was that of blood. I remembered the woozy feeling I had felt and shuddered. I couldn't pass out before dinner. I didn't want Brielle to get in trouble. I also didn't want Danica to get in trouble for leaving us.

After a few minutes, I decided there was nothing from my first connection that could help find Zora, except for the part about the "Realm," which I still didn't understand. I moved on to my last connection.

There hadn't been any smell of blood in the last one because Zora's wounds were older. However, I hadn't observed much with the fairies in the room.

When I thought all was hopeless and that I had better get dressed, something occurred to me. It was like being stuck on problems during a math test. I would think and think, unable to find an answer. Then suddenly the answers would come to me. The same thing had just happened with my thinking about Zora.

I remembered the musty smell. It hadn't just been a musty smell. Something was familiar about that specific stench.

I concentrated on the odor. I wracked my brain for answers, knowing there was one somewhere. I just had to find it.

Then I realized it reminded me of the tang of animals and the faint scent of hay. I remembered hearing a crunch under my feet when I went over to Zora and then the scratch of the hay when I collapsed to the floor after being one with her. And then I knew.

Zora was being kept in a barn!

I couldn't believe I hadn't realized it earlier. The odor was flooding my nostrils now. I could remember it clearly. All of those years riding horses with Dina had paid off. I remembered brushing my horse, Lucy, after spending the day riding. Dina had always complained of that musty smell.

Everything fit together like puzzle pieces after that. Everyone believed Zora was in a Fairy Realm. No one would have ever thought anything different. However, Zora was not in the Fairy Realm, that I knew for sure. I knew what Zora had been trying to tell me. Her mention of the "not in the…Realm" finally made sense. She was trying to tell me she wasn't in a Fairy Realm, the Element Fairy Realm, specifically. But I knew where she really was.

Zora was in the Human Realm!

I jumped from the bed, all of my dizziness and aching now gone from my body. I knew where Zora was. Her time was running out and I had to act quickly. I ran to my shoulder bag and took out Zora's journal. I put my cross necklace on for luck and quickly prayed I would have enough strength for what I was planning to do. I scribbled a few words on an unused piece of paper in the journal. I left it open on the table beside my bed. I hoped the right elf would find it.

I knew I would need some kind of weapon. I put my shoulder bag over my head and started opening drawers and cabinets, but there was nothing I could use. Dismayed and disappointed, I realized I would just have to take my chances. Maybe I could find something on the way out of the palace.

Getting out of the palace was the tricky part. I hoped Jacqueline wouldn't want to start her guard duty again so soon. I opened the door and ran out of the room, colliding right into Brielle. The pot of tea she was holding flew into the air with some of it spilling onto the carpet. With catlike reflexes, Brielle caught the handle as it fell to the ground.

"Ramsey, what do you think you are doing?" she yelled. She held out her hand and helped me up.

"I don't have time to explain. I have to leave the palace," I said quickly.

"What? Why?" she asked.

"I know where Zora is," I blurted out.

"You know where Zora is?" she asked.

"There's no time. I have to get out of here."

I tried to run past her, but she grabbed my arm with her free hand. "Not without me you're not. Now tell me where she is," Brielle demanded.

"Why do you even want to come?" I wondered.

"For the same reason I wanted to spend time with you today," she explained. "You're not like the others, judging me because I'd rather have fun than sit all prim and proper all the time. You're different."

"Why does everyone keep saying that?"

"Because it's true," she said, shrugging her shoulders.

"You can't come to the Human Realm with me, Brielle!" I cried. My hand flew over my mouth. I had just told her where Zora was.

Brielle grinned. "Oh yes I am! You can't fight Element fairies without help."

"But you are a princess!" I protested.

"That doesn't matter. Surely by now you must have figured out that I'm not just an ordinary royal." I grimaced, realizing the truth in her words. "Why do you have to go alone anyway?"

"I don't really have proof that she's in the Human Realm. It's just a feeling, but a strong one. It would take too long for me to explain my reasoning to Queen Taryn, and the soldiers won't be here until tomorrow morning. I have to do this now," I said.

"Then you have no choice. I'm coming and that's that," she decided.

I sighed. I knew I had to let her come. Otherwise, she would tell the Queen. Then the guards would stop me, and I wouldn't reach Zora in time.

"Fine, do you have any weapons?" I asked.

"No, but we can get some. Drink this tea and follow me. It will help clear your mind."

I gulped the scorching hot liquid and followed Brielle down the stairs. She took me to a room that smelled heavily of smoke. It was faintly lit by firelight. I could see swords and other weapons hanging from the walls and lying in piles on the ground.

"What is this place?" I asked.

"It's the palace's weapon room. The guards store extra swords and daggers here," Brielle explained. "Do you know how to use a sword?"

"No. I grew up in the Human Realm, remember? Kids there learned how to play baseball, not fight with weapons," I said.

Brielle gave me a strange look and then shrugged. "Then you will just carry a dagger. Anyone can use a knife," she said.

Brielle picked up a five-inch dagger and placed it into a sheath. She handed it to me, then found a sword for herself. We attached our weapons to belts and tied them around our waists. I noticed Brielle hadn't bothered changing for dinner either.

"Why didn't you change?" I asked.

"I…I had a feeling."

"You had a feeling?"

"Yes," she said. "I had a feeling you would remember something about Zora."

"And just how do these feelings come about?"

"They just do," she said.

Before I could question her further, she took my hand and pulled me out the door. After shutting it quietly, we both tiptoed through the halls. I was surprised we didn't see any guards. I remembered what time it was and then understood. Everyone was preparing for dinner.

"Are there guards outside?" I asked.

"There should be, but not many are on duty at this time," she said.

She pointed to a room emitting music and laughter. I nodded and continued to follow.

"And even if they were, we could take them," she added.

Not knowing how to respond to that, I simply followed her out the palace doors.

***

The night air was chilly as we left the palace and stepped onto the bridge. About halfway across, Brielle let go of my hand and climbed onto the railing.

"What are you doing?" I asked.

"You need to get to the Human Realm, right?"

"Yes," I replied.

"Then we need a body of water to make an elf circle," Brielle reminded me.

"I'm sorry, I almost forgot."

"How else were we going to get to Zora?" she asked.

"You're right. Let's go," I agreed.

I waited for her to jump down from the bridge and onto a tiny strip of land. Then I climbed onto the railing, prayed I wouldn't break my neck, and jumped. I landed unsteadily but without injury.

"How do we know this will take us to the barn where Zora is being held?" I asked.

"We don't," Brielle admitted.

"What if we are nowhere near it?" I wondered.

"In the Elf Realm, nothing is a coincidence. There is a reason you figured out where she was being held here, now. She will be somewhere nearby. And if not, we will walk until we find her. Just trust me."

"I trust you," I told her, knowing I had no other choice.

"Then let's dance again," she suggested.

"Doesn't it have to be midnight to go into the Human Realm?" I asked.

"No, not in Tarlore. Queen Taryn put restrictions everywhere except in this city. She wanted unlimited access just in case we had to make a quick escape."

"Make a quick escape from what?"

"From the Element fairies, of course. If they attacked the city, we would hide in the Human Realm. I can explain in more detail when we are not in the process of saving your sister. Hurry now; the sooner we get out of here, the less chance we have getting caught by the guards," Brielle told me.

She took a step forward and began the elf circle dance. I joined her a second later, and together we made a perfect, flattened portal.

With one deep breath, we joined hands and stepped into the circle, vanishing from the capital city Tarlore, from the Queen, from Stellan and Addison, from the guards, and from the Elf Realm.

~18~

Sisters

The bright morning light blinded us as we appeared in the Human Realm. The twelve-hour difference between the Elf Realm and this Realm meant it was eight the next morning here. I rubbed my eyes and took a look around.

We stood in a large open field that seemed to stretch on for miles. I could hear grasshoppers chirping and bees buzzing, and felt the beginning of a hot, humid day. Wildflowers swayed in the breeze. The landscape was gorgeous. However, I wasn't here for the scenery.

Where was the barn? Would we be able to find it?

"Let's start walking," I suggested. Brielle nodded and we began.

We walked for miles under the blazing sun. Sweat trickled down my face as we trudged through the field. But no matter how far we traveled, we didn't spot any signs of a barn.

Noon passed and our stomachs grumbled with hunger. I fished through my shoulder bag and withdrew the ripe fruit from the Birchwood City orchard. Brielle thanked me and stuffed the fruit into her mouth. We ate as we walked. The heat was exhausting, especially with our heavy clothes. In the Elf Realm, it was considerably cooler, yet still a comfortable temperature. Here, we were baking. I transferred my dagger to my shoulder bag so I could loosen my belt and allow air into my shirt and onto my hot skin.

Hours passed as we traveled further. Our toughest challenge began when we reached the base of an incredible hill. Looking up, I almost cried. How would we climb this hill in our exhausted condition? My head still throbbed and my legs ached from our adventures in the city the day before. Brielle didn't seem any better.

But sitting atop the hill was what motivated us. Even with the blinding sun, I could make out the shape of a farm. Sitting next to a silo was an immense wooden barn.

"Brielle, I think that's it!" I cried, pointing to the hill.

The Princess nodded. "It's worth a try. Let's get moving."

The sun was setting when we finally reached the top. Brielle and I hugged and sighed with relief.

"Let's rest for a moment before going in. We need strength," Brielle suggested.

We ate the rest of the fruit and lay for a while on the grass. After walking for so long, we were both completely drained. We knew we couldn't continue so soon. We meant to rest for just a moment, but I should have realized those kinds of plans didn't always work out. Because before we could stop ourselves, we fell asleep.

***

My eyes flew open to pitch darkness. I swore and felt around for Brielle. When my hands found her arm, I jarred her awake.

"Brielle, wake up!" I whispered. "We fell asleep and we have to get moving!"

I heard Brielle groan and sit up. "What time is it?" she asked. She was obviously too tired to tell the time herself.

"It's almost ten," I informed her.

"What? That means we slept for almost four hours!"

"Keep your voice down!" I scolded. "We are lucky we weren't caught out here." I grabbed her hand and pulled her up. "Come on, we have to find Zora."

Brielle nodded. We had a bit more energy because of our nap, so we ran as quickly and quietly as possible to the barn.

"Wait," Brielle said as we grew closer, "what's our plan?"

"What's our *plan*?" I asked, a little confused.

"How are we going to get Zora out of there, walk the ten miles back to the pond, and then cross into the Elf Realm?"

"I don't know, but we have to try our best," I said. "It doesn't have to be midnight when we cross into the Elf Realm, right?"

"Not if we go back the way we came. The restrictions don't affect that part of the Human Realm because of Tarlore," Brielle explained. "It's the only portal that never has a time limit."

"Then that's one good thing. Let's just hope we can run fast enough," I said.

"Is that all the plan you have? Really? It won't work," she told me.

"I know it sounds crazy, and it probably is. But I don't have another plan. I wasn't prepared for a return to the Human Realm, and I didn't have time to think. Let's just get Zora out of there and make the rest up as we go along. I have no idea what else to do," I admitted.

"Okay. I'll trust you. But we had better hurry," Brielle said.

I nodded and prayed that the simple plan I had would be enough to get us through this alive.

We crept to the side of the barn, our feet rustling slightly in the grass. I held my breath as we walked. I was afraid Finn and his followers would hear us. When I could feel the hard wood of the barn, I found a small peephole and peered through it. I motioned for Brielle to come closer.

I immediately recognized the musty smell and the very faint trace of blood; I knew we had found the right barn. I couldn't see much of anything through the darkness, but I could make out the outline of a body slumped against the wall.

"I think I see her," I whispered to Brielle.

"Are you sure?" she asked.

"No, but I'm pretty sure," I told her.

"Say her name. See if it's really her," Brielle suggested.

I nodded. "Zora, is that you?" I whispered a little louder, "Zora?"

The shape moved and a small moan escaped from its mouth.

"Zora?" I repeated.

"Maybe it isn't her," Brielle said.

"Hush, it has to be," I retorted. "Zora?" I repeated one last time.

"Ramsey…," the shape whispered.

I turned to Brielle. "It's her. I recognize her voice from the connections."

"Well, don't just stand here telling me. Say something back to her!" Brielle suggested, gesturing toward the barn.

I nodded and looked through the peephole. "Yes, Zora, I'm here. How can I get in there?"

I heard her cough and then moan again. "There's only one door and Wynter is guarding it."

I turned to Brielle. "We have to figure out a way to get in there without being heard."

"Give me a second to think," she said.

I waited for a few moments, then Brielle's eyes lit up.

"What?" I asked.

"Just stand back, all right? I can't believe I didn't think of this before," Brielle said.

I nodded, unsure of Brielle's next move. She unsheathed her sword and placed the tip against the barn wall. My eyes widened as a faint glow appeared on the sword. Brielle moved the glowing sword in a door shape and then the glowing ended.

She freed the huge slab of wood and set it gently on the grass, creating a passageway into the barn. It was small and crude, but big enough for us to step through without getting cuts and splinters.

"Let's go," Brielle said.

"What was that?" I demanded to know.

"I'll explain later. We don't have time to chat. Come on," she said.

Still baffled, I followed her and stepped into the barn. I pushed away all thoughts as I saw Zora. I ran over to her and hugged her as tenderly as I could manage.

"Thank God you are still alive," I said.

"Just barely, it seems. We have to get out of here right now before the Element fairies hear you. They treated my wounds, but I'm still weak and dehydrated. I need to see a healer very soon." She saw Brielle and gasped. "What is the Princess doing here?"

"It's a long story," I told her.

"I won't ask again until we are safe. But then you had better explain everything to me," she said.

"I will, I promise. As long as you start explaining things to me," I said.

Her eyes widened, and then she nodded. "Fine, it's a deal."

"Can you walk? We need to get out of here now," Brielle reminded us.

"Yes, I think so. Oh no…," Zora groaned.

"What?"

"The oath," she said. "I swore an oath, Ramsey. We can't escape."

"Can't it be broken somehow?" I asked.

"I don't think so…." She sighed.

"Yes, it can," Brielle told us, giving me hope like a beacon for a ship.

"How can it be broken?" Zora wondered.

"By making a new oath to Ramsey that you won't tell Finn," Brielle explained.

"Sounds too easy. How do you know that?" I asked.

"How do you think I get out of the promises I make to my mother? If I didn't break a few by promising a random stranger that I *will* go into the city after promising the Queen that I *won't*, I would never see the light of day."

"I'm not even going to ask," Zora said quietly.

"I wouldn't either," I agreed. "But it's proof that Brielle's idea works." I looked at the door where Wynter supposedly stood guard on the other side. Wondering why no one had heard us yet, I turned back to Zora, realizing I didn't have time for questions. "Okay, Zora, make your promise," I instructed.

Quickly, Zora said the oath. A new ball of glowing light left her and flew into me. The sensation tingled for a moment and even hurt a little, but then all was still. Zora was free. I took her hands in mine and helped her to her feet. She brushed the dirt off her ragged clothes and looked at me expectantly.

"Are we going to leave?" she asked.

"Right, let's go," I said.

We followed Brielle back to the makeshift doorway, but before we stepped through and out of the barn, we heard the sound of fluttering. The noise moved closer and closer until we knew fairies were right outside the main door.

"It's them," Zora whispered.

"We have to hurry," Brielle said, stepping through the makeshift door.

I urged Zora forward, but she refused to move, like she was frozen in place with fear.

"Come on," Brielle urged.

The door swung open, and our eyes locked on the entryway.

Finn stood in the doorway with Wynter and Lura by his side. A flame flickered in his palm, lighting the room. All three of them appeared shocked and livid. I reached my hand into my shoulder bag, unsheathed my dagger, and clutched it tightly. I wasn't going to let them stop us from getting out of here. I wasn't going to fail after coming this far. We had to escape this. Otherwise, Stellan and Addison would go to prison, and Zora, the Princess of the Elf Realm, and I would be tortured or killed. That couldn't happen. For me, it wasn't an option.

Using their sparkling wings, the fairies flew into the room and planted their bare feet on the ground only a few feet from us. Their beautiful faces shone in the firelight, making them glow. They appeared both mesmerizing and cruel. I could see the danger in their eyes.

"What have we got here?" Finn asked.

"It looks like Ramsey finally figured out where her sister was, Finn," Lura said. "It's about time you used your mind for once. However, I guess you really aren't that bright. If you were, you wouldn't have come here."

"And she brought a friend," Wynter pointed out, her tone alluring and ice cold.

Finn's attention went to Brielle. He stepped forward to get a good look at her. I saw Brielle take a step back against the wooden wall. Her eyes shone with panic. I saw her hand grip her sword. I hoped to God that she really knew how to use it.

"This isn't just any friend, Wynter," Finn yelled exuberantly. "This is Princess Brielle of Tarlore, Queen Taryn's daughter!" Finn laughed. "What a great catch we have here!"

Wynter and Lura joined in the laugh. My entire body stiffened. They were going to kill us. I should have known, but I was too focused on finding Zora to think about the dangers of being caught. Finn walked over to Zora and me. His flame was so close it almost set my hair on fire. I shivered.

"Did you really think you could save her, Ramsey? When I told you not to come back, I meant it. Now, not only will Zora die, but so will you and your princess," he said menacingly.

"No," I said as confidently as I could.

"What?" he asked. He seemed surprised by my protest.

"I didn't come all this way to watch my sister die. I won't let you hurt her, me, *or* Princess Brielle."

"How are you going to stop us?" Wynter asked from behind Finn.

"Very easily," I told them, the corners of my lips pulling up into a sardonic smile.

"And how's that?" Lura asked, amusement in her tone.

"With the power of an elfen holding a sword," I said.

I nodded once.

Before the Element fairies could begin to grasp what I said, Brielle took her sword from its sheath. It gleamed in the firelight, looking sharp and commanding. With one quick move, she lunged forward and shoved it deep into Wynter's stomach. I had to look away. The water fairy screamed in pain, and I heard her drop to the floor. Brielle pulled the sword out just as Wynter took her last breath.

"Wynter!" Lura gasped. She ran to the water fairy and crouched over her lifeless body.

Meanwhile, Brielle had backed up against the wall, shaking with sobs. A look of pure horror spread across her face.

"Brielle, snap out of it! Keep fighting!" I shouted.

"I…killed her…," Brielle sobbed. "I…never thought…." She slumped to the floor.

Realizing Brielle was in no shape to continue, I jumped up and took out my dagger. I had to do something.

Finn, who had paid no attention to his dead companion, threw his head back and laughed, a blood-curdling sound that made me feel nauseated. Then he looked at me with eyes as red as fire, full of hatred and wickedness.

His hands grabbed my shoulders.

The hot fire he sent from them made me drop the dagger and scream in agony. The burning went right through my shirt and to my skin. I could feel my flesh ripping open, and the smell of it made me sick and dizzy with queasiness and pain. Smoke rose from my body and around the room. Finn kept his malevolent gaze fixated on me as he slowly burned me alive.

Zora started screaming, and pounded on Finn's legs, but it didn't do any good. Finn was too powerful, and I wasn't strong enough to break his grip. Shocked by the pain, I could do nothing but shriek.

"Brielle, Brielle, please do something! Get up!" I screamed through the torture.

Finally, Brielle came to her senses and raised her sword, ready to strike at Finn. He removed his hands from my shoulders, which sent me dropping to the ground with a *thud*. I wasn't able to hold myself up. I couldn't even move. The throbbing was so unbearable that I could barely keep my eyes open to watch Brielle and Finn's encounter.

Finn raised his hands in the air and sent waves of fire toward Brielle and her sword. In quick jolts, she swung the sword around to block the flames. She dashed around the room in what seemed like a great blur. Light from the fire cascaded around the walls. I was afraid the wood would catch fire. The fighting continued for a while, and I could see that Brielle was tired and breathless. Finn didn't look the least bit fazed. But nothing changed. No one gained an opportunity to really strike.

Every flame Brielle's sword caught caused it to increasingly glow from the heat. Brielle finally dropped the sword with a loud cry. The blade was now red hot and had started to melt out of shape. But Brielle wouldn't back down. She jabbed in and out at the fire fairy with her fists, but he was quick and his wings gave him the ability to dodge the blows.

Meanwhile, Lura had stopped grieving over Wynter. She made a gesture with her hands that sent a giant funnel of wind to surround Brielle. It carried her up to the ceiling and twirled her around. With another gesture, the funnel disappeared and Brielle dropped to the hard floor. Her head hit the ground and she was out.

I screamed in horror and anguish as I watched blood seep around the Princess. I couldn't let her die! I couldn't give up this easily!

"Zora, get out of here!" I screamed.

Zora had to leave. At least one elfen had to live through this. I *couldn't* and *wouldn't* fail completely.

"I won't leave you!" Zora retorted.

"Don't argue, Zora. Just go!"

"No!"

"Zora, please, listen to me! You have to get away!" I begged.

I didn't know if it was the certainty in my voice, or just pure luck, but Zora listened and headed toward the doorway. But she stopped when she saw what Finn was about to do next. Lura had her by the shoulders an instant later.

Satisfied with the attack on Brielle, Finn turned around and walked back to me. I ignored Zora's cries and rose slowly to my feet. Filled with rage, I kicked Finn in the worst possible place. Human or fae, it still worked as long as they were male. The attack sent him to the ground in pain, but not before he reached his hand outward and grabbed me, trying to pull me down with him. Thankfully, he was only able to grab hold of the necklace with my name on it. He yanked it from my neck and fell to the ground. The necklace burned in his fiery palms.

Wasting no time, I picked up my dagger and staggered over to him. I raised it into the air and brought it down hard on his right shoulder; I was too weak to aim directly at his chest. He yelled with fury as I removed the dagger, preparing to strike again.

From out of the corner of my eye, I saw Lura hurtling herself toward me. I didn't have time to react. She was on me in an instant, bringing us both to the ground. Zora rushed over, now out of Lura's grasp. She took the dagger from my hands and pushed the sharp end into Lura's back, making the air fairy cry out with rage and despair. As Lura's eyes began to close, her hand flew up and sent a wave of air right into Zora. Already weak, she was no match for the air fairy's power. She hit the wall and slumped to the floor, unable to get back up again.

I threw the now-unconscious Lura off me and looked around. Finn was slowly getting up; the fire radiating from his hands was hotter and more menacing than before. I tried to get up as well, but I didn't have the strength. The burns on my arms sent waves of pain through my body. The effort of using the dagger and falling to the ground had taken all of my lasting strength. I gasped for breath through the pain and the putrid reek of smoke. Finn got to his feet and started walking toward me once more.

I screamed in agony both outside and inside. *I did everything I could! It has to be enough! Oh God, oh God!* I sobbed and screamed with everything I had. I screamed my sorrow to Zora and Brielle. I begged Finn to have mercy. I had never felt so broken and frightened. It was my worst moment, my worst feeling. My heart thundered wildly in my chest, as my last seconds passed by in a blur.

"Please," I cried, "don't. Please don't kill me," I begged, even though I knew it was no use.

"It's too late to beg, Ramsey." Finn said darkly. "I wanted to know your secret, but killing you will have to be good enough. It will at least put an end to everything. I will never have to worry about you again."

His hands rose up into the air. The flames flickered from his palms, ready to end my life. I screamed one last time as the fire shot out, left his hands, and made its way onto my already burning body.

The last thing I saw before the flames struck was a large hawk flying into the room and crashing into Finn. Everything was on fire as I felt myself fall to the ground.

Then I was gone.

~19~

Betrayal

The darkness was unbearable. It was all around me. I could see nothing. I thought death would be an escape, but it only brought on a terrible darkness I could hardly bear. It wouldn't go away or leave me alone. It was making me crazy.

Why was it so dark? I thought Heaven was full of light. Was I even in Heaven at all?

All I could think about was Zora and how I had failed her; left her to burn as I had, the flames licking at her as they had for me…

The flames! The burning! It was still there, I realized, all over my body. Every part of me was covered in the fire, tingling like needles shoved into my skin. *Oh God*, I thought, *I am still alive.*

I could still feel.

But should I fight…or should I let go? It would be so easy to let myself slip away….But no, I couldn't let go. Giving up wouldn't get me into Heaven. It wouldn't get me anywhere worthwhile. I struggled to hold on. I thought of how much Zora needed me. If she was still alive…No! I couldn't think like that. If I wanted to live, I had to be strong and optimistic.

I focused my mind on those I loved. Maybe my memories of them would give me the strength to recover. I thought about Stellan and Addison, but they couldn't hold me. Neither could thinking of Brielle or Aaliyah. Nothing I thought of was strong enough.

Then the Stranger's emerald eyes came into view in my mind. I didn't waste time wondering why he was enough to hold me again. I focused my thoughts on him. I could feel myself coming back, but slowly. I had hope inside of me once again. I just needed a few more moments.

Then his image disappeared. Thinking of him had helped, more than anyone else, but it wasn't enough to let me open my eyes. I needed more. What else could I do?

Then I heard a voice.

"Ramsey! Ramsey, please, wake up. Ramsey, don't die on me. Don't leave us."

I grabbed onto that voice. I allowed its call to pull me forward. It was my last chance to live. If I didn't grab hold of it now, I knew there would be no other chance.

"Ramsey, Ramsey! Ramsey, come on! Come back! Open your eyes, Ramsey!"

I was getting closer. Just a little bit more….

"Ramsey, everything is okay! Zora is alive! You did it, Ramsey! Now come back to us!"

Zora was alive! I finally had enough strength to open my eyes. I had a stronger reason to fight. I hadn't failed after all.

Stellan's face was the first thing that came into view.

"Oh, Ramsey, thank God," he said. His hand brushed my hair.

"Stellan…," I croaked. Tears formed in my eyes. They were hot and stung my cheeks. "How bad is it?"

"Bad," he admitted.

I moaned.

"But you will live. Galen is here and he is healing you. Just hold on," he told me.

"Stellan, you have to keep her awake. The healing will work better if she is awake. Otherwise, she won't receive all that I can give her. And remember, this may not be enough to heal her completely," Galen reminded him.

"I understand," Stellan snapped, his features showing both anxiety and heartbreak. He looked back at me. "Ramsey, you need to stay awake, all right?"

"Okay…," I whispered. "Stellan…it hurts so badly," I said through my tears. "It hurts."

"I know it hurts, but it will get better, all right? Everything will get better soon," he said tenderly, bending down to kiss my forehead.

"Do you promise?" I asked.

"I promise," he said gently.

I winced and my eyes started to close. It was too hard to stay awake. I just wanted to sleep. I would even accept the darkness again if it meant sleep. The exhaustion was so incredible….

"No, Ramsey!" he cried. "Stay with me."

"Where's Zora?" I asked.

I wanted to stay awake. I needed something to keep me awake. I hoped seeing Zora alive would help me hang on.

"She's okay. Galen already healed her."

"Zora…," I moaned.

She was at my side a few seconds later.

"Ramsey, I'm here," she said, taking my hand in hers, the only part of me that wasn't on fire.

"Hi, Sis," I said.

"Ramsey, you were so brave. I knew you would rescue me." She smiled, tears clouding her eyes.

"I'm glad you are safe," I said. I struggled to say the words. I was so weak.

"Me too," she replied.

"Stellan…did you get my note?" I asked.

He nodded. "It was clever of you to leave it in Zora's journal. After you didn't show up at dinner, we looked all over Tarlore and the palace because we knew Brielle was gone as well. We finally went to your room. When we noticed the journal, it was Addison's idea to look through it."

"Addison?" I asked.

"Yes, she is here," Zora told me.

"I saw a hawk," I told them.

"Yes, both Aditi and Galen came with us," Stellan told me.

"Does the Queen know?" I asked.

"Yes. She would have sent more with us, but I told her I could only use my ability on one person at a time. I took Addison and then Galen. Aditi flew here by herself. We got here just in time."

"Yeah, you did," I muttered.

"How's it going, Galen?" Stellan asked.

"The healing is working, but not fast enough. I'm not sure she can survive this without more healing power...power that I simply do not have," he said ominously.

I started shaking with fear. I couldn't die! Not now! Not after knowing Zora was okay! Not after knowing it was all over.

"She has to make it!" Stellan and Zora said together.

They exchanged a glance I didn't understand. Zora seemed confused. It appeared as though Stellan was worried about something other than whether I lived or died. What was happening?

"You said she would be okay, Galen," I heard Addison say.

"I know, but the wounds are extremely serious," he said gravely. "My power is already drained...."

"We won't just let her die. What can we do?" Addison asked.

"I can heal her." I heard Brielle's voice from the other side of the room.

"Brielle, is that you? Are you okay?" I asked.

"I'm fine. Galen healed me right away," she replied.

I saw Brielle walk over to me and kneel beside Zora.

"What were you saying, Princess? Can you truly heal her?" Galen asked.

"Yes. It's part of my ability," she said.

I realized Brielle had never told me about her ability. And I had never asked.

"What ability is that?" Zora asked.

"Let's just say that jewels give me various abilities," she said.

"Jewels?" we all said at once. I heard Aditi's voice in the mix as well.

"I can use jewels to do different things. Ramsey, remember when I dried your clothes?"

I nodded, refraining from speaking because the pain was so great. It *had been* very strange.

"Well, I used a ruby to generate enough heat to dry them," she explained.

"How does that work?" Zora asked.

"I have a special connection with gemstones. When I hold a jewel in my hands, I can channel a specific ability from it," she explained.

"That is really strange," Stellan admitted.

"So? I have more power than all of you put together. I have various abilities because of the jewels," Brielle said, holding her head up high.

"How can you heal her?" Zora asked.

"Each jewel has its own ability. Rubies for heat, sapphires for cold, pearls for cutting things…."

"Is that how you got in the barn?" I interrupted.

"Yes," she confirmed. "I touched the pearl from my necklace to the sword. It received the ability and was able to cut through the barn wall."

Confused faces looked at Brielle.

"Once again, I can't help it if my powers are unique! If you all want to know every detail of my ability, I'll explain it to you over tea when this is over!"

"Can we please get to the point of this long explanation? Ramsey doesn't have time to waste," Galen reminded them.

"Of course," Brielle replied. "Emeralds can be used for healing. So if I have an emerald, I can heal her."

"Do you have one?" Galen asked.

"No," she said crossly. "I would, if my necklace hadn't been ruined. It fell off when I was injured. Then when you guys came in like heroes and kicked Finn to the ground, his flaming body burned it to a crisp."

I now knew why Brielle was such a jewelry hoarder. The memory of her necklace with every jewel imaginable floated through my mind. It left when I realized the question I should have asked right away.

"I almost forgot! What happened to Finn?"

"He got away before we could stop him. But he did receive some nasty wounds from Aditi," Stellan said, looking over at her.

I strained my neck just in time to see her grin with satisfaction.

"I went after him, but lost his trail," the guard explained. "At least the other two are dead."

"You mean the other *one*. The air fairy is still breathing. I healed her after Zora and Brielle," Galen corrected.

"She is? I thought she was dead! Why would you heal her? I'll kill that witch for throwing me around!" Brielle said, clenching her fists.

"No! Ramsey comes first," Stellan demanded.

I witnessed another perplexed glance from Zora.

"Where am I supposed to get an emerald?" Brielle asked.

"I have one!" I remembered. "The shoulder bag you bought for me in the city has an emerald on the front!"

"Oh, yes! I remember now! Where is it?" she asked.

"I dropped it when Finn attacked me," I said, feeling a wave of dizziness crash over me from all the talking.

"I've got it!" I heard Addison shout.

"Bring it over," Brielle instructed.

"Here," Addison said, coming to her side and handing her the bag.

Brielle started picking at the emerald. "It won't come loose!"

"I'll help!" Aditi volunteered.

In an instant, she shape-shifted into her hawk form. She flew over to Brielle and ripped at the bag with her beak. Soon the emerald was free and in Brielle's hands.

"Hurry, Brielle. I can't stay awake much longer," I whispered.

"Just hang on for a few more seconds," she said.

Brielle knelt down beside me and started rubbing her hands together. I could see the emerald begin to glow and then turn her pale hands green. She placed her glowing green hands over my stomach and pressed down. I cried in pain and struggled to stay conscious.

"I know it hurts, but it will be over soon. My kind of healing isn't always gentle. It just doesn't work that way. Everyone's powers are different," she told me.

"I got that!" I screamed.

"Just hang on!" Brielle shouted.

Zora stroked my hair and tried to calm me down. But the pain was just too great. I was ready to scream again, when suddenly I didn't feel anything anymore. I mean, I didn't feel any pain. Everything was fine. I was perfectly fine.

"There," Brielle said, standing up. She wobbled a little, but Aditi, back to her elfen form, was there to steady her.

"Thank you, Brielle," I said, feeling new strength flow into my veins.

Brielle nodded and sat down against the wall to rest.

"Ramsey, can you get up?" Zora asked.

"I'll help you," Stellan offered.

"Thanks," I said, and put my hands out to him.

He took them and brought me to my feet. Before I could give him the kiss I desperately wanted to share, everything went black. Then colors began flashing before my eyes. I tried to open them, but it felt like someone was holding them shut. What was happening to me?

A picture formed before my eyes.

It was a baby elf being rocked by his mother. The mother was Aaliyah. I realized I was watching Aaliyah rocking Stellan as a baby! The pictures started changing. I saw everything. Stellan's whole life flashed before my eyes. I saw his first day of school, I saw him playing with Addison, and I saw the first time he received his ability. How was I able to see this? Had I passed out and this was a dream? Or was it real? What was this?

I continued to watch the memories pass by. I realized how wonderful it was to see and to know, no matter how strange it felt. Stellan had had a very good and peaceful life, except for the death of his father. This entire experience would have been completely amazing if what I saw next had never happened.

The next picture was like a huge stab to my heart. I felt my whole world crashing down as the image formed. I wanted it to stop, and I didn't want to believe it, but nothing I did could make it go away.

It was Stellan, but he wasn't alone. I saw him place the "S" necklace around her neck. I recognized it from his memories. His father had given it to him before he left for war, to signify how much of a man he had become, and to help Stellan remember his father no matter what happened.

Then I saw Stellan bend down to kiss the one person my life had revolved around for the past week.

He kissed Zora.

My eyes were finally able to fly open. I was too stunned and heartbroken to cry. Wordlessly, I released Stellan's hands and backed up against the wall. How could he? How could he have done this? He had not only betrayed Zora, but he had also betrayed me. He had been with Zora when she disappeared and then he had kissed me. *How could he?* It was all I was able to think. I was so shocked I could barely breathe.

I repeated the question aloud as I hit the wall. "How could you, Stellan?" I couldn't think of anything else to say. My heart was broken in two.

"What? What's wrong?" he asked. He obviously hadn't seen what I had seen. He didn't know that I knew.

I steadied myself as a sudden realization came to mind. "Does anyone know what day it is?" I asked, ignoring him completely.

"Midnight came a few minutes ago, so it's early Monday. But in the Elf Realm it's still Sunday," Zora said quietly.

"No, what is the *exact* date?" I asked, getting annoyed.

"It's June seventh in the Elf Realm," Galen confirmed.

"*Happy Birthday to me*," I sang, my voice cracking, just loud enough for everyone to hear. "I'm sixteen today, you guys. You know what that means?"

I had lost track of the days in the Elf Realm, too concerned with finding Zora to pay attention to my birthday approaching.

"You received your power, didn't you?" Brielle asked, awe creeping into her voice.

"Yes, I did. But I wish I hadn't." The tears finally started pouring. I was shaking so hard I could hardly see straight.

"Why? What is it?" Addison asked.

Zora walked over to me and took my hands in hers. She gasped and took them away before I began to see her memories. She knew what my power was because of the special elf gesture. She looked into my eyes and I nodded slowly. Then she walked quickly over to Addison and whispered something into her ear. Addison replied back to her. Zora's eyes widened. She whispered again and then walked back to me. Addison was left with her mouth hanging open.

"Stellan…you didn't," she said, disbelief and horror wracking her features.

Zora put her arms around me and held me. "I'm so sorry, Ramsey. I had no idea. I'm so sorry."

"No, Zora, I'm sorry," I told her. "I didn't know…I wouldn't have if I had known…"

"What's going on?" Brielle asked.

I ignored her.

"How could you?" I repeated again to Stellan, who I noticed was finally putting the pieces together.

"Ramsey, I…," Stellan began to say.

"No! You have no right to speak to me! I trusted you, Stellan! I trusted you! How could you do this? You kissed me knowing you were with Zora. You kissed me while my sister was fighting for her *life*. How in the Realm could you do this to us? You said you cared about me!" I screamed at him. I couldn't control my rage and heartbreak any longer. It was like an erupting volcano, an unstoppable force.

"I didn't mean to hurt you, Ramsey, and I didn't mean to hurt Zora! We were only together for a short time. It wasn't a deep relationship."

"It sure *looked* pretty deep when you put that necklace around her neck!" I cried. "How can you even say things like this with her standing *right here*?"

"How did she know that?" Galen asked. "Ramsey, what is your power?"

"When she holds both of your hands, Ramsey can see your memories. She can see what your whole life has been so far in a matter of seconds," Zora explained.

Zora took the liberty of explaining my new power in more detail to the others. Meanwhile, I was busy screaming my head off at Stellan.

"Stellan, I thought you really cared for me!"

"I do care for you, Ramsey! Remember your promise to me? You said you would remember that I cared about you no matter what."

"That promise means nothing now that I finally understand it," I said sternly.

"I believed what I had with Zora was important, but when I met you, I realized how wrong I was," he tried to explain.

I would have none of his pathetic excuses.

"How can you say that? She was *dying*, Stellan! And you didn't even bother to tell me you had a dying girlfriend!" I shrieked.

"I didn't know what to say. I was afraid you wouldn't want to be with me. That you would think less of me...."

"Well, I sure don't want to be with you now!" I shouted. "What did you think would happen when I found out? You must have known it would come out sooner or later. Or were you hoping I wouldn't be able to rescue my sister?"

"Don't say that, Ramsey! It's not true!" he protested.

"You betrayed my sister and broke my heart. Once we return to Birchwood, I don't want to see you again," I said, anger spewing from my mouth and forming into words.

For a final touch, I picked up my shoulder bag and took out the "S" necklace I remembered was still lying at the bottom. I waved it in the air then threw it in his face. "I think you might want this. Maybe you can give it to the next girl you betray."

I turned my back on him and ran into Zora's open arms.

"I'm sorry, Zora," I said.

"You didn't know, Ramsey. It's not your fault," she said, her eyes clouded with tears.

I hadn't thought about what this meant to her until now. She had been betrayed by Stellan too, but she was staying strong for my sake. I loved her for that.

"Let's go home, okay?" I suggested.

She nodded, and I followed her out of the barn. I heard Galen ask Addison to help carry Lura, who was still weak after being healed. Aditi had shape-shifted and flew ahead of us down the hill. Brielle shouted an ugly name at Stellan and then ran to catch up to us.

I looked back and saw Stellan walk out of the barn last…and completely alone.

~20~

The Long Walk Home

The walk back to the portal was the longest of my life. We could have teleported with Stellan, but no one seemed interested in doing so. He didn't seem to want to himself. Everyone was too hurt and shocked by what he had done. Even Galen, who knew next to nothing about me, felt sorry for Zora and me. He also needed to remain with Lura. He had healed her, but she was still weak, and he didn't want her to escape. He and Addison carried Lura silently the whole way. Brielle asked why we were bothering to take her with us, and Galen responded, "She's a prisoner."

Brielle thought that was a poor excuse to keep her alive, but she didn't pursue it after that. I could tell even she was too tired to fight anymore.

Aditi soared high over our heads. She circled a couple of times and then went a little ways ahead of us. She always came back just to make sure we were okay. I wished I were a shape-shifter. I wanted to fly far away from all this. Our slow procession to the portal was agonizing. It just gave me more time to relive everything that had happened.

How could *this* happen? How could I manage to find and rescue Zora, and then get punished for doing so? How was that fair? The endless tears stung my cheeks. I bit my lower lip to keep from sobbing again. It took me a while to become silent. I spent most of the return trip wiping my tears and clearing my throat. Zora was slightly better off than I was. She cried as well, but I think it was more for me than for herself. Our reunion should have been a happier one. Because of Stellan, it hadn't been.

Stellan remained at least ten feet behind us for the entire journey to the portal. He hadn't spoken one word since we left the barn. I was glad. I didn't want to hear his voice again. I didn't want to see his face again.

I looked back at the barn that was slowly crumpling to the ground. We had set it on fire before we left. We didn't want any humans walking in it to find the dead body of a water fairy and blood everywhere. Galen and Aditi explained it was the only way to hide all the evidence. I also think everyone wanted the barn destroyed because of the terrible events that had taken place there. Maybe they thought burning it would help erase the memories, help us find peace. I knew the memories of this day would linger with me forever, like a scar.

I wondered if Stellan had ever truly cared about me. I thought he had. He said he did even after I confronted him. But how could someone who cared act in such a dishonorable manner? Why hadn't he told me from the start? Why had he kissed me? I remembered his words: "*I believed what I had with Zora was important, but when I met you, I realized how wrong I was.*" Was that the truth? If it was, could I ever forgive him?

I couldn't answer the question my mind repeated over and over again. I didn't have an answer yet. I placed my right hand over my eyes to get the thoughts out of my head.

"Ramsey," Zora said.

"Yes?"

"I know everything seems terrible right now and a huge mess, but I want you to know something."

"What?"

"You are my sister and I love you," she said.

"I know," I said.

"And I won't ever turn my back on you again."

"You never did," I told her.

"I let our parents take you away," she reminded me, averting my gaze.

"You were only a child, Zora. I read the journal. I know how hard it was for you."

"It was hard for both of us," she said, looking up at me.

I nodded. "By the way, your power isn't cruel, Zora," I told her.

"What?" she asked.

"In your journal, you said you didn't like your power. I think it's cool. Maybe you could try it on me when we get back. God knows I'm going to need help getting to sleep."

"Not funny, Ramsey," she said sternly.

I smiled the best smile I could manage, knowing she was right. Brielle joined us a few moments later. "I just wanted to say that Stellan is a horrible rat. Both of you are way too good for him. If you want, I could have him put in prison," she offered.

"You are not helping the situation, Princess Brielle," Zora told her.

"Oh, sorry." She looked down at her feet. "And by the way, don't call me Princess. Ramsey is my friend, and she calls me Brielle. Since you are Ramsey's sister, you should call me that, too."

"Thanks, Brielle. But no more prison offers, all right?"

"Fine." She sighed. "Let me know if you change your mind."

"Will do," Zora replied, a slight smile on her face.

Brielle could make anyone smile. Her special qualities were anything but serious.

I remained silent throughout the conversation. I didn't want to talk about Stellan, whether it was criticizing him or crying over him. I hoped the pain would go away if I refrained from talking about him. It might have been wishful thinking, but I hardly cared anymore.

A screech from Aditi told us we had finally arrived at the portal. My head hung low as we slowly made our way.

***

"You go first, Aditi," I told her as she went back to her elfen form.

She nodded. "All right. Once I'm through, send Galen and Lura. Princess Brielle, you come after, and then Addison. The rest of you can decide what to do after that." With a nod, she turned her back to us and jumped into the portal.

Galen went next with Lura, who was just beginning to regain consciousness. Brielle gave Stellan a nasty glare and then went as well. Addison followed quickly after. The three of us were left alone with each other. Before I could react, Zora had jumped into the portal. What kind of game was she trying to play?

"Ramsey, please wait," Stellan said.

It was painful to hear his voice, and my emotions were in turmoil. I shook my head.

"Please, Ramsey. Just listen to me for one second."

I didn't respond, so he took it as a yes. "I did a terrible thing. I know it was wrong. I should never have kissed you before telling you about Zora. I should have told you from the beginning. I was going to tell you, but then…," he trailed off and shook his head. "Ramsey, I can't change what has happened. But can't you just look past that for a second and remember how you felt about me up until this point?" he pleaded.

"It doesn't matter how I felt about you, Stellan. Our entire relationship was a lie," I said bitterly.

"No, it wasn't. I care about you…*so much.* I feel things for you that I've never felt for anyone else. And it doesn't matter how short of time we've known each other. I know in my heart that what I feel for you is real. Can't you say the same?"

I bit my lip, refusing to respond because I didn't know what to say.

He stepped forward, reaching out to me but then letting his hands drop to his sides as he thought better of it. "I…I just want you to forgive me, Ramsey. Can you please? Can you *ever* forgive me?" he asked.

I thought about it for a moment. Could I forgive him? I probably could. Did I want to? No way.

"Ask me about it in the morning," I said sarcastically.

I turned around and jumped into the portal before he could say any more.

***

Zora and Addison were waiting for me when I arrived. I went back to Zora's arms and waited until I stopped shaking before I spoke.

"Where are the others?" I asked.

"Galen and Aditi took Lura and Brielle to the Queen. We are to meet them there shortly. However, you can go to your room if you want. Everyone would understand," Zora said.

"No, I'll come with you. It's the right thing to do," I said. "I should face the Queen."

They both nodded and helped me get back over the bridge. As we walked to the palace, I heard Stellan climbing onto the bridge and following us.

Eder stopped us before we reached the palace doors.

"Can we talk?" he asked, looking away from me once when he noticed Zora's presence. However, he didn't say anything about her return. Instead, he waited for my answer.

"Sure," I said, hoping he had changed his mind and was going to let me in on a few of his secrets.

He led me away from Zora – who clearly wanted to say something but didn't have the chance – to a secluded area near the palace.

Not removing his hand from under my elbow, he asked, "Are you okay?"

"I've been better," I admitted.

He didn't comment on the fact that I should be happy about my sister being safe, and I was grateful. Even though he had no idea of what went on between Stellan and me, he respected me enough to leave the subject alone after noticing how upset I was.

"I just wanted to express how relieved I am that you're safe," he told me, so earnestly that I felt tears welling up in my eyes.

His eyes became wide with shock. "Hey, it's all right," he said, pulling me into his embrace.

Even though I knew it was probably inappropriate to be hugging the Queen's guard in front of my sister and Stellan, I couldn't deny the sense of comfort I felt at being in his arms. He was the strength I needed in such a bleak situation.

He released me from his grasp and stepped back, clearing his throat in doing so. I could tell he was back to his professional mode. "Has Zora told you anything of your secret yet?"

I shook my head. "There hasn't really been…enough time."

"She's avoiding it. She doesn't want you to know," he said abruptly.

"You don't know that," I retorted. "Once she's back home safe, she'll probably be open to telling me."

Eder shook his head. "No, she won't. I was expecting this…."

"There you go!" I said. "Back to being vague again."

"I'm sorry; it's just the only way…."

"Stop," I said, "you've already told me the story. Thanks for the hug, Eder, really, but I've got to go meet with the Queen."

I started to walk away, but his next words stopped me cold.

"I'll tell you if she won't," he said sincerely.

I spun around, my heart beating rapidly in my chest. "You mean…you know my secret?"

He exhaled deeply. "Yes."

"Why didn't you tell me before?"

"I was told to allow Zora to tell you," he explained.

"Told by whom?" I asked.

Before he could respond, Zora came up and started tugging at my sleeves. "Come on, Ramsey," she said, "it's time to go."

"Wait, we're in the middle of something here," I replied.

"No," she said sternly, with anger filling her voice. "We leave *now*."

Confused as to why she was acting so harshly, I looked from her to Eder and back again, trying to decide my next move.

However, I wasn't the one to make it; Zora was. She pulled me away from Eder and led me toward the palace doors, where Stellan was waiting with a suspicious look upon his face.

"Zora!" I cried. "Stop. I'm serious!"

She paid no attention to me. I was surprised she could be so strong after being tortured for months.

"She won't tell you!" I heard Eder yell. "Trust me! You have to find another way!"

I couldn't even reply; Zora was pushing me through the palace doors. The last thing I saw as I turned around – before the doors swung shut – was a concerned Elvina resting her hands on Eder's shoulders, as if to calm him down…or maybe even to restrain him.

***

Once inside, Danica, Thane, and Jacqueline took us to the Queen. We followed silently up the many flights of stairs to her quarters. Galen, Aditi, and Brielle were already there with her. I saw Lura being heavily guarded by Wren and Gavin. The two shape-shifters' eyes never once drifted away from the air fairy.

Lady Cora was sitting with the Queen and Brielle, who was clinging to her mother's side. When we entered, Queen Taryn stood up and approached us.

If I hadn't been so upset, I would have taken time to admire the beauty of Queen Taryn's small "apartment." All I had the heart to notice were the elegantly decorated walls, carpet, and bed. The traditional green and brown elfin colors were utterly magnificent.

"Welcome home, Zora," Queen Taryn said. "I am glad you are safe at last. I'm glad *all* of you are safe."

"Thank you, Queen Taryn," Zora said.

We all repeated Zora's words soon after.

"I know you all must be tired, so I will make this brief. While what Ramsey and my daughter did was foolish, reckless, and extremely dangerous, it was well worth it. You not only rescued Zora, but you also captured an air fairy, killed a dangerous water fairy, and managed to scare off a highly trained Element fairy general," she said.

I noticed how Queen Taryn failed to mention it was Brielle who had killed Wynter. Maybe Brielle hadn't told her. I wondered who Queen Taryn thought had killed her. But I wouldn't mention anything. Brielle had taken it pretty hard, and I didn't want her feeling worse about the situation.

Queen Taryn started to speak once more, so I focused back on her words. "You also did this all without one bit of disturbance from humans. Well done." She waited a moment before continuing. "As for the trials of Addison, Stellan, and Ramsey herself, consider them nonexistent. You have proven that bringing Ramsey from the Human Realm was the right thing to do. You will always be remembered for your courage. Now, I know you are all tired, so, goodnight."

We all said goodnight to Queen Taryn and the others and left them to discuss Lura's fate. Stellan was considerate enough to teleport to his room and leave us alone. It was better that way. Zora, Addison, and I walked slowly down the stairs to our rooms.

"Will you be staying in my room?" I asked Zora as we went down the hall, trying to push the eerie occurrence with Eder to the back of my mind.

"Of course I will. Anyway, no one gave me a room of my own," she reminded me.

"Good," I said.

Once again, I didn't want to be alone.

Addison's room came before ours, so we said goodnight to her there.

"I'm glad you two are safe. I'm sorry about all the pain my brother has caused. Believe me, I had no idea about any of it."

"We kept the relationship a secret because we had no idea whether it would work or not. We didn't want anyone hurt if we decided to break things off, so we decided to wait until we were more serious. That never happened, as Stellan said. Don't think I will ever hold what happened against you. I know Ramsey won't either. You will always be my best friend," Zora said, hugging Addison tightly.

"She's right, Addison," I agreed, and gave her a hug as well.

"Goodnight," she said, walking into her room.

"Goodnight," we both replied before she shut the door.

"Let's get some sleep, all right?" Zora suggested.

"That sounds like a wonderful idea," I agreed.

I walked with her into our room. Zora took a shower, something she hadn't done since she was taken, and I prepared to go to bed. I gave Zora my nightgown and changed into my navy sundress. It would be all right to sleep in for now. Throwing down my tattered shoulder bag, I went to the nightstand. I picked up Zora's journal and handed it to her when she was done showering.

"I believe this is yours," I said.

"Thank you. I'm glad it helped," she said as she took it.

"It did."

Before we got into bed, I noticed something.

"Zora, you might want to take that Mood Diamond off your neck," I said with a slight smile.

"That's probably a good idea." She unclasped the necklace and tossed it onto my shoulder bag. "I hope I never have to use that again."

"Me too," I agreed.

We were too tired to do or say anything else, so we climbed into bed and blew out the candles.

"Zora?"

"Yes?" she replied.

"Outside…with that guard…why were you acting so…harsh?"

I heard Zora take a sharp breath and then slowly exhale. "I'm sorry. I just wanted to get inside the palace. I can't explain it, but I felt like I wasn't really safe until I was inside."

I nodded, understanding her reasoning completely. However, I had one more question for my sister before we fell asleep.

"What he said, about you never telling me my secret…it's not true, is it?" I inquired.

"Let's leave those things for another time," she told me quietly. "Right now, we both need rest."

Not satisfied, but knowing I shouldn't push her, I said, "Okay. Goodnight."

"Goodnight," she replied, turning away from me.

A few minutes later her breathing became even, and I was left alone with my thoughts.

Zora's homecoming should have been a happy one. It wasn't in the least, no matter how grateful I was that she was safe.

It wasn't enough to celebrate yet.

***

I slept undisturbed, and I was glad to see Zora safe and sound when I woke up later. It was five on Monday morning in the Elf Realm. Feeling rejuvenated, I got out of bed and took the much-needed shower I hadn't been able to do last night. I redressed in my navy dress and went to wake up Zora.

"Time to get up already?" she asked.

"Yep, we should get down for breakfast. We don't want anyone worrying about us, do we?"

"No," she agreed. "What am I supposed to wear?"

"Uh, I have no idea. Maybe we can borrow something from Brielle. Let's go and see her now," I suggested.

"Sure, let's go."

We hurried up to Brielle's room. I hoped she was still there and hadn't left for breakfast yet. Thankfully, when we knocked on her door, she opened it quickly.

"Hey! Come on in," she invited.

We stepped inside and sat down with her on the couch.

"Zora needs fresh clothing, and come to think of it, so do I. Can we borrow something?"

"Certainly. I have just the things for you," Brielle told us.

She went to her wardrobe. After fishing through it for a few moments, she came back with two sundresses. One was green and the other brown. I took the green one and Zora changed into the brown one. The dresses were simple yet pretty, with embroidered vines at the bottom of each.

"Thank you so much, Brielle," I said, once we were dressed.

"You're welcome. I'm glad I could help."

"We should really get down for breakfast," Zora reminded us.

"Right, let's go," I agreed.

We ran down the stairs and into the dining hall. We sat down at just past five thirty. We made sure to sit far away from Stellan, who was with Addison and the ten guards a few chairs down. I felt bad for ignoring Addison, but I knew she would understand.

I didn't look at Stellan. Instead, I kept my eyes on Zora and Brielle, who were silently comforting me.

I didn't want Zora to pity me, because Stellan had hurt her too. But she told me that things had changed for her after she was taken, were put into a different perspective. Being alive was all she truly cared about, at least right now. She would grieve for her lost relationship, but it wasn't what most concerned her at the moment.

I wasn't hungry, but I forced myself to eat something. I knew I needed the nourishment, no matter how bad I felt about Stellan. Breakfast passed quickly. I was ready to return to my room when I saw Addison approaching. I smiled as she walked over to me.

"We're leaving at noon," she said.

"So soon?" I asked, taken aback.

"Queen Taryn says it's for the best. She is expecting a great deal of company from around the Realm in three days for the summer, and they need to prepare."

I nodded. "Okay."

"Meet us on the bridge at noon," she confirmed.

"All right, see you then," I told her.

I watched Addison go and then joined Zora and Brielle, just in time to avoid Stellan's gaze as he walked by.

"We are leaving at noon, Zora. We need to meet Addison on the bridge."

"No! You can't go so soon!" Brielle shouted in protest.

"Queen Taryn has guests arriving in three days. She needs our rooms for them," I explained.

"Oh, yes, I remember now. I'm sorry we are making you leave," Brielle apologized.

"Don't be. We need to get home anyway," I told her.

"Yes, I miss Birchwood City too much to stay away any longer," Zora agreed.

I nodded. "But let's not talk about leaving for another couple of hours or so, okay?"

Brielle and Zora agreed, so we put leaving out of our minds. Brielle told us she had a surprise and dragged us up to her room.

Once inside, she brought out two large baskets with shiny green bows. She handed one to each of us and sat down on her brown couch. They were very heavy. We stared at them for a moment, not sure of what to say.

"Open them!" she cried.

"Brielle, you didn't have to," I protested.

"Just open them," she demanded.

I sighed. "Fine."

I sat down and pulled the bow off the top of the basket. Then I carefully took off the lid and peered inside. Sitting delicately in a nest of dried grass was a large egg. It was silver with blue spots. The blue spots shone like jewels. It took me a minute to realize they *were* jewels. They were sapphires! I placed my hand over the egg; it felt warm to the touch. My mouth hanging open, I looked up at Brielle, who was grinning from pointy ear to pointy ear.

"Is this what I think it is?" I asked.

"It depends on what you think it is," she said sweetly.

"How did you have the time?"

"I have my ways," she explained.

By now, Zora had opened hers as well. I scooted over to her and looked inside her basket. She also had a very large egg. This one was also silver but had red spots. Zora's egg was decorated with rubies.

"Brielle…oh my," Zora exclaimed.

"Am I right, Zora? Are we looking at dragon eggs here?" I asked.

"Yes," Brielle and Zora both said.

I squealed with joy and clapped my hands, careful not to drop the basket.

"Brielle, how did you get these?" Zora asked.

"Like I said, a princess has her ways."

"Are you saying that when these eggs hatch, we will have baby dragons?" I was still trying to put things together.

"They won't be babies very long, that's for sure. I hope you have a big open field for them to live," Brielle said.

"Oh, we do, but, Brielle, this is too generous. Dragons are so rare," Zora reminded her.

"It's all right, truly. You need something to remember me by anyway. They're orphans. Both mothers were killed in the war."

"That's too bad," I said, momentarily saddened by the thought. I felt better when I realized this was a chance for Zora and me to give them the love they deserved. "So how big are we talking here?" I asked, still admiring the beauty of my egg as it sparkled in the light. "And when are they going to hatch?"

"They get big, as in *very* big. The humans didn't get the size wrong in their fantasy books. Dragon eggs take about two to three years to hatch. These will probably hatch by the end of summer or the beginning of fall."

"Wow, dragons by fall. Amazing," I whispered.

I couldn't believe I was going to have my own dragon! It almost didn't seem real.

"How do we take care of them? I have read only a little on dragons," Zora said.

"Don't worry, Zora; you have no idea how easy it is. I have a dragon myself, but he is off on a holiday at the moment." Brielle giggled. "Just make sure they have plenty of room and enough food. Eventually they will just fly off and find their own meals, though, so make sure to tell them not to feast on any farms that provide food for the elves in your city. You must set rules right away."

"Can we communicate with them?" I asked.

"Sort of," she replied, "dragons are highly intelligent. They can pick up almost any language. Common is like a second nature to them. Be glad we don't speak our own elfin language anymore like we did when our Realm was first created. That would be tough for a baby dragon to learn. At first, you won't be able to understand the dragons. You will be able to pick up some of their body language and noises, but it takes years to fully understand Dragon Tongue. Their language is a lot more complicated and advanced than ours."

"So they can understand us, but we can't understand them?" Zora clarified.

"Yes. Personally, I think the system works well. I wouldn't want to hear my dragon discuss plans to disobey me!"

We laughed and hugged Brielle, repeating "thank you" numerous times. I was so happy with my new dragon egg I nearly forgot about Stellan. I sighed and rubbed my dragon egg gently. I couldn't wait until the end of summer.

Finally, things were looking up a bit.

~21~

Wise Goodbyes

I pushed the door open and walked down the stairs of the palace, clutching my dragon egg basket, my shoulder bag slung around my neck. Carefully setting down both the bag and the basket, I leaned my arms onto the bridge railing and looked out across the water. It was a little after eleven, and I was early for our departure, but I hadn't wanted to remain inside the palace any longer. I didn't want to risk seeing *him* until it was absolutely necessary.

The crystal clear water beneath me was beautiful and completely mesmerizing. I watched the water sparkle and dance as it bobbed over stones and helped tiny fish swim along the streams. The water's gurgling soothed me. I closed my eyes and just listened to the calming sounds.

"This truly is a wonderful place," a voice said beside me.

Left to my own thoughts, I hadn't noticed the Queen join me until she spoke. My eyes flew open.

"Hello, Queen Taryn," I replied.

"You're out here quite early. You missed my formal farewell to your friends."

"I'm sorry. I just needed some time to think before we left," I admitted.

"I see. I thought your troubles were over. Sure, there is still your secret to think about, but that will be dealt with in due time. You rescued your sister, saved your friends from prison, made many new friends, and you are leaving with a dragon egg," she pointed out.

"Yes, those problems are solved and I leave here today with many things to be thankful for. But I now have a new problem I hadn't expected."

"How so?" she asked.

"It's a long story," I said.

"We have time."

"I don't know…," I trailed off.

"Trust me," she said, "I'll only listen."

I nodded, and told her everything about Stellan and me. I told her about how much we seemed to care about each other. Then I told her what had happened in the barn. It felt good to tell someone who hadn't been there, someone who could just listen and not be affected. She didn't know Stellan, not really, so it was easier for me to speak about him. When I was finished, I had fresh tears clouding my vision. Queen Taryn was silent for a moment and looked at me intently.

"I can't tell you how to fix your problems or how to feel. However, I can tell you one thing. Remember that your power is a very special gift. You have the ability to see things others can't. You can tell when someone is lying or telling the truth. I know your first experience was an unhappy one, but you will have many more that will turn out differently."

"I hope so."

"Why don't you try it on me?" she suggested.

"What? Oh no, I couldn't possibly. You are the Queen. It wouldn't be right for me to know about your whole life."

"If it will help you, Ramsey, then it won't matter to me. Here, take my hands," Queen Taryn said.

She put her hands out to me and nodded in encouragement.

"Are you sure?" I asked.

"Yes. Go ahead."

I bit my lower lip and slowly reached my hands out and placed them over hers. A large, bright flash of color hit me, then the pictures started to form.

I saw Queen Taryn's birth and childhood, when she was Princess Taryn. I saw the love in her parents' eyes as they watched her grow. I saw her live a beautiful life in the palace. A few of the pictures were sad. Her parents' deaths, the war, and the death of her husband, the King. However, most of the images were happy. The most wonderful memory was of Brielle's birth. I could see Queen Taryn's love for her daughter as I watched the Princess grow. Even among the turmoil and sadness, Queen Taryn truly enjoyed living and being the Elf Realm's leader.

The pictures ended, and I was left smiling in the darkness behind my eyes. I opened them and released my hands from hers.

"Thank you," I said quietly.

"See? Your power can show brilliant things as well. It's also very informative. Before seeing those memories would you have guessed that I liked to ride bareback on a horse?"

I smiled. "Never."

"Then you have learned something about your queen, haven't you?" she asked.

"Yes," I admitted.

"I have to find Princess Brielle so we can see you and your friends off from the palace. Excuse me for just one moment," she explained.

"Wait!" I called as she turned to leave.

"Yes?"

"I remembered what your power was when I saw your memories," I told her.

"How I know what others are doing even when I am not around them?"

I nodded. "You knew when Brielle and I went after Zora. Why did you let us go?" I asked.

"I let you go because I believed in you."

I was taken aback. The Queen of the Elf Realm believed in me, even though I was only a confused elfen from the Human Realm.

"I don't know what your secret is, Ramsey. But I do know you are special to this Realm. Whatever you may need to do to help us in the future, I trust you."

I was speechless as she walked away. Before opening the palace door, she turned to me one last time.

"And that also means I know about Brielle's wild lifestyle."

"I'm not sure she realizes you know," I said.

Queen Taryn smiled wryly. "Well, she thought she could use her topaz gem to hide. When she uses it, it blocks others elves' powers. My power is stronger. I'm far older and more experienced than my young daughter."

"I have to admit, your daughter's power is very confusing and strange to me."

"That's Brielle for you," she said. She laughed and then vanished into the palace.

Smiling, I turned back to the water. I liked Queen Taryn very much. She was real. She wasn't a high-and-mighty royal. She was like any other elfen, just with a little more power. More importantly, she understood her daughter and allowed her to make her own decisions. If only Brielle knew that I wasn't the only one different in this Realm....

I waited on the bridge until I heard the palace doors open once again. Out came the high guard, Queen Taryn, Brielle, Lady Cora, Addison, Zora, and...Stellan. I took another look and realized Thane and Aditi were missing, as well as Eder and Elvina. I wondered where they were. I picked up my shoulder bag and made sure my dragon egg basket was still safely by my side.

The guards lined up in a row outside the palace. Queen Taryn stood in front of them with Brielle and Lady Cora. Addison and Zora walked over to join me with Stellan lagging slowly behind. We stood facing Queen Taryn as she began to speak.

"It is time to bid you farewell. We have admired your courage and enjoyed your company. Now, you must return home, and we must prepare for our summer guests. We will always remember your time here."

I wished I could have spoken with Eder before leaving, but my problems with Stellan had distracted me. Now, I desperately wished to converse with him. He had told me to wait until I found Zora to worry about anything else. I had found Zora, so now I felt I had the right to get some answers.

But there was no time left for that now. We were leaving, and he wasn't present. I would just have to take his advice and let things happen when they were meant to.

Before the royal entourage retreated into the palace, Danica walked over to me.

"Here," she said, handing me a white card decorated with green and brown flowers. "I would like you to attend my wedding in July.

Your sister may come too, along with anyone else you care to bring. I don't want this to be the end of our friendship. I would like it if we got to know each other better, without me having to protect you." She smiled. "You truly are a special elfen."

"Thank you," I whispered, suddenly unable to raise my voice any higher.

My vision grew blurry once again. We were truly leaving Tarlore. I wouldn't see anyone here until July. It seemed like a lifetime ago that I was in the Human Realm. How long would it feel like before I was able to return to Tarlore?

Danica squeezed my hand, then left me. I put the card in my shoulder bag.

"Goodbye, my friends, I wish you well on your journey," the Queen said.

With a wave, she turned and went back into the palace. Brielle had started to follow, and then at the last second she turned around and ran over to us. When she reached where I was standing, she hugged me tightly.

"See you at the wedding," she said. I could tell she was trying to hold back tears.

"Wouldn't miss it," I replied, my voice cracking.

I watched her go into the palace, tears streaming down my cheeks. She was a wonderful friend, no matter how strange. The guards and Lady Cora followed Brielle. I turned to Zora, and was about to say something about leaving when the palace doors swung open again. I turned to see who else was running back for a goodbye and gasped. It wasn't for a goodbye at all.

Instead, it was Thane and Aditi, pulling a very resistant Lura toward us. She looked refreshed from her healing the previous night, but was still dressed in her own clothes, splattered with blood. Her blonde hair looked unruly and tangled. Yet her face showed the same cruelty and cold beauty it had before, and her smile was still dangerous. We waited silently as they passed. As they crossed the bridge, Lura turned to face me.

"You think this is over, elfen? It's not. You will not live to see your next birthday, no matter what power you now possess, no matter what secret you hold within you. Tell your little plaything he had better watch your back, because Finn will come after you. Don't underestimate him. Don't ever think you are safe," she spat.

Thane angrily pushed Lura forward into a waiting carriage that read *Prison* on the side. The horse pulling it went into a gallop, and Lura was gone. Thane and Aditi walked passed us without a word, and retreated into the palace.

I was left shaking with anger and fear. I knew Lura had called Stellan my "plaything" just to anger me. She had been in the barn when I confronted him.

The fear came from her warning. No matter how much I hated to admit it, I knew what she said was true. Finn would be back. He was still out there. I just had no idea when he would come.

My frown quickly turned into a smile when I saw a large golden dragon soaring overhead. I sighed and gazed at the sky as we walked through the busy streets. Soon, I would have a dragon as well. I thought about what it would be like to watch my own dragon flying up in the sky.

It was a great way to bid farewell to Tarlore.

~22~

Decisions, Decisions

The journey back to Birchwood City was long, tiring, and mostly silent. I spoke only when addressed directly, and I refused to be anywhere near Stellan as we walked. The only ones who talked frequently were Addison and Zora. Being best friends, they used the journey to catch up on lost time. They laughed and giggled about school and friends, but became serious when Zora described her life as a prisoner.

I tried to ignore most of their chatting. I didn't want to laugh with them. I didn't want any more excuses to cry. I just wanted the trip back to pass quickly so I could be home. Then I would sort out my problems with Stellan. Now was not the time. I hadn't decided what I would do about the situation yet.

The trip took three days and two nights. Addison tried to lighten the mood by singing and playing her fiddle, but she was the only one who sang. Zora couldn't, because we would all pass out, and neither Stellan nor I was in the mood. I enjoyed the music even so. It was pleasant and comforting as I lay awake at night, trying my best to fall asleep. Zora still refused to try my idea of singing me to sleep.

On the last day of our trip, Stellan tried to talk to me more than once. He would tap me on the shoulder, but I would just walk faster. I was afraid to talk to him because I didn't know what I would say. But after about the fifth time, I finally responded.

"What, Stellan?" I asked in annoyance.

"Can we talk?" he asked.

I shook my head. "I need a bit more time."

"All right, how much time?"

"I don't know," I told him.

"Ramsey, please," he begged.

"This isn't easy for me, Stellan," I told him.

"I know."

"I don't think you do," I retorted.

I locked my eyes onto his. He looked down. "How much time?" he repeated.

"We can talk when we get home," I said, not knowing whether that would be enough time or not. But I had to say something to get him off my back.

"All right, I'll hold you to that," he said.

I ignored his comment and walked ahead.

***

Stellan didn't try talking to me again. Instead, he walked a few paces behind me. Addison and Zora led the way back home. By noon, we had reached the field right before the city.

A short time later we walked through Birchwood City's gates. I sighed with relief at the familiar sights and smells. Although I had spent only a short time here, I knew it was my home. It had always been my home. Now I could share it with my sister. I smiled as I thought of having family in the house. I wouldn't be alone any longer.

Zora came over and gave me a hug. "We're home!" she cried.

"I know," I said, though I wasn't quite as enthusiastic.

I was upset and confused about the choices I would have to make soon. I wanted to rejoice with my sister but couldn't summon the energy.

We walked through the busy dirt streets. As we passed, elves shouted congratulations and welcomed Zora home. A few elves even came up and talked with us for a while. Some hugged Zora and said they were glad she was safe. The sun was shining and everything was right…except for one thing. I would have to deal with that later.

Elves everywhere cheered and praised me for rescuing my sister. I finally felt welcome somewhere. I belonged. These elves were proud of me. I was accepted. And I didn't have to hide my ears anymore. This was truly my home. I felt a little of my despair ebb away.

Then I remembered my human family back in Wisconsin, and a wave of melancholy came over me. I hadn't thought about my old life much since coming here. I didn't miss them as much as I thought I should. But I knew it wasn't because I never cared for my human family. I had just been too preoccupied with my new life and the challenges it presented. I wondered how often I would think of my parents, Dina, and Carmen in the time ahead. However, I knew no matter how much things changed for me, for better or worse, my old life would be with me, in the back of my mind and in a place in my heart. I would never forget what led me here.

Zora and I stopped by Aaron's shop on the way. As welcome-home presents, he gave both Zora and I a beautiful gold and silver interlaced chain necklace. We thanked him and went into the streets again. Stellan and Addison had gone ahead to see Aaliyah before us. Enjoying the time away from Stellan, I walked happily down the roads with my sister.

We were tired from our journey when we finally arrived at Aaliyah's house. We needed to see her before we could rest. When we walked through the door, she ran over and hugged us both. Tears fell as she embraced us. I smiled the whole time, relishing the sweetness of the reunion. I had brought my sister home. I made many elves happy with her return. I felt elated by this accomplishment.

"Welcome home, Zora," Aaliyah said through her happy tears.

We all hugged and rejoiced together, and Addison joined in as well. We had lunch after the tears dried, then Zora and I went home. We put our things away, including our dragon eggs, which we placed beside our beds. Then we spent the remainder of the afternoon talking and finally getting to know each other.

I told Zora everything about life in the Human Realm. I told her how hard it was, about my loving adopted family, my ditzy sister, and my best friend, Carmen. She told me she would talk about her life another day, because it involved the one elf I didn't want to discuss. I agreed.

Addison wrote through Zora that a welcome-home party was on the schedule for us tonight. The elves wanted to celebrate Zora's rescue from the fairies. They also wanted to officially welcome me to the home and the city of my birth. I was home at last.

And here to stay, I thought to myself happily.

I dressed in the red velvet gown Brielle had purchased for me in Tarlore. I hadn't had a chance to wear it to dinner, so I decided now would be the perfect time. The dress had beautiful black lace at the bottom and across the waist, very elegant and regal. I paired it with my pearl necklace, earrings, and bracelet from Aaron's store.

Zora wore a deep blue dress with a green band around the waist. She paired the dress with black shoes similar to mine and a sapphire necklace, bracelet, and earrings. We left the house feeling elegant and festive.

The party had already begun in the town center. I hadn't noticed the open area around the big fountain before tonight. We could hear music playing and the laughter and celebration of elves. We looked around in awe at the wondrous place. Candles lit the entire area with a beautiful glow of flame. The fountain spouted clear water, shining under the full moon. Everyone looked regal and happy. *Elves sure love to party*, I thought to myself. And this was a time of celebration. I wished the Stellan problem would disappear for a while so I could feel happy too.

Zora left me to greet old friends, and I decided to look around for someone I knew as well. The first friend I spotted was Blaire. She wore a lovely green dress with brown lace trim. I ran over to her.

"Hey!" I greeted.

She turned around and smiled. "I heard you were home! Welcome back, and congratulations on rescuing your sister."

"I couldn't have done it without you, Blaire. The Mood Diamond helped a lot," I said over the roar of the music. I left out the part about my near-death experiences with it. It wouldn't be appropriate conversation for a party.

"I'm glad," she said.

We parted ways when I caught sight of another friend, sitting on a chair and listening to the music, his small legs swinging to the sounds.

"Mac, what are you doing here?" I asked. "I thought you had gone to the Flower Fairy Realm."

"I did!" he replied. "But when I heard word that a brave elfen and her friends had rescued her sister from Element fairies, I had to return!"

"Thank you for coming! And may I say, you look quite handsome in your suit," I complimented.

"I knew I would! Now go and enjoy the party with your friends. We will talk again soon, and you can tell me all about your travels."

"All right, I'll see you soon!" I called as I walked away.

As I turned to survey the area, I realized that I didn't see Stellan anywhere. Had he come to the party at all? Or had he remained home because of me? I felt oddly guilty.

I walked around in search of something to do. I didn't really feel like dancing, and I didn't even feel like visiting with friends. I had no interest in reliving my travels just yet. The stories would always end with the remembrance of what Stellan did.

Instead of joining the party, I took a seat on a small wooden bench. I hadn't really wanted to come to the party, but I had agreed for Zora's benefit. I had to support and welcome her home the right way.

Sighing, I looked up at the beautiful stars in the sky. Each star twinkled brightly in the clear night. The sight was mesmerizing and soothing as I gazed upward. Lost in thought, I wasn't aware of the music becoming a great deal slower. I was holding on to the deep power of the sky's comforting palette.

A shadow appeared before me, distracting me from the beauty of the sky. My eyes widened in shock as I gazed upon a different form of beauty.

The Stranger held out his hand.

"Would you like to dance with me?" he asked, with his emerald eyes and their sparkling silver slashes dancing in the moonlight.

Should I? Stellan's image flashed across my mind. I hadn't decided yet what I would say to him. Maybe dancing with someone else would be inappropriate.

But as his eyes watched me, waiting for an answer, I realized it didn't matter. I wanted to dance with him, and I wasn't going to say no. I owed it to him, after all, because thinking of him had helped me through the last few days. It was only one dance; just one dance with this beautiful-eyed elf.

"Yes," I said, breathlessly.

I took his hand in mine. Being careful not to allow both of my hands in his, I followed him to the fountain. I didn't want to see any memories tonight, especially from someone I hardly knew, even though the idea was tempting.

I placed my arms around his neck and he placed his around my waist, holding me close. At first, I could barely breathe. His nearness threw me into a whirlwind of emotions. I looked into his eyes, and he smiled, just slightly. And suddenly, I felt completely at ease with him as we glided together. I felt *warm*.

We danced slowly for one song, and neither of us seemed to notice when the next song began. I never took my eyes off his. He kept his emerald gaze locked on mine.

Dancing with him was heavenly, an experience I wished would never end. I finally found the relief I needed; all the tension seemed to slip away. For the few moments I was in his arms, everything was pure bliss. I didn't have worries. I didn't have anything else to think about but dancing with him. He was so…*refreshing*, and so unlike anyone else in my life. *He* was different.

Another song came and then another. We didn't notice the time pass. We didn't speak. We just swayed to the music. The comfort he exerted was so precious, and I was afraid that at any moment it would all slip away. I found myself leaning in, resting my head on his shoulder so his cheek touched mine. I felt my face redden, making me glad that he wasn't able to see.

His grip on me tightened, and I did the same. It was like we were both fighting to stay together, and not allowing anything to ruin this moment between us. My breathing quickened as I realized how close we were. I was all too aware of his hands resting on my lower back, their imprints like sweet flames that seemed to go through the thin fabric of my dress and onto my skin.

I wanted to say something to him. I wanted to tell him all I felt just now, but I couldn't find the words. A jumble of phrases clouded my mind, making me unable to form coherent sentences. I exhaled deeply; I didn't know whether it was from the frustration I felt at not being able to speak, or the relief I felt at being in his arms.

A new, faster song began, and it seemed the enchantment between us began to ebb. I looked up at him, not knowing how to proceed. His fingertips brushed a strand of hair from my face that covered my eyes. He watched me for a moment, and the beauty of his gaze mesmerized me. We were still close, and the connection we shared was impeccably intimate. Still, no words were spoken between us. But that didn't matter. We didn't need words. All that needed to be said was found in our eyes.

In that moment, I forgot Stellan. I forgot the kisses we had shared. I forgot the butterflies I felt whenever he held my hand or called me beautiful. I forgot that he told me he was falling for me, feeling things he had never felt before. I forgot him, and instead, I focused on the Stranger. I remembered every detail of our previous encounters: The way his eyes seemed to penetrate my every emotion; the way I lost all traces of normal speaking function when he was near; the way just the thought of him gave me a balance; and the way it felt to be held by him, every part of me alive and feeling sensations I didn't know existed until now.

Then I wondered, *what if?*

What if *he* kissed me? What if *he* told me I was beautiful? What if *he* told me he loved me?

What would I say in return?

Before I could think of an answer, he backed away from me, bowed slightly, and walked away into the crowd. I watched as he looked back and smiled at me one last time before he faded among the elves.

Suddenly, I felt strangely empty, as though he took something of mine along with him as he went. I didn't know what it was, or what exactly had just happened. I hadn't even learned his name.

He was still the Stranger to me.

***

My head was still whirling from the party as I walked back home. I had danced with the Stranger. Time had seemed to pass quickly…but it had been incredible. During that short time with him, I questioned whether or not I would throw away Stellan for him, if he asked.

But he hadn't. He had walked away, leaving me breathless and confused.

So where did that leave us? Nowhere. It would be nearly impossible for me to deny the connection we had, but there was one little problem. I didn't know him. I didn't know his name, where he lived, who he was. All I knew were his eyes, and that wasn't enough for me…*not yet*.

But I did feel a new strength in me, a new confidence. Dancing with the Stranger was just what I had needed to get over the heartbreak of Stellan. Everything was clear to me now. I knew what I had to do, and the choices I must make.

I couldn't stay upset or sad forever. If I did, I would miss out on life, miss out on the happiness that I deserved here, where I belonged. It was time to throw away my sorrows and face a new future. I couldn't dwell in the past. I couldn't let it hinder me. I couldn't let it break me. It was time to start moving forward.

I didn't return to the party after those last dances, and I hoped Zora didn't notice, or mind my leaving. I couldn't remain there after dancing with the Stranger, feeling so different from before. I was sure of myself now, confident in my decisions. But the feeling was foreign to me, and I didn't know how I would use this new certainty.

Feeling alive and hopeful, I was about to open the door when I felt a hand on my shoulder. I knew who it was even before I turned to look at his face. Stellan took one of my hands and led me away from the door. I followed him without complaint. I had promised him we would talk. And now that I knew what to do, what to say, I was okay with speaking to him.

We went behind my house and stood in silence for some time. Then I sighed.

"Are we going to talk, Stellan, or can I go to bed? It's been a very long day."

It took him a while to reply. "I'm sorry, Ramsey."

"I know," I said.

"I'm so sorry."

"I know," I said again, wiping away newly fallen tears. I hadn't wanted to cry tonight, especially after the wonderful evening with the Stranger. I couldn't help thinking of him, even with Stellan standing right in front of me.

"I never meant to hurt you," he told me.

"I know."

"What I did was terrible and senseless."

"I know," I repeated.

"I was telling the truth when I said what I had with Zora was nothing more than a few dates and a necklace. We were friends for years, much like she and Addison were, so we decided to give being together a chance. I thought it might go somewhere, but now I see it couldn't have. Not after meeting you," he told me.

"I know."

"I love you, Ramsey."

"You what?" I looked at him, completely surprised.

He shook his head. "I can't say for certain if it's love or not. We've only known each other for a short time. It's just that when I met you, everything I thought I was certain of disappeared. You unraveled me. What I say to you, I want to be perfect. Instead of worrying about myself, I worry about you. Whenever I walk, my feet lead me to you. Even my ability wants to take me to you, which makes it really hard to get to work, by the way."

I stifled a laugh. My heart was so heavy, but with what emotions, I didn't know.

Stellan shook his head, like he was struggling for a way to express his every thought and feeling. "And just the thought of losing you drives me crazy. I can't lose you, Ramsey, because without you, I'll just keep unraveling until there is nothing left of me."

I couldn't say anything back to him. I didn't know *what* to say. Part of me felt the same way. It didn't matter how long we had known each other, and it didn't matter what he had done. But I wasn't sure I *wanted* to love him. And I wasn't sure I could really forgive him.

I wanted to move on with my life. But did that "moving on" include or exclude Stellan? Could things ever be the same between us after all that had happened?

"Ramsey, please say something. Anything," he pleaded.

I breathed in deeply, choosing my words carefully. "I can't say it, Stellan. I can't give you the answer you want," I told him straight out.

He looked down. I saw his heart break in that instant. But I had to tell the truth. He started to walk away, but I stopped him.

"I can't say I love you, Stellan, because I haven't said *I forgive you* yet."

"Please say it," he said, as he turned back toward me. He made sure to only take one of my hands, a new light in his eyes.

"I forgive you," I said.

"Thank you," he replied, pulling me close. "I promise, I –"

"No more promises, Stellan. We'll deal with the rest another time. Just…make me forget that you hurt me," I told him.

His hands went around my waist, and he pulled my body toward his until we were barely an inch apart. I looked into his eyes. I put my arms around his neck and stood as tall as I could to reach his face.

"I love you, Elf Girl," he said.

I smiled and leaned my head forward so my lips were close to his left ear. Before we shared our most magical kiss, I whispered the words he wanted to hear.

"I love you too, Stellan."

~23~

Only Until the End of Summer

It was July seventh, one month after my sixteenth birthday, one month after I rescued Zora, and the date of Stellan's eighteenth birthday. Was this a coincidence? By now I believed there were no such things as coincidences when it came to magic. I didn't think Stellan's birthday being exactly one month after mine had extreme importance. It was just a cool thing to think about.

Walking the short distance from my home to Aaliyah's, and clutching Stellan's present in my hands, I took time to reflect on just how far I had come in the last several weeks. I went from being an awkward human girl with weird ears to an elfen with a magical ability, a big secret, and a great-looking boyfriend to boot. I *had* come a long way.

However, I knew I still had a long way to go before I truly found myself, the deep inside self. That couldn't happen until I knew my secret. For now, I was finally enjoying my new life, and that was enough.

I knocked on Aaliyah's front door, though I knew I didn't have to; I still hadn't broken the human habit of knocking. I didn't think I ever would. It just seemed respectful to me, and I wanted to remember and honor a few of my human customs. They were a lasting part of me.

I hoped Stellan would like his gift. I was still very new to this Realm, so I had relied on Mac, who had decided to remain in the orchard, for Stellan's present. As a gnome, Mac had spent a lot of time underground before coming to the Elf Realm. In his travels he befriended a dwarf who gave him a special talisman. It was a flat disk, rimmed with silver and with a gold center, which hung from a string as a sort of necklace. Mac said it protected the wearer from evil.

After explaining the difficulties I had searching for the right gift, Mac had decided to give his treasure to me. The talisman was a perfect gift, and I was grateful to Mac. Stellan would surely be happy with it as well.

I was surprised when Zora and not Aaliyah greeted me at the door. Usually, the gentle elfen would be there to greet her house guests. I wondered if she was just too busy getting ready for Stellan's birthday dinner.

Zora had a solemn look on her face, but this didn't surprise me all that much. Since her return to Birchwood, she was wary of Stellan, still hurting from his betrayal. I didn't blame her, nor did I expect her to forget anytime soon, but I hoped she would eventually be able to make peace with the situation and move forward. She deserved peace after everything she had gone through during her abduction.

Zora liked to keep a safe distance from Stellan, only coming around Aaliyah's when he wasn't home, which was usually when he was with me. I did my best to spend time with Zora – without Stellan – but it was sometimes hard to find a good balance, considering I wanted to be around those I loved most all the time. I wanted Zora to be happy, so I would continue to find ways to even things out until she was ready to leave the past where it belonged.

I stepped through the doorway, ready to be greeted by smiling faces and party decorations, but I received the exact opposite.

Aaliyah had tears in her eyes, and her face was almost drained of color. She looked way too pale, even for an elfen. Addison wasn't much better. She also looked teary-eyed, and her expression was that of pure despair and worry. What was going on?

I looked over to Stellan, whose own expression was grim. He was holding a letter in his hands, and I wondered how it was tied to their sad moods.

"What's going on?" I asked.

"Aditi just dropped off this letter," Stellan told me. "It's from Queen Taryn."

"What's wrong? Did something happen to Brielle? Is everyone okay?" I asked, starting to panic.

"Everyone in Tarlore is fine," Addison said, with a slight sharpness in her tone. "But everyone here…*is not*."

"What is she talking about? What does the letter say?"

"You had better take her outside, Stellan. Talk to her in private. This is…a very *delicate* subject," Aaliyah said.

Now I was full-on panicking. My hands began to shake, so I quickly set down the present onto the dining room table.

Stellan nodded and took my right hand, keeping the letter clutched in his left.

"Mother is right," he said, and then a rush of wind crashed over me and we were outside the house.

I needed a moment to catch my breath. When I was steady, I looked up at him.

"What does the letter say?" I asked again, my voice quivering with every word.

"It…Look, Ramsey, this letter doesn't change anything. Times may be rough for a little while, but that doesn't mean that we can't get past it…."

"Stellan, just tell me what the letter says," I pleaded, fear gripping me so hard that I found it difficult to breathe. "Please."

"It says that it's time for me to go to war," he said solemnly.

"What?" I asked, my voice barely above a whisper. "Why?"

"I'm eighteen, Ramsey. Most elves must go at this age and serve for two years. Only elves with powers needed in the war are requested, and I am one of those powers. My 'teleporting' will allow me to escape and reach enemies quickly. My power will help the war effort. I used to think my ability was important to me, special…Not anymore…."

"No," I said. "Queen Taryn can't do this. She knows how much we've been through….She can't do this."

"She doesn't have a choice either. She has to do what's best for the Elf Realm," he told me.

My heart was breaking. I couldn't believe what I was hearing. Stellan and I had gone through so much in a short amount of time. We were just beginning to truly connect again after what had happened between us. He couldn't leave me now. He simply couldn't.

"Don't go," I told him. "Don't leave me."

"Ramsey, I don't want to, but it's not that simple. I have a duty to this Realm. I have a duty to fight for the safety of all elves, for *your* safety. I can't just ignore that."

"But I need you here. I need you with me. I still haven't found out my secret…I might need your help. What if Finn comes back for me? He's still alive…."

I thought of every excuse possible to make him stay, but even as I rattled them off one by one, I knew they weren't good enough.

"Stellan, please…I'll do anything…"

"Stop, Ramsey. You're just making this harder. You…you have to accept this," he said.

"How can you say it so simply? How can you talk about leaving so calmly as if it doesn't matter?" I asked.

Stellan threw his hands in the air as he cried, "Don't you think this is difficult for me? I don't want to leave you, Ramsey! I don't want to leave knowing you could be in danger, knowing you could need my help. Just the thought of it scares me. But I have to go."

Tears fell from my eyes as he put his arms around me. I held on to him tightly, not ever wanting to let go.

"When do you have to leave?" I asked quietly.

"The last week in August," he said.

"That's only a little more than a month from now. It's too soon."

"I know."

"I want to go with you," I decided.

He held me tighter. "You can't, Ramsey. You have to go to school in September. Your place is here with Zora. She's waited fifteen years for you to come home. The two of you need each other."

"I need *you*," I said.

"It's only two years. I know our love is strong enough to last…to wait."

"I don't want to have to test it," I told him outright.

"I don't either, but I can't escape this. You know it as well as I do."

I nodded, although I wished I didn't have to accept it.

"My birthday present to you makes perfect sense now; before I thought of it more as a novelty gift. Now it will come in handy," I said sarcastically, remembering that the talisman supposedly warded off evil. Stellan would soon be facing a lot of evil.

"What's the present?" he asked.

"I can't tell you. You have to open it yourself. That's how birthday presents work," I teased.

"Then let's go open it," he suggested, a smile finally reaching his features.

He took one of my hands once more, and then led me back into the house as if nothing had happened. As if nothing had changed.

But it had.

~24~

One Answered Question

It was July fifteenth, the day of Danica and Thane's wedding. I sat in a church pew, Stellan on my right, and Zora on my left. I waved to Brielle, who was sitting near the church altar with Queen Taryn. We had arrived yesterday in the capital, after another long journey from Birchwood City. It felt great to be back. Tarlore was like a second home to me now.

I remembered my first visit here. So much had happened since then. I could hardly believe how little time had passed since I rescued my sister and then found out Stellan was going to war.

Zora and I finally cleaned out our parents' room. I realized that keeping busy kept my mind off Stellan's inevitable departure. We gave most of our parents' belongings to Aaliyah, but kept a few personal items for ourselves, including our mother's jewelry. Actually, Zora took most of it, because she was the hoarder. We kept those few things safe in our vanity drawers and turned the room into an incubator for our dragon eggs. They grew closer to hatching with each passing day. We set up two nests for them to lie in and always had a fire lit to keep them warm. We were both excited for their hatching. We had even started thinking about names but hadn't decided on our favorites yet.

Addison had come to Tarlore this time with all of her belongings. The Queen had requested that Addison be her personal messenger. Only a day after Stellan's letter arrived, Addison received her own, this one summoning her to Tarlore as soon as possible. Queen Taryn valued Addison's power and wanted her to live at the palace and stay by her side, as a special member of her high guard.

Two elves I loved would now be leaving Birchwood – both Addison and Stellan. However, Aaliyah, Zora, and I knew Addison had to accept. It was a wonderful opportunity for her, an honor. Things wouldn't be the same without Addison, but I trusted Brielle to keep her company and send letters with Aditi about how she and everyone at the palace were doing. Addison could even use her ability to write us herself. Even so, it was hard to imagine Addison not returning home with us after the wedding. I felt like a part of me would stay in Tarlore with her when we left.

Thinking of Addison leaving Birchwood reminded me yet again of Stellan going off to war. I felt my eyes dampen just thinking about how soon it would be until he left. We had only until the end of summer....

Stellan noticed my despair right away. He leaned over and whispered, "This is a joyous occasion, Ramsey. Forget about me leaving for a little while, all right? Please?"

I nodded, and promised to try my best, and he gave me a quick kiss on the cheek. I squeezed his hand even tighter. I was surprised it hadn't started turning purple.

Stellan was wearing the talisman. When he first put it on, he swore never to take it off, especially while he was away at war. I liked the idea and hoped it would comfort him somehow, even though it was just a piece of rock.

I rid my mind of sad thoughts when the music began playing the traditional wedding march, but with a bit of an elfin touch to it. The musicians played medieval fiddles, and the elegant sound comforted me and kept me from shedding any more tears.

Everyone turned to watch as Danica walked down the aisle. Thane proudly escorted her. Many of the most traditional customs in the Human Realm had their own flair in the Elf Realm.

Danica looked radiant in her white gown. *At least that doesn't change*, I thought to myself. However, as she walked closer to us, I noticed a green flower in the center of her abdomen tied onto the dress by a green sash around her waist. *Elves just can't live without green*, I thought to myself, almost giggling. Her black hair was pinned up in an elegant fashion, and a diamond tiara added to her sparkling beauty. I knew the tiara was Brielle's idea. I could see her grinning as she admired the jewels atop Danica's head.

Thane was handsome in his brown suit, which suited him perfectly. Their personalities came to the forefront on this happy day – and I realized I had never seen them without their guard uniforms until now.

As I watched the happy couple recite their marriage vows, my mind buzzed once again, but my thoughts settled on a different aspect of my new life. Perhaps it was because I was back in Tarlore, back to the place where I had finally figured out where to find my sister in the Human Realm. For a dark moment, I was back on the palace bridge where Lura had threatened me, saying that Finn would come back for me someday soon.

Dozens of questions ran through my mind as the elfin couple said their vows. I couldn't ignore the questions, because I desperately wanted answers. Even though I had rescued my sister from Element fairies – the reason I was brought here in the first place – confusion still clouded my life.

When would Finn return? Would I be prepared?

When would Zora finally tell me about my secret, and was the wooden trunk connected in some way? A few days after my return to Birchwood, I tried breaking the lock, with no success. I uttered the words to a spell in the book, but when I reached my hands out to touch the lock, they were burned severely, making me cry out in pain. I threw the book away and didn't try again.

Other than that one occasion, I hadn't paid much attention to my secret since bringing Zora home, especially with Stellan leaving so soon. I was putting myself on hold for now. Soon, however, I knew I would have to face the hazy details of my past that surrounded me, waiting to be discovered.

Would I ever see Eder again, whom I noticed wasn't present at the wedding? Would I ever learn the answers I still wanted from him? He had told me that rescuing Zora was only one piece of the puzzle; how would I find the other pieces? He had also said that he knew my secret, and that someone had informed him to wait for Zora to tell me. Who was that someone, and would I ever find out?

Why couldn't I stop thinking about the Stranger, even when Stellan would soon leave for war? What was his significance, and would I ever encounter him again?

Most importantly, *would I ever* have one day without anything major to think about? A day where all that mattered was the weather outside and the company I shared? *Probably not,* I decided. That was my life, at least for now.

Until I figured a few things out, problems and issues would follow me wherever I went. Nevertheless, I could be happy at the same time. It would work out if I found a balance. I would *make* it work.

I was the Elf Girl, and no matter what troubles came my way, I would be the one to shape my future.

A future I was prepared to fight for with endless determination.

***

I received an answer to one of my questions when we returned home, without Addison, a few days later. Unfortunately, it wasn't a very good answer.

I walked into my room while Zora checked on the eggs. Stellan planned to take me out to his restaurant later that night, and I was excited about seeing him. We wanted to spend as much time together as possible before he had to go.

As I opened my wardrobe to choose an outfit, my eyes briefly scanned the room. I noticed something unusual, something out of place.

Lying on my bed, perfectly centered on my pillow, was a note. Confused, I picked it up, wondering who could have left it there:

See you again soon, Ramsey. Don't forget that. Don't forget me.

I dropped the note and screamed. Zora ran into the room to see what was wrong, and I looked down at the note, now lying on the wooden floor. Shaking, I could still read the name signed at the bottom, the one name that could unnerve me so completely.

Finn...

Acknowledgements

Words cannot even express the gratitude I feel for the many people who have contributed to my successes today. However, I will do my best to give them the thanks they deserve.

First, to Maryanne Grabo, my mother, my reason for existence, my support system, who acted as my reader, my agent, my proofreader...and a bunch of other positions I can't remember because there are so many. She has been with me every step of the way, and without her, I can honestly say that I wouldn't be a published author.

To Scott, my father, who encouraged me to write, even though he isn't much of a reader. And for introducing me to coffee. It really helped with the writer's block!

To Yia Yia, my grandmother, who read my book for teens and loved it anyway. To my family, for supporting me and promising to buy my book even when they had no idea what it was about...as long as I autographed it for them.

To my closest friends, for being great marketers for the book, giving me my personality, and keeping me sane through all the stress. I, "Marcel" (happy now?), am very grateful for all you have done for me.

To my fellow choir geeks, for taking the edge off as we belted out choral numbers and for putting great songs in my head as I sat down to write.

To my English teachers, Mrs. Hudaj and Mrs. Schwane, for *cacophony* and countless other big words.

To Emily Young, my best friend, proofreader, and original cover designer. Through all the ups and downs of writing, editing, and publishing, she has remained by my side, continually providing the added encouragement, hope, and strength only a best friend can do, and giving me a good laugh when I desperately needed one. Without her, my life would be far less interesting.

To my editor, Patricia Lantier, PhD. She taught me so much, helping me grow as a writer. She transformed my manuscript of ideas into something readable. With her help, my writing became a novel.

To Vasilena Slavova, my graphic artist. You brought my creativity to life in the cover and portrayed the perfect vision.

To Angela and Booklocker.com. for believing that my novel was worth publishing. They made my dream a reality.

To everyone who has supported me by buying my book, spreading the word, or even just saying congratulations or asking me about my writing – every bit has made a difference.

Finally, to God. It always comes back to Him. Without Him, I wouldn't have this passion for writing. Without Him, I wouldn't be who I am today. *Thank you.*

About the Author

When she's not spending countless hours writing or absorbing book after book, Markelle is active in Chamber Choir, Theater, Varsity Tennis, Bible Club, Destination Imagination, running, taking care of her two cats and four rabbits, and spending time with friends and family. At the age of fourteen, she began taking a serious interest in writing. Two years later she completed this, her first novel, as a Junior in high school. Her plans are to attend a 4-year private college in Wisconsin and earn her degree in Creative Writing. And yes, she definitely believes in fairies.